After The Leaves Fell

Ella Justice

For the girls who thought they were hard to love and the men who prove them wrong.

Author's Note

Hey reader!

While After The Leaves Fell is a closed door contemporary romance with no explicit on-page intimate scenes, it does deal with heavy topics. I always want my readers to feel comfortable and know what to expect, especially when it comes to sensitive subjects. This book contains a cancer diagnosis (past and present), abandonment issues, brief moments of suspense throughout and a full scene of suspense with guns present, brief mention of deaths within the healthcare world specifically in the labor and delivery specialty and explores themes of grief and family trauma.

That being said, interwoven with these deep and often difficult themes is a story of a two people falling in love despite it all. There is plenty of banter, swoon-worthy scenes, romantic gestures, and moments that will have you kicking your feet and giggling at Jason and Oakley's antics. Welcome to the As The Seasons Change world, and happy reading.

BEFORE THE LEAVES CHANGED

1

There are moments in life that bring an undeniable shift. The world holds its breath, and in that moment, the very trajectory of *you* changes. A few people live for those moments. They crave change, the high the comes with altering their path at any second. To others, life just...happens. It doesn't bother or excite them. It simply is. Then, there are those filled with dread. It's all unstoppable, and it scares them regardless. For me, it wasn't the inescapability of change that hurt. No, it was the hollowness that followed being left behind that scarred.

Call it intuition, but I knew just over the horizon, the promise of the inevitable was barely starting to stretch its fingers towards me. Like the changing of the seasons, my life needed to feel the cold, to be *forced* to transform into something new, but the colors were going to be *oh*, so beautiful.

At least, that's what I prayed for.

"We have to call it," I argued. The travel nurse blinked back at me in surprise.

"I've been working in labor and delivery for ten years—" she started, squaring her shoulders and stretching the pink scrubs we both wore.

"It doesn't matter. Make the call," I interrupted, tired of this conversation already. The only reason I was even involved was because Ash begged me to say something.

Ashley Mancini, the curly-haired nurse standing by my side in the dark hospital hallway, was one of the few who claimed to enjoy my presence. My co-worker and roommate was a short little thing, petite, tan skin, with tight black curls, and she was almost in tears over this patient.

Around the same time Ash had convinced me to work on the labor and delivery floor with her, she tried to convince me we would be great roommates. She then offered me the master bedroom in the townhouse she was trying to rent and to make my lunches for a month. We moved into our new place the next week. Within a few months, she'd worn me down, becoming the closest thing I had to a friend.

Don't tell her I said that.

"Tina, think about that momma in there–" Ash began, sniffling.

"We need to give her more time." Tina held out a hand, like she held authority over women's bodies and their ability to push out a baby. "She really wants—"

"She *wants* a healthy baby. She *wants* to survive this with as little trauma as possible." I looked at her, drawing every scrap of energy I had left in this last hour of our twelve-hour night shift. "We have to follow protocol. Call the doctor before this becomes an emergency c-section and your license is in question."

Her eyes widened—I knew she wanted to keep fighting me, to prove her ten years of experience had power over my twenty-five years of life. But I knew things too. I knew that if you didn't control a situation, it would control you.

And you would lose.

"Fine, Oakley," she said with a sigh. "I'll make the call. But can I give you one piece of advice?"

I was too worn out to do more than raise my eyebrows.

"Try caring about people. You're the most unfeeling nurse I've ever met." She huffed, pushing past me to the nurses' station, hopefully to call the doctor.

Beside me, Ash blew out a breath, her usual cheeriness creeping back onto her face.

"Thank you, Oakley." She pushed her frizzy ponytail over her shoulder. "She needed your..."

"Unfeeling words?" I smirked.

"Don't listen to her. You were advocating for a patient! There was no way she'd make it through another two hours without a doctor consult. You made the right call." Ash glanced towards the nurses' station. "Tina's contract is up this week, so don't worry—she'll be gone before your next shift. Are you heading home now?"

"I finished up my charting, and Anita said I could go once that was done. Hopefully, I can get an extra hour of sleep before you try to drag me out tonight."

Saturday nights were girls' night, mandated by Ash and our other two roommates. They went every week, but I only went when forced, usually when they were going somewhere with edible, cheap bar food.

"Or you could come to the gym with me as soon as I get off. Think about it: you could spend time with me—"

"And meet the gym guy you've been trying to set me up with?" I walked towards the locker room, ready to get out of my scrubs. A small, mischievous smile stretched across her face.

"Girl, a perfect guy isn't going to appear out of thin air," she argued as we reached the locker room door, where my comfy sweatpants and the keys to my old white hatchback were ready to get me out of there. She never seemed to understand I wasn't looking for a guy at all, let alone a perfect one.

"See you later, Ash. Tell your boyfriend you're hitting on guys at the gym for me again. He loved that *so much* last time."

Ash didn't have time to argue—someone called her name, and I took my chance to rush into the locker room. After changing out of my sweaty scrubs and clocking out, I got into my car and finally started the drive home.

I turned on my *Comforting Music That Won't Make You Cry* playlist and let the soothing music wash over me. After only a few miles, the trees were the perfect level of suffocating. They crowded every inch of space, and I could finally breathe.

My Tennessee born and raised heart loved it; too many trees meant I was home.

Downtown Nashville's early morning lights started to fade into country roads as I drove into the outskirts of the city. Maples and oaks reached high into the sky on either side of the freeway as I merged into early morning traffic. It was the beginning of September, but the temperature was dipping in the mornings, and the leaves were hinting at change. They promised bright reds, burnt oranges, pops of yellow on big, floppy oak leaves stretched over the rolling hills. It was going to be hauntingly beautiful.

Pulling into our driveway, I only had to tug the ancient gear shift twice, this time to put it into park, before glancing at my phone with a groan, forcing myself to open the text I'd left sitting since it came in at two in the morning.

David: Oaks, baby, u up? when can i see u?

David had been a blind date out of pity for my roommate Tess, who couldn't get him to stop asking about me. They worked at the same accounting firm, and we'd met briefly when Tess forgot her lunch at the house a month ago.

Though a tough businesswoman, Tess had a hard time saying no to people she couldn't prove wrong with a spreadsheet. So, when David asked if he could take me to this new bar in town I 'had to try', she said I would love to.

Tess knows no date ever goes well at the bar. It's basically gospel. But when she volunteered to make me meals for a month if I put her out of her misery, I tried *not* to be my usual self. *How bad could David be?*

First, he called me 'baby' when we met and existed in his own personal cloud of cologne. The smell was so overwhelming, I had to hold back a gag—and I dealt with the aromas and fluids of birth regularly without blinking an eye.

Next, he insisted we sit at the bar, not a table, though plenty were open. He proceeded to watch every girl who walked by, constantly stared at my chest, and had to 'go to the bathroom' when it was time to pay.

Long story short, not my type.

But Momma raised me right, so I typed out a response.

Oakley: Unfortunately, I don't think I'll have time to see you again.

Oakley: Stop using so much cologne and actually take a girl to dinner sometime. I think your success rate would improve.

After hitting send and turning off the car, I grabbed my bag and slowly made my way to my front door. It swung open as I reached for the doorknob, revealing a professional Tess Bedford, a large coffee in her manicured hand. Her long, thick strawberry blonde hair, blown out and pageant ready at all times, combined with her thick twang, gave away her deep Southern roots.

She had these bright green eyes that looked into your soul like she wanted to know you, and unless you were an awful human, she genuinely did.

"Oh, hey, Oakley! Sorry, I've gotta run. The new intern keeps takin' all the good coffee in the office." She grinned, even as I looked pointedly at the still-steaming coffee in her hand. "You know this is fixin' to be gone before I hit the freeway."

I gave her a small smile then glanced back at my texts. Gentle-hearted Tess needed to be warned. Given the entitlement that seemed a core part of David's personality, I had no hope he wouldn't confront her.

"Tess, I might've sent a grumpy text."

"'Might've' is your way of sayin' you did, and you don't regret it but I probably will for you. Show me the damage, sister."

With no shame, I handed over my phone and watched her eyes widen like they were going to pop. After a moment or two of her gaping, I yawned and grabbed my phone back.

"Oakley, how am I gonna face this man?"

"Act like you've got no idea. It's not your fault I'm a grumpy love-hater." I shrugged. Ash had given me that nickname when she tried to set me up with a guy and he cried at the end of our date. He got clingy, so I put him in his place. Honestly, I thought I'd been plenty nice about the whole thing.

"Okay, I can do that." She stepped out of the house as I stepped in, still mumbling to herself as she wandered towards her car. As I went to close the door, she shouted, "Bye, grumpy love-hater!"

"Go get your coffee, little miss sunshine!" I shouted back as I shut the door.

As soon as the lock clicked into place, I practically ran down the hallway, climbing up the stairs to my room on the second floor. I opened my door, dropped my bag on the floor, and changed for bed as fast as possible as the night replayed through my head. It was exhausting to deal with so many priorities battling for my attention—like how the patient's bleeding wouldn't stop, verging on a scary hemorrhage, or her freshly born baby needing respiratory help and getting admitted to the NICU.

It was hard not snapping at the new parents to focus. It hurt watching them show their emotions so openly without feeling a twinge of longing. It was frustrating hearing Tina call me unfeeling and uncaring when I knew the real cost of growing attached. I was relieved when reality faded away as soon as my head hit the pillow.

***

Ring, ring, ring.

I groaned, rolling over and trying to silence my alarm.

Ring, ring, ring.

Finally getting a hold of my phone, I sat up at the caller ID flashing across the screen.

Jackson Tennen.

I read the name again, not believing my eyes.

The phone stopped ringing as I stared at it, grief and regret and hurt creating a perfect storm in my tightening chest.

Tucking my dark, wavy hair behind my ear, I set the phone down on my blanketed legs and twisted my fingers together. Did I call him back?

I couldn't watch him walk away again, watch him abandon our family. Abandon me.

But this was *Jack.*

When the phone rang again, I found myself answering before I could think it through.

"Hello?" I answered, my voice low and scratchy.

"Oakley?" That was him. The eldest Tennen sibling was identifiable by his deep grumble.

"Jack?" I whispered, not believing what I was hearing.

"Hey, Oaksy." His attempt to butter me up by using my nickname pissed me off. I pushed away the warm memories of a toothless Jack trying to pronounce 'Oakley', dubbing me 'Oaksy' for the rest of my life and huffed.

"What the hell, Jack? This is still your number? Where are you?" I started, letting my anger take hold. Jack and I were always straight with each other. At least, we used to be.

I paused, and the vital sign machine sounds I'd know anywhere filled the silence.

"Jackson Tennen, are you at the hospital right now?"

Another pause. I couldn't breathe.

"You're the only one I could call."

2

I flipped on my blinker as I changed lanes, the trees that had brought me such peace only hours before doing nothing to calm my racing nerves.

Jack, the backbone of my childhood, had cancer.

Bone sarcoma.

Like Momma.

God help him, he was terrified. I'd never heard his voice shake before, not even when Pa lost his job during Momma's first round of chemo. Hunter, the third Tennen sibling, understood parts of what was happening, but he'd been too young to help out much, unlike high school-aged me and Jack. Mallory, the youngest, was too little to understand. I'd been terrified, but Jack had been solid. He made a plan and executed. Then, he left home and never came back, started his own life away from us. Away from the burden.

But this? This was bigger than even he felt he could handle.

So, he called me.

The last time I saw my older brother was years ago, in Boston.

Jack left home as soon as he graduated high school, more than ready to escape our small town and the pain riddling our house. He called me out of the blue after years of no contact, wanting to see me. I'd taken the weekend off from my nursing program, lied to my parents, and used all my meager savings on a plane ticket. After Boston, I thought maybe I'd gotten my brother back.

Until he disappeared for the next four years. Again.

As I readjusted my tight grip on the steering wheel, Ash's name popped up on my phone. I hit answer and put the call on speaker before setting the phone back in my cup holder.

"Hey girl, I just saw your text. Are you sure you're okay going by yourself? I could get my shift tomorrow night switched around and try to get a seat on your flight," she proposed, the concern clear in her voice. She'd never met Jack, and she didn't know the rush of overwhelming trauma this news brought. She didn't know I hadn't spoken to my brother in years. I didn't talk about it, but she knew me. "Or I could find a flight—"

"Ash, it's okay. I grabbed the last seat on this flight, so I doubt you'd be able to find anything worth buying at this point." I took a deep breath, trying to calm some of the panic I felt.

"How is this working with him getting off work?"

I smiled shakily to myself. She was giving me a task to focus on other than the pressure building in my chest.

"He said the military is giving him leave; he's already on

disability because of the accident. He's taking the time he needs to get everything figured out."

Apparently, my big brother had joined the army, working as an engineer on a base in Arizona for the last four years—not that any of us knew he was even still alive.

He'd been in an accident. There was a wire issue that malfunctioned right into him, and some shrapnel from the explosion tore through his leg. When they did routine blood work, his white blood cell count was astronomical. After a few more tests, they found the source of the flagged labs. That was all he told me before I booked my flight.

"And all his stuff?"

"He said everything he needs fits into one suitcase." I let out a long exhale as I took the exit to the airport, looking for the long term parking sign.

"Huh. Impressive."

A muffled man's voice suddenly came through the line. Ash mumbled something back, but I only caught the end. "—just one second for an emergency situation is all I ask, *acci-denti. Chi ti credi di essere -*"

Ah. The piece of work boyfriend. He definitely deserved Ash's emotional-outburst ramblings. Although she was born and raised in New York, her father was a proud Italian American that made sure his only daughter knew the language.

"Anyway, Oakley, you were the best person to call. You're so calm in these situations. You'll get it all squared away, *cara.*" As much as I enjoyed her angry ramblings, the term of endearment felt like a tight hug I needed but wouldn't accept. I pulled into a spot in the parking garage, giving what she'd said some thought.

Yes, I was reliable. Yes, I was the person people could call to fix a problem. But something was draining me. Not just this situation, but my life.

I tried to come off as someone who didn't care, someone unfeeling, which was why I rarely got attached. I told people exactly what I thought. I was feisty, blunt, and brutally honest while preferring to keep to myself.

But I had a secret: I cared too much.

It was easier to be unattached than to feel all the hurt and pain that came when someone inevitably left you behind.

That was the secret I lived by, the secret that might be slowly killing me. Because somewhere inside, I was *tired*.

So, I simply agreed when people told me how calm and reliable I was in hard situations. I lived up to it, even though everything in me begged to differ. I wasn't all those things—I was just skilled at shoving my emotions down deep enough to ignore them screaming to be let free.

"It'll all work out. Who knows, you might even be back in time for family dinner tomorrow night." Ash forced a laugh, but I knew how Jack coming back would rock my fragile family to their core.

It'd been eight years since he'd set foot in Tennessee, since he'd been inside the childhood house that formed us. Momma and Pa rarely talked about him anymore, their tears dried after years of abandonment. Eight years without a word, no sign of life from their son.

Now, he was sick. Momma would feel that pain stronger than most.

"Oakley?" Ash whispered. "We're all here for you, okay?

It's okay to rely on other people sometimes. Seriously, you're not in this alone."

Turning my car off, I sighed, contemplating how I could possibly tell her every thought racing through my head. Stepping out of the car, I shut the door and walked to the back of the car, popping open the trunk as I answered.

"Thanks, Ash. I'm good. I've got it handled." I grabbed my carry-on, setting it on the ground and extending the handle. "I'll text you when I know what the plan is."

"Okay. Good luck, and seriously, call if you need anything." Ashley's voice dropped to a conspiratorial whisper. "Or if you find a hot man on that plane and need to spill some tea."

I rolled my eyes. Hard. "Uh huh. Thanks Ash." I barely heard her response as I hung up. Tucking my phone in my back pocket, I shut the trunk before turning right into a brick wall.

As I swung an arm to steady myself, my carry-on started to roll away before crashing to the ground with a bang. In my desperate flailing, my other arm latched onto a strong bicep. That fact clued me in that the wall I ran into wasn't made of brick. Not at all.

It was made of man. A built man.

I felt the arm I was clinging to wrap around my waist, keeping me upright. The heat made its way to my cheeks as my mind realized what was happening. Forcing myself to look all the way up, I inhaled sharply at what I found.

Dark brown eyes met mine. The intensity and lightness mixed there were such opposites, but somehow, with the way they gazed into my soul, their contradiction made sense. Startled by his striking eyes, I took in everything else about this man. He was tall, towering over me, which was impressive. This guy had to be well over six feet.

His shoulders were broad, the chest I'd plowed into wide and muscular. You could tell by looking at it—or running into it—that he was strong. I allowed my gaze to roam over his face.

Simply put, he was beautiful in a gruff, manly way. He had some stubble, though not enough to be called a beard, dark blond hair that dropped down across his forehead, the shaggy locks his only hint of boyhood. Thick brows accentuated those deep brown eyes; they quirked up at my obvious analysis of his face, and I finally noticed the phone pressed against his ear.

Flustered, I pushed against his chest, stumbling backwards as his arm dropped from around me.

He chuckled at my frantic movements before speaking into his phone.

"Hey, sorry, man, I gotta go. But everything should be set." His voice was deep and gravelly, exactly how I imagined it would be. I rubbed my temples lightly before pushing my untamed hair behind my ears. "Yeah, see you soon. Good luck, brother."

Ending whatever call he was on, this guy turned and gave me a cocky half smile. Something in me settled.

"Sorry, I wasn't paying attention."

"No, no, you're alright," I replied calmly, gaining back some of my sanity. Impressed at how convincing I sounded, I continued, "Neither was I. Sorry."

The silence stretched on for a moment, and I saw a debate in his eyes. Then, his gaze skated over my face.

Assessing *me*.

He gave me another half-smile, and something about it looked oddly familiar. I couldn't place it, but I knew I'd seen it before. Returning his smile with a hesitant one of my own, I broke the silence and asked, "Have I met you before?"

Surprisingly, his smile strained before he slowly shook his head. "If we had, would you have forgotten me?"

"Would you?" I challenged, giving him a hard stare.

"So you're one of those girls who needs to be complimented, eh?" he said with just enough of a smirk that I rolled my eyes and registered a slight accent I couldn't fully place.

"Well, considering people 'round here don't talk like that, I assume you're not from this side of the Mississippi." I tilted my head and smirked back. "So you don't understand that 'round here, we don't need to ask for compliments. We have our own ways."

"Oh yeah? So if a guy from Canada wanted to fit in, how would he compliment a beautiful woman in an airport parking garage?" He stepped a bit closer, and I had to lift my chin to meet his gaze. He was good—too good. As I crossed my arms, something foreign zipped through me. I searched for something to put this overconfident stranger in his place.

"See, that's the thing, hotshot. I can't teach you how to be a southern gentleman." I smirked as he put his hands on his hips, playing along with whatever this was. "It's something y'all are either born with or you're not. A true lady can tell the difference real quick."

"I see. Well, humor me for a moment, Miss Southern

Lady." He grinned mischievously then he leaned forward until our faces were almost touching. That feeling rushed through me again, and I recognized it.

Excitement.

This guy could hold his own. I liked it. It was different from the hurt and fear that had taken up residence in my head, and I surprised myself by latching onto it, if only for a second.

"Give it your best shot." I smirked back at him.

"Considering I just swept you off your feet, I don't think it should be too hard." He grinned even harder when I scoffed. There were only inches between us now, and I was close enough to see a damn sparkle in his eye. He was enjoying this as much as I was. "I definitely learned something today."

"Oh yeah?" I challenged. "How to run into unsuspecting women?"

"No. That I could never forget a southern lady like you. A true Canadian gentleman can tell the difference."

He looked at me, and I looked at him. The wind picked up, blowing through the open sides of the parking garage, shuffling a few early fallen leaves towards us, and I felt like it was trying to tell me something. As the air shifted around me and the leaves crinkled while they tumbled, this moment felt important.

I was disrupted from our little stare down when my phone buzzed. Pulling it out of my pocket, I saw a text from Jack.

Jack: Let me know if everything is okay with the flight

The flight. I only had about forty-five minutes to get checked in, through security, and to my gate. I didn't have time to share flirty moments with random guys in parking garages, no matter how good it felt to have his arm wrapped around my waist. Glancing back up at my mysterious stranger, I already saw the understanding in his eyes.

"Sorry to cut this short, but I've really gotta go." I held up my phone as if that was somehow proof. "Keep working on that southern gentleman thing. It has potential. And thank you for catching me. You know, after you ran me over."

He gave me a small laugh before his eyes drifted over to my luggage, still sprawled out in the middle of the parking garage, then moved towards it before he spoke.

"Well, at least let me make it up to you by getting your luggage, ma'am." He pulled my bag up, and 'thank you' was on my lips when his eyes shot to mine. They weren't full of mischief and interest anymore. They were pissed and confused. "You're a fan? A puck bunny? Of course you are. I can't catch a break."

"Excuse me?" I asked, completely thrown off. What the hell did he accuse me of?

"You heard me. Was this whole conversation planned?" He came closer as he spoke, and this time, I didn't want to stay in his space. In fact, he reminded me of every reason why I hated talking to guys. "How long have you been waiting around? Stalking me to get your chance? You know what, I don't even care. Stay away from me, and I won't file for a restraining order. I know better than to fall for stuff like this."

I opened my mouth to defend myself, but he marched away with a huff.

"I have no idea who you are, you self-centered psycho!" I hollered after him, but he was gone, walking away as quickly as he'd come. With my own annoyed huff, I leaned down to grab my luggage, trying to piece together what set this guy off. "I hope I forget I ever met you!"

The only thing I had on my rarely-used luggage was a cheap Nashville Rebels #1 fan tag Pa got me for my birthday as a joke, since I never paid attention to his favorite sport unless forced. As I glanced at the player featured on my luggage, everything clicked into place.

That smile *was* familiar.

But we'd definitely never met before.

I'd watched that man smile on TV in my parents' house many times in the two seasons he had played for the Rebels.

Those dark eyes on that tag were the same ones that had checked me out, flirted with me, then turned to disgust.

Jason Westerman. Star forward. Pro hockey all-star.

My mystery man.

What an asshole.

My whole life, I've needed an outlet for strong emotions. Sitting on a cramped flight for two hours, pissed off at a professional hockey player who bowled into you with his hotness, then called you a puck bunny pissed me off. Adding that I was about to reunite with an estranged brother with a cancer diagnosis and had no opportunity to belt out angry songs made for a grumpy Oakley.

And yes, I'd googled "puck bunny" and was plenty offended.

Screw you, Westerman.

Thankfully, the relief and sorrow in my brother's eyes as I stepped out of the Uber at his apartment swept the anger away. I'd silently stalked inside, not ready to fully face him yet.

"Really, thank you, Oakley," Jack said for the millionth time as I tucked a few more t-shirts into his suitcase. He wasn't lying—everything fit in one suitcase.

I glanced at my big brother, his somber face filled with tension as he slouched in his hospital issued wheelchair. With his short, dark hair and pale skin, he looked sick.

He *was* sick.

But I knew, despite how bad he'd hurt me, that I was going to do everything I could for him, even if I couldn't trust him.

"Jack, I'm real angry with you, but we're family. I would've been out here when the accident happened—"

"I know, I know, but it's been years, and I know that's my fault. It's all my fault, and I'm sorry for that." He took a deep breath, rubbing his hands back and forth on his armrests in a self-soothing motion. "I just want to go home."

"Have you talked to Momma?" I took a seat on the bed facing him. We'd been dodging any mention of his plans once he got to Nashville. This felt big, overwhelming.

"No, no. I don't know if they'll want to see me at all, and

with *this?* This can't be an over-the-phone conversation." He paused, thinking. When my big brother needed to get something out, you had to give him the time and space to do it. So, I waited. A few moments passed before he finally met my gaze. "I'm twenty-six, Oaksy. I haven't spoken to them since I was eighteen. I can't put that on them. I can't be a burden. I *can't.*"

"Jack—"

"No, Oakley. I won't do that to them." He sighed, wheeling himself forward to look at the contents of his suitcase. "One of my buddies from college moved to Nashville a few years ago, uh, for work. We've stayed close. He has an apartment downtown, near the hospital the military set me up with, and he offered me a room. I don't like it, but it's the best situation."

Now I was the one taking a deep breath. The pain in his eyes made me feel helpless. Jack didn't ask for help. I vividly recalled him at ten years old, standing in the kitchen, covered head to toe in flour, trying to explain in his surly Southern accent that he could do it himself. He'd grown into a man and lost the accent in the years since, but that stubbornness seemed to still be there.

"Thank you for calling me," I said softly. His gaze snapped to mine. "Jack, our family misses you. No matter how rightfully upset they're gonna be, we'll get through the storm—"

"Because we can hang on to each other," Jack finished our momma's favorite phrase to use when we were kids. "You're all grown up, Oaksy."

I held back the words I wanted to scream.

I had to grow up.
You left me behind.
You abandoned us.
Instead, I nodded at him.
"We're gonna get through this. Together."
Even though I meant every word, panic raced through me. Could I really do this? Could I forgive him, care for him, watch him live through our worst nightmare?
I didn't have a choice.
"Thank you for coming." Jack sighed, glancing at the time. "I have another favor to ask."
"What type of favor?" I asked warily.
"Family dinner." His smile was grim. "I need to face them. Tomorrow."
He was finally coming home.
I prayed we would survive it.

3

Sierra: Hey, Oakley! I know it's been years since we've talked, but I heard you're working in labor over at Vanderbilt. Amazing!

Anyhow, I moved back to Nashville for a research project. Remember that one we did on music therapy? I brought it to the doctor I'm working under, and he LOVED it! Especially the piece you did on mental coping strategies with different beats and melodies. He was wondering if you'd be interested in chatting more about your research and possibly joining our team? Let me know if you'd be interested, and if so, when you're free to chat???

I read over the text one more time as we waited at the baggage claim, waiting for the bag full of Jack's life and enjoying the humid air that proved he wasn't hiding in Arizona anymore.

Sierra was a classmate from nursing school, but while I'd

graduated and started working, she'd gotten her master's in clinical research. When we did that research project, I became obsessed with how music affected the brain. There was so much we didn't know about how the mental game affects our healing process. If we could understand and use music to heal our psyche, it would be such a powerful tool, an amazing way to heal.

Growing up with a mother who used music to heal during her battle with cancer opened my eyes. The science, the healing, the emotion—it became my beacon, my light in the never-ending darkness.

To have Sierra reach out was a dream come true. If she'd sent that text last week, I might've said yes.

I glanced over at Jack.

Research was a part of medicine I was scared to explore. It wasn't as controlled as my nursing job, where I clocked in for twelve hours and clocked out. Certain problems had protocols and solutions. Research was a different world, one with much less structure. It meant change.

My world just got flipped upside down. Jack needed me. Momma would need me. I wasn't sure I could add a passion project to the mix, even if the thought made me feel alive. So, I tucked my phone in my back pocket and rocked on my heels, watching Jack's luggage hit the carousel with a thump.

It took us thirty minutes to get his luggage, find my car, argue about helping him get his wheelchair in the car, and finally get on the road to his friend's place.

"You sure you have the right address?" I asked for the third time as we pulled up to a high rise in the heart of downtown Nashville, Johnny Cash playing low in the background.

It was a stunning building, with at least a hundred floors. The windows were pretty, but they had to be a privacy issue.

"I'm sure, Oaksy." Jack scratched at his chin, obviously uncomfortable with being more specific. My fingers tapped against the steering wheel, the old nickname grating.

We pulled up to the building, and the valet service came towards us. I started to put the car into drive and find other parking, but Jack stopped me, rolling down the window and listing a room number and code that had the valet widening his eyes and asking for my keys again.

"Just let them take it. It's covered in the rent." Jack shrugged, moving to get out of the car before groaning in frustration. He muttered a few curse words Momma would've been shocked to hear as he tried to balance on his one good leg on the busy Nashville sidewalk.

"You know, you could show some patience," I grumbled, opening the trunk to grab his wheelchair. I pulled it out and set it on the sidewalk, unable to ignore the pure annoyance on his face. "Come on, let's get you settled in the lap of luxury."

With another huff and a roll of his eyes, I got Jack situated in his wheelchair before turning to see the valet waiting for my attention.

"We'll bring the luggage up to the suite, ma'am," he declared with a little bow that made me wildly uncomfortable. I wasn't the type of person people bowed to. I drove an old car, wore the same tennis shoes from my junior year of college, and would never be described as extravagant.

"Um, thank you, sir?" It came out like a question, and for the first time since we'd left the airport, Jack fully smiled.

Sure, he was laughing at me, but it was a win. "Just the large suitcase; you can leave the carry-on in the car please."

With another deferential nod, the valet got in and drove away. Convincing myself my car wasn't being stolen, I sighed, pushing Jack's wheelchair. We made it two feet before he dug his good foot into the ground, lurching us both forward as the wheelchair came to an abrupt stop.

"What the hell—"

"I don't need to be pushed around like some invalid, okay?" His words were harsh.

"Jack, I pushed your wheelchair through both the Phoenix and Nashville airports. What's the problem?" I asked, genuinely confused. He ignored me, staring up at the beautifully intimidating building. An idea popped into my head, and sadness pierced my soul. "Is it because of this place? Or your college friend?"

He sighed again, and I knew I'd nailed it.

"Listen, Oakley, me and this guy go way back. I've always been the tough guy, the one who fixes problems, and he's a little larger than life. Seeing how successful he's been...he definitely doesn't have his little sister wheeling his pathetic ass around because his life is falling apart." Jack's voice got louder and louder until his words came out in an angry rush.

"Listen to me," I demanded, rounding his wheelchair so he could see my face. "I don't know who this friend of yours is, but I know who you are. You are Jackson Oliver Tennen. You've faced hard and unfair things your entire life. When kids in school made fun of you because you had a hard time reading, you learned how to build a telescope. When Pa picked up double shifts and Momma was in the hospital, you helped out by doing pickups and drop offs, supporting each of us. You were the one at back-to-school nights. You were the one who got Hunter to football practice. You stepped up when things were tight. Every. Single. Time."

His eyes were shining, and the harsh lines softened a bit as my words sank in.

"What you're handling now is different from what you've faced before. I may not have been old enough or brave enough to stand up to those kids or help the way you did, but I'm here now. Things changed. You're not the one they rely on anymore, and you don't have to do this alone, Jack." I reached out a hand, stiffly laying it on his arm as he blew out a breath. "But you do have to suck it up, swallow that stubborn pride you use as a shield, and let people help."

The noises of the city came back to us as I waited for his response—cars rushing by, people talking loudly on cell phones and hustling past. All I could focus on, though, was my big brother, wrestling with himself in front of my eyes. Despite what he'd done, no one should ever have to come to terms with all he had. No one should have to do it alone.

When he finally let his eyes meet mine, determination replaced self-pity.

"Okay."

That was it?

"Okay?"

"Yeah."

"I give you a pep talk to refute your sad, pathetic 'I'm in a wheelchair and my friends from college are cooler than me' idiocy, and all I get is an okay?" I asked incredulously. He smirked, and that was when I knew he could survive this—at least for now.

"Yep. Now, would you please push me inside so I can see the lap of luxury I'm gonna be living in?" His eyes still carried uncertainty and sadness, but his tone was teasing.

"It would be my honor, lieutenant drama queen."

I think our jaws hit the flawless marble floor when we entered the building. An artsy glass light fixture hung from the high ceiling, and once we rode up the elegant elevator, I realized Jack had pushed the button for the top floor.

Top floor of a building like this? He really *was* living in the lap of luxury. I had to bite my lip to keep from asking what this guy did for work again. I was leaning towards a trust fund.

When the elevator finally opened, only a few doors lined the long hallway. Jack nodded towards our right, and once we got to the correct door, we were faced with a keypad. With all the confidence in the world, he hit some buttons, and the pad flashed green. Glancing back with apprehension that matched mine, he pushed the door open.

If we thought the lobby was luxurious, it was nothing compared to this apartment.

Mostly because of the view.

As I pushed Jack into the main living area, I was stunned by the open layout, gorgeous kitchen, and the wall of floor-to-ceiling windows showcasing downtown Nashville in all its glory.

"What was it you said he did again?" I finally whispered reverently. Jack just coughed uncomfortably.

"He said my room is over here. I'm gonna go check it out

real quick," Jack declared, avoiding my question and wheeling himself down the hallway. "Hang out here for a second."

"Uh, okay?" I responded, thoroughly confused. There must be something seriously wrong with this college friend to make Jack act so strange. But watching my brother wheel himself away, his broad shoulders and strong muscles limited by an injury and the crushing weight of what was to come, I understood the need to just take a minute.

Deciding I probably needed a minute too, I stepped toward the glass. Everything looked so small. People were going about their business, trying to build a life worth living. From up here, they all looked so tiny, so insignificant.

They weren't. They all needed someone to take care of them, but once they were finally okay, they would move on. They wouldn't need someone anymore.

Getting left behind is inevitable.

Interrupting my train of thought, I heard the distinct sound of buttons being pushed on the keypad. This was either the buddy from college or the valet, so I turned around and brushed my hair back as the door swung open.

"What the hell?"

4

Those beautiful dark brown eyes pierced mine once again, but this time, instead of feeling all fluttery and flustered, I was pissed.

So royally pissed at this stupid man and at the stupid universe for putting him here.

Again.

"You broke into my apartment?" Jason Westerman fumed. "Are you actually insane? I'm calling the cops."

"Oh, please do, you egotistical jerk!" I yelled back, my face flushing with heat. "Damn, you really can't pull your head far enough out of your ass to see the truth, can you?"

"See what truth? That you're an obsessed puck bunny?" His face turned red, looking unnatural on him. "You track me down at the airport, pull that whole innocent southern girl act, and now you're standing in my living room? What else do I need to see?"

"Don't act like you know me at all!" In my fury, I took two steps until I was right up in his face, his hand still poised

30

to call the police. "You have no idea who I am, and there is no way I would go through that much trouble! I don't have the time, asshole!"

Shit, he really was even more beautiful up close.

That pissed me off even more.

"Oh, really? Then who the hell are you? How did you get into my apartment?" he shouted back at me. At that moment, Jack wheeled himself down the hallway. The sound of the wheels against the hardwood turned my face from Jason Westerman's stupid one.

"Jase? What's going on?" Jack asked, confused. Looking at my brother then back at Westerman, I took a step back in shock as the pieces clicked together.

Jason Westerman was my brother's buddy from college. As Momma would say, slap me sideways and call it Sunday.

Interrupting my train of thought, the man of the freaking weekend grabbed my elbow and turned towards Jack.

"Hey, Jack. I'm so sorry, man. I don't know how she got in here—"

"Uh, I do," Jack interrupted, looking between the two of us.

If I didn't get out of here soon, my rage was going to burn me alive.

"What?" The idiot had the gall to sound surprised.

"Yeah. You wanna get your big mitts off my little sister, Westerman?"

It took a full thirty seconds for the bonehead to figure it out and drop my elbow, stepping back in surprise. Those well-defined eyebrows shot up so high, they practically disappeared into his shaggy mop of hair. Crossing my arms,

I glanced back at Jason, giving him my best unimpressed look.

"I, uh, oh shit, I—" the poor fool stuttered.

Yeah, I'd be pretty damn embarrassed too. Deciding to put him out of his misery, which was more than he deserved, I pushed past him and only stopped with my hand on the door handle, glancing back at them both.

"Call me when you're ready for a ride to dinner, Jack. I'm gonna run home and freshen up." He gave me a small nod as Jason gaped at me. "And tell your 'buddy' here to get a grip on that ego. You are on the top floor, after all, and if his head gets any bigger, he'll fall right through the hardwood. I'd hate to have to rescue my brother from death by jackass."

With that, I marched out the door, slamming it as loud as I could behind me. The small rush of satisfaction didn't last as long as it should've. It felt like ten years before the elevator finally arrived, and my whole body fidgeted with the need to escape.

Once I made it to the ground floor, I stormed to the valet, scaring the poor man half to death.

"I'll get your car right away, ma'am," his panicked voice squeaked out, and before I could say anything, he was off. I took a deep breath. Everything about this place made me feel like dirt, from the fancy valet driving my ancient hatchback to the idiot professional athlete who lived there. I needed to get in my car, and I needed to sing some songs from my *I Hate Men* playlist.

It was truly the only cure to my anger.

After the frantic valet got my car and I apologized with as much grace as I could offer, I turned up my music. The best of Miranda Lambert and Carrie Underwood's anger at the male species filled my speakers, and my voice went hoarse from screaming the words as I pulled into my driveway, but I felt better. Still wildly angry, but better.

Until I saw Ash and *the* boyfriend arguing on the porch.

Turning off my car, I closed my eyes and laid my head back against the headrest.

What was this, argument day? I wasn't normally a contentious person. Feisty? My siblings would say so. Opinionated? Sure. Ready to go to war if someone disrespected my people? Definitely.

But those weren't things I saw as strengths. While most people defined me by them, I tried everything I could to push those traits down, to cover them up. Those are things people always used as their excuse as they walked away.

But when someone came for my people, it was like they awoke that part of me in a split second.

Apparently, a hockey player accusing me of being a puck bunny did it too.

A FREAKING PUCK BUNNY.

Something knocked against my window, and the noise jerked me upright. My eyes flew open to see my roommate, Tae, smiling at me through the glass with concern in her big blue eyes. Glancing back, I saw she'd pulled her car up next to mine in the driveway.

Sighing, I grabbed my phone and keys and opened the door. As I stepped out, I heard pieces of commotion from the porch.

"Do you even love me, Ash? I do literally so much for

you, and you literally don't ever do a thing for me," the boyfriend whined.

"Welcome to the soap opera," Tae said, throwing an arm around my shoulders I tried my best not to shrug off. "Are you okay, honey? That was some serious sighin' and ponderin'."

Tae Sutton was deep south royalty, a freelance journalist and blogger by day and a bartender by night. Apparently, the bartending was a social outlet, since she in no way needed the extra cash. But that was Tae—all reckless abandon and whimsical fun.

She used her free arm to push her thick blonde curls over her shoulder and set those baby blues on me, worry in her gaze.

"Just a real long day...a long weekend, actually." I glanced at my friend and her absolute ass of a boyfriend. "I have a feeling it's about to get longer."

"He really is the worst. Bless his heart." Tae sighed. "I'm sorry you're the one who always ends up facin' him. I'm too nervous to try again after last time."

We both huffed at the memory of that spineless excuse of a man bursting into tears and telling Ash he couldn't understand what Tae was saying. Tae's accent got real thick when she was angry—thicker than her normal, which was *thick*. She wasn't afraid to pick a fight if she needed to, with a whole lot of south and sass thrown in there for good measure. But she knew if the boyfriend felt stupid, he'd whine to Ash.

To be fair, he was pretty stupid.

Deciding I would get my luggage later, I let Tae's arm drop and made my way to the porch.

"Donovan, you don't mean that!" Ash said tearfully, trying to reach towards him. "My friends need me too. You can't ask me to ignore them. I promise, I love you. Please!"

As I reached the steps, my fury from a certain hockey player quickly redirected to this particular brand of idiot. Seriously, who did he think he was? When I was within a few feet of them, the boyfriend finally looked over at his audience, and his eyes widened when they landed on me and Tae.

I kept my face neutral, but on the inside, I was grinning. I'd always been good at striking fear into people who deserved it. Momma said my eyes said a whole lot more than my words. Every time good ole Donovan and I faced off, I was grateful Momma was always right.

"Hey, Ash. You alright?" My eyes sought hers first, and the tears there spoke for her, her cheeks flushed with heat despite the fall air. "Donovan, you need to leave."

"You can't—" he started sputtering, and I glared.

"Private property. I can and will call the cops on you." I gave him a saccharine smile. "You do *not* wanna push me right now. You've already made Ash upset, and that doesn't seem like you are *literally doing so much* for her. So I'm gonna say it one more time. Leave, or it's fixing to be a real long day for you."

His scrawny Adams apple bobbed as he gulped, and he glanced back at Ash one more time before shoving past me. He practically stomped to his car, throwing a fit like the little boy we all knew he was. He didn't even look back as he climbed into the truck his rich daddy bought him, the tires squealing dramatically as he peeled out of our neighborhood.

Turning back to Ash, I could tell she was about three

seconds from a breakdown. Shoving down my bone-deep weariness, I put an uncomfortable arm around her shoulder and guided her inside. I knew it was bad when she didn't even make a comment on me willingly showing affection.

"Come on, Ash. Tae got mint chocolate chip at the store this week, and it's calling your name." I patted her shoulder awkwardly as we made our way to the kitchen. Tae strutted in ahead of us, grabbing bowls and spoons as I got Ash situated on a barstool at the counter. She was shaking, but the tears were still controlled.

"Ash, what's going on?" I prodded. Tae started scooping insane amounts of ice cream into each bowl. She had even pulled out a fourth one, presumably for Tess, who hadn't made an appearance yet. It took a few seconds, but finally, Ash met my eyes and sighed.

"You said you'd never say I told you so, but I feel like I need to hear it right now." She rubbed her eyes, looking exhausted. "I can't help how I feel about him. He's like a drug; I keep going back, and I can't stop. He's not always like that."

Tae and I exchanged a look. He *was* always like that—normally worse.

"Darlin', we all know you're a romantic. But that boy? He doesn't treat you the way you deserve. He's been raggin' on ya about everythin' and nothin' since y'all first started up, and it hurts our hearts to see you broken down by a man who doesn't even deserve you." Tae spoke slowly, looking into Ash's eyes as she said what we'd never wanted to. "You deserve someone who will love you for every piece of you, not someone trying to turn you into someone else, hun."

Ash just sniffled, looking like she was about to burst into another round of tears, as I pushed her bowl and spoon forward. Silently grabbing both, she dug into her ice cream and let the sugar take her away. Tae and I grabbed our own bowls, watching Ash like she could break at any second.

"Hey y'all, is Oakley back—" Tess stopped mid-sentence as she came into the kitchen, eyes widening while she took in the depressing scene.

Ash tapped her spoon mindlessly against her bowl, her light brown eyes completely bloodshot, her curls frizzy and matted at the same time. Tae fidgeted with the hem of her white sundress, fixing to get a permanent worry line from watching Ash with furrowed brows.

I held out the fourth bowl of ice cream as Tess slowly walked over. Accepting the bowl, she glanced at Ash then back at me and Tae with her eyebrows raised. I mouthed 'the boyfriend', and she simply nodded, understanding crossing her face. She leaned against the counter, facing Ash as she continued tapping away.

Finally, Ash stood.

"I'm going upstairs. I promise I'll talk through everything later. I need to be alone right now." Without waiting for a response, she turned and made her way to her room, her retreating footsteps the only sound breaking the tenuous silence. Gathering the rest of the empty bowls and depositing them in the sink, I turned to Tae, who started filling Tess in on the latest round of drama.

"I'm sorry you had to walk into that on top of everythin' else, Oakley," Tess started gently, her eyes wide as Tae finished the story. "How's your brother?"

"He's doing alright." I sighed, rubbing my eyes. The exhaustion from the day was starting to hit me full force.

Tae and Tess exchanged a quick look then glanced back at me with sympathy. I stiffened, wanting to avoid any more looks like that. If I was going to survive the drive to my parents' place and the high emotions my brother's homecoming was sure to bring, I was going to need a shower.

So, I gave them a noncommittal nod, conveying who knows what, before trudging up the stairs, leaving my luggage and my perfectly ordinary, well-controlled life behind.

5

"Ohhhh, so you think I shouldn't kiss him 'cause he just got braces?" Mal tilted her head, running a brush through her long, dark hair while looking at me in the mirror. From my spot lounging on her bed, I could see the tubes of lip gloss littering her vanity and the random sticky notes around the mirror in front of her.

Things had changed drastically since my younger sister took over the room we used to share. Everything yet nothing had changed in my parents' small, three bedroom house on the outskirts of La Vergne, Tennessee, where I'd spent my whole life.

Every time I drove down the one lane road to the house at the edge of a small, rural neighborhood, I felt a pang of hurt. We were one tax bracket away from a trailer park, and I'd never thought we had nothing until I left. Until I had something.

"That's not what I said, Mal." I sighed, lying back all the

way and covering my eyes with my arm. "I'm just saying, it's something to be aware of when kissing a boy. What if you're trying to use tongue and cut it? Think of the infection risk."

"Um, why would I use tongue?"

I felt the bed dip next to me as Mal's disgust rang in the air. I'd had few good experiences with tongue, so it was valid.

"I don't know, Mal. It's a way of kissing." I sighed again, the weight of the day resting firmly on my shoulders. Jack had the good sense to call Momma and let her know he was back and coming to dinner. He even told her he had news, and it would be hard to hear. So, Reba and Dolly were blasting, and Pa was solemnly staying out of my frantic Momma's way, out on the deck 'manning' the grill.

"Well, I don't think it's gonna be my way of kissin'." Mal pulled the arm covering my eyes away and leaned over so I didn't have a choice but to look at her. "You okay, Oaksy? Momma always says two sighs in a row is a sure sign."

"A sure sign of what?" I sat up to face her.

"I dunno. She just says a sure sign." Her cute button nose scrunched, dark hair curtaining her face as she tried to think. She got Momma's southern belle looks through and through. "She always says it in that tone, ya know? The one she uses when she's tryna explain a dramatic situation to Pa?"

"Oh, trust me, I know the tone." I laughed at my sweet little sister. "Just tired."

She grabbed my hand and squeezed it tight.

"Mal, know whatever Jack says tonight, it's gonna be fine. I'm helping him, and I'll get it handled." As I spoke, Mal nodded and dropped her head, drawing her hands into her lap.

"I don't even remember him, Oaksy," she whispered. "He's a stranger. Why should I care when he's never even cared to call?"

There weren't any words. Nothing could replace the years he'd chosen to miss.

"You don't." She glanced up, confused, her eyes begging for me to explain this away. "That's on him to fix, with all of us. But we should at least give him the chance."

The words tasted sour in my mouth—everything in me wanted to punish him for how he'd abandoned us, but as I watched my sister curl in on herself again, I knew I couldn't. I hated seeing the weight fall heavy on her shoulders. She might be older than her years, but Mal still deserved to be a kid.

"Don't think all this change is gonna stop me from showing you who's boss 'round these parts," I drawled.

Her eyes widened a fraction, and she began to scramble off the bed, but not before I pounced. Not caring that she had just spent an ungodly amount of time brushing her hair, I put her in a headlock as she pawed and clawed at my arm.

"Oakley! Ugh—" she squealed between laughs as we wobbled on unsteady legs.

"You know the magic words, Mallory Louise. Come on, let's hear 'em!" I taunted, keeping my grip light. She giggled and grunted again, trying to kick my legs out from under me.

"Girls!" Momma hollered at us from down below. "Hurry on down here please!"

"You heard her, Mal! Quick! Say the magic words!"

"Ugh! Fine! Oakley Mae Tennen is my favorite sibling, and I would go fishin' with her over any soul in the universe!"

Mallory screamed. I let her go immediately, and she thumped to the floor with a huff. "Jeez, Oaksy—and people think brothers are the worst!"

"Oakley! Mallory! Quit rough housin' and hurry yourselves down here!"

"Yes, ma'am!" we called out in unison. As we headed for the stairs, I looped an arm around my baby sister one more time in a rare hug as I geared up for the looming conversation.

"For the record, I would go fishing with you over anyone in the universe too, Mallory Louise Tennen." I squeezed her to my side. She rolled her eyes but proceeded to wrap both arms around my waist and gave me a squeeze back. Then, in a swift move only our brother Hunter could have taught her, she poked me in the ribs. *Hard.* My arms reflexively let go, and Mal's laughter trailed her as she booked it past the boys' old room and down the narrow stairs.

"Mal!" I hollered as I ran after her.

Jumping down the last step, I rounded the hallway and jolted to a stop when those all-too-familiar, piercing brown eyes met mine.

"You've gotta be kidding me."

Jason freaking Westerman was the only one who heard my grumble, since my parents were currently staring at my older brother in shock. Momma grasped Pa's hand tight as they stood in silence, Jack's face even paler than earlier.

"Momma. Pa." He took a moment to clear his throat. "I know you probably don't want to see me, but I needed...I needed to be here."

Mal shuffled awkwardly on her feet as she stood behind

Pa, and the tension filling the space threatened to drown us all. Jack glanced helplessly at me, but I simply stared. He needed to do this on his own. The hulking hockey player stood back, glancing apprehensively at me once before turning back to the shitshow.

"I-I'm sorry. I'm sorry I left and I'm sorry I never called and I-" Jack's apology cut off as Momma lunged for him, arms tight around her boy's neck. Pa, as always, stood silently behind her with a supportive hand on her back. When she pushed back, wiping tears with the back of her hand, she was smiling.

And I knew we would all move on for Momma's sake while none of us ever truly healed.

"You're back now, and that's what matters," she declared, and Pa nodded. That was that, and my chest started to tighten. Momma's eyes finally moved from her boy to the giant man trying to melt into the hallway walls. "And who are you?"

"Jason Westerman." Jason stuck out a hand, which Pa gave one firm shake. "We were roommates at Boston College."

"You were living in Boston?" Mal asked, hurt still lacing her tone. I took silent pride in the way she didn't immediately forgive Jack either. Jason's eyes widened, and I think he finally realized how deep this went.

Jack nodded once, his eyes catching on the teenager he'd never known.

"Hey, don't you play for the Rebels?" Pa asked, a light returning to his eyes.

"Yes, sir. Got traded two seasons ago."

"I thought he was dropping you off, not making a house call." I interrupted, making no effort to cover my sharp tone. Jason gave me a pleading look as Momma gave me a disapproving one.

"Oakley Mae Tennen. I'm so sorry for that tone of hers, Jason. Despite her manners, what my daughter means to say is, you are more than welcome in our home anytime," Momma declared. I opened my mouth to argue, but she raised her eyebrows. "Now, quit bein' ugly, Oakley Mae. You're fixin' to be on dish duty tonight."

"I'm on dish duty every Sunday dinner," I protested, but Momma raised a hand, effectively silencing me, fussing over my big brother as the tension seeped out of the room on her command. My eyes drifted quickly past the hulking man as Jack gave a pained smile, his hand mindlessly rubbing his thigh. The combination of stress and travel must've made the injury flare up, causing additional inflammation and swelling. I caught his eye, giving a long glance to the leg before moving back to his eyes. He grimaced and gave me a slight nod back.

Injury agitation confirmed.

I pushed off the wall and headed to the kitchen to find supplies. Hearing a teary Momma already demanding to know everything we'd missed, I opened our medicine cabinet and grabbed a few things. Strangely, the medical tape I needed to reinforce his bandage wasn't where I normally stocked it. Shuffling a few things around, I finally caught sight of it up on the top shelf. This cabinet was already free-hanging above the counter, so the top shelf was a good bit above my head. I stood on my tippy toes, my fingertips barely grazing it.

I blew out a frustrated breath, debating climbing onto the counter, when a muscular arm reached above me, grabbing the sports tape so easily, I could scream. Startled, I whirled around, only to smack into that same broad chest that pissed me off on sight.

Time slowed as my gaze rose to meet those brown eyes once again. My stomach fluttered as I realized how close our faces were, and the earnest look on his stupid face took my breath away.

I hated it.

I waited for him to back away, but he didn't. Instead, his eyes searched mine. Slowly, as if trying not to startle me, he held the medical tape between us.

A peace offering.

"H-hey," he stammered, his deep voice piercing through me. "I, uh, I wanted to explain some things."

I took in his hesitant expression and his sideways smile as he rubbed the back of his neck with his free hand.

"Explain?" I retorted. He winced, crossing his arms in front of his body. There was almost no space between us, and I took a step back to avoid more physical contact than necessary, but I'd backed myself into the counter, giving me nowhere else to run.

"Yeah. I was an absolute jerk," he said softly. "Jack explained everything, why you were at the airport and my apartment, and it's crazy we ran into each other in the first place. I need you to know, I'm not normally like that. I just— you can imagine how hard it is to trust people when I'm, well..."

"I actually can't imagine," I stated, giving him no leverage. His eyes widened and his shoulders tensed, like he finally realized I wasn't going to make this easy.

"Oakley, I'm sorry, okay? I had this psycho ex-girlfriend and some bad fan situations. It puts me on edge, and I'd just gotten back from an away game we'd lost, which isn't an excuse, but when I saw your suitcase tag with my face on it and then you showed up in my apartment—"

"You jumped to the most logical conclusion: that everyone is obsessed with you?" I spat. In my head, I knew it made sense, but my heart was still annoyed. He'd done the unforgivable: wounded my pride. "Listen, I get that your life is different from mine, but being an absolute ass to a girl you just met is self-centered and ignorant."

"I know. Can we please start over?" His striking eyes pleaded with mine. "Jack's told me about you for years. The legendary Oakley Mae. That's not how I wanted to meet you for the first time, and I'm so sorry. Can we pretend that never happened? I promise I'll be more of a southern gentleman. You can even show me the ropes."

My thoughts raced. Jack had talked about me? Why would he do that? Did he explain how he'd abandoned us too?

Him quoting our first conversation only made me more confused. I didn't like that. I liked clear, predictable, and that was the most frustrating part. Because he got under my skin. Nobody did that.

"Oakley?" His voice brought me back. I'd zoned out hard, staring into his eyes as my thoughts whirled. Then, my mind stuck on one.

He'll leave you too.

One reason was all I needed. Escaping his trance, I shook my head and made a decision.

"Not in your wildest dreams, Westerman." I tried to sound confident as I grabbed the medical tape from his hand and walked around him, my blunt words stunning him enough to make an escape. "I told you before—you're either a southern gentleman or you're not. And I don't have time for lost causes."

6

People can be a lot of things: funny, annoying, helpful, sad, selfish... Humans are beautiful myriads of feeling and light and life.

They can also be incredibly stupid.

"What do you mean you're not gonna tell them tonight?" I seethed, barely holding in my anger.

"I just came back home, and she's worried about my leg already. Maybe we should deal with that news now," Jackson argued back. We were quite the sight, in our tiny downstairs bathroom, his wheelchair maneuvered to fit between the toilet and the wall so he could prop his injured leg on the tub. I sat with my supplies on my lap next to his leg, unwrapping his bandage.

"You know how pissed she's gonna be if you don't say anything tonight?" I whisper-shouted, trying to keep our voices down. Momma had knocked on the door twice before I hollered at Mal to distract her.

This day had lasted ten years already, and I was anxious for it to be over.

"I know, Oaksy. Let me think," he grumbled, slumping back in his wheelchair.

"Don't call me that," I finally snapped. Jack sat up straight. "You don't get to call me that."

Silence sat between us, soaking up every drop of tension.

Finally, Jack spoke, his voice barely a whisper.

"I'm sorry, Oakley." He leaned forward, trying to catch my eye.

"It's going to take more than sorry to fix this," I said softly, the anger dissipating as hurt took charge. "And it starts with being honest. You have to tell them."

"I don't know if I can, not when I just got them back."

Shaking my head and shooting him one more disapproving glare, I focused on his injury. If I didn't, I would say things our relationship could never recover from.

The skin was angry and inflamed, the serrated cuts across his thigh significantly worse than when I'd wrapped them earlier. Taking a cold cloth, I started to dab at the skin. Jack winced, pulling in a sharp breath as I tried to clean off the wound.

"We have to avoid an infection, Jack. It's draining, which is a good sign, but I'm gonna put..." I explained as I reached towards my pile, only to realize I didn't grab my antibacterial spray. Letting out a groan, I looked at the door, which seemed pretty well blocked by Jack's wheelchair. Maybe if I turned sideways?

"What do you need? I can call Jason—" Jack started to say.

"No," I barked, cutting him off. Jason was the reason I'd forgotten it in the first place. "Let's call Mal."

"Oakley..." Jack sighed, like he always did when he was about to be my parent instead of my brother. "He apologized and explained, didn't he?"

He had. He'd infuriatingly made sense, but he was overly confident and defensive and arrogant.

"Doesn't mean we're gonna be friends, Jack. The guy has a serious ego issue," I mumbled, cleaning out the small wounds littering my brother's leg until he'd let me call Mal.

He sighed again. I hated that sigh. It always made me feel like the world was on Jack's shoulders, and I'd put it there. When he didn't say anything, I looked up to find him assessing me.

"What?" I snapped, too much on my mind to have this conversation.

"He's a good guy, even though he was wrong for insulting you." His face was a sober mask. "He's had so many people treat him wrong, and he doesn't let it bring him down. Don't be one of the people who treats him wrong, not when I've talked you up so much."

The emotional whiplash was killing me, but I matched Jack's hesitant smile. Sitting in the bathroom that held so many memories of fighting to brush our teeth first, singing songs as we cleaned, and patching up skinned knees, I knew, despite my anger, that I would gladly take Jack's sighs and parental speeches any day, just as long as he was still here to give them.

"I'm still angry at you, but...I'm glad you're home, Jack." My voice was filled with emotion I tried not to show. Jack's face softened, and he reached over to pat my hand before sitting back in his chair.

"I'm sorry I left for so long." He stared down at his hands. "I-I just hope I'm strong enough to stay."

"Don't do that," I said. He didn't even look up. My heart stuttered at what had brought him home. "This won't be like last time, Jack. I promise."

"It can't be, Oakley. I'd rather die than let it be like that again."

When his somber eyes met mine, I was brought back to the days when it felt like we'd lost both of our parents to Momma's cancer, and my chest tightened.

Before I could respond, a loud knock rattled the door. It cracked open, hitting the side of the wheelchair softly before Jason popped his head in.

"Sorry. I was sent by Mallory to see what was taking so long?" he said, his eyebrows drawn in, looking so far out of his element. "I think she's tired of distracting your mom."

"Well, Oakley refuses to ask you to grab her something she needs—"

"And Jack is trying to get out of telling our family about why he really came home."

If Jack was going to throw me under the bus, I could play that game. I even matched his glare.

"I thought that was the whole point of being here? Of coming home?" Jason asked, crossing his arms and trying to look at Jack. It was jarring that these two were close enough that they talked like this. "You have to tell them, brother."

Jack didn't answer; he just glanced at his friend before focusing back at his hands.

He must've been so scared. This, all of this, was going to change our whole world. *Again.* Life was cruel like that. It got you comfortable, and then it took your biggest fear and put a spotlight on it. You had no choice but to face it.

If Jack could face this, maybe I could face some of my own issues. For him.

The small ones, at least.

"Fine," I huffed, moving my pile of medical supplies to the side and trying to maneuver my leg over the wheelchair, where Jason had taken a step back.

"Oakley, despite what you believe, I'm capable of—" Jason started as he stood his ground against me. I respected it, but I also needed him to move.

"I know, you idiot. I just...I didn't want to shout over—" My leg got caught on Jack's wheelchair, and I stumbled the last bit towards the door. Jason's arms shot out, grasping me under the elbows and pulling me upright. I jerked my arms back but had nowhere else to go. "Huh. Nice reflexes."

"Why do you sound so surprised?" Jason asked with a smirk.

"I'm not. Now." I huffed, pushing a palm against his chest and shoving him into the hallway. At first, he looked at my hand against his firm chest with confusion. Then, he glanced up and finally took a step backwards.

When we were fully in the hallway, I removed my hand from his chest and shut the door as Jack yelled, "Be nice!"

"No promises," I shouted back at the same time Jason hollered, "Only if she is!"

I rolled my eyes and crossed my arms. Jason mirrored my stance hesitantly, as if he really expected me to come at him.

"The antibacterial spray is in a white bottle with a green top. It should be on the top shelf of the medicine cabinet," I whispered, meeting Jason's surprised eyes. "The one where we talked earlier. Could you grab it for me, Mister Hockey?"

"Mister Hockey?" he whispered back. "And why are you whispering?"

"It felt right, and I stand by it." Now, I was whispering harshly. "And *we* are whispering because my brother is proud and stubborn and doesn't need his little sister hollering orders at his friend across him while he sits in a wheelchair. And these walls are extremely thin. So, this sacrifice of being so close to you saves his dignity a bit and gives him a chance to think about telling them—"

Mal's laugh echoed down the hallway, and I whipped my head around to make sure none of my family was close enough to hear us. When I turned back to Jason, his hands had moved to his hips, his head leaning in, like he was really listening.

"I don't know you, okay? But you seem to know Jack, enough to know he'll do anything for the important people in his life, even if it's misguided and hurts him in the long run. Like not telling our family about his cancer because he doesn't want to burden them and then telling our family only because I asked him to." I sighed, forcing my voice into a more relaxed whisper. "He's going to have a lot of choices taken away from him soon. I might be mad at him right now, but I don't want to take another choice away if I can help it."

"So standing out here with me—"

"An unfortunate yet necessary sacrifice for the independence of Jack." I gave him a strained smile as I reached for the door handle. "Think you can handle grabbing that spray, hotshot?"

He paused, looking at me intently.

"What?" I snapped, still whispering.

"I can't figure you out, Oakley," he said at full volume. "You flirt with strangers like a professional, you have this cute little southern accent but your words are weapons, and you can be so damn feisty—"

"Do you have a point?" I started, flustered as he stepped closer.

"Good hell, I'm getting there." He cut me off with a grin. "I hope you can accept my apology, because I'm not going anywhere, and I don't think you are either."

Despite the way we were trying to clear the air, it felt like it only thickened around us, locking us in the moment. "I'll consider it—but only for Jack's sake."

"I won't give up on this, Oakley." He dropped back to a whisper, something that felt intimate and genuine as that deep voice flowed over me. Shivers raced through me, and my defenses went up stronger than ever.

"Oh, I'm not worried. I'm more stubborn than anyone. Don't get your hopes up, hotshot."

He shook his head, chuckling as he looked at me with something new in his eyes. Trusting Jason to get me that spray, I made the treacherous journey back over the wheelchair and settled into my spot on the tub. When I looked up at Jack, he was still staring at his hands, like they held the answers. So, I focused on gathering my supplies back into my lap.

"Okay."

My eyes shot up to his. He looked grim but determined. "Yeah?" I asked hopefully.

"I asked you to give Jason another shot. You asked me to tell them." He nodded as if that was it.

"Jack, you shouldn't do this because of me. You should do it because you can't truly come back until you're truthful with the people who make it home." As I spoke, the door opened, and a bottle of antibacterial spray was chucked at me. Snatching it with both hands, I rolled my eyes at Jason.

"Nice reflexes." He grinned before he looked between us and raised his eyebrows. "So, are you doing this?"

This time, when Jack and I looked at each other, we shared a small smile of understanding. A truce of sorts.

Then, a look of completely warranted apprehension.

Telling the family about Jack's cancer went almost exactly how I expected. Momma broke out into sobs, Pa held her hand and comforted her, and Mal sat by herself with her own tears before looking back at me for confirmation. Hunter, who was FaceTimed in from his dorm room at the University of Tennessee, was silent save for an occasional question. He'd call in a few days to share how he really felt about it, after he'd had time to process.

The unexpected variable was Jason. The rest of my family had taken a seat in the living room with Jack in the center, fidgeting under all the attention. Jason stood behind the couch with me. My brother had called him the same day he'd called me, so we both already knew. We'd both already decided how we would react to this conversation, and for those few silent moments, I enjoyed not being alone.

I tried to ignore him shuffling closer. I tried to ignore the goosebumps that sprang up at the near contact.

I couldn't ignore him when he leaned close and whispered, "Are you okay?"

His breath caressed my cheek, and I fought back a shiver.

"Oaksy? What do you think?" Mal's eyes were filled with tears, but her face was stoic, like she was trying her best to be brave. Momma had set the phone with Hunter on the line propped up against the couch, now gripping Jack's hand tight. Pa was standing, a hand on Jack's shoulder, his other hand linked to Momma so they made a tidy little circle of grief, just the three of them, the way they always did.

Stepping away from Jason Westerman and his deep brown eyes, I fidgeted with my hands as I rounded the couch. Mal jumped to me, wrapping her arms tight around my waist as Jack silently pleaded for help.

So, I went clinical.

"From what we know right now, Jack's case is manageable. His official diagnosis is osteosarcoma, which as we know is the most common form of bone cancer." Momma's eyes widened, but I kept going. "They caught it early enough. It's still localized in his injured leg. He begins chemotherapy soon, which will hopefully shrink the growth and prepare him for surgery to have the tumor removed. He should be able to fully recover, just like Momma."

Jack gave me a thankful nod as Momma started to hope. Her frown softened, and she gripped Pa's hand a little tighter. I felt like I needed to warn her.

"To be honest, this will be hard. The treatment, combined with the natural spread of the cancer and trying to heal from an injury, well, it'll wipe him out. His body's going to be exhausted, but with time, the hope is he'll heal completely." I tacked on a small smile to try and lessen the blow, and Momma turned to Jack, asking a million questions.

The pressure in my chest grew a bit, and Mal looked up at me with those sad eyes, like I carried the weight of this for her, for all of them.

Like he could sense my thoughts, Pa put up a hand, and Momma stopped her chatter. He rarely gave an opinion he didn't believe with his whole heart, even if that meant staying silent, so when Pa spoke, we listened.

"I need to say one thing. Our family has been through this before, and it put a lot on Oakley and Jackson's shoulders." Pa waved me off when I tried to protest, that Tennen stubbornness lighting in his eyes. "This time will be different. We will face this together."

Then, he nodded, and that was it.

Momma nodded in agreement, and I wanted to scream. The words meant more than I could ever explain, and yet they weren't enough. Again, the true pain was being put away, wrapped in a neat bow, like it didn't need to be looked at any closer.

They didn't know what we went through before, because they *weren't there.*

How could I trust that this time would be different? How could I feel love from my parents and yet feel so utterly abandoned by them?

Feelings I'd tamped down since I'd moved out of this

house and away from the pain started to roar back to life. And not for the first time, I understood how Jack could never look back.

It was all too much, too out of my control.

Placing a kiss on Mal's forehead, I unwrapped her arms from around my waist and made my way to the back patio. The pressure in my chest was growing, and I focused on getting outside, away from all the sorrow and uncertainty.

I needed to get out. I needed to detach. It was too much.

As soon as I made it onto the back patio, I felt like I could breathe again. I rushed to the railing, leaning over and taking in deep gulps of air.

I needed to be strong for them. Even if they promised this time would be different, we weren't different people. We were just older versions of those who barely survived last time.

As I took another deep breath, the pain in my chest started to recede. Not enough, but it was fading. My hands moved to my temples as they attempted to rub the stress away.

"Are you okay?" That damn deep voice. It shouldn't have made my heart skip. I shouldn't have turned around and met those brown eyes. "Oakley?"

"Yeah?"

Embarrassment washed over me as I turned. He'd seen all that. He knew what a mess we were.

"You good?" Those eyes were full of concern, not pity. They shouldn't be. We had one moment of understanding. That didn't change anything between us.

"Yes sir. Right as rain." I grimaced, whipping back

around to face the tall oaks covering our land, the edges of the leaves starting to turn orange. It was hinting at fall, like the trees knew we needed to warm up to the change before they exploded with color, that we needed time to come to terms with losing it all. I felt Jason stand next to me. "What do you want, Westerman?"

"Well, after world peace and the Stanley Cup, I would love to understand some of these southern sayings." He smiled, and I scoffed at his attempt to change my focus.

"Oh yeah?" I tried to laugh. "Makes sense you'd be struggling. With that tiny brain and all the hits you take, there can't be much room for learning new things."

"Ouch, Oaks." He pressed a hand to his chest, as if I'd stabbed him there. "Most people would offer to explain them to me."

I turned to face him, his dark eyebrows practically disappearing into his hair. I got lost for a second, thinking of how it was possible for him to have such shaggy hair and a boyish smile and yet be all man. His height. His build. His presence. He was intimidating, to say the least.

"Maybe I'm not most people," I quipped back, fighting a smile. Ready for another witty comment, I was taken aback when his smirk dropped, and he looked at me. *Really* looked at me.

"Yeah, I'm getting that." He tilted his head to the side and examined me further, like he was still trying to figure me out.

Uncomfortable, I shifted my gaze to our backyard, to where I spent my childhood until he spoke again.

"Bless your heart."

I whipped my head around. "Pardon?"

"What does that mean? I've heard people say 'bless your heart', and I have no idea what it means. I don't know what you just said either."

This poor Canadian looked so bewildered, but the lightness between us started to feel a bit like it did when we first met in that parking garage—like he was just a guy I found attractive, joking around like he could be just as attracted to me. And like I had then, I took the emotional reprieve this moment offered.

"'Pardon' means 'excuse me'. 'Bless your heart', well, it has several meanings depending on the context," I offered, but he still looked at me like he was lost in a sea of questions only I held the answers to.

"If it's said like 'oh, bless your heart'," I said in my most condescending tone, "it means 'you're an idiot'."

Something, let's call it recognition, dawned on his face, followed by offense.

"But 'bless your heart'," I said in my most grateful, upbeat tone, "means 'thank you so much'."

"How in the world can one phrase mean those two things?" he asked incredulously, his whole face scrunching in thought.

"I don't make the rules, Westerman. I just live here." I tried to school my face back to an indifferent mask.

"Jack used to say this one all the time in college, and every time I asked him what he meant, he always said 'oh, bless your heart', which I now know means he was calling me an idiot."

"But a pitied idiot."

"That's even worse!" He looked so offended, I couldn't

help but chuckle. "He'd say 'slap me sideways and call it Sunday', and if you tell me that has multiple meanings, I might lose it."

"Oh, that one is a Momma Tennen special. She always says that," I explained, letting the nostalgia of Momma and her many sayings take over me as I glanced back towards the house and let out a breath. "It's a saying for when you're surprised, or something is different than you thought it would be."

Thoughts of Momma brushing my hair back as I fell asleep and holding my hand when I was upset ran through my mind. She had rough hands, calluses from her guitar and growing up on a farm scratching across my skin. It was my favorite feeling in the world, because like her sayings and songs, it was my momma, even if I hadn't let her do anything like that in years.

"What is that about?" he said, bewildered.

"What do you mean?" I asked, instantly defensive. He motioned a finger, circling the area around my face in an exaggerated motion.

"Your whole face looked, dare I say it, not pissed off or worried." He grinned wide, and I rolled my eyes at his enthusiasm.

That was the problem, wasn't it? I was always either pissed off or worried, sometimes a combination of both. How much longer could I be the person who bore it all?

Did I even want to be that person anymore?

"You zone out hard when you're thinking," he said softly.

"Yeah. Ever since I was little. Momma always said I had

so many thoughts, I couldn't think and be in reality at the same time. Ready to leave me be?"

"Not even close. Are we gonna be friends now, OT?"

"OT?"

"Yeah. Oakley Tennen. Also overtime." He grinned lazily, as if he hadn't just given me a nickname. "I think it's gonna take me a little longer to get through to you that I'm a guy worth knowing, but an overtime win is always the sweetest."

Stunned, the only response I had was a very eloquent, "Ah."

"Yep. Okay, OT. What about 'if the creek don't rise'? Does that mean they're waiting on the creek to determine what they're doing? Why in the world do people talk in code around here?" His voice was a deep, rich yet light combination that kept blowing my mind.

"I think the correct southern sentence you're looking for is 'why do people talk in code *'round these parts'*," I corrected. "If someone says they're gonna make it 'if the creek don't rise', it means they're gonna make it unless something stops them."

"Why don't they say they'll be there unless something comes up?" His deep timbre pitched higher as he got more confused. I let a giggle go free and immediately slapped a hand over my mouth.

I didn't giggle. *Ever.*

Westerman caught on to my surprise, and his eyes widened. We stood at a standstill as a grin broke over his face and he raised a finger.

But I couldn't move, because his full smile was breathtaking—a little bit mischievous boy, a little bit full grown man, and a whole lot of getting under my skin.

I was annoyed at him. I was attracted to him.

And I couldn't get my damn face under control.

"I knew it," he declared smugly as that finger lingered between us. I lightly smacked his finger out of my face.

"Knew what?" I asked, ashamed to admit how breathy my voice sounded. He leaned against the railing, far too casual with all this tension coursing between us.

"You light up when you're happy, even though you don't seem to let yourself," he said as if telling me about the weather. "It makes you even more beautiful."

A flurry of emotions bombarded me, and I didn't know what to say.

"Oaksy!"

Both of us turned to face Pa, who glanced between us with confusion.

"Yeah?" I croaked out.

"Sorry to interrupt, but your momma is currently reheating all the food and doesn't want to have to do it a second time. She already had to stop herself from begging Hunter to drive home so all her babies could be close. I don't think she could handle it if her green beans went soggy." He chuckled as he looked between the two of us again. "Mal was also asking if you brought her an outfit for her, uh, her hangout with the Letcher boy."

"You mean her date, Pa?" I joked, trying to relieve some of the tension. Pa's face scrunched up like he'd eaten something sour. "It's in my car. I'll go grab it before we eat."

"Thanks, kiddo." He turned to Jason and put a hand on

his shoulder as if they were old friends, not people who'd met one hour and two traumatic conversations ago. "If the good Lord ever blesses you with daughters, you best be ready for a heart attack every time you blink."

Then, he turned his gaze towards me, and it softened as he released Jason's shoulder.

"And if you're blessed enough to have one as loyal as my Oakley, you're a special man," he stated proudly as I blushed. Trying quickly to come up with something to get us out of this situation, I was surprised when Jason spoke up.

"I only hope I can be deserving of someone so special, sir." His eyes met mine. "And maybe, I'll get to be someone special to her too."

Somehow, I felt like we weren't talking about imaginary future children anymore. My heart wanted to believe him, that he wanted to know me.

But another part of my heart wanted to argue with him again, grumble that a part of me was still hurt. I wanted to explain how he couldn't say things like that and not mean them, that he couldn't play with emotions like it was a game, scream he wasn't going to be another person to walk away because I'd never let him get close enough for it to matter.

"Well, this has been fun and all, but I'm gonna get that outfit before Mal gets her panties in a twist."

I moved past Pa, but I couldn't help but look back, trying to ignore the determination I saw glittering in Jason's eyes.

It wasn't until we had finished dinner and I was driving home that I realized: the pressure in my chest went away when Jason Westerman made me smile.

7

There was something to be said about living with a bunch of 20-something girls. Not good or bad, but something. Nothing could rival searching for your black tube top while the girl across the hall yelled to borrow your shoes. As soon as the elusive top was in my hands, Ash was at my door, still hollering.

"Please, Oakley? I promise not to spill a drink on them." When I gave her a look, she smiled sheepishly. "This time. Last time was a series of unfortunate events."

"By that you mean Donovan got hammered and knocked the drinks *and* the cheesy fries onto your feet, which were wearing my shoes? It took me a week to get them to stop smelling like cheap beer and old cheese, Ash."

"He won't be there tonight. It's girls' night. Plus, that was just one time."

"It's a pattern of behavior," I tried to say softly, but it was hard to keep the frustration from seeping in.

After their big fight last week, my normally bubbly and

happy friend was practically comatose for two days. Then, Donovan came groveling when I wasn't home, which seemed far too convenient of timing. Ash forgave him, and I'm trying to forgive her for *that*.

"Do we have to talk about this right now? Tae and Tess want to head out in the next thirty minutes, and neither of us are anywhere close to ready for downtown." She tried to sound sassy, but her voice trembled. Closing my closet, the white boots left inside, I flopped down on the bed, my long legs hanging off the side and resting on the floor. I'd only agreed to go out because this bar had cheap bar food, and I needed a distraction from my life. Ash laid down beside me, her feet dangling and kicking restlessly against the mattress.

"Ash, I don't want to say everything that's wrong about him, but I feel like I need to say you deserve better."

"But—"

"But what? You think you don't deserve more?" I snapped, taking a deep breath to calm the protective instinct rising to the surface. "This life has enough challenges on its own. You don't need a guy who makes it harder."

"I'm not like you, Oakley. I can't walk away and never think about it again. I obsess over every little interaction, and I know I'm way too attached. I know, but I can't help it." She took a deep breath, and I tried not to let her words sting. "You don't care. I care too much. It's why we're best friends. It's also why we can never talk about our romantic relationships without it ending in a...well—"

"Argument?"

"I was going to say heated disagreement. Oh, what does that lady Tae always listens to call it?"

"Brene Brown! She calls it a rumble!" Tae called from the bathroom down the hall. I hadn't wondered if they were eavesdropping, but at least now, I knew they were. I sat up to yell back.

"Y'all gonna come into the room to be part of this conversation?" I hollered down the hallway.

"Nah, you're doin' great, Oakley!" This time, it was Tess who hollered back, and I could hear her smiling.

"Yeah, we can hear just fine from here!" Tae added.

Heaving a big, dramatic sigh, I flopped onto my back again.

"We always rumble about this. Ash, I want to support you in everything, but I can't support something that makes you so unhappy, something that is draining the joy out of you." I tried to keep my voice soft and understanding, but it came out more like I was scolding a little kid.

"So basically, you don't support my relationship."

I opened my mouth to respond, but Ash kept going.

"I mean, I get it. Sometimes, he makes me feel awful. *Porca miseria*, he can be a jerk." She let out her own big sigh —the Italian came out when she was particularly stressed. "But sometimes, I want to feel cared for, like I matter. Don't you ever want to feel like you're wanted for every single piece of you? In a romantic way? There's nothing wrong with wanting to feel connected to someone, Oakley."

I didn't want to point out that she said nothing about *him* making her feel cared for and loved. Silently, I took it as a win that she wasn't delusional. But her words still pierced me, the longing she felt to be loved like that. My heart pounded, disagreeing that those feelings were a good idea. Connection meant pain and sadness and grief. It meant getting left behind when it was all over.

"I don't think a guy should determine all of those...those feelings, Ash. You should determine how you live your life."

"Let me work through this one, okay? I've got too many thoughts flying through my head. I'll come to you when I need to talk through them, I promise." She pushed off my bed and looked towards my closet longingly. "About those shoes—"

"Ash, we aren't the same size. Every time you borrow a pair, you complain the whole night about your feet sliding around."

"Just because something *appears* to be a bad fit doesn't mean it's not *exactly* what you need." She smirked as she sashayed out of my room, the tense feeling between us seeping away. "Now, come on, my hot bestie, you've had a long week, and you're not getting out of going. Let's PARTY!"

An hour later, we were glammed to the nines and jamming to some country as we made our way into the city, Tae our driver for the night. We miraculously found a parking spot only a block from their favorite spot, Tin Roof, a low-key bar for locals in Midtown. It had a different vibe than Broadway, the famous street in the heart of downtown Nashville where bachelorette parties were a dime a dozen and personal space was a commodity, not a right.

As we made our way to the entry line, guided by the strings of lights glowing above the entrance, Tae strutted to my side, so full of confidence, she never minded when I distanced myself from her friendship. She simply pushed her way back in.

We fell in step behind Tess and Ash, who chattered excitedly about some new country artist. We walked quickly, since the warm nights now held a chill as soon as the sun set. The sidewalk to the bar was lined with hotdog carts and trees starting to turn red for autumn.

"How's that brother a' yours doin', hun?" she asked, her accent washing over me, thick as honey and just as sweet.

"He hasn't told me when his chemo is set to start or when they've planned his surgery, but it's all going to be in the oncology center." I shrugged, trying to play off the dread that started to creep in. History was repeating itself, only worse this time. This time, I knew what was coming and yet had no idea what to expect. "He's so stubborn."

"Must be a family trait." Tae poked me in the side and giggled as I swatted her hand away. "He's stayin' with that friend of his, right?"

The image of Jason giving me that breathtaking smile as he pointed his finger in my face and called me beautiful flashed through my mind, followed by the moment I pushed his firm chest as we stood alone in the hallway, whispering like we were more than acquaintances. My cheeks instantly flushed, and I turned to hide my reaction from my overly-observant roommate.

"Oakley..." she drawled slowly. "His friend is hot, isn't he?"

I kept my eyes down.

"Oh my stars, you totally flirted with him. He's got you

feelin' all hot and bothered!" Her eyes were as round as saucers.

"No, he pisses me off," I said resolutely. "When I dropped Jack off, he accused me of being a crazy fan and breaking in. He threatened to call the cops."

"You're kiddin'!" she exclaimed. Tess and Ash whipped their heads around to look at us. "What did you do?"

At this point, we'd made it to the end of the line. Outside the bar was humming with energy, typical for a Saturday night. We settled into waiting, hints of music filtering through the door, and Tess and Ash turned to face us and crossed their arms.

Ash took the lead, speaking over the buzz of voices surrounding us. "Wait, what's going on?" Before I could speak, Tae was off.

"Oakley's brother's new roomie, his friend from college, is apparently super hot and gets our Oakley here all flustered like we've never seen, but she's decided she's angry at him 'cause he accused her of breakin' into his place and bein' a crazy fan." She spoke so fast and with so much excitement, you'd think I told her I'd gotten front row tickets to a sold-out concert.

"What?" Ash exclaimed at the same time Tess practically screamed, "Is he a music guy or somethin'?"

"No," I replied vaguely, hoping they would move on to the whole 'accused me of breaking in' thing. But no, they all looked at me expectantly, barely even blinking. "He plays hockey for the Rebels."

Three. Two. One.

Tess and Tae squealed in unison, each grabbing one of my arms as Ash whipped out her phone, typing furiously.

"What's his name?" Ash shouted.

"Is he any good? How tall is he?" Tess asked at a concerning volume for her.

"Oh, hun, this could go either way. It's a rough sport with some rough lookin' men. But some of those hockey players... Get it, girl!" Tae's voice got louder and louder.

"Y'all. Chill," I hushed them. People in line were side-eyeing the group of screaming girls. "He's a cocky jerk."

"Oakley Tennen. You better give us a name, or we'll start saying random players and googling based on your reaction," Ash said with a tenacity so at odds with her generally sweet and bubbly disposition. "Oh! Tae, there's some cowboys behind you. Turn around and—"

"Fine, fine! Westerman." That was all she was getting out of me.

It only took two seconds for her to plug it into her phone and her jaw to drop.

"Oakley. Are you kidding? This man is *fine*! Like, he's not a boy, he's a *man*," she exclaimed in a semi-hushed whisper. Tae and Tess dropped my arms and surrounded Ash to see whatever extremely attractive picture she'd found of the hockey player.

Ugh. He bothered me so much.

But I wasn't hot for him—I was just plain bothered.

I crossed my arms, ready to defend my position. I hated Jason Westerman, even if he had made me giggle.

Before they could say anything else, the line started

moving. Tess's head popped up, and she pulled Ash's arm as we all surged towards the entrance.

"Oaks, this guy *is* a man." Tae threw over her shoulder as we all shuffled forward. "Do you have his number? He should meet up with us! You look hot tonight."

I glanced down at my black leather tube top and dark denim skirt I'd paired with my favorite brown cowgirl boots and gave Tae a sarcastic smile.

Jason Westerman was a professional athlete, one who probably dated models and blonde, aspiring hockey wives. I was a grumpy southerner with an attitude from the rough side of a small town. It would never work.

When he could have his pick of anyone in the world, he wouldn't pick me.

"Oh, for sure. I'll totally ask the guy who threatened to *call the cops* on me and makes me angrier than a rattlesnake in a rainstorm to interrupt y'all's sacred girls' night. Absolutely not. I don't have his number, and no," I raised a hand to stop Ash's response, "I will not ask my brother for it. Listen to me on this one. I know y'all think I'm some grumpy love hater—"

"Oh, honey, we don't think that. We know it," Tae declared, dramatically flipping her big blonde curls behind her shoulder before snaring me with a look. She was walking backwards in high heeled, knee-high cream boots and a denim mini skirt, which was as impressive as it was terrifying. "And he only *threatened* to call the cops, right?"

"Not the point." I looked to Tess for some sort of backup, but all she gave me was a sympathetic shrug. "The point is, in the few times we've interacted, we've only gotten along for more than a minute once."

"Those are pretty bad odds," Tess said with a supportive smile. The other two shot her a look, to which she waved a hand in the air. "Oh, get off your high horses. Y'all have stopped seein' a man for far less."

"Yeah, but those men didn't get me as flustered as this man gets Oakley. And..." Tae said, still walking backwards. There was now only one bachelorette group between us and the inside of this bar. "You said y'all have interacted a few times, yet you've only told us about the one. I reckon something happened in those other two instances that would make us even more *Team Westerman*. The fact that you're feelin' anything other than indifference towards this man is huge."

"Ma'am," the bouncer interrupted in a bored tone, holding a hand towards Tae as she continued to walk backwards. Tess was already handing her ID to the other bouncer as Ash and I searched the deep depths of our purses for ours. Tae turned on a dime, her ID already out and ready to go.

"There ya go, hun." She smiled sweetly at the unimpressed bouncer as he scanned hers and handed it back.

As soon as we made it through the doors, Tae and Tess were off to find us the best table. The atmosphere instantly pulled us in, high top tables lining the walls, along with several booths, a dance floor in the center, dim white lights, and loud rock country from the band at the front covering the room in a nightlife ambience I'd only ever felt in Nashville. The bar sat at the start of the dance floor, the kitchen tucked back behind it all. They'd already started decorating for the new season inside, with fake fall leaves twisted into the string lights and a scary apple cinnamon tequila shot added to the menu.

It was packed, typical for a Saturday night, but Tess and Tae were renowned for finding a table, whether through good timing or sweet talking some poor fools, so I had faith as they beelined through the crowd. Music and chatter surrounded us, cocooning the crowd in a comforting aura of liveliness.

Ash lingered with me, and as she hooked her arm with mine, I glanced down to see worry in her eyes. In her stilettos, she was definitely more city than country.

"Girl, I'm so glad you came out tonight, but are you sure you're okay? You've had a lot going on, and you never get red-faced about a guy," she shouted over the loud music and giggled into her hand, as if she was already mentally replaying me getting flustered about it.

I took in the way she glanced up at me, like she was willing to accept anything I felt. Maybe I could tell her.

"I just—" I was cut off by a buzzing in my purse. Dropping my linked arm with Ash, I stopped walking and dug around for my phone. *Jackson* flashed across the screen, and my stomach instantly dropped.

"Oakley?" Ash grabbed my arm. "Everything okay?"

"Um, I-I don't know. I have to take this. I'll catch up with y'all in a minute." I was already moving towards the bathrooms, ignoring Ash as she shouted after me. The bar was loud, thrumming with music and conversation that was already hurting my head. The hallway leading to the bathrooms was probably the quietest I was going to get. Pushing past a trio of giggling drunk girls and trying desperately to shove down my frustration, I held the phone to my ear.

"Jack?" I answered frantically.

"Oakley? Hey, uh—" a deep, melodic voice that was definitely not my brother's answered. My spine straightened on its own, and my head instantly flew through a million different reasons why *he* would be calling me.

"Westerman, what the hell? If you're calling me as a joke—"

"What? Damn, woman, you never give a man a chance to explain, do you?"

"That feels pretty hypocritical, don't you think?" I snapped.

"Fair enough, OT. I didn't call you to argue with you, as fun as that is," he replied, and I told my heart to stop doing whatever that nickname was making it do. "It's about Jack. He, uh, he's not doing good."

"I'm going to need a lot more than that detailed report, Westerman." I forced myself to go clinical. "Is his injury infected? Does he have a fever? Has he been nauseous or throwing up? What's his blood pressure at? Does he—"

"Oakley, I'm not gonna lie to you, I haven't checked half those things. He's dead asleep right now, but he hasn't eaten in two days and he's been throwing up a few times a day, that I know of, for the past week. Obviously, I'm not a medical professional, but I do have a bit of experience with pre-game anxiety. With him starting chemo..."

"Pre-game anxiety?" I repeated, my mind still scrambling to form a thought. "You think he's anxious? About chemo starting soon?"

"I repeat, I will not overstep your expertise here, OT. If you're thinking hospital, I've definitely repped his weight before, so I could get him to the car even if he's dead weight." As he spoke, I rolled my eyes at the way he just *had* to drop that he could bench Jack's weight. "But from the way he's withdrawn the past few days, the not eating and the way he completely shuts down when I mention his cancer, this dumb jock says he's extremely nervous about starting treatment."

I mulled over his words, leaning back against the wall. "So, Mr. Dumb Jock, if you've got this all figured out, why are you calling me?"

He hesitated. I pictured him rubbing the back of his neck nervously like he did at family dinner. "He starts chemo tomorrow morning at 10."

"On a Sunday?" I asked, bewildered.

"On a Sunday," he confirmed. "He didn't want anyone to know, but he needed a ride."

"Westerman, you better be ready to open that ridiculously expensive door at 9."

"The code is 1235. Muffins or pancakes?"

"You do realize 1235 is one of the first codes someone would try if they wanted to break in?" I huffed as I slammed the door with my foot. My hands were full, my big work bag with Jack's paperwork, healthy snacks, a paperback about World War II he'd mentioned he wanted to read, extra headphones, and a charger for my brother's first day of chemo over my shoulder while I balanced three still-steaming herbal teas from the coffee shop down the street in a flimsy cup holder.

"And you realize there are five security guards and a top of the line alarm system, making it one of the most secure buildings in Nashville?" Westerman's deep voice carried from the kitchen, but I couldn't see him—which was concerning, because he had an open layout, and he was no small guy.

As I moved to put my stuff on the granite island, he popped up, holding a tray of fresh muffins. I pushed my frizzy, unkempt hair out of my face and took a long sniff. Apple cinnamon. It made his apartment smell amazing, like the epitome of cozy fall.

"Did you bake those?" I asked, not able to hide my shock. Barely concealing a chuckle, Jason set the muffins on the counter and shut the oven door. As he stood there with bright blue oven mitts on and a flour streak across his tight black t-shirt, I couldn't help but chuckle back.

"First of all, I feel like that was your judgmental laugh. Secondly, yes I did. Baking is the family business. You got a problem with that?"

"Oakley?" Jack's hoarse voice interrupted us. He was standing by the doorway, hobbling to the barstool next to me.

Jason had sugar coated it.

My brother looked like death. His skin was pale and lifeless, and while his eyes were still cool and calculating, they were completely bloodshot and a little glazed over. His whole body sagged with exhaustion, as if holding himself up was taking all his energy. My heart dropped.

He hadn't even started chemo yet.

"Oaksy—Oakley, what are you doing here?" he rasped,

obviously having just woken up. Even in high school, he woke up at 5 A.M. on the dot, every single day. We used to joke that Momma's farming blood had infected him. I couldn't imagine that had changed since his time in the military.

That small spot of pressure started to slowly pound in my chest.

"Jackson Oliver Tennen, why didn't you tell me you started chemo today?" I asked, not bothering to hide the hurt and anger in my voice. Yes, he was sick, but that didn't excuse him for being stupid.

Jack's head whipped to Jason, who was meticulously arranging and rearranging the muffins on plates. "You said you wouldn't call my family."

Jason was all nonchalance, his arms crossed as he leaned back against the counter in a relaxed stance, the opposite of the tension radiating from Jack and his clenched fists.

"I didn't. I called your nurse." He smiled innocently then nodded towards the muffins. "My Grams says these are best when they're straight out of the oven. Eat up, you two. I have no doubt our friendly neighborhood nurse here wants to get there at least fifteen minutes early."

"J, for real, man?" Jack starts up again. "I was going to—"

"No, you weren't. I would apologize if I overstepped, but she deserves to know. Someone in your family deserves to know." Jason pushed off from the counter, grabbing a muffin from the island. "You need support. That's the whole reason you came back here."

I don't know when I had started rubbing my temples, but the moment Jason's eyes zeroed in on the motion, my hands dropped, and I crossed my arms.

"Jack, if anyone understands not wanting to ask for help, it's me." I tried not to sound frustrated. "You asked for a week to settle in, and we all respected that, but you can't be stubborn right now. This is going to be hard. It's going to try to break you—physically, emotionally, mentally. As much as it physically pains me to say this, Westerman is right."

"I'm sorry, what was that?" Jason smiled smugly. "Can you say that again?"

"Shut up." I glared at him before focusing back on Jack. "Jack, you have a support system. I'm a *nurse*. You chose to come crashing back into our lives while you're going through this huge, horrible life-altering event, and you're not going to tell me when you start chemo? Are you kidding me?"

"Oakley, I've put you through enough. You've dealt with *this* enough. You have your own life to live—"

"Jackson Oliver," I interrupted, releasing his arm and crossing mine. I gave him a stare that hopefully conveyed the full depth of his stupidity. "Did you forget we were both there? Nobody told us what was going on, and we didn't get a choice about anything. We did what we had to because that's what we do for family. This time, we're choosing to be in this with you, so do all of us a favor and swallow your pride."

Taking a deep breath, I reached across the counter and grabbed a muffin. While Jack hung his head and tried to figure out his next words, I took a huge bite. It was okay.

Fine. It was probably the best muffin I'd ever had. I gave credit to his Grams.

Out of the corner of my eye, I saw Jason smiling way too smugly as I took another big bite. He nodded to the baked good in my hand and raised his eyebrows. I could almost hear that slight Canadian accent. *'Pretty good, eh?'*

I rolled my eyes.

"You're right." Jack gave me a single nod. "I'm sorry, Oakley. I'll send you my schedule. I would be grateful if you could help me—but *only* when you have the time."

Popping the final chunk of muffin in my mouth, I quickly chewed, swallowed, and dusted my hands of crumbs. Then, I grabbed a tea and slid it in front of him.

"Great. Now drink up. Water is best for chemo prep, but a little chamomile and honey won't hurt."

"I'll grab my shoes," Jason announced, starting to make his way around the island. I whipped around to face him.

"Wait, why are you coming? Don't you have hockey? Or literally anything else to do?" I stuttered, turning to face him as he crossed by me. Instead of continuing, he stopped about two inches from me.

I was aware of every bit of that space.

"Nope, it's your lucky day, OT. We had a pre-season game yesterday, so Coach gave us today off." He crossed his arms, not so subtly flexing his muscles as he looked down at me. Crossing my own arms again, I tried not to react as they brushed against his, staring up at the nuisance.

"I don't need your help—"

"It's a good thing I'm not going for you then, isn't it?" His eyes changed a bit, turning less casual and more frustrated. "Jack's been there for me, and I've tried to be there for him ever since we were stupid eighteen year old kids far from home in Boston. He's a brother to me. Whether you like it or not, I'm a part of the support system too. So, get off your high horse, your highness, and let me help my best friend, eh?"

With those biting words, he pushed past me and laid a hand on Jack's shoulder briefly, whispering something in his ear before heading down the hallway.

I watched as he left, mulling over his harsh truth. My cheeks burned with heat.

"When did that little crush develop?" Jack asked, and even his sick, raspy voice sounded far too smug.

"Shut up and drink your tea."

8

The first time I felt like something was wrong, we were loading Jack and his new crutches into Jason's nice SUV.

Had I expected him to drive some sort of totally impractical sports car? Yes, I did.

Had he humbled me enough that I held my tongue?

Also yes.

I handed Jack the bag and stepped back so Jason could shut his door. That's when I felt *it*. This distinct feeling of eyes on me. The hair on the back of my neck bristled, and I flipped around. All I saw was a flash of blonde whip around in the crowd of people, another busy day in the heart of the city. Fighting a shiver, I pushed it down. I was full of nerves and on edge. I needed to focus on Jack.

"Oakley?" I jumped as Jason's voice brushed my ear.

Swirling around, I smacked right into his chest. Thankfully, he had those infuriatingly quick reflexes and caught my arms to steady me.

I let him.

"Sorry, I just... I'm a little on edge." I looked everywhere I could but him.

"Yeah."

That cold tone was his only response as he let go of my arms and turned to get in the car, grabbing the keys from the valet and giving him a much warmer smile and kinder words.

I was disappointed he'd lost his smile and sick that it was my fault. The cold didn't fit him.

After a silent car ride, during which we all stewed in our own thoughts and looked out our respective windows, we pulled up to the hospital. Slinging my large bag over my shoulder and hopping out of the car, I walked over to where Jason was already helping Jack get situated with his crutches.

After a few mumbled directions, we found our way to the oncology center to check Jack in. I wasn't familiar with chemotherapy scheduling, but here in the South, where Sundays were for the good Lord and good food with family, the sterile waiting room was almost empty.

When the nurse called for him to go back, he glanced at me and Jason standing beside him before taking a step away.

"I'm doing this part by myself," he stated gruffly.

I blinked, not expecting to fight him on this twice. "Jack—"

"Having you come this far is all I can take. I don't know if I can handle a physical reminder that I'm useless right now."

"Man, you're not—" Jason stepped closer to me as he attempted to persuade Jackson.

"I know. I do. I just... Please, just let me do this part on my own." He swallowed. "My pride needs this. *I* need this."

Suddenly, I didn't see the strong, military man who'd grown up without me. I saw him when he was eight and I was seven, holding my hand as I cried. The girls in my class were being real mean. They'd told me I was too sassy. I sang too much old country music. My family was poor, what they considered white trash. They'd taken a vote and decided I wasn't a girl who could be a best friend, so I was kicked out of the group.

Heartbroken, I ran into the forest and sat against the dark bark, fall leaves crunching beneath me as I hugged my knees to my chest, bawling with all the force and feeling of a hurt child. It was Jack who'd chased after me, who'd sat next to me and pulled me close.

"Oaksy?" he'd said, stoic as he'd always been. "Things get hard a lot. I know sometimes, you feel alone at school. But you're not alone, 'cause I'm there. I'm your family. Family is always there, even when you can't see them. Don't cry, Oaksy. Even when you don't want to remember, I'm there."

And then, one day, he wasn't. I had to be better than that. I had to be.

I knew I had to give Jack this. This chance to prove to himself that he could face it. This chance to show him family could be there, even when he wasn't there for us. Putting a hand on Jason's arm to stop his pleading words, I gave Jack a small nod.

"We'll be back in three hours. We can go get lunch at Tucker's after." I smiled softly. Jason's arm flexed under my hand, and I quickly pulled it away. "You better be ready for some brisket, because that's what you owe me for this. I can't believe we're leaving."

I allowed myself one eye roll, and Jack's face flushed with gratitude.

"Thanks," he whispered.

With one quick look at Jason, Jack grabbed the bag from my hand, slung it over his shoulder before readjusting his crutches, and turned away from us, following the nurse, who attempted to relieve him of the bag.

He stubbornly refused.

After the door swung closed, I let out a breath.

He could do this. I had to believe he could do this.

Jason and I just stood there, like we needed a moment to convince ourselves it would all be alright.

"So, what do you wanna do for three hours?" I asked hesitantly.

After a minute, he shifted to face me, and for once, his emotions weren't on display for the world to see, like he wanted to be guarded from me.

I didn't like it.

"Are we going to fight?"

"I'm sorry, Jason." I grimaced, unable to meet his eyes. "I'm not exactly a ray of sunshine, okay? I've always been like this. Having him back, having him be sick, I just...I can't..."

My hands rose to my temples, slowly rubbing circles as I fought down the sudden emotion trying to claw its way out.

"How hard was that for you to say?" he asked.

Glancing up, I took in his small smirk and the hesitant truce in his gaze.

"Cheering against the Rebels level," I answered softly, and he let out a short laugh as I lowered my hands.

"Good answer," he muttered with a hesitant smile. "Well, this is your city. What do the locals do?"

"You ever been to Riverfront Park?"

As soon as we were on the walkway, tall maples and tulip poplars surrounding us, it was a balm to my soul. There was a section of the path where the sidewalk curved, and right before it took you away from the water, you could see everything: the bridge going across the river, the hundreds of trees lining both sides, the city buildings in the distance. I stopped there, leaning against the railing and staring at its beauty. Jason mirrored my stance, and I got a few moments of silence before he spoke up.

"Is there a reason you always escape to look at the trees?"

My face scrunched in confusion.

"At your parents' house. When things got heavy, you went to a spot where you could see the trees. You dropped your brother off at chemo and you apologized, which I know could not have been easy for you." He gestured out to the trees in front of us. I rolled my eyes at him, which earned me another hesitant smile. "Now, we're with the trees. Why?"

I *had* always run to the trees, especially when I was younger. Everyone at the townhouse knew the front porch, with a perfect view of our big oak tree and its wide floppy leaves, was my thinking spot.

"I'm not sure what it is." Looking out at the tree line again, I bit my bottom lip in thought. He waited, and I found myself rambling. "Ever since I was little, it was an escape.

They didn't need anything from me. I remember stomping on the crunchy leaves during the fall and looking up at the sun through the leaves in the summer. I used to tell Jack I loved the trees because they weren't afraid of change. I hate change. My family was always changing. It was all overwhelming. Then, Momma got sick, Jack left and didn't look back..."

We were silent for a moment. A glance at Jason showed the understanding in his eyes.

"I guess I admired how steady they were in the face of change, how they adapted to their beautiful leaves leaving them behind over and over again. I wish I had that."

My cheeks heated as I realized everything I'd shared. "You didn't ask for all that. Forget—"

"Oh, no way, Oaks, you don't get to take it back." He grinned as I winced. "But I get it. The ice was the same safe place for me. It was the only thing in my life that wasn't changing, the only constant I had. It saved me."

Curiosity spiked against my will. It hit me then: I didn't know anything more about him than Pa had shared about his hockey stats, which were apparently impressive.

Glancing over, I took in how he looked out across the river with a contemplative gaze, crossing his arms and leaning against the rails with his whole body. I wondered who Jason Westerman truly was. If the cocky, golden retriever thing was an act or just a facet of who he was. If the arrogant, angry man I encountered was a defense mechanism or real.

"Saved you from what?" The words escaped before I could stop them, but I couldn't deny it: I wanted to know more about this man who cared about my brother enough to go toe-to-toe with me.

With a small smile and a dip of his head before he turned to meet my gaze, I had a feeling that there was so much more to Jason.

"You really want to know?"

"I asked, didn't I? Come on, Westerman. Share."

He chuckled before his smile dropped, taking on a more solemn tone. "My mom didn't care to be a mom, and I never knew my dad." Even though the soft smile stayed, I could see the hurt in his eyes. "Mom wanted to stick it to him, show him she didn't need a man. We bounced around a couple of women's shelters until one day, I guess she decided she didn't even care enough about sticking it to him to keep me around anymore."

My heart raged at the thought of a mother abandoning her child. He must have felt like an inconvenience.

"How old were you when she..."

"Left me at the shelter? I was five. She did have the courtesy to call my grandparents a week later and let them know the general area they could find me."

"Are you serious? She just left you there?"

"I haven't seen her since. No one knows where she is, or if she's even still alive." He shrugged as if it didn't bug him anymore. Aside from the small gleam of hurt in his eyes, I believed it really didn't. "So, my grandparents discovered they had a grandson and became legal guardians of a five year old after their estranged daughter left them a voicemail out of the blue."

"When did the hockey start?" I was intrigued by how

such a hard beginning to life could turn into what he was today, how he could be so happy all the time when he'd been hurt so deeply. He'd been so completely left behind.

"When I hit about ten and started to understand, I had a lot of anger. My Gramps, a true Canadian man, signed me up for hockey." The sadness in his eyes started to mix with amazement. "Whenever I hit the ice, everything went away: the anger, the guilt, the sadness, the abandonment. It was just me and the cold air, gliding around without a care in the world. And I was really good at it."

"Ah, I was wondering when the cocky hockey player would return," I joked lightly, giving him a chance to jump out of the deep end we'd wandered into. He took my offer, giving me a wide smile.

"Listen here, OT. Just because you're obsessed with me—"

I rolled my eyes. *Hard.* He laughed until a loud buzzing came from his jean pockets. As he took out his phone, his eyes lit up, and he took a step back.

"Sorry, I gotta take this real quick." He turned around, answering the phone and putting it to his ear. "Hey, pretty lady."

My heart dropped. I didn't want to name the emotion that started to grow in my chest, so I let gratitude take its place when my own phone buzzed.

Pulling it out of my pocket, I grimaced at a new text from Sierra.

Sierra: I don't want to push you AT ALL, but I remember

how passionate you were about this. Would you be willing to set up a meeting? I'd be a horrible coordinator of research if I let an AMAZING nurse get away without doing a little groveling ;)

Taking a deep breath, I read over the text again.

"So, you gonna text them back or leave them hanging?"

I whirled around, suddenly backed into a hard place by Jason Westerman. Again.

"You gonna read my text messages after I didn't eavesdrop on your phone call with your girlfriend?" I definitely shouldn't have said that. His eyes widened with joy, and I held back a groan.

"Oh, yes, my girlfriend. She was wondering if you liked the muffins."

"What? Your girlfriend asked about the muffins?"

"Yeah, it's her special recipe, you know." He leaned forward and had the audacity to wink at me. "Since you think my Grams is my girlfriend."

It shouldn't have been physically possible for my cheeks to get hotter, but they did. "Ah."

"Ah. So, what type of text is the kind of text that makes *the* Oakley Tennen flustered?"

"None of your business."

"Neither was the sob story of my childhood. But you got that, so it's only fair."

"I—"

"You looked pissed. I appreciate that." His eyes softened.

"You appreciate me being pissed?" I raised my eyebrows before crossing my arms in front of my chest. "You piss me off to no end, Westerman. I get the feeling you don't like it when we argue."

"I think Oakley Tennen being pissed is the equivalent of saying you care." His grin widened. "And my whole goal is to make you care, just to spite you. What did the text say?"

"Again, it's none of your business," I huffed, annoyed by his persistence.

"Again, yes, it is."

"What will you do for me if I tell you?"

"You flirting with me, OT?" He grinned smugly.

"If you count being annoyed out of my mind flirting, then sure. Whatever pumps up that little ego of yours, hockey boy."

"First of all, it's hockey *man* to you. Second, as a hockey man, I could take the phone by force. But I'd rather not take a knee to the groin, so I'm asking nicely." He gave me that dazzling smile again. "Wouldn't it confuse the hell out of Jack if we came back as friends?"

"Whoa, don't push your luck there, Westerman. We're not friends."

"What was the text, Oakley? A boyfriend? A medical emergency? Are you joining my fan club? Oh—"

"Fine! Here, read it for yourself!" I shoved the phone into his hands, the text thread still open. "Congratulations. You annoyed your way into a secret."

He was already engrossed in reading. "You want to do music therapy?"

"It's just an idea. But it's bad timing." I sighed with resignation, reaching to take my phone back and putting it back in my pocket.

"Bad timing how?"

"My brother came back and has cancer? I have a demanding full-time job with an abnormal schedule? My family needs me right now? I have people who count on me, Westerman. You might be unfamiliar with the concept—"

"You can lash out all you want, but it doesn't change the fact that you're making excuses." He reached up, slowly grabbing my wrists from where my hands had started rubbing circles on my temples. We both froze. I didn't know how to react to the energy buzzing between us from those two insignificant points of contact. His voice dropped so low, it was almost a whisper. "You do that a lot."

"Yeah," I barely whispered back, my wrists in his firm but gentle grip as I struggled to breathe.

"You want some unsolicited advice?"

It felt like anything more than our whispers would break the moment, and we both wanted to stay a little longer.

"I get the feeling I don't have a choice."

"'Life moves pretty fast. If you don't stop and look around once in a while, you could miss it.'" He returned to normal volume, his voice sounding like he was trying to end a big speech.

"Do you always give unsolicited advice in a weird voice?"

He looked at me like somehow *that* was the dumbest thing that had happened in the past five minutes.

"No, but I always quote Ferris Bueller in that voice."

"What?"

"You're kidding." He dropped my wrists in a dramatic

fashion, almost forcing a giggle out of me. *Almost.* "You've never seen Ferris Bueller? An eighties classic? He keeps skipping school?"

"I don't—"

"Oakley, let me believe you forgot that line. Please." This was ridiculous, but I tried my best nonchalant shrug instead of telling him he was obnoxious.

"Care to elaborate on the teachings of..."

"Ferris Bueller. Yes, I would." Taking a deep breath, he stepped close to me, and I blamed the chill breeze when I shivered. "You do have a lot going on, and you always will, because that's life. It doesn't stop moving and changing. Change is hard for you. Don't let it be hard."

"Don't let it be hard?" I mumbled, and then strong hands were cupping my face, Jason's thumbs on my temples. "What are you—"

"I figured you could focus on my words more if I took care of this part for you." He searched my eyes for permission. "That okay?"

"No." I felt anything other than okay. Unsteady, shocked, scared. Then, I looked into his eyes, focused on the light pressure of those strong hands in my hair. "Don't stop."

He let out a breath, and as his thumbs started moving in circles, a strong mix of calm and unsettled rushed through me.

"I know we don't know each other well. I made a horrible first impression, and you're a piece of work. But I know Jack. He only speaks when he means it, and every time he's ever spoken of you, it's with awe. He would always say his sister was meant to change the world." I struggled to breathe as emotion clogged my throat. "As someone whose entire career revolves around making split second decisions, I say try. If you never give it a shot, how do you know if you missed something that could change your life?"

I hated that he was right. This research was something I'd been wanting to do for a long time. It would help people handle their emotions, their traumas.

Anyone had access to music. Once they learned how to utilize it and what helped them heal, they could do it on their own. They could do it when they got left behind.

The way Momma taught me.

When Jason's hands fell from my face, they pulled me from my thoughts. He had that cocky smile on his face, but his eyes were hesitant. *Cautious.*

"Fine," I whispered.

"Fine?"

"Yeah." I rolled my shoulders back, infusing my voice with false confidence. "There's no harm in checking it out, right? Seeing where it could go."

"Exactly." The caution left his eyes, and the way he smiled at me was unnerving. "But don't worry, OT. This doesn't make us friends."

"Are you sure you don't want to come up, Oakley?" Jack mumbled, barely able to get the words out. After picking him up from chemo, he insisted on lunch at Tucker's, even though he was falling asleep standing up, which left Jason and me to carry the fairly normal conversation. We were still in a tentative truce from our conversation by the river. I only rolled my eyes twice. It was strange.

"It's all good, Jack. Let's not test how long me and Westerman can go without killing each other." Glancing at Jason, who had started making his way back towards us after talking with his apartment's valet, Jack finally gave me a small smile. "You'll make it to December, Jack. I believe it."

The surgery to remove his tumor was confirmed. Best case scenario, they could operate in December.

"December." He nodded.

That was the goal, our new lifeline. We just had to make it to December, and then all of this would go away. I didn't know if Jack would go away too, but I was sure Jason would. Why would he stay when December passed and Jack didn't need him anymore?

"Momma is all set to come tomorrow. I don't want you switching around your work schedule and not sleeping enough because of me." Jack's stern face almost made me laugh, but I would take it as a win that he would allow someone to be at every chemo session. "Thanks. For today. Having your support meant a lot."

"Even if it was forced on you?"

"Yes, Oakley. As usual, you were right. Get outta here and go live your life," he said as Jason reached us where we stood closer to the automatic doors, foot traffic moving around us.

"Get some sleep, alright?" I turned to Jason, pinning him with a stern look as I readjusted my bag on my shoulder. "You're in charge of making sure he rests *and* eats dinner. You boys got that?"

"Yes, ma'am," they replied in unison, both grinning before Jack started to tilt a bit to the side. Jason reached out a hand to steady him.

"There's a bench right inside, man. I'll make sure Oakley here gets in her car without starting an argument with some innocent bystander."

I glared at the annoying man as Jack made his way to the bench inside the lobby.

Jason tilted his head at me, like he was slowly figuring something out.

"Why are you looking at me like that, Westerman?"

"Get dinner with me sometime."

My head reared back. "Pardon?"

"Oaks." He stepped forward. I chafed at the fact that I had to tilt my head up to meet his eyes. He was such a big presence. "We got along for more than two minutes today."

"Did you forget the part where you ignored me half the morning because you were frustrated?"

"You are pretty frustrating." He gave me that smile again. "But I don't normally feel comfortable sharing my childhood with people like that. They always get this look. I wanted to tell you, and you didn't get that look."

"How did barely getting along lead to..."

"Asking you out?" When I gave him a pointed look, he continued with a grin. "Pick a reason. To make up for how I've acted. To prove I'm a good guy. To finally figure out what goes on inside your head. To get to know my best friend's little sister. To go out with a beautiful woman in the town she calls home."

I stood there, in the streets of downtown Nashville, stunned. That was...oddly refreshing.

I was saved from having to answer by the elderly valet, whose name tag read Bill.

"Miss Tennen, your car is ready for you whenever you are."

I returned his smile as I took my keys from his outstretched hand. "Thank you, sir."

He nodded before he turned around. I took a deep breath before forcing my flustered self to walk towards my car. When I was rounding the front to get to the driver's side, Jason called out from his spot near the doors.

"Should I pick you up on Friday, OT?"

I glanced at him, then my brother slouched on the bench inside the beautiful building.

I'd only have Jason until December—if I ever had him at all—and that wasn't a risk I could take.

"In your dreams, Westerman."

Then, I raised two fingers to my head and saluted him. Without waiting for a response, I got in my car and turned on my *If Screaming Was A Song* playlist to drown out all the feelings that out of body experience had created.

9

"This is your fault! All your fault!"

"Baby, I—"

"I can't do this! I can't!" The shrill yelling was two seconds from bursting my eardrums. It didn't help that my arm was getting the life squeezed out of it.

Ignoring the patient's husband, who was trying to coach her through some breathing thing that we were way past the point of doing, I zeroed in on Amber.

When she'd arrived barely thirty minutes before, sweating and screaming and definitely in transition, I sprang into action. Getting her quickly on the bed and forcing her to focus long enough to check her cervix and place an IV were my priority. She was completely dilated, measuring ten centimeters and plus three station. Long story short, her body was ready to give birth. All the baby needed was a few good pushes. She was past active labor, past getting an epidural or doing her breathing exercises, past *sanity*.

When something has to happen and there's no force in

the world that can stop it, your body forces you to choose how you react. The adrenaline hits, and you subconsciously pick a path. Either your mind goes blank, succumbing to the panic, and all you can do is freak out, or you zero in. You turn on another mode, another level of yourself, that only comes out when there is no other choice. Clinical, detached, and sane.

Medicine was the only place where I was on another level, a level on which I could make decisions that so deeply affected another human being and feel confident in them. So, when Amber's doctor barely made it through the door and her baby's heart tones were too low, I told her to push before the doctor even had her sterile gloves all the way on.

When Amber screamed at her husband and gripped the life out of my arm as I held her leg, the response was immediate.

"Amber!" I shouted, barely catching her attention. "Focus. You're having a baby. You don't have time to freak out. I need you to hold that breath and focus on pushing with everything you've got. Can you do that?"

Her eyes connected with mine, and she nodded, determination taking over. I loved this part, when they recognized how their life was about to change and they embraced it, let it fuel them.

I envied it.

"Okay, she's having another contraction. Amber, we need to get the baby out on this next push, or we might have to use a little extra help, okay?" Dr. Farrow said calmly from her position at the foot of the bed.

"Right here, Amber. Push!" I coached, watching as Dr. Farrow brought another new life into the world.

That baby girl might have had low heart tones towards the end, but she came out just as shrill as her mother. Once the baby was doing okay, everything had been fully delivered and sutured, and Dr. Farrow and the other nurses left the room after congratulating the couple, I turned to ask the new mother if she wanted something to eat. Before I could open my mouth, she gripped my arm tight again.

"Thank you, Oakley. You got her here." Her eyes filled with tears, and I gave her a forced half smile.

"I just hollered at you."

Amber and her husband laughed, even though I hadn't meant it as a joke. Then, she glanced down at her brand new daughter and looked back at me with somber eyes.

"She's our miracle baby, you know? We've been waiting for her for so long, and now she's here." She sniffled, holding out a finger for her daughter to grasp as I shuffled uncomfortably. "We were actually taking a break from infertility treatments. For all our planning and trying, she came when we least expected it."

"She decided to make quite the entrance," I said, this time attempting a joke, and surprisingly, they both grinned. A warm feeling broke through the anxiety in my chest. I'd never spent this long after a birth in a patient's room, and I wasn't sure what I was doing.

"Yeah. That all moved pretty fast. I feel like I missed it." Amber sighed. "Oh, it's like that quote you like, honey! The 80s one?"

The husband, whose name had gone in one ear and out the other during all the chaos, smiled lovingly at his wife. "Life moves pretty fast. If you don't stop and look around once in a while—"

"You could miss it," I finished the quote subconsciously. The husband was now smiling big, and I had definitely noted he said it in the same weird tone and voice Jason had. Was that a guy thing? The 80s movie quotes and voice thing?

"You a Ferris Bueller fan?" he asked.

"Um, no, sir. Just heard that quote recently," I replied quickly, and a wave of tiredness hit me. Lord, I had so much charting to do. "I'm gonna go grab you some snacks and give y'all some time, but if she starts rooting around like she's looking for food, go ahead and start breastfeeding. I'll be back in fifteen minutes to check on everything and help with that if you need. Congratulations."

They chorused their thanks as I headed out, shutting the door softly behind me. I leaned against the wall for a second, and for some reason, the first delivery I'd ever seen flashed into my mind.

It was during my student clinical in the oncology center— what I'd thought was my dream job: helping people with cancer, like Momma.

I'd met the nurse who was going to show me the ropes, and he took me to the first patient's room. The woman couldn't have been much older than thirty, and the young girl grasping her hand, tears streaming down her face, couldn't have been much older than ten.

Too young. They were both too young. I was too young.

I didn't even make it past the door. They all looked at me —the nurse, the woman, her distraught daughter. They needed someone to make it better, and I couldn't. I couldn't.

So, I ran, trying to catch my breath, getting lost in the maze of the hospital and breaking down in a hallway.

I remembered leaning against the wall, trying to rub out the pain in my chest as I slid to the floor, forcing myself to breathe.

"Hey, there's a storage closet a little further down the hall if you need a place to really break down." A cheery voice broke through my haze of panic. I glanced up at the curly haired nurse, who held those hospital-issued blue and pink striped baby blankets in one hand and pointing down the hall with the other.

If I was thinking clearly, I would have told her to leave me be or ignored her entirely. But I couldn't breathe, couldn't stop seeing the haunted look in everyone on that floor.

"It's too much," I rasped, the words leaving scratches behind as they clawed their way to the surface. I focused back on the floor, my hands moving from my chest to my temples, trying to soothe the stress away.

"What is?"

"All their pain," I whispered. "How am I supposed to feel their pain, watch them leave people behind? People who need them?"

Silence. I hoped she'd walked away, left the strange nursing student on the floor to hyperventilate and deal with the emotions she couldn't face.

Then, a hand stretched in front of me, and I glanced up.

"Come with me."

I blamed the lack of oxygen for the way I grabbed her hand like a lifeline. With my arms wrapped around my stomach, I followed her down the hallway to a set of closed double doors.

She scanned her badge, and the doors swung open. This part of the hospital was different. Pictures of babies and families covered the walls, and there was a man and a very pregnant woman talking at the nurses' station. The nurse marched me right past them, down a hallway with a lot of activity I wasn't expecting.

She spared me one glance to make sure I was following and then strode into one of the rooms. When I walked in behind her, for the second time in an hour, I froze in the doorway. There was screaming, there was blood, and there was a very panicked man and a very in pain woman. How was this any better than the sterile type of pain I'd just witnessed?

"Stand over there." The nurse pointed, and I simply listened. I watched as she talked with the other nurse, who was coaching the woman through some type of breathing exercise.

I watched as both the nurses took control of the room. I watched how when the doctor came in, they worked as a team. I watched how the pain was replaced with joy, the nurse simply the person who knew the answers, who could lessen the pain and worry, who knew the probable outcome was good. They knew the science, they knew the protocols, and they made the decisions. The pain in the room was short, and it was never the focus.

It was something I could face. It didn't overwhelm me. There were solutions to problems in a chaotic environment. Pain led to an expected outcome. There were no haunted eyes or imminent death, no seeing the same pain over and over again until they were gone. I could do this.

After the baby was born, the nurse who led me here walked

over as the now-calm couple ooo-ed and ahhh-ed over their newborn.

"So, what did you think?" She smiled, like she already knew my answer.

"Are y'all hiring?"

She just laughed. "What's your name?"

"Oakley Tennen." I stuck out my hand for her to shake, and she laughed again.

"Ashley Mancini, but my friends call me Ash." Grinning, Ash shook my hand. She looked me over, and the crinkles by her eyes deepened as her grin widened. "You can call me Ash."

"Good work, Oakley. I didn't think she was going to get that baby out without a vacuum." Present-day Ash grinned as she pushed off the wall beside me, walked over to the nurses' station, and plopped in her chair. I followed, pulling my hair out of its extremely messy low ponytail and regathering it into a sloppy low bun as I slid into the seat next to her. I woke up the computer in front of me, shrugging as I began typing into her digital chart.

"People get so hysterical," I grumbled, but I couldn't forget how it felt when they'd laughed at my joke—when it felt like I was sharing in their joy, not just avoiding their pain.

"Alright, thank you, ladies. Have a great rest of your night!" Dr. Farrow interrupted my thoughts, giving a small wave as she walked by, and we all chorused our goodbyes. As soon as she was down the hallway, Ash turned to me.

"So..."

"So?" I responded, trying to focus on work.

"How are things going with the hockey player?"

"You mean the hockey prick?" I responded automatically.

Jason and I switched so frequently between arguing and flirting, it made my head spin. Sometimes, he made me livid, and other times, he made me feel light and safe. We were walking a strange line, and Jack had definitely noticed over the past few weeks of chemo runs and Sunday family dinners.

"You're hiding something," Ash sang, rolling her chair closer to mine.

"Nope." I kept my eyes focused on the screen, although nothing was processing.

"Then why are you zoning out?"

"I'm not zoning out. I'm charting. Don't you have patients? A job to do?" I snarked at her, trying to think of anything other than Jason Westerman and his smug grin that drove me nuts.

"My girl is a first-time momma who's barely three centimeters and has beautiful heart tones. I've got plenty of time for this," she replied with a smile. "What did he do now to get you so out of sorts? Wait, did he kiss you?"

I gave up on pretending I was charting and turned to face her, gripping the arm rests.

"Ash, are you for real?" Despite my tone, she nodded happily. "No. We can barely stand being in the same room. We go back and forth between arguing and being fine so much, I never have any idea what he's thinking. One minute, we're snapping at each other about the stupidest things, and the next, he's asking me to dinner. I mean, good hell, does he actually think I'll say yes when five minutes before, we weren't speaking? It's just—"

"No. Way," Ash interrupted, the smile falling from her face as she stared. "You care. You care what he thinks and what he does. Oakley, this is huge!"

I blinked slowly once, twice. I opened my mouth and closed it. I couldn't care about Jason. He was probably leaving my life in a few short months.

So why couldn't I say it? I shook my head, more at myself than anything.

Ash started in again, but thankfully, the call light went off in Amber's room.

"Gotta go." I stood and quickly walked away, trying to deny that I cared.

I denied it when Ash brought it up again as we walked to our cars.

I denied it to myself as I drove to Jason's apartment.

I was so busy denying it, I didn't see the cyclist flying through the crosswalk in front of Jason's apartment building. I'd made it a bit of a routine to go way too early to pick up Jack so I could get us hot chocolate or herbal tea and sit with my thoughts in the coffee shop. The mornings were getting chillier every day, and the warm drinks made the fall days a bit cozier. Normally, I was well rested and ready to face the day with this new routine, but normally, I wasn't coming off a shift I didn't tell Jack I was picking up. I wasn't normally consumed with Ash's allegations of caring.

When the cyclist hit me and the herbal tea flew everywhere, I barely got my hands out in time to keep from banging my head on the pavement. Asphalt scraped my palms, and I hissed in pain as the same sensation went through my knees. Today was not the day to wear running shorts, it seemed.

My mind raced, and I couldn't remember if I had the right of way or not, if this was my fault or not. Sounds jumbled as people tried to get my attention, but their voices didn't matter when a hand landed softly on my back.

"Watch where you're going!" I knew the anger in that voice. It was normally directed at me. "Oakley? Oakley, are you okay?"

I raised my head enough to see the concern in Jason's eyes. He grabbed my arm, steadying me as I slowly got to my feet. The fog in my brain started to clear as I took in the crowd and the flustered cyclist, itching for a fight. Which was hilarious, since he was about half Jason's size. Everyone was half his size, but the man who'd hit me was rail-thin, fingers twitching, a threadbare t-shirt and worn shorts his only protection against the cold humidity that ruled the mornings as we inched closer to October.

Embarrassment washed over me as people rubbernecked to get a good look at the girl who'd just gotten run over by a bike. Fantastic.

"Jason?" I barely whispered, and whatever Jason heard in my voice had him wrapping an arm around my shoulders and guiding me the rest of the way across the street.

"Tell your girlfriend to watch where she's going next time," the guy stammered, his accent definitely not from around these parts. Few people from the South would get angry without making sure the other person was alright first. I would've asked, since I *was* raised right, but my head wouldn't stop spinning.

"How about you stop at red lights and apologize for nearly running over a woman?" Jason angrily snapped back. The cyclist started to protest, but Jason tightened his grip around my shoulders and held up a hand. "Shut your mouth before I shut it for you."

With that, he turned and guided me to his apartment. We didn't speak until Bill handed over his hockey bag with a silent nod. A fuzzy connecting of the dots almost happened, but then, it was gone with a wave of nausea. Without consulting me, my arms wrapped around Jason's waist to stabilize myself as I fought to stay on my feet, my hands clenching his shirt.

"Whoa, Oakley?" he asked as he caught my weight. "What's going on?"

"I'm—" I covered my mouth with a hand. "I think I'm gonna puke or pass out or..."

My voice drifted away as Jason quickly guided us into the building. We got to the elevator, his eyes assessing me all the way up to his apartment, his arms wrapped around me as he gingerly got me settled on the couch before going back into the kitchen. As I sat there, the nausea finally faded, and the world came back into focus. My head was throbbing, even though I knew it had never hit the ground.

Everything else seemed okay, save for my hands and knees, which were bleeding, risking an infection with the amount of dirt and gravel in the scratches. My soaked shirt clung to my skin. Pinching it between my fingers, I pulled it away and saw the redness on my chest where the tea had exploded. Damn me for asking for extra hot tea so I could avoid Jason longer. A lot of good that did me, seeing as I was now sitting on his pristine white couch.

His white couch, and I was covered in dirt and tea.

Horrified, I stood.

Too fast.

I swayed, and those strong arms caught me again.

"Oakley? Sit back down—"

"I'm all dirty-"

"And bleeding." He held up a package of Band-Aids, medical tape, and an ice pack. "I don't care if you're dirty, Oakley."

"No, I need to go. I need to change before Jack wakes up and sees—"

"Hey, hey, look at me, Oaks," he commanded sternly. "Don't worry about that right now. Sit down and let me look at these cuts, okay? Or, I don't know, should I take you to the hospital? Do you think you might have a concussion? Sorry, I'm not normally the one trusted with the medical stuff. I can take Jack to chemo, but that's about all I've got."

As I looked up at him, he seemed so genuine, so flustered and out of his element but willing to try because I was hurt. I took a deep breath and winced when pain in my ribs flared.

"No hospital. I didn't hit my head. Grab some water, and I can clean out the cuts. Do you have any antibacterial spray?" I asked. He nodded. "Great. I'm gonna sit at the counter—"

"Nope, you're going to sit on the comfortable couch." He held up a hand, the silencing effect only slightly marred by the sheer amount of medical supplies he was holding, but the way he went stern again made me listen. "Start cleaning your hands and knees while I grab you a new shirt."

He guided me back to my seat on the couch, setting the medical supplies beside me, and quickly got a washcloth wet. He handed it to me before hustling down the hallway to his room. I sat there, the washcloth in my hands, and tried to process. When Jason got back, I hadn't moved, and he didn't comment. He handed me a huge sweatshirt with *Lethbridge Hockey* in block letters across the front. We both stared at the sweatshirt in his hands for a moment, and when I went to grab it, his gaze zeroed in on my chest. I opened my mouth to holler at him about manners when his eyes widened.

"Hell, Oakley, is that a burn?"

I glanced down to where the redness had only grown since my initial assessment. Groaning, I pulled the fabric away from my skin again.

"Hot tea. I thought..."

"Take your shirt off."

"Excuse me? That's not how southern gentlemen do things—"

"Oakley, I'm not joking right now. What do I do for a burn like that?" He sat beside me and reached for the hem of my shirt. I swatted his hands away, which hurt my battered palms. I glared at him through my grimace.

"Back off, Westerman. I'm fine. The skin is just irritated."

"Oakley. Shut up."

I narrowed my eyes at him.

"You preach to Jack about letting people take care of him. Let someone take care of you for once."

"This is not the same and you know it. Jack is having life-altering chemotherapy, and I—"

"Got run over by a bike. I saw it, Oakley. That guy hit you going full speed downhill, like he was aiming for you." He huffed, as if the thought was making him angry all over again. My thoughts were jumping everywhere, trying to understand why he was so upset. "So if you could please shut up for five seconds, stop arguing, let me look at that burn and clean off your hands, I would appreciate it."

That speech was subpar at best. No groveling or begging to take care of me. No telling me it wasn't that bad and it would be fast. Maybe it was the straightforward way he told me to shut up, or the genuine look in his eyes when he looked at my minimal injuries, like he needed to do something about it.

I reached for the hem of my shirt and pulled it over my head.

10

Nothing about this was sexy or sensual as the shirt stuck to my skin and Jason had to help pull it off. Once I was shirtless and exposed in nothing up top but my comfiest cotton bra, Jason glanced over my burns, a single glance to confirm I truly was fine before he grabbed his spare sweatshirt from where it sat in my lap and pulled it over my head. My hands shook as vulnerability swept through me. I had no control. If my body wasn't hurting in so many other places, I might have felt pressure start to build in my chest.

Once he finished redressing me, he silently went about cleaning the rest of my injuries. Neither of us said a word as he carefully dabbed the dirt and asphalt from my cuts. Whenever I hissed at the sting, he would pause for a moment, glance up, wait, then start again. I tried to focus on something else, anything else, but the only other thing that caught my attention was the smell of detergent coming from Jason's sweatshirt I was currently drowning in. It was clean and fresh, and I couldn't stop breathing it in.

Jason only spoke after he'd cleaned both hands and was working on my knees. With my leg across his lap, I barely heard him at first.

"What would you have done if I hadn't been there?" he asked softly.

"What?"

"If I hadn't been heading to practice at that exact moment, what would you have done?" He paused, glancing up at me. I was so used to Jason joking around and smiling, or being frustrated and angry, I wasn't sure how to handle him like this.

"I would've gotten in my car and used my first aid kit then taken Jack to chemo." My eyelids started to flutter closed when a sudden thought jolted me awake. "Jason, are you supposed to be at practice right now?"

He didn't answer; he simply moved my other leg so both were across his lap. The movement swung my body, and I leaned my head against the armrest. Random things, like the softness of the couch or the pumpkin spice scent in the room, stuck in my brain. He would be the type of guy to light a scented candle. The thought had me glancing up at the man who was becoming harder to hate by the second.

Focused on cleaning out my knees, he didn't meet my gaze or answer my question. His brows pulled together, like getting the asphalt out of my scrapes was worth missing work. But I had no energy to fight it. I closed my eyes, letting him.

"Why are you doing this?" I mumbled.

"You're not alone in this world, Oakley." He spritzed the

antibacterial spray on each of my knees, and I hissed at the sting. "Why don't you let your family support you the way you support them?"

"They don't need that in their life," I whispered. "Why are *you* doing this?"

"Because I need people. Can't survive this world without them," he muttered back, his voice low and gruff. "Family isn't always blood. If it was, I wouldn't have anybody."

We never truly have anybody.

My legs shifted off his lap, and he resettled them onto the couch. My eyes fluttered open as his face hovered over mine. Those eyes saw too much.

"Are you sure you didn't hit your head?"

"Just tired. This lady came in laboring—" I cut myself off, but he was more observant than I'd ever give him credit for.

"Are you serious? I thought Jack said you lined up your schedules?" He shook his head, still leaning over the couch where I laid. As he spoke, he took a pillow from where it was wedged between me and the back of the couch.

In a swift movement, he reached behind my head, his fingers sneaking into my messy hair, lifting my head and adjusting the pillow behind it. He did it so quickly, so smoothly, I didn't have time to respond. When he shifted back, reaching a hand across to brace himself on the back of the couch and caging me in, my heart beat faster.

"I picked up a shift."

There was no way I was telling him I needed the extra cash. My car was making an unnatural sound, Mal's birthday and Christmas were coming up, and Momma's church choir group needed some 'anonymous donations' for their fall concert in a few weeks. But he didn't get to know that because he didn't get to know me.

"Why would you—"

"I don't need you to take care of me, Westerman," I muttered, and I couldn't take the words back. "We don't need to have anything to do with each other when you'll be gone after this is all over anyway. I don't *need* to be around you. I need..."

My ramble faded as I lost the battle with sleep. As I drifted away, I barely caught Jason's answer.

"Maybe you're right."

Those words stayed with me when I woke up hours later to an empty apartment and a text from Jack explaining Jason had taken him to chemo and dropped him off before heading to practice. No mention of me, which meant Jason had gotten Jack out the door without seeing me.

Those words pierced my heart when I snuck out of Jason's apartment, grabbed my washed, dried, and folded t-shirt, and made my way to my house wearing his sweatshirt.

And they hurt as much as I'd tried to hurt him with mine.

Family dinners were always magical.

When the weather was good, Momma would hang her twinkle lights and make us eat on the back porch. When she was sick, if she was home, we would wrap her real good with blankets and push her wheelchair outside so she could still be part of it. As the sun set and the sky went alight with stars, the twinkle lights would shine bright enough that you could still see the first line of towering oaks and maples past the back deck. There was always laughter, and in the soft glow of the night, we would spend hours eating, talking, arguing, and being together.

As the seasons turned completely from summer to fall, there was a crispness to the air that lent itself to back porches and twinkle lights with cozy jackets and apple cinnamon candles, a few of Pa's special candles lining the deck to keep any lingering bugs away.

Not super magical, but that was about the only downside of living in Tennessee.

That, and good-for-nothing Jason Westerman.

"Oh my Lord, you are such a child!" I hollered as Jason pulled another strand of hair out of my once-neat low bun. For the past ten minutes, I had been trying to help Momma cook dinner by chopping onions for the soup. Jason was supposed to be helping with the rolls, but every few minutes, another strand of my hair got pulled out or a flash of flour came inches from my eyes *and* my onions.

The stupid pleading look Jack flashed at me when he suggested we help with dinner so he and Momma could go over the chemo schedule was *not* enough to make up for what I was having to endure. If Jack thought forcing us to be alone would stop the tension, he was wrong. Dead wrong.

"I'm a child?" Jason challenged with a cocky smirk as he flicked another bit of powder at me. At that, I dropped my knife on the cutting board and turned to face him, my hands on my hips. I was grateful for the orange UT apron Momma forced me to wear, because more flour came flying at me the instant I turned.

"Westerman! I'm not kidding. Knock it off." I hurried to try and get some of the flour off the front of my apron, which only stuck to the onion juice coating my fingers. "You'd think you were raised on the streets. Did no one teach you manners?"

In my frustration, it took me a second to realize the air had changed. As I glanced up at Jason, the playfulness was gone, and a frown marred his face. It didn't look right there.

"I—"

"I'm just trying to loosen you up," he said shortly, turning back. "I may not be up to your standards, your highness, but at least I'm not a stick in the mud."

He rolled his shoulders back and shuffled on his feet, readjusting his weight. A grimace replaced the frown for a second, and I knew he was hurt—not from my careless words, but something physical. He'd been doing that the whole night.

I shouldn't care if he was hurt. The man infuriated me, and it infuriated me even more how much I wanted to demand he sit down and let me take a look at the injuries from his game last night. He would never know I watched every second of it. That after watching him dominate on the ice, I spent an hour scrolling through his social media, soaking up every piece of the man I could find, feeling misplaced jealousy over every girl pictured hanging off him, no matter how old or photoshopped.

I knew with a few sharp words, I could make him let me help, just like he'd done to me. We hadn't talked since the bike incident the week before. My hands had healed, but I didn't believe either of us had healed from our conversation. Instead of trying to take care of the arrogant man, I turned back to my cutting board and resumed angrily cutting onions.

"That's the best insult you could come up with? Did you get hit in the head at practice?"

Now it was time for him to drop the dough he was trying to roll out.

"You keep saying stuff like that, like you think I'm stupid." He stepped closer, crowding my space. "That's fine, Oakley. I think you're too stuck up to consider anyone else's feelings besides your own. Because you 'don't need anyone', right?"

With that soul crushing statement, he reached over and pulled out my hair tie. My head shot up as the entire tangled mess fell around my face. Using my forearms to push the hair back, I turned to where he was waiting with his arms crossed.

"Are you serious?" I shrieked.

"Stop being a buzzkill and have fun for once."

At that moment, Mal came bounding into the kitchen and picked a piece of dough from Jason's semi-rolled out mound. Her eyes widened as she took in the tension.

"Y'all okay?" she asked unabashedly, lips smacking as she chewed on the raw dough.

"Yes," I answered as Jason said, "No."

I rolled my eyes at him, but he already had his focus on Mal.

"That Letcher boy still hanging around?" he asked. "A

couple weeks ago, you were trying to figure out if he was worth more than a first date. Any decisions?"

"Still undecided. Unfortunately, boys my age don't have a high maturity level." She sighed like that was the burden she must bear then came around to my side of the counter and wrapped an arm around my waist before smiling at Jason, her sweet young face scrunched in thought. "But as Oakley always says, what are boys compared to rocks and mountains?"

"Oakley always says that, huh? I thought she didn't watch movies."

"Oh, she doesn't, but 'Pride and Prejudice' is mine and Ash's favorite." Her scrunched face turned to a radiant smile as she wrapped both arms around my waist and squeezed. "She's kind of like the captain of the Rebels you were telling me about, the one who's real loyal and sacrifices for the team? That's Oaksy, except she sacrifices the fact that she hates lovey dovey stuff to make her people happy. Lame that it's a sacrifice for her, but whatever."

Trying to avoid getting my onion-flour hands on her, I gave her a small smile.

"That's great, kid. Does she ever have fun while she's sacrificing for everyone else?" Jason asked, and Mal just giggled. Before she could answer, Pa called out from the back deck.

"Mal! Could you come set the table?"

"Comin' Pa!" she called back. As she released me and rounded the counter, she smiled mischievously at Jason. "She needs lots and lots of help with that. Best of luck!"

"Hey!" I yelled, but the screen door to the back deck was already slamming closed behind her.

"See, OT? Take it from the kid."

"She's fifteen. Also, I don't need to take advice from kids," I retorted, crossing my arms in frustration as I faced him. "Someone around here has to be an adult, Westerman."

"Being an adult doesn't mean you have to be a killjoy," he said, crossing his arms. "Jack is serious and grumpy, but you've got this shrill undertone that takes it to a whole other level."

Shock and anger coursed through me. Before I could think it through, I reached across him, grabbed a handful of flour, and threw it in his stupidly handsome face. Flour puffed in the air between us, and to my chagrin, once it cleared, all that tension remained. The white flour was caught in his stubble, covering his cheeks but leaving those expressive eyes clear. He was angry, but something like amusement also swirled there.

That made me just plain angry.

"You haven't heard shrill yet." I grinned at his powdery face. Instead of stepping away and letting me have a win, he stepped closer.

"Oh, I definitely have. Real recently," he replied with an infuriating smirk, like he knew exactly how to get under my skin.

"You are so arrogant, infuriating, a big child who—" He stopped my rant when he stepped so close, his chest touched mine. Startled by his proximity, I gasped, and my eyes snapped to his.

"You keep assuming you know me. It's really starting to

piss me off." He took a deep breath, like he was trying to keep himself from saying something he'd regret. "You told me I didn't know you, so I'm trying to, but you're making it really hard."

For a moment, we both stood there, chests heaving. He was too close, too overwhelming, too annoying, too arrogant, too handsome, *too much.*

"Why?"

"You want me to tell you why you're making it hard?"

"No. I'm sure you'll do that all on your own." I shrugged, trying to find the right words and gesturing to him. "Why do you want to know me so bad? Why do you keep trying and asking me to dinner and invading my space when I make it so hard? It's frustrating for both of us to keep doing this when we don't even get along."

He paused, pinning all his unnerving focus on me.

"Jack is important to me, and you are important to Jack. By relation, that makes you important to me." He smiled, the white flour still caking his lips. "I'm loyal to my people too, Oaks, even when they push me to my limits. We're similar, you and me."

He looked at me expectantly for a minute, and then it clicked, probably only because we'd already mentioned the movie.

"Pride and Prejudice, Keira Knightly version?" I barely whispered. He leaned a bit closer, so close, he had to tilt his head to keep from bumping noses, and my heartbeat picked up. My body leaned towards his involuntarily when something thumped on my head, trickling through my hair and puffing in front of my eyes. That powdery grin widened to a full smile, and the arm that had come up over my head while I'd been embarrassingly entranced came back to his side.

I opened my mouth in shock, but he just started to walk backwards towards the living room, leaving me at the kitchen counter flushed and startled with my hair down, covered in flour and onion juice, completely unraveled by the hockey prick.

"And we're both so stubborn." He shot me a ridiculous wink. "Hey, Momma Tennen, is there a bathroom I can use? Turns out, Oakley gets too excited about making rolls."

11

The rest of the night went exactly how one would expect after the flour showdown in the kitchen. While Jason was in the bathroom, washing the flour off his face, I was digging in his jacket for his car keys and hiding them in my parents' closet. Apparently, while I was in the bathroom trying to get the flour out of my hair, Jason was telling Momma and Mal that the flour fight had been a result of me trying to make a move and Jason trying to lighten the mood after letting me down gently. I didn't find out until after an *entire dinner* of my little sister and Momma glancing between me and Jason, mistaking the anger for post-rejection embarrassment.

Pa was the first one to break the awkward tension around the table.

"Y'all know what we need?" He leaned towards a giggling Mal. We all knew what was coming, and I dropped my spoon in my soup with a plop and leaned back with a groan. "The only thing that makes an Oakley Mae frown into an Oakley Mae smile."

"Pa, I don't—"

But Momma had already jumped out of her seat, unlocking her phone plugged into the speakers. They always kept the speakers out on the back porch where we had Sunday family dinners, because music was as essential as the meal itself. The country classic *'Fishin' in the Dark'* came through the speakers as Momma turned up the volume. With that beginning beat, Jack started tapping along on the table just like he used to, and we all paused for a moment. Then, Pops hopped out of his chair, already bouncing as he reached my chair and extended a hand. Letting out a noise of protest, I reluctantly took his hand and let him pull me up. Like he'd done since I was a little girl, he pulled me into a loose waltz hold and moved us in a jaunty dance.

My family sang the words we all knew by heart, and just like every time I was in a bad mood, I fought a smile all the way through that first verse.

At the chorus, Pa spun me out dramatically and shouted, "Come on, Oaksy!"

Finally giving in to my ridiculous family, I let out a loud laugh and belted out about fishing in the dark where the cool grass grows. Momma was spinning in her own circle, singing at the top of her lungs, and Mal had come around the table to hesitantly grab Jack's hands. Even though he was still sitting, he was swaying along and carefully spinning our little sister as we all danced under Momma's twinkle lights. If Hunter were here, he would pick Mal up and throw her over his shoulders as he spun. I missed my younger brother for a moment before Pa twirled me again. I was breathless with laughter and from singing so loud before my eyes finally settled on Jason.

While he had a small smile on his face, there was something sad there, almost longing.

That was when it struck me: he didn't have this. At least, not here. Jason Westerman had his team, his friends, his fans, his puck bunnies, but his Gram, the only family he had, wasn't here.

Family isn't always blood. If it was, I wouldn't have anybody.

The longing in his eyes was the same as when he'd said those words.

He was missing family, the people and connections he needed to survive. At that moment, the great, big, cocky hockey player was feeling the absence of someone who knew him as well as my Pa knew *'Fishin' in the Dark'* was what I needed to smile.

When his eyes met mine, there was a split second when I wanted to go to him, comfort him, tell him he could be a part of our family. That we'd take care of him.

Our eyes met, and he gave me that sad smile. I gave him a nod of understanding in return. Then, I stuck my tongue out and let Pa spin me away as Jason's rumbling laugh finally came out to play.

After dinner, it took Jason and Pa about thirty minutes to find the hidden keys. Finally, forced to stand on the porch to make sure Jason didn't break my fragile brother as he helped him into the car, I set Momma straight.

"I didn't make a move on him," I tried to argue. "He has a big ego, Momma. He probably thinks every girl is in love with him."

"Maybe they are," she mused, having turned her attention to where Jason stood, his impressive ass and strong back facing us as he got Jackson and his injured leg settled in the back of his car. Once he shut the door, he turned back towards us.

"Momma Tennen. Oaks." He nodded to each of us, and then his gaze zeroed in on me. I hated the way it made my heart beat faster. "You think we could hit five minutes next time?"

He started rounding the hood of his car, walking backwards and keeping his smug face on mine. Momma looked at me in question, but I knew what he meant.

There was no way I could stand getting along with Jason Westerman for five whole minutes.

So, when he reached his car door, eyes still on me, waiting expectantly for an answer, I waited. And when he pulled on his car door that didn't budge, his gaze falling to the thin fishing line I had looped around his driver's side and back seat door enough times it effectively barred them closed, I plastered a smile on my face that only grew when his wide eyes met mine. Then, he smiled back, respect and something else gleaming in his eyes.

Maybe we could do four minutes.

"Do I have to keep repeating myself, Westerman?" I said, taking a step back towards the house. "Only in your dreams."

His grin grew as he raised two fingers and saluted me, like I had the first day Jason Westerman asked me out.

With a tilt of my head, I saluted him back and left the hockey player behind, only to think about him for the rest of the night.

The leaves were changing fast. I dreaded this part of the year, because soon, everything would change, and my trees, one of my sources of peace, would be completely different. I watched the big, strong oak tree in my front yard, wrapped in a blanket Ash knitted for me last Christmas. My thoughts liked the fresh air.

My phone rang from the cushion beside me, and Hunter's name flashed across the screen. Smiling softly at the unexpected call, I answered and put him on speaker so my hands could sneak back under the warm blanket.

"Hey, Oaksy," he said. "How's my favorite older sister?"

"Your only older sister is fine. How's my favorite younger brother?" I said back, already smiling softly at the calm happiness Hunter brought with him everywhere. Ever since we were little, me and Jack were grumpy and stoic and blunt. Hunter and Mallory were like little balls of sunshine in comparison.

"Classes are good. Football's even better." Hunter was a running back for the University of Tennessee, and though it broke my parents' Roll Tide hearts, the full ride scholarship significantly lessened the blow. "Y'all still coming out for the homecoming game?"

"Yeah, we'll be there. I have something that afternoon, so I'll come later than everyone else, but I'll be there, Hunt." I snuggled deeper into my blanket. "Jack's coming too. He promised he'd take it easy, but I don't think anything could stop him from being there."

"Why?" The fierceness behind his words startled me. "Jack's been fine on his own for years. He's never bothered to even let us know he was alive. So why now? Because he's sick?"

"Hunter Tennen," I reprimanded sternly, but I understood. Oh, how I understood.

"Have you ever asked him, Oaksy? I know it hurt you too, that it left you to put our family back together. How can you just forgive him?" He blew out a breath of frustration. "Sorry. I just—does he even realize he left us? How that felt to be abandoned?"

Leaning my head against the back of the couch, I sighed and did exactly what I had to do: I worked to put my family back together.

"I'm going to be real blunt with you here, Hunter. You have no idea what it was really like when Momma was sick. Jack worked real hard to shield you from the worst of it. Pa was going through the motions, thinking his wife was going to die at any moment, which would've been fine if they didn't have four young kids. Instead, it left me and Jack to raise y'all for two years before Momma went into remission."

A memory flashed across my mind from the years I'd tried to forget.

The windows were open so I could see my trees, blowing in humid air that promised a warm spring through the cold kitchen. Momma was in the hospital again, so Pa was there too. He went from work to the hospital then straight back in the morning. They were rarely home these days. When Pa came home, or even Momma, it was always with this feeling like we were just waiting for them to go again, which left me and Jack in charge most of the time. That day, we were making dinner, and since we didn't have the car, Jack had taken the bikes to drop twelve-year-old Hunter off at football practice. Five-year-old Mal sat at the counter, her tongue sticking out in concentration as she drew a picture for Momma.

The phone rang. I set the spoon down on the countertop, turning the burner to low so my attempt at mac n' cheese wouldn't burn. Again.

Picking up the landline, I answered with all the grace of a stressed, exhausted, angry fifteen year old.

"What?"

"Pardon me, I might have the wrong number. Is this the Tennen residence?" the woman on the other end drawled.

"Yeah," I grumbled, narrowing my eyes at the mac n' cheese. We couldn't afford to buy another box this week.

"Who am I speakin' to?"

"I'm not telling my name to no stranger," I sassed, ready to hang up the phone. Momma always told me to let people talk before I stopped listening, but sometimes, people had nothing interesting to say. Mal chose that moment to try to get my attention. The lady droned on.

"I'm looking for Jackson Tennen's parents. I'm from La Vergne High? He's had an awful lot of tardies recently that need to be brought to their attention."

"Oaksy! Oaksy, look—"

"Are your parents there? Or is there a better time?"

"I drawed you and me and—"

"If he keeps bein' tardy and skippin' detention, he won't graduate on time and—"

She kept going. Mal kept trying to show me her picture, which wasn't of her parents taking her fishing. It was me and Jack taking her fishing.

Jack might not graduate? No. It was too much. When was Momma coming home?

A bad smell reached my nose, and I knew my mac n' cheese was burning again and Mal needed her parents and Jack might fail school and Momma might die and Hunter almost missed football today because we forgot it was a Thursday, and it was all too much.

"SHUT UP!" I yelled into the phone. "Listen, lady, Jack is doing his best. Our momma is real sick and my pa is trying to help her, so that leaves me and Jack to run this family. He's only sixteen, and he works so our brother can play football and I can feed us and nobody is helping us and we need our momma. She might die and we need her. We need her to sing and make biscuits and be our momma. Without her, Jack is the only one. He will graduate and leave this house and not have to be our parent anymore and get to be my brother again, so don't get your panties in a twist over things that don't matter. Because of you, I burnt my mac n' cheese. AGAIN."

I hung up the phone before rushing over to the old gas stove and moving my pot of mac n' cheese to an unlit burner. It looked like only the edges were crisped, but that didn't soothe my rage.

"Oakley?" I turned to see Jack holding a sniffling Mal, both watching me with wide eyes.

"Sorry," I huffed, tears swelling in my own eyes.

"Where's Pa?" Mal asked between little cries. "Where's my momma?"

Jack didn't say anything else. He walked over and tugged me to his side, holding his two sisters until our tears subsided, and then we ate the burnt mac n cheese in silence. The next day, after school, Pa came home. He drove me to soccer practice then took Mal to see Momma. I never asked, and Jack never said.

But Pa came home because Jack had seen me break.

Hunter huffed at my words.

"Yeah, I know. I was there, Oaksy."

"No. You were at football practice, and school, and friends' parties. You were being a kid because Jack stepped up to be a parent. You felt the pain of Momma being sick, but you didn't feel the burden of running the family in the meantime."

Silence hung over us as I let those words sink in.

"Was it too much? To be around us?"

"I think so," I answered honestly. "I think we healed from everything that happened when Momma got sick in different ways. For you and Mal, I think it taught you to embrace the people you have around you, to find joy in all the little moments."

"But for you and Jack, it taught you to push people away,

that you can only depend on yourselves," he said, as if this was revelatory for him. It felt a little revelatory for me too.

"I don't know, Hunt. But I do know for Jack, he needed to take care of only himself for a while. Once he was sure Momma was better, that the cancer was really gone and we were gonna be okay, I don't think he could be that anymore." I sighed. "And bless him, I don't think he knew how to be our brother anymore. It doesn't make it right, and it sure as hell doesn't mean I forgive him, but I do understand him."

Hunter went silent again, and I watched the wind blow, knocking a few loose leaves to the ground.

"I'm sorry, Oaksy. I never—" He stopped, and I heard the emotion in his voice. "I never realized how much that put on y'all. Do Momma and Pa...?"

"They've brought it up before, and I try not to blame them." I shrugged, even though he couldn't see me. "It's hard. But Jack..."

"Is he—" That emotion clouded my baby brother's voice again. "I know you said he'll be okay, but will he really?"

"Honestly? I don't know, Hunt." I took a deep breath. "I'm worried about this crushing his spirit more than anything."

"How do we avoid that?"

"I don't know. I only know the medicine." I sighed again, snuggling deeper into my blanket as a crisp wind tried to cut through my layers. "I just..."

"Oakley, have you seen this?" Ash hollered as she came barreling onto the front porch in her fluffy robe and slippers. She must have been deep into a romance movie marathon, the way her curly hair stuck up in every direction and she smelled like buttered popcorn. "Your boyfriend is on the news!"

"Well, that sounds way more exciting than our depressing conversation. Please tell us, Ashley," Hunter piped up from where I still had him on speakerphone. The fact that he knew her voice was a testament to how many times she'd interrupted phone calls like this.

"I'm only gonna say this once. He's not my boyfriend. He will never be my boyfriend. We can barely stand each other. Plus, he's Jack's best friend, and there's only so much grumpy Tennen that sunshine guy can handle," I declared with an eye roll, moving my phone to my lap when Ash made herself comfortable next to me.

"Whoa, you've got a thing for Jason Westerman, sis?" Hunter beamed through the phone. "If Jack and him are really as close as Momma says, that means something. He's gonna lead the Rebels to the Stanley Cup finals this year."

Ash nodded vigorously, as if she knew anything about hockey, and once again, I wondered how nobody could see past Jason's charm.

"Yeah, fine, he's good at hockey, but he's also cocky, arrogant, gets defensive real fast, and loves to push my buttons and—"

"I thought you were kidding," Hunter interrupted. "She really does like this guy."

"Does no one around here listen to the actual words coming out of my mouth?"

"Oakley, it's not the words you were saying. It's how you were saying them," Ashley said with a giggle before she shoved her phone at me. "I have a Google alert set for him, since I know you try to ignore his existence—"

"Ash, that is not normal."

"Shush." She huffed, forcing the phone into my hands, pressing play on a video.

The clip was from a sports channel showing some type of Thanksgiving style set up in a gym, full of kids grabbing food and toys and smiling big. My confusing thoughts couldn't find a reason we were watching this. It was only the first week of October. We still had almost two months until Thanksgiving, and I saw no evidence of Jason anywhere in this video. As the camera panned the room, the newscaster's voice came through Ash's phone speakers.

"These kids are treated to a full Canadian Thanksgiving meal, along with donated toys, fun gifts, and a whole array of new hockey gear. The event normally lasts the holiday weekend, giving the kids a full Thanksgiving experience. This is part of the "Fostering Worth" program, founded and funded by Alberta's own Jason Westerman."

The camera cut to a video interview between the same newscaster, an older gentleman wearing a retro Hockey Night in Canada tie, and a smiling Jason Westerman. My eyes latched onto Jason, taking in the way he seemed so genuinely happy but looking like he'd rolled out of bed for this interview.

"Jason, in the past, you've kept very quiet about your involvement with this growing program and your connection to the cause. This year, you wanted to share a bit more about this program and what it means to you. The floor is yours."

"Thanks, Ed. I appreciate you having me," Jason

started, his Canadian accent more pronounced than normal. "I started "Fostering Worth" as a way to give back to the system that kept me alive. I spent a short time in a foster home, and that experience changed my life. I know what it's like to feel unwanted, and so many kids in the foster system feel that way. Even when I was given a home with my grandparents, I still felt lost, but I found my place in sports, in hockey. I want other kids to feel that, to understand they have worth, to feel like they belong in this world. That's really the mission of "Fostering Worth", and I'm so grateful to the staff and volunteers who connect with these kids and help them feel that worth when I can't be there in person."

Pictures of Jason over the years with groups of kids, smiling, playing hockey, eating food, and excited to see him, played across the screen as he spoke. It cut back to the interview, and for the first time, Jason looked a bit nervous.

"Now, you've been a part of this league and many more public organizations for a long time. Why come forward and share this one so close to your heart now?" Ed asked, and I almost grabbed Ash's arm at the forwardness of the question.

On screen, Jason sighed, running a hand through his hair before giving a small smile.

"I don't want any of the attention on me, but I want to use the platform I've been given to bring some awareness. I realized recently I want people to know who I am, that this is a part of me, and sometimes, the fame and money that comes with being a professional athlete can seem like all that matters." He shrugged. "I'm just your average guy who happens to be good at hockey. I also happen to believe the impact we make on people is what defines us, and I'm hoping what I leave behind shows who I really am."

"Thank you, Jason. Now, about this season..."

Ash slowly grabbed the phone back and locked her screen as my mind raced. My thoughts flew a million miles a minute, and I could only land on one.

"Oakley? You okay?" Ash asked hesitantly.

"Is she totally freaking out? Because it sounds like the guy she's trying to hate is a pretty golden dude. I mean, he started a foundation for foster kids?" Hunter, who I'd forgotten was still on the phone, sounded like he was on the verge of fangirling. "You might—"

"I got hit by a bike," I blurted.

"I don't really see how that's relevant," Ash ventured, like she was trying to grasp my crazy but having a hard time.

"No, I...ugh. I got hit by a cyclist, and Jason took care of me. He cleaned my scrapes and let me sleep on his couch. He missed practice to take care of me, even though I was mean to him. He never told Jack I picked up an extra shift and got hit by a bike and still came to take him to chemo." I was rushing now, and I could hear my accent getting thicker as my panicked words flew. "He never told him because he knew I didn't want him to know, and then, he was lonely at family dinner, and I understood him. He needed people. I've been awful to him and he needs a place to belong and—"

"Oakley, breathe," Hunter commanded through the phone. "What are you trying to say? You got hit by a bike?"

"I think she's trying to say she cares," Ash said, a mischievous smile on her face.

"What do I do?" I muttered, mostly to myself. "He just...
He needs people, but I can't stop pushing him away."

We sat in silence for a minute, and then my baby brother
spoke up as the voice of wisdom he rarely got to be as a
younger sibling.

"Sometimes, the best way to change how you feel is to do
the opposite of the feeling you already have," he said then
sighed. "If everything in you wants to push him away, do
something that will pull him closer."

Closer was scary, but everything in my life scared me. I
sat with that thought for a second, thinking through what I
could do, when my heart broke for Jason.

"I think I know what he needs."

12

"**O**akley. Calm down for a second and breathe, sweetheart." Momma grabbed my shoulders as I tried to quickly load the mashed potatoes into the serving bowl. "Everythin' looks great. It'll be fine."

I huffed out a breath, pushing my freshly-curled hair behind my ear. I'd forced my whole family to dress real nice tonight, and when Ash saw me all flustered and trying to make the Costco pie look like it was homemade by putting it in a nice dish, she practically shoved me into a festive gray sweater dress. She was surprised when I let her and even more surprised when I asked for help with my hair.

"Momma, it needs to be—"

"No, it doesn't," she huffed, forcing me to stop scooping and turn towards her. "Honey, a nice gesture doesn't need to be perfect."

"But I'm not doing a nice gesture, Momma. I'm...this..." I stumbled with my words until I crossed my arms and took a deep breath. "I'm not a "nice gesture" person."

"That doesn't mean you don't care, Oaksy. You care a whole lot." Momma put her hands on her hips, and I took in the love in her eyes. Her wild hair, so similar to mine, was piled haphazardly in her attempt at a fancy updo. Thinner than before chemo, she was still stronger than she'd been in years. She had smile lines around her eyes, and her foot was tapping to the old school country Pa had playing. Not even Johnny Cash could soothe my nerves now. "You have a hard time showin' it. You get scared of gettin' attached."

"Momma—"

"No, Oakley Mae. You can't deny it. But you seem to also believe you don't have anythin' to give." She reached out, placing her hands on my forearms and looking deep into my eyes. "You have so much to give. And when you give it, you fear it can overwhelm people, but what do I always tell you?"

I sighed, but she stared into my soul like she would wait there all day.

"I'm like the best kind of music. Not everyone has the same taste, but everyone can recognize quality."

"That's right sweetheart. Now, about Jason."

"Oh lord, Momma. We don't even—"

"Hush. You're tellin' me you're gettin' all flustered, which you *never* do, over a man you don't even like?"

It took everything in me not to roll my eyes. Momma hated when I rolled my eyes. Thankfully, we were inter-rupted by a loud knock on the door. When I turned back to finish scooping the potatoes as Momma answered the door, I heard the voices moving towards me. Most of the dishes were still sitting on the counter, all sprawled out and waiting for the guys to get here before we moved them outside. My eyes surveyed the roasted ham, sweet potatoes, rolls, green bean casserole, pumpkin pie, and a special maple cream pie it had taken me forever to find. Google said it was a holiday favorite up north, apparently.

"Yeah, we're playing New Jersey on Wednesday. That'll be our first game of the regular season, so—" Jason stopped talking when he entered the kitchen and saw the food. Digging the serving spoon into the giant serving bowl of mashed potatoes, I turned and dusted off my hands on my dress. I tried not to fidget as I waited. His eyes finally moved from the food to me, wide with shock.

"Happy Canadian Thanksgiving!" Mal hollered excitedly as she came into the room, holding out her hands for knuckles. Jason turned away from me for a second to bump his fist against hers then focused back on me.

"Canadian Thanksgiving?" he asked. I gave him a smirk, trying to break the tension.

"You know, ham and mashed potatoes?" I gestured to the food. "Are you even Canadian? Embarrassing, not knowing your own holiday among a bunch of Americans, Westerman. Really, your Grams should scold you for that."

With that, something clicked in his gaze, and he realized this was for him. We'd given him our family to borrow for the holiday he was missing with his. The soft smile he gave me only lasted a minute before it turned into something else, more of a smirk, and my heart skipped.

"Well, don't just stand there. Everyone grab a dish and let's get this goin'," Momma commanded, and everyone jumped into action.

But Jason didn't move. He watched as I tucked my hair behind my ears again and stepped out of the way.

"J, you gonna stare at my sister and make a cancer patient carry the green beans for *your* damn holiday?" Jack snapped, holding the rolls in one hand and trying to pick up the green bean casserole with the other. He was finally off crutches, but that didn't mean his balance was any good. My face heated, and I grabbed the green beans from my grumpy older brother and quickly went outside.

Not a word was said, yet I felt caught.

After the food was devoured and the dishes cleared away, we sat in our small living room and shared Thanksgiving memories. Even though it was still early October and way too early for our own American Thanksgiving, I felt grateful I even had a family to share a holiday with, even when we felt a little fragile. As I watched my sister laugh at Jason's theatrical storytelling, I hoped he would get that too, even if he annoyed me.

I stood from my spot on the couch, and Pa caught my eyes from where he sat with Momma, who was deep in conversation with Jack about the difference between classic country and pop country. My brother, who always opted out of Momma's singing lessons, seemed engrossed. He'd been doing that recently, trying to be invested in what we loved, trying to make up for lost time. I guess we were all trying to be *more*.

Heading towards the door, I jerked my head, letting Pa

know I was heading outside. He nodded once before turning back to Momma and her expressive argument for the classics.

Once I was on the back porch, I finally took a deep breath as I plugged my phone into Momma's sound system. Pretty soon, fall would fully be here, and our family dinners would move inside. They always lost a bit of their magic when we weren't accompanied by the birds chirping and the sun setting as we ate, Momma's twinkle lights acting like stars above us. Shuffling my country playlist, I smiled when Shania Twain's *'Honey, I'm Home'* came on. The happy tune had me nodding along as I leaned over the railing.

I heard the back door open then shut as footsteps got too close to the stereo.

"If you touch my music, I will kill you."

"Shania Twain? Really?" Jason's deep grumble, full of judgment, grinded my gears.

"Oh, so you *are* cultured enough to know her music but *not* cultured enough to appreciate it?" I glanced over my shoulder.

"Coming from the girl who doesn't know movie quotes?" he fired back as he came to rest against the railing with me. We faced the dark outline of the woods, the sun having long since set. "What would you Southerners say to that? Sorry, 'around these parts'? The pot calling the kettle black, OT."

I scoffed. I didn't need his opinion.

"What is it about the music for you anyway? Why is it so important to you?" he asked, turning his face towards mine. I turned to him, and the soft glow of the lights barely illuminated his slightly crooked nose, probably broken from hockey, stubble, and inquisitive eyes. He was handsome *and* intelligent, but he didn't need to know that.

"My momma is a musician. She sings, plays the guitar and piano, can read and write music, the whole bit." I shrugged, trying to keep things light. "It's always been a part of my life, even though I don't sing—"

"Why not?" he interrupted, turning his body even more towards me. "I heard you belt that fishing song. You can actually sing."

"I'm going to ignore the fact that you called it *'that fishing song'*, and your offensive surprise," I huffed.

"Well, that wouldn't be very Oakley Tennen-like," he replied with another smile. "And you're deflecting. Come on, Oaks. Let's hear about the music. Why don't you sing?"

"Momma always wanted me to sing, like her." I sighed. "I enjoy singing fine enough but not performing. I listen to music and sing by myself because that's my outlet. I'm no performer like you, Westerman."

"If only you were so blessed." He grinned, and it was an effort to not grin back.

"I don't think my general dislike of people would make me a successful hockey superstar. You can be friendly and charismatic sometimes. It's annoying."

"Wow. Was that a compliment? I can't believe this." He nudged my shoulder, and I nudged it right back.

"Oh, come on. You know you're a big deal."

"I'm an ordinary guy." He had a smug smile on his lips, but it felt off. "I'm a Canadian with anger issues who got good at hockey."

"Anger issues? You're defensive, but anger issues seems a

bit far," I prodded slowly, since that smile of his had faded away. He shook his head a bit. "You really don't think I'll let you get away with a comment like that, do you, Westerman?"

"It happens in the moment. I'm not actively angry all the time, and hockey gives me an outlet. But it feels like it's always simmering there, covered up. When it comes out, it *comes out*. Like when you get happy. Normally, you're cool and collected and grumpy, but you have these moments of joy that shine through. They're powerful when they do. I'm normally a happy, easy-going guy, but I have these moments of anger and defensiveness that are powerful and sometimes take me by surprise." He said it fast, like he wasn't sure how I would respond.

And I wasn't sure how to or why he'd told me that. We both sat there, taking in each other's words in a rare moment of silence. The music continued to play in the background, the words of *'Keeping Score'* by Dan + Shay making my mind wander until Jason spoke again.

"Are you ever going to admit you planned a Canadian Thanksgiving for me?" he asked softly. I kept my gaze focused on the dark trees and night sky.

"I don't know what you're talking about," I answered just as softly.

"Momma Tennen didn't do a good job taking the credit." He chuckled. She had played along a bit but not enough, saying she was happy to move Sunday dinner to Monday once she'd been informed of the holiday and that Jason wouldn't be able to go home due to his schedule. The way Jason's eyes had burned into me then was new.

"Well, you can't be the only one with a secret side," I grumbled, annoyed he'd seen right through me.

"Of course not. How could you live if I was better than you?" I shot him an unimpressed look, and his grin softened as he spoke again. "Is this about the bike incident?"

"It's about a lot of things, Jason, and I'm not a saint. I don't cook, so it really *was* mostly Momma." I shrugged, trying to downplay the whirlwind of feelings that led to this night. Jason took a moment and looked at me the way he had during dinner. Then, he glanced back at the house, where faint strains of laughter mixed with the music.

"Your family is amazing." He spoke softly, looking at our small, rundown house.

"We aren't always like this," I responded and instantly wished I could take the words back.

"Jack told me a bit," he said, and I couldn't help but wonder what version he'd been told. "Is that why it's hard for you to trust people?"

"How am I supposed to trust someone to *choose* me when the people who are always supposed to simply belong to you couldn't stay?" I asked, looking out at my trees again. "Nothing is promised. My family loves me, but when everything happened, I got left behind, again and again. They promised we would be okay, but it was out of their control. Believing someone will stay with something they have no real tie to? It doesn't make much sense."

With those words, I turned, ready to face the disbelief, to see a happy, cocky man who didn't understand. But when I looked at Jason, all I saw was understanding.

"Don't freak out, but we're more similar than you think,

Oaks," he started softly. "You have all these amazing connections, and yet you choose to be alone. I have few real connections, and yet I choose to be with people, even when the lack of depth makes me feel just as alone. We've created these barriers around our trust to avoid getting left behind."

As much as I hated to admit it, he was right.

"But our music tastes are where I have to draw the line." He grimaced, and I grinned as I registered the newer country song playing, singing about two people fighting but not wanting anyone else. *That's Why We Fight* by Ella Langley and Koe Wetzel.

"Can't handle the country, Westerman?"

"When we get dinner, I get to pick the music."

"You still believing I'll go out with you?" I scoffed, shaking my head at him.

"I'm taking your advice, OT." He leaned forward and got real close. My breath hitched despite myself. "I'm dreaming about it, and let me tell you, it's a damn good dream."

"We have dinner together every Sunday, Jason, since you've decided to make yourself a regular at *my* family's house. There's no chance we're changing the music," I declared, putting my foot down. He opened his mouth, but I held up a hand to silence him. "No, you can't annoy your way into this one. It's not happening. We're not even friends."

"Do we need to start arguing again to prove that? It's been a while since we've gotten into a good fight."

"One week is a while? You literally locked me out of your car on Monday until we hashed out Jack's chemo schedule," I reminded him. "You play a professional sport, Westerman. In a few days, you're booked 'til the summer, and we don't know what Jack's schedule will look like past December. You don't have a lot of control here."

"No, guess I don't."

His words drifted into the night air, settling thickly between us as he gazed out into the darkness again.

"You worried about the season starting?" I said, trying to focus on anything other than how defeated he sounded.

"This year is our year. I can feel it." He finally smiled, giving me that cocky grin I didn't realize I missed. "But this doesn't mean you're getting rid of me, Oaks. I have enough time to convince you not to hate me."

With him grinning at me, the world alive around us, I knew he didn't need time.

I already didn't hate him.

Maybe I even understood him.

13

"Momma, it's really fine. I don't mind driving up on my own." I tried to not sound frustrated as I filled my water bottle at the sink. Grabbing an apple from the bowl on the counter, I finished putting the last of the things I needed for work into my bag.

"Oakley Mae, you said yourself you will only be gettin' a few hours of sleep before that secretive meeting you're havin' and then drivin' four hours, not even considerin' the traffic, to get to the hotel?" Her scoff was a thing of southern sass legend. "Not on my watch, young lady. Now, Jason is a perfectly nice young man your brother has invited to come with us on this family weekend as a thank you for his hospitality, and he made special arrangements with his team at the beginnin' of his busy hockey season to support a family who ain't even his blood. He said he was more than happy to give you a ride."

"Momma! You already talked to him?" I stuttered,

appalled at the gall this woman possessed. She was like a dog with a bone when she set her mind to something.

"Of course I did. I knew you'd pitch a fit, even though Jack said you two have been gettin' on so well recently. Things seemed to have turned around since you planned him a whole Thanksgiving meal. That was quite the peace offerin', sweetheart." Her voice hinted at something, and my cheeks burned. "Is there a problem with drivin' together?"

Yes, there was.

Jason Westerman was officially under my skin.

He even invaded my thoughts when I went fishing alone, and that was my sacred time.

And no, I hadn't said yes to going out with him, no matter how many times he brought it up. He'd slip it into conversations or I'd randomly get a text about it. In the past month or so of knowing Jason, I'd coldly rejected him every time, but I was finding my resolve weakening with every new ask.

So yes, being trapped in a car with him going into a weekend when we would be spending time with my family—who loved him almost more than they loved me—and then pretend like seeing him joke with Mal and talk hockey with Pa wasn't breaking down my control was a problem.

"Oakley? You zonin' out on me?" Momma's voice cut through my thoughts, because I had absolutely been zoning out.

"I'm here Momma. It's fine. I'll just drive—"

"Oh, perfect. I'll let Jason know!" Her excited voice cut me off before I could say 'by myself'. "Love you, hun. Drive safe, and we'll see you tomorrow night when you and Jason get in. Have fun but not too much fun, okay? Bye!"

The call ended, and I was left stunned. I stood at my counter, shock and a slight feeling of betrayal coursing through me. When my phone buzzed in my hand, I wasn't surprised to see a text sitting there from the man himself.

Westerman: *So we're carpooling to Knoxville, eh?*

Westerman: *I have practice until 2, wanna come to the rink and we can head straight from there?*

Westerman: *I'll even let you pick the music, but if I have to listen to that 'Night and Fish and Moon' song for four hours, I'm picking the snacks.*

It felt like he had the upper hand right now, and I needed a little safety. A bit of control. So, grabbing my keys and heading towards my car, I quickly typed out my response and hit send.

OT: *We're taking my car.*

As far as night shifts went, this one was pretty normal. I had two patients, and only one delivered on my shift. I tried to connect more with them, intentionally this time, but I never knew what to say. Maybe I was just the most unfeeling nurse they'd ever seen.

Climbing into my car, I turned on my comfort playlist before heading home to sleep for a few hours before my meeting.

I couldn't believe I'd agreed to meet with Sierra and Dr. Grouse. How did I think I could do this? I couldn't even connect with patients when I tried. But then I remembered, of all things, Jason's words, the words that convinced me to reply to Sierra in the first place after he'd intrusively read her text.

If you never give it a shot, how do you know if you missed something that could change your life?

He was so annoying.

Taking a deep breath, I started my car and headed back home. Most of my comfort playlist was, in fact, Nirvana. I listened to country most days, but when Momma got sick, I went through a phase where any country song reminded me of her, and it hurt too much. So, when I needed to *feel* and tuck those feelings out of sight, I turned to Kurt Cobain and his angry guitar.

After my drive through the city, a quick shower, and what could really be considered a glorified nap, I pulled out my slacks, white blouse, and undereye concealer to make myself presentable.

Sierra was waiting for me outside the research facility, a remodeled building downtown, two cups from the coffee shop down the street in her hands. Shifting them to shake my hand in her firm grip, she grinned like I was already saying yes. She was confident like that.

"Hey, Oakley! Thank you so much for making the time to meet with us." She pulled back and handed me a cup. She looked different from when we were in school together, her blonde hair pulled away from her face in a professional updo, slacks instead of scrubs gracing her tall figure. "I think you're going to be excited about what we have going on here. Dr. Grouse will explain more, but I can't wait to hear your ideas on getting this program off the ground."

"Thank you for the opportunity, Sierra." I gave her a small smile, letting my professionalism keep me calm. "This research means a lot to me. Do you really think I can help?"

"Oh, I do." She turned to the facility, gesturing for me to walk inside with her. "I believe you are exactly the person we need."

As I walked in the doors, I felt it. The air shifted, like something important was clicking into place.

Like that piece of me exhausted by life caught a glimpse of something new.

I felt alive.

***

Dr. Grouse's words of praise and excitement raced through my head as I headed towards the marked entrance Westerman told me to enter in the very thorough instructions he texted this morning. It made me both roll my eyes and smile as I entered the hockey arena, and I was tempted to ignore his instructions, if only to piss him off.

It was fun to make *him* roll his eyes for a change.

There was something about the crisp air in that building; it felt fresh, like Pa teaching me to glide at the church Christmas skate night. When the kind old man who checked me in led me to the practice area, I knew it would forever feel like Jason too.

When I saw Westerman, number 26, next up on the offense drill, I was mesmerized. I'd seen him skate the one time I'd watched his game. I'd been impressed and a little attracted.

But it was *nothing* compared to watching him up close. Up close, I could see *him*.

I could see his strong legs pushing into the ice and gliding as if he was born to do this. I could see the floppy hair sticking out from the back of the helmet, which should not have been as hot as it was. But the worst part was that damn sexy, lopsided smile he wore while he powered towards the defenseman, juked around him with that mix of intensity and casualness that was uniquely him, then slapped the puck top shelf above the goalie's left shoulder.

An ordinary Canadian my ass.

I was already breathless, caught off guard by his hockey skills and how handsome the joy on his face made him, when he skated by me to get back in line.

He was looking over the stands until his eyes caught mine, and he came to an abrupt stop—right in front of me. That lazy smile turned into his full, breathtaking one. Lifting a gloved hand, he waved, a small one right next to his helmet, like a little kid.

I waved back, a small smirk on my lips.

A whistle sharply rang out across the ice.

"Westerman! Stop flirtin' and get on the line!" Tim O'Connell, the head coach of the Rebels, hollered across the ice. Turning around, Jason raised his stick in acknowledgement then turned back to me and gave me a mini salute. This was becoming a thing, and I couldn't deny it made my heart flutter.

Every. Time.

Jason took his place on the line like his coach asked, that cocky grin of his firmly in place. Surveying the arena, I could see why he loved it, why this was his safe place. He truly looked like he belonged here. Something inside me was jealous of that.

"Oakley!" Most of the guys were exiting the ice, probably headed to the locker room, but on the other side of the plexiglass, Jason stood. "I'm gonna go shower and change. Meet at the front?"

"Sounds good," I replied as I stood. Before I turned, I gave him my own mini salute, matching his grin as I did. That started as my move, and I couldn't let him steal it.

Taking my bag, I ducked into the closest bathroom, quickly shedding my business casual attire from the meeting and pulling on leggings and an oversized sweatshirt. Summer had definitely ended as we headed towards the end of October, and the air now had that cool feeling only fall in Tennessee could bring. I stared in the mirror taking in my wavy hair and tugging at my oversized sweatshirt. There was a new light in my eyes. I felt lighter than I had in weeks, and for the moment, I wasn't focused on the pressure of taking care of anyone or the fear of change.

I was focused on hope instead.

As I exited the restroom, my bag slung over my shoulder and a small smile on my face, a flash of blonde caught my eye. Right next to the entrance where I was supposed to meet Jason was a petite blonde woman, looking like every hockey wife on social media, dressed in designer overalls with perfectly styled hair and sporting a good-sized pregnant belly.

Who was this woman, and why was she waiting where Jason asked me to be?

She turned to me, recognition lighting her green eyes and a smile spreading over her face, and something in me braced for whatever this would be.

"You must be Oakley Tennen." She grinned wide. "Your brother is that grumpy military guy, and you are as pretty as I imagined. Of course, I only had descriptions to go off, since Colin and Jason both refused to let me look you up on social media, which was annoying, but it's okay, because I knew I'd meet you soon!"

"Uh—"

"Sorry, I have a habit of being overly honest and spilling all the information I know about people and freaking them out." She smiled and shrugged. "I'm Ivy. I'm married to Colin Kreuger. Jason is over at our place all the time, and let me tell you, I have been so excited to meet you! That guy can't stop talking about you. This world can be a little flashy sometimes, so finding good people is a rough go."

I opened my mouth to speak, but once again, Ivy's eyes lit up with another thought, and her somewhat endearing motormouth took off again.

"J said you work in labor and delivery?" She barely paused for me to nod. "We have to be best friends! This right here is my first baby. I promise, I'm not normally this chubby, and my tummy doesn't normally stick out this far. I just have so many questions, and my mom isn't exactly the type to share these things, but now I have you! What do you recommend for people to pack in their hospital bag? My doctor said my blood pressure has been too high and I have to be induced early. Do inductions take longer than normal labor? I mean, I don't know how long we'll be there, and Colin is a chronic over-packer and a worrier, and he has done all this research on, um, oh what is the medical word Dr. Farrow used—"

"Pregnancy induced hypertension?" I threw out when she paused for breath. She grabbed my free hand tight with both of hers.

"Yes! Yes, that's it! Do I need to be worried? Colin tries to help, but neither of us know much about having a baby. Both youngest kids, so we're spoiled and with no younger sibling experience to pull from!" She was interrupted by a big, burly arm wrapping around her shoulders and pulling her into a tight hug before the big, burly owner of said arm placed a kiss on her forehead. Ivy dropped my hands to lean into his body, as if his presence instantly calmed her chaotic energy.

"Hey, baby," the man who must be a defenseman of the Nashville Rebels, Colin Krueger, gruffed. He was known for getting into fights, being a little grumpy and a lot brutal with his words on and off the ice, according to Pa. He played rough, and it showed. I never would've put him and spunky Ivy together, with her petite frame and his towering one. But anyone seeing how he looked down at her as she pecked his lips could tell, this man was whipped. His eyes practically glowed with love as he watched her open her mouth to chatter again.

"Colin, perfect timing! This," she gestured to me and raised her eyebrows, "is *the* Oakley Tennen."

Colin's eyes widened, and I felt scrutinized as his eyes raked over me. What was Westerman telling these people?

"So you're *Jason's* Oakley," he said with absolute finality, like it was a fact that somehow, me and Jason belonged to each other. My shoulders stiffened. "Nice to meet you."

"You too?" My words came out as a question, and I searched for something else to say as Ivy moved her hands to cradle her stomach. Perfect. I'd take pregnancy questions over whatever was happening with me and #26. "To answer your question, high blood pressure can be an issue. When are you due?"

"We have an induction date set for November 16th." Colin's gruff reply accompanied Ivy's enthusiastic nod.

"Oh, that's a few weeks away. In my opinion, since your doctor is aware and has already set an induction date for that reason, I wouldn't be overly worried about it. Grab a blood pressure monitor for home to keep an eye on it if you want and don't be afraid to go into the office or the labor and delivery unit if you start feeling more off than normal or have a string of high pressure reads. Dr. Farrow is a provider I work with a lot, and she keeps cases like these well-monitored."

"I love it when you talk medical."

I whirled around, coming face to face with the man behind that mesmerizing voice. We were going to have a serious conversation about him talking to these strangers about me when I wasn't distracted by the way his damp hair had a slight curl to it, the smell of his shampoo wrapping around me like a warm blanket. It brought me back to when his shirt stretched between us like a peace offering, hot tea soaking through mine. I'd thought it was the detergent I was smelling, but it wasn't. It was *him*. We locked eyes, and there was that weird look on his face again, almost like he was, somehow, proud of me?

"Jason, you should've introduced us to Oakley sooner. She calmed my fears way more than Colin's panicked research." Ivy promptly ignored Colin's noise of protest as I turned back to look at her. "Seriously, thank you, Oakley. You're a godsend. Oh, we should totally have a girls' night!"

"Ivy, don't smother her." Jason moved to stand directly behind me. His hands landed on my shoulders, and I stiffened before involuntarily melting into his touch. My mind fought my body, telling me to step away, but I didn't. "OT still has to survive a whole road trip with me, and what did you say? My ego comes with a danger of causing death by jackass?"

Even with his touch burning through my sweatshirt, I could do witty banter.

"Truer words were never spoken, Westerman." I turned my head to look up at him behind me, smirking. His hands stayed on my shoulders, sliding slightly down my arms in a comforting motion. I allowed it. "You ready for my road trip playlist?"

His eyes twinkled as he let out a groan, dropping his head to my shoulder to try and hide his smile.

"As long as I get to pick the snacks," he grumbled against my sweatshirt, and I giggled. Again. I freaking giggled. He lifted his mischievous eyes to mine, letting me know he hadn't missed that. Playfully pushing his head away, I turned back to see Ivy and Colin still there, wildly amused looks on their faces.

This had to be one of those out-of-body experiences.

"We're burning daylight," I laughed hesitantly as I shrugged out of his grip, stepping towards the door. "It was nice to meet y'all."

After a quick goodbye, Jason pulled on one of his old ball caps as we made it through the front doors and a few steps into the parking lot before he tried to turn me towards his car.

"Westerman, this was the deal. If I have to endure your presence for four hours in a confined space, I get to do it on my terms," I declared, stopping in the middle of the lot, crossing my arms and pointing in the opposite direction. "My car's that way."

"Oakley, come on. You know that piece of—" He stuttered only for a second when he caught my glare. "Adequate-for-driving-short-distances car barely makes it to your parents' place. It's not the safest choice."

Stubbornness rose in me like a physical force.

"A cocky hockey player isn't the safest choice either," I retorted. As soon as the words left my mouth, their double meaning caught me by surprise. Jason's eyes widened as he took a step closer, and I knew he caught it too.

"Is that why you keep trying to claim we aren't friends?"

"We're *not* friends. We're acquaintances on a good day, enemies on a bad one."

"I think we're more than 'not friends'." He stepped forward, his face close, hands propped up on his hips. The way they were held away from me made every other part of him feel so much closer. "'Not friends' means you're indifferent."

"So does enemies."

"No, OT." He gave me a grin, like he was trying not to tease me but couldn't help it. "Enemies means there's a whole lot of feelings involved."

"Yeah. Hate, dislike, tension—"

"Tension, passion, a focus on the other person."

"You're twisting it. We're only in each other's lives because of Jack."

"Sure. Because your brother is a good friend, you tolerate my presence."

"Weren't we talking about my car?" I retorted.

"Yeah, but you don't think I'm safe. Despite what you try to convince yourself, we *are* friends, friends who argue and care for injuries and plan holidays. Hate to break it to you Oakley, but we aren't enemies anymore. We're friends with enemy-level feelings."

I tried to roll my eyes, but then I looked at him—really looked at him. He had a small bruise on his cheekbone, one fading into a light yellow. I knew if he took off his shirt, I'd see a bruise on his ribs from the hit he took two nights earlier during their away game against Florida. He still couldn't help but shift his weight from the pain in his hips from whatever injury he got weeks ago.

He wasn't safe. He was temporary. I couldn't care about him.

But as he looked into my eyes with an intensity I couldn't avoid, I knew I already did. Those feelings of annoyance were turning into something else every time he was in my space, and that made him even more dangerous.

"We're not," I protested. "You're a stuck-up hockey player who assumes things and gets on my last nerve."

"And you're my friend's stubborn little sister who picks fights for no good reason," he retorted with a grin. "So, should we grab that dinner tonight before we meet up with your family?"

It wasn't humanly possible to roll my eyes any harder.

"I'll take that as a maybe on dinner. Car's this way." He jerked his head back.

"Then we're driving separately, because my car is that way." I pulled out my keys and dangled them between us.

"You're going to be ridiculously stubborn about this, aren't you?" he asked, almost resigned.

"Yep. Pick your path, Westerman."

He groaned then snagged my keys, pushed past my shoulder, and started towards my car, slinging his bag over his shoulder in a move way too attractive to be real.

I smirked, and he hollered back at me, "You're killing me, OT."

As I took a step to follow him, pleased I'd won our little battle of wills, my phone buzzed. As I pulled it out of my bag, a second social media notification buzzed. I frowned. I hardly ever used social media, but curiosity took over. I opened the message and felt the blood drain from my face.

JASON WESTERMAN IS OUT OF YOUR LEAGUE. GET OUT BEFORE YOU GET HURT.

When the sudden shock lessened, I quickly clicked on the notification to open the app and go to the profile that sent the unsettling message. It had no profile picture, no followers, and only followed one account: Jason's.

What the hell was this?

Taking a deep breath, I tried to think. Some crazy fan had somehow seen me around Jason and lost their delusional fantasy of Jason being theirs. They were insane but harmless. Right?

"Oaks, you coming?" Jason's voice jolted me back to the moment.

As I looked at him, halfway across the parking garage, I remembered the way he reacted when he thought I was stalking him—his security system, his ball caps pulled low over his brow, the way he checked over his shoulder when we were in public.

Concern wrinkled his brow, and I knew I wouldn't tell him. Clicking the screen closed and trying to forget for the both of us, I nodded, trying to leave the fear behind. Road trips were for good playlists and tolerating hockey players, not amateur stalkers.

14

Jason didn't even give me a glance before he said, "No."

"You don't even know what I was going to play."

"Is it country?"

"Nope."

"Liar." He reached over, tickling my side. I yelped, surprised, and jerked as far away from him as I could in my small passenger seat.

"Focus on the road," I huffed as I pushed his hands and body back to his side, ignoring the goosebumps erupting at his touch. "Fine, the first song is country, but there's a good mix on this playlist. It's my happy music, so don't you dare laugh."

"Alrighty, Oaks. As you wish." He winked, using one hand to drive, the other hand resting on the center console.

"Princess Bride'. That was too easy, Westerman." I smirked, but inside, my heart was pumping, wondering if he would like my music. "This song is one I have to belt at the top of my lungs, and there is no other way to listen to it, so buckle up, buttercup."

"First of all, I see what you did there. And second, I look forward to being serenaded by *the* Oakley Tennen. Please, proceed."

Without hesitating, I clicked play on 'What Hurts The Most' by Rascal Flatts.

As soon as they sang about hearing the rain on the roof of that empty house, I was gone.

Nothing else existed but me and those emotional lyrics. That was the magic of music. It made you soar, made you cry, made you fall in love or want to wreck a cheating ex's car. It made you *feel*. Feeling was something I couldn't seem to get right, but when I listened to music, it gave me a place to try. It let me feel for a few minutes at the top of my lungs and then go back to life as if I hadn't felt at all.

There was a slight pause between 'What Hurts The Most' and 'Come As You Are' by Nirvana, and I heard a soft, "Wow."

"Wow what?" I asked, prickly insecurity creeping in.

"Wow, I feel like that song unlocked a whole other side to you." He smiled over at me, but his eyes held something more, something tender, something that quickly turned mischievous. "It was actually pretty cute how into it you were. You didn't even let loose that hard with 'I Love To Fish at Night'."

"Oh, shut up, Westerman. You're talking over Kurt Cobain, and that's a special kind of blasphemy that even the best groveling won't excuse you from." My voice felt all tight, and I prayed he wouldn't notice. Heat scorched my cheeks.

What in the world made me sing in front of him? "And you know it's '*Fishin' in the Dark*'."

"I'm glad you showed me how you use the music. I've been wondering how it's an outlet if you're not performing, but it makes sense now." He paused. "It's all starting to make sense now."

"What is?"

"The way you work."

I glanced over at him, confused.

"When we first met, I figured you were defensive and obstinate."

"That's a big word, Westerman."

"Impressive, eh? Anyways, it took me a few arguments to see you're not defensive, you're guarded." He looked over at me, as if to emphasize his words. "There's a difference. You don't keep feelings out. No, you're holding it all in so tight, it has nowhere to go. That's why the music is so important to you. It gives you an outlet without feeling like you're bothering anyone."

My jaw dropped. No one ever just *got* me. I wasn't sure if I even did. Jason Westerman, after completely piercing my soul, held out his palm to me.

"You can pay for my therapist skills with our dinner date. I'll take a handful of those sour patch kids as a prepayment, though."

***

Everything under me was rumbling and shaking as I quickly blinked my eyes open. A solid string of curse words in a thick

Canadian accent flooded my ears as my eyes slowly took in my surroundings.

Was I still in my car? Check.

Were we still on the freeway? Apparently, we had barely pulled off to the shoulder.

Was Jason still in the car? At this point, he was already at the front of the car with the hood popped open.

Shaking the rest of the sleep from my eyes, I jumped out of the car and hustled to his side. Now, I might know nothing about cars, but from the smoke drifting from my hood, it didn't look good.

"Oakley?" His voice was strained.

"Jason?"

"Remind me why we took your car?"

Because I was ridiculously stubborn, and for some reason, I needed to have some advantage over Jason. It was stupid.

"I don't need anyone to help me, Westerman." I snapped, angry at the situation more than him. His head reared back, and as he took in the car and my shivering where we were stranded on the side of the road, I saw the moment he decided to fight back where he'd given in earlier.

"How's that working out for you, Oakley? If your mom hadn't forced you to carpool with me, you would be stranded halfway to Knoxville on the side of the freeway with the sun setting and no working car by yourself. That's not safe."

He took in a ragged breath, as if it hurt him to think about.

"I know, okay? I know. How much do you think this will cost?" I barely whispered, already deep in my head about how in the world I was going to afford this. I didn't have time now to pick up extra shifts, and who knew what the research job would pay? It was a passion project, not a money move.

"I don't know, but we really should've taken my car. Dammit, I tried to tell you this, Oakley, but you're so stubborn when it comes to anything to do with me." His voice raised a bit, not enough to be yelling but enough to make me realize he was genuinely upset, and my chest tightened. Everything was changing, and there was nothing I could do to stop it.

"You act like you have this right to take care of me, but who gave you that right?" Using both my hands, I pushed against his chest. "You're sweet to my sister, you take care of my brother, you're kind to everyone around you, and *we're not together*. No matter how many times you ask me out or make me feel important, I'm not that girl, Jason. I can't care about one more person as deeply as I want to care about you because...I...because—"

My breaths were coming shorter and shorter, making it harder and harder to breathe. As the pressure in my chest became crushing, I felt rough hands gently cradle my face. All the sounds around me were swimming, and Jason's mouth was moving, but I couldn't hear any sounds. Then, he moved slowly, his thumbs reaching up to my temples to make slow circles. He brought me closer so I could feel his chest rise and fall.

Slowly, I matched my breathing to his. Slowly, he came back into crystal clear focus. Those brown eyes. That stubble.

The jawline and the lips I dreamed of kissing.

His voice finally reached me.

"I don't have the right to take care of you, but don't get it wrong, Oakley Tennen. I care about you. There's nothing I want more than to see you love yourself the way everyone around you wants to love you. The way I want to. I'll never apologize for wanting just a piece of that love to come from me."

My body sagged against him, and I let him wrap those strong arms around me, because I couldn't do it alone anymore.

———

"Sorry, sir, there's nothin' else I can do." The gravelly voice of the man behind the reception desk sounded like sandpaper. "All towns from Nashville to Knoxville are pretty well booked up now, what with the big game and the fall colors all fixin' up to be right pretty. I can give ya two single rooms, but they'll be at opposite ends, seeing as that's all I have open."

With a sigh, Jason's tired eyes met mine. This was the only motel in the tiny town the tow truck had brought us to, and we were too far in the boonies for an Uber. Or a taxi. Or a rideshare. Or a bus. Jason checked them all. We were well and truly stuck, and there was no way we were taking separate rooms so far away from each other in this rundown place. So, we were stuck in that too.

As if my nerves weren't already fried.

Even I couldn't deny the shift that had happened between us after my meltdown. The care with which he treated me. The way he, without even thinking about it, laced his hand with mine as we wandered the grimy hallway to find our one-bed room for the night. The way I let him, and even squeezed his hand when he glanced down at me as we reached our door.

"You ready for the one bed trope?" he asked, a grin in his voice.

"Pardon? The what now?"

"Oh no. Do you not read romance books, Oakley?" he exclaimed as he fit the key into the lock, turning it easily and pushing open the door.

The room was everything I expected. Tiny. Disgusting. Wallpaper and décor straight from the seventies. And, sure enough, there was only one bed. Tucked in the corner sat a chair. Not a couch—a wooden chair.

I dropped my bag on the solitary chair then reached over it to get the small lamp turned on, smirking at his shocked tone.

"Do I seem like the type of girl who reads romance books?"

A chuckle met my ears as he took in the tacky wallpaper. It felt like we could get murdered here and no one would housekeep afterwards. Our only light source was the tiny lamp on the nightstand by the chair, and it gave off just enough of a dim glow so we could see where things were.

"Well, you did serenade me with '*Before He Cheats*' earlier, so I guess the obvious answer is no."

"Hey, just because a girl likes some Carrie-Underwood-hate-men music doesn't mean she necessarily hates romance." I shrugged, turning to face him. "This one, however, doesn't believe in all that stuff. Is the starting forward of the Nashville Rebels a romance book lover?"

He put his hands on his hips, disgruntled. Somehow, he made that look hot. Hot and disgruntled. Hell, I needed sleep.

"Okay, first of all, we'll be circling back to the 'all that stuff' comment. Second, so what if I do?"

"I'd be surprised, since you so harshly judged my emotional singing of '*What Hurts The Most.*'"

"I pulled an OT and gave a blunt opinion." He smiled at my little giggle, which resulted in another finger at my face. "Two in one day? As you Tennens say, slap me sideways and call it Sunday."

My heart warmed even more at him using Momma's favorite phrase. I knew we both felt the exhaustion from the events of the day, including our argument on the side of the freeway. Still, I could grudgingly admit, I appreciated that Jason was with me. I needed his ability to make me giggle.

"To answer your insensitive question, no, I'm not a big romance reader. Grams, however, treats them like the South treats sweet tea."

"An essential good?"

He snapped his fingers and gave me a quick point before he turned and started grabbing clothes from his bag.

"Exactly. The only time I can get her to talk about herself and not fuss over me is when she's talking about those books. So, we talk about her books a lot. You ever read *A Thousand Boy Kisses* by Tillie Cole?" he asked with so much passion, I had to hold back another giggle.

"Is it bad if I say no?"

"Honestly, not sure. That one had Grams torn up for weeks. She would cry every time she talked about it. And the ending? I bawled when she told me, and I'm a grown man." His hands were back on his hips, the shirt and sweatpants he'd pulled out abandoned on the bed. Now, I let a full blown smile out as I grabbed my toiletries and a change of clothes.

"Grown man is a bit of a stretch," I said as I started to move past him. I'm not sure what possessed me to touch him. Maybe it was how he held me after the pressure in my chest got too strong. Maybe it was the way he bawled at the plot of a romance book for his Grams. But instead of passing by, I put a hand on his chest and froze.

Completely froze.

We both stared at where my hand rested, his chest rising and falling with his breaths as they caught and sped up, faster and faster.

What was this? This pull I felt towards him? This desire I had to tell him all my fears, all my wants, everything I wouldn't tell anyone else?

I barely felt my change of clothes and toiletry bag fall from my hands, hitting the floor with a thud we both ignored.

Those strong, warm hands framed my face, those thumbs drawing lazy circles on my temples. My eyes jumped to his.

Jason Westerman's deep brown eyes always baffled me. They could be wildly intense and completely carefree all at once. They were safe and yet so dangerous. In that moment, I was lost in the mix I saw there. It was like he was trying so hard to tell me something with a look while holding everything back from me at the same time.

"Oaks?" he whispered.

"Jase?" I whispered back. I'd never called him that before.

"You good?"

He shifted a little closer, and I could feel his warm breath against my face.

"Right as rain." My whisper was barely audible.

He started to lean forward, and I watched his gaze flick to my lips and back to my eyes, searching. I wasn't sure what he found there, but my heart prayed he found a resounding yes. It didn't matter the question.

His lips hovered over mine, millimeters from shattering our tenuous friendship, when a familiar song broke the silence.

I'd never been annoyed to hear *'Fishin' in the Dark'*, but when we both jerked back, I knew we'd lost the moment.

"It's Pa," I whispered, trying to cling to some piece of whatever we'd been pulled from.

After a beat, Jason gave me a sad smile. His thumbs tapped against my temples, hands still cradling my face. Then, he pulled my head forward a bit, his lips meeting my forehead. They lingered for a second, and my eyes fluttered shut. When he pulled away, the ringtone was almost over, and I slowly blinked open my eyes to meet those browns again.

"I knew there was a reason I didn't like that song." His voice was gruff. "Answer it, Oakley. I'll hunt down some food."

Still in a trance, my head moved in an imperceptible nod. Giving me a small nod back, he let me go and grabbed his wallet. The song ended, but I wasn't jumping to grab my phone.

"I'll be right back. Keep the keys just in case. You'll have to let me back in." He went to the door, but before he opened it, he turned back to where I was, still speechless.

"Oakley?"

"Yeah?"

"Don't stress about the car, okay? Let me take care of this."

He took my stunned silence for a yes, leaving without another word.

That emotional rollercoaster drained my will to stand, and I collapsed onto the bed, leaving my things on the floor.

15

'*ishin' in the Dark*' blared from my bag again. I leaned over—that's how ridiculously close together the chair and the bed were—and plucked my phone from where I'd stashed it. Hitting answer, I raised the phone to my ear and resumed my sprawl on the bed.

"Hey, Pa," I answered, trying to keep my voice even.

"Hey, kiddo, y'all okay? I know you texted Momma that you're just gonna stay in town for the night, but are you sure?" His calming voice brought tears to my eyes. I clenched them shut. "We can come get you both."

"Don't leave Hunter and everyone on our account. Jason already tried to see if there was an uber or something we could take, but we broke down in the middle of nowhere. There's a rental car place, but it closed before we got into town. That's the backwoods, I guess."

"Makes sense. Told your ma it was all taken care of, but she didn't believe me." He sighed gently, and that was when Momma's worried voice took over.

"Well, what I couldn't believe is y'all took that car! Your Pa has been tellin' ya to look for a more reliable one for months now, Oakley Mae. You're askin' for trouble."

"I know, Momma." Sighing, I reached an arm up and draped it over my eyes. "It's on my to-do list. Don't worry, Jason gave me a talking to about it, so all those bases are covered."

Had I already brought up Jason twice in this conversation? Yes. Yes, I had.

Did I hear the embarrassingly long pause and muffled whispers from my parents while I was still thinking about that interrupted moment with Jason? Yes, yes, I did.

"He's taking good care of you, kiddo?" Pa finally said, choosing his words carefully. "And it sounds like you're letting him?"

There were so many thoughts bouncing around in my head, it was hard to separate them all. Exhaustion took over, and I could hardly keep my eyes open.

"Yeah, I guess I am," I almost whispered. "I'm exhausted, so I'm gonna head to bed. I'll see you tomorrow."

I barely heard Pa's 'love you' and Momma's frantic 'wait' before I ended the call and sat up, knowing if I didn't change my clothes and wash my face now, I never would. I quickly rushed to the bathroom, grabbing my stuff from where I'd left it on the floor, scrubbed my face clean, tugged on my over-sized t-shirt and boxer shorts, and settled back on the bed.

It felt like no time had passed when I felt a strong hand lightly shake my shoulder then gently push the hair behind my ears. I couldn't remember my eyes closing, but they slowly blinked open, and a smile spread over my face as I took in the all-too-familiar scruff, chocolate brown eyes, and messy hair. My hand reached out towards where he sat on the bed, not listening to my head and doing whatever the hell it wanted.

"Hey, you're really handsome." The sleepy words tumbled out of my mouth, and only when the chuckle met my ears did I realize I was not, in fact, still asleep. Sitting straight up, I rushed to straighten my hair and adjust my shirt. "Um, I didn't—"

"Don't even try to take that back, OT," he said before he reached forward and grabbed the takeout containers from the chair. "If I'd known you sleep like the dead, I definitely would've taken the key."

Embarrassment swept through me again as I realized I was supposed to let him in. I grabbed his arm as all the thoughts became clearer and the brain fog cleared.

"Oh, shoot. I thought I'd hear you knock, and I'd be able to let you in and—"

"Oakley, Oakley, calm down. It's fine, Gary from the front desk let me in."

"Gary?"

"Yeah, for the price of taking a photo as bragging rights to his sons that he met me."

"Ah."

"Yep. You want a cheeseburger?" he asked as he popped open the containers, the sweet smell of greasy food floating through the air. I couldn't remember the last thing I'd eaten, and starving was a light term for the feeling as my hands involuntarily started moving towards the food.

"Jason Westerman, you are a king among men." I basically groaned as I wrapped my hands around the cheeseburger and took a bite. With my mouth still full, I mumbled, "I take back every time I tried to hate you."

As I happily took another bite, the amused chuckle I expected never came. Swallowing my mouthful of burger, I turned and saw those eyes gazing at the untouched burger in his hand. Even from his profile, I could tell he was thinking hard.

"What's wrong?" I asked softly, scared of the answer.

He turned slowly to face me, his expression a storm of emotions I didn't know how to interpret.

"You tried to hate me?" he asked, eyes searching mine. "For real, Oakley, not kidding around?"

"In the beginning, yes," I answered honestly. "It was safest."

"There's that word again." His eyebrows drew together in confusion. "Safest for what?"

"For me. My pride was hurt."

I blamed it on exhaustion. That was what had me pouring out my heart to someone who didn't want it.

"Pride?"

"Jason." I lowered my burger and shifted so I could look at him head on. "You called me a puck bunny and a stalker. Even though it pissed me off, it was also embarrassing. Who in their right mind wants a hot guy they were flirting with telling them they seem crazy?"

"There's so much to unpack here. One, it's good to know this attraction goes both ways, OT. Two, I'm so sorry I ever made you feel like that. Can I please explain the whole story?" His eyes pleaded with mine, and although I was exhausted, my body thrummed with energy at his sincerity. I gave him a small nod before he continued. "I got drafted six years ago, when I turned twenty one. I was young. After I started making plays and getting some media coverage, every piece of attention I got went straight to my head—especially attention from women."

He paused, trying to gauge my reaction.

"Ah," I said, trying to hide my unwarranted jealousy from those seeking eyes.

"I wasn't a good guy, Oaks. Grams told me to shape up, that this wasn't how she'd raised me, but I didn't listen. After my first season, I went to visit Jack and some buddies at university in their senior year. He told me his little sister was coming, that he hadn't seen her in years, and he had this feeling we'd get along."

I remembered that trip I took to Jack's. He'd introduced me to his friends, all nice enough guys but none of them Jason. There'd been so much going on that night—so many unresolved issues between Jack and me, the crushing realization I couldn't force him to come home, finally accepting he'd left me to pick up the pieces of our family on my own. I thought if I'd shown him I could fit into his new life, he would come back into mine.

He didn't.

But the way Jason was looking at me, I knew there was something about that night I was missing. I put my burger down in the box and grabbed a napkin for my messy fingers, more confused than ever.

"Jason, I remember visiting Jack, and we never met. I'm sure of it." I swallowed. "I would remember."

"You're right. We never met." He sighed, giving up on his

burger too, setting it next to mine before fully facing me. "Before you showed up, I got absolutely hammered and went off with some chick from the bar. I woke up the next day with a massive hangover and a royally pissed off friend. Jack gave me a talking to I hadn't gotten in years; it was the wake up call I needed. It was always me, Grams, and Gramps growing up. They were all I had, and when I lost Gramps, I think it broke a part of me that wanted to let people in. But Jack, through some hard times, became a brother. He became one of my people, and I had let every single one of my people down.

"So, I decided to stop with all the women and just pick one. That girl I'd gone home with that night was persistent and didn't know about hockey, so she seemed like a good choice."

He ran a hand over his face, and I knew we were getting to the part of the story that caused him so much grief. Again, I blame the tiredness and the pain of these memories for both of us, but I reached out, resting my hand over his and giving it a squeeze. In solidarity.

"We were on and off from that time up until two years ago. On top of being manipulative, she tried to drain my accounts. When I tried to confront her about it, she laughed. She said I couldn't tell when someone was using me, that I was so desperate to feel connected, I couldn't tell when it wasn't real. That playing me had been one of the easiest things she'd ever done."

Jason gave a humorless chuckle. "Turns out, she knew exactly who I was, and dating me was exactly the cash con she and her drug dealer boyfriend were looking for. I don't even want to think about the money she stole from me. Tracking her down and proving she'd taken it without my consent would cost more of my sanity than I was willing to give her. She already broke my ability to trust that a woman could want anything more than my money and fame." He took a deep breath before starting again. "I've always believed most people are good, that for every good man, there is a good woman. Gramps used to say, 'You will find someone who matches your worth, and that's when you'll be grateful you put in the work to be worth something.'

"I need you to know, I didn't used to be worth much at all. A piece of that broken man lashed out at you when we first met, but I'm not him anymore. I've worked hard to find more purpose in my life. I'm glad we didn't meet back then, because you would've been even less impressed with that idiot. I try every day to not be that guy, and I hope you can see that."

We were silent for a moment, our hands connecting us as all that hurt sat in the air. He wasn't meeting my eyes, like he had some reason to be ashamed.

"What was her name?" I asked softly. His eyes snapped to mine in surprise, tilting his head to the side in confusion.

"Rachel. Why?" he answered hesitantly.

"Well, if I'm going to be hating this woman until the end of time, I need to use her name when I curse her." I gave him a cheeky smile. "Makes the hate more solid that way."

"I see. Is that what you did with me?" He gave me a half smile, the sadness and hurt still lingering in his eyes. "Cursed my name in your head?"

I couldn't blame the tiredness for what I did next. Nope,

this one I blamed entirely on Jason. On the way he let me see a vulnerable side of him. The way I now understood he was only doing what I did in trying to hate him: protect his heart.

So, when I reached out my free hand, letting it caress his cheek before settling my palm firmly against his scruff, I blamed it all on Jason Westerman.

His hand tightened its grasp as his eyes searched mine.

"I tried to hate you, Westerman. I try to pretend I still hate you, but it's all talk. I guess my heart knew it wasn't what it seemed, even if my pride didn't want to hear it." I took a deep breath. "It's your fault, really. You get on my nerves, but you made it impossible for me to truly hate you. I see the man you are, and he's worth a hell of a lot."

I took inventory of every place we touched, trying to memorize this moment, this man. Slowly, I removed my hands from his and reached for my forgotten burger. I could feel his stare but promptly ignored it until he picked up his own food.

The next few minutes passed in comfortable silence as we ate, pondering all that just passed between us. A million thoughts ran through my head, and I found myself coming to a scary realization, one that had been forming for a long time, slowly building through every interaction we'd had.

The Jason Westerman I had created in my head was wrong—so wrong. The man sitting across from me was more than irritating comments and cocky bravado, more than a professional athlete and a hot guy. Even though he was all those things, he was also *more*.

We finished our burgers, and as I wiped my sticky fingers on the napkins, Jason started cleaning up our mess. I reached for my own box, but he pulled it from my hands and gave me a look.

"I got it, Oaks. I'm gonna toss these and then change for the night." He barely met my gaze, reaching one hand into his bag and grabbing some clothes off the top. "You wanna pick a side of the bed?"

I'd barely nodded before he was in the bathroom, taking our takeout boxes, his change of clothes, and a whole lot of tension with him.

Sighing deeply, I tucked myself into my chosen side of the bed, closest to the door. After tossing and turning for a second, the sound of water running in the bathroom reminded me I wasn't alone.

I was about to share a bed with a man.

And not any man.

The man who'd snuck into my mind and refused to leave. The man who told me about one of the worst experiences of his life and then ate burgers with me and got ready for bed as if emotional conversations and bedtime routines was something we did. The man who made me feel like I could be more than cold and unattached.

A man who understood how it felt to be left behind.

My heart sped up as I thought about what it would feel like to wake up next to him, to sleep knowing he was right there, peaceful and unaware of the world around us.

Those racing thoughts were interrupted when the bathroom door opened, flooding the wall opposite me with light before it quickly flipped off. Jason turned the corner, and when he saw me tucked into bed, a small smile snuck across his face.

"What?" I asked as he put the clothes he had been wearing earlier into his bag. "What's that smug smile for?"

"Smug smile, huh?" He laughed, turning to look at me before climbing into his half of the bed. His arm grazed mine, and I practically jumped out of my skin. Goosebumps spread quickly, and I cursed all that was good and holy.

"Your resting face is pretty much a smug smile," I laughed nervously.

"That's fair. You have to admit, it looks damn handsome on me." He gave me his brilliant, full smile this time.

Yeah, it did look pretty damn handsome.

"Every time we hang out, it seems like we're forced together." He turned, laying on his side, facing me. Like a gravitational pull, I followed, facing that scruff and those deep brown eyes. "And yet, it doesn't feel forced. It feels like the easiest thing I've ever done."

I gulped, not ready to answer the questions in his eyes.

"Even when I pick a fight with you?"

I expected him to laugh. He didn't. Instead, he reached out, pushing a stray lock of hair from my face before bringing his hands back between us.

"Even then, because if you didn't care at all, you would've ignored me. Instead, you let me bother you. Figuring out how you work has been my favorite type of puzzle." That smile would be the death of me. I glanced away, trying to think of anything to dissolve this tension—or maybe to lean into it. I wasn't sure yet what I wanted. "Hey OT?"

"Yeah?" I whispered.

"Tell me something good." He looked at me expectantly.

When I blinked blankly, he groaned. "Come on, Tennen. You're telling me you've never heard of 'Me Before You'? British guy in a wheelchair and girl with crazy outfits? It's a really good love story."

"You know, for a macho-bro-professional-hockey-player, you sure know a lot of romance movies and books," I said, giggling. His smile broadened in acknowledgement of the giggle. "I haven't seen it. Sorry to disappoint."

While I gave him a noncommittal shrug, he shifted closer.

"You never disappoint me, Oakley. From that first time you sassed me, you've never disappointed me," he said in that serious tone of his. "Now, tell me something good. Not something that makes someone else happy—something for you."

He watched me patiently, and I found myself telling Jason something I hadn't told anybody.

"I got a job offer today, to do that research on how music can help in the healing process," I whispered, talking quickly. "It would just be assisting the doctors doing the research, but I did a project on this in nursing school, and my partner showed it to her boss. He's a neurologist, and he just received funding to start a new project, and he wants to do mine. He wants to do *this*."

I stopped my rant to take a breath and suddenly felt self-conscious. Tucking my hands between my cheek and the pillow, I took in the way Jason was looking at me—and I kept going.

"When Momma got sick, I wasn't scared. Not at first." I paused, biting my bottom lip.

"You were fourteen when she started chemo, right?"

I nodded.

"I'm not sure if I didn't process it, or if I didn't believe she was actually sick. Then, one day, Pa came home and found her on the floor with a four-year-old Mal trying to wake her up. She went to the hospital, stayed there for a few months, came home for a few weeks, then ended up right back in a hospital bed." I shook my head at the memory. "That first year...it was literal hell. Pa didn't know how to take care of everything, so he focused on work and Momma. Jack took care of us. We split responsibilities. I cooked, he got us where we needed to be. We both did the grocery shopping and the cleaning, because Momma was sick, and Pa..."

"He couldn't handle it all," Jason said softly, reaching a hand towards me. Shifting, I lined up our fingers as they rested together on the mattress. In a second, his big hand was covering mine. Something about that sudden contact made me blink back tears.

"I remember the first time I visited the hospital. It was the second year she was sick, and we weren't sure if she was gonna make it. Jack was barely holding it together. He was tardy and getting and skipping detentions daily. Even worse, he wouldn't talk to us anymore. To me. I could feel my brother fading away, and I was powerless to stop it. Pa was physically there, but he wasn't Pa anymore. Mal and Hunter were struggling, Mal not understanding what was happening, Hunter angry at the world. I couldn't imagine cooking another meal. I hated cooking and trying to explain what was happening and not understanding it myself. I felt so *stretched*. Then, I visited Momma. I walked into that awful, tiny hospital room, sure she was gonna die, and she was listening to '*I'm a Survivor*' by Reba McEntire."

"A country song?" Jason asked, his fingers moving to lace through mine. I squeezed his hand, not sure how to share this part of me.

"Are you surprised?" He chuckled, and I gave him a small smile. "Momma was so weak, she hadn't spoken in days. But when she listened to her music, she would sing. Her body wouldn't let her talk or move, but she could listen. She could *sing*."

My voice broke, and Jason's hand tightened around mine. I took a deep breath, taking his strength.

"After that, I would bring her new music during my visits. I would play music in the house, especially when we were fighting. Pa and Jack responded best to Johnny Cash. I loved '*Fishin' in the Dark*' and Nirvana. Hunter would only calm down to Jack Johnson, and Mal needed Taylor Swift for a tantrum.

"Music wasn't just our escape; it saved us, all of us. We know so much of our healing process is mental, but I don't think we've fully utilized how much of an impact music can have on us, how the melodies and beats encourage the production of certain hormones. There's some research, some developed therapies, but there's more to discover. I know it." I paused, trying to control my breathing. "Jason, this could save people the way it saves me."

Vulnerability suffocated me. I'd never told anyone what I'd told Jason, and yet, I knew he'd understand. He'd understand the desire to have a purpose, to take the hurt and the pain and turn it into something else. Something *good*.

"Oaks, I've said it before and I'll say it again: I love when you talk medical." His eyes were shining with pride. "You're so intelligent, it blows my mind."

"Thanks, Westerman." I smiled softly. Even with the energy coursing between us, my eyelids started to droop, exhausted from the day and sharing. As my eyes lost the fight to stay open, a soft chuckle met my ears and then gentle lips touched my forehead.

"See you in the morning, Oaks."

As I drifted into sleep, my fingers still laced through his, I realized there was something else good, something else just for me.

These little moments with Jason, when we weren't fighting and when I wasn't determined to hate him, made me happy. After tonight, I saw us for what we truly were: a girl trying too hard to make sure her people were okay and a man fighting every day to be better so he wouldn't disappoint his.

He was right. We were more similar than I'd ever wanted to believe.

16

"You sure everythin' is okay? I mean, you haven't been rude to him a single time, sweetheart. Sassy for sure, but have you decided to finally stop hatin' the poor boy?" Momma shouted in her pitiful attempt at a whisper. She decided to bring this up while we were standing at Hunter's football game in Neyland Stadium, surrounded by endless chatter, music and announcements from the speakers, and the general noise that came from a large event, especially a huge rivalry game in the south, where my baby brother was the star running back in his senior season.

Thankfully, Jason and Jack went to grab some food from the snack bar. Unfortunately, his absence led to an intense inquisition from Pa, Momma, and Mal. I pulled at the sleeves of my orange and white hoodie, trying to hide my hands from the cold.

"Momma. I already told you," I sighed, glancing to Mal

for help, but she was hanging onto my every word. "As much as he still bothers me to no end, he's a good person."

"Honey, botherin' is exactly what a man does when he wants you, and gettin' bothered means you want him back," Momma stated, like that wasn't the most scandalous phrase I'd ever heard come out of her sweet Southern mouth. I turned towards Pa for help, only to find him nodding along.

"It's true, Oaksy." He grinned. "I've never seen two people more bothered than you two. Plus, your momma here's been griping about finally getting some grandkids, so it's about time—"

Out of the corner of my eye, I saw Jack and Jason making their way back down the metal stadium steps. I shot Pa a glare so strong, he turned and shut his mouth quickly before smiling way too big to be inconspicuous. Jason looked from Pa to me, confusion written on his face. I shrugged, and he took Jack's seat next to me. Surprisingly, Jack didn't say anything. He took a seat next to Pa, wobbling a bit as he lowered himself down.

Even with the crutches gone and the chemo working, Jack looked weak. His skin was pale, eyes bloodshot, but he refused to stay home. He was adamant that his life wasn't going to be stolen by cancer.

The desire to be present, to make up for what he'd missed, especially with Hunter and Mal, was almost palpable every time I spoke to him.

"Popcorn?" Jason asked, pulling me from my thoughts. We stared at each other as I shook my head. He smiled under the brim of his worn *Westerman's Baked Goods* hat, and the memory of those lips against my skin last night came flooding back. The gentle touch from such a strong man was burned into my soul.

Turning back to the game, I focused on ignoring the way Jason Westerman made me feel for the rest of the game. Which was next to impossible, considering he nudged my arm when country music played over the speakers, cheered as loud as the rest of us when Hunter scored a touchdown, bought Mal a giant foam finger, and fit in like he had always belonged in my family.

In my life.

For the first time since Hunter started to play for them, I was extremely grateful UT's defense was having a rough year, since a close game meant less time to pay attention to the guy sitting next to me. I focused on the field, screaming as Hunter took the ball and ran a 45-yard touchdown to secure the win. On my feet, I smiled as everyone cheered before glancing at Jack to share this moment. This moment meant more than a touchdown. This was a moment Jack missed when he'd left, that he would miss if he left us behind again.

My brother watched, emotion clear in his expression for once, as our baby brother lived his dream—the dream only made possible by Jack's sacrifices. Jack stayed sitting, and I knew the only reason was because he couldn't stand, history repeating itself as I watched someone so strong become so weak in front of me.

As the players geared up for the field goal, I couldn't take it anymore. I couldn't watch my family fall apart again.

I couldn't be the one left behind to put it back together when Jack left.

Again.

That thought, as selfish as it was, consumed me.

Shoving past my family, I muttered something about using the restrooms. Muffled calls followed me, but I booked it up the stadium steps before anyone could catch me. Shoving through excited fans, bumping shoulders with girls in cropped sweaters and men with beer bellies, I finally made it to the closest restroom. The smell of popcorn, hot chocolate, and sweat surrounded me in the crisp fall air, along with the roaring buzz of excitement and groans of disappointment from the crowd.

Since I'd bolted in the middle of a field goal during a close game, there was no line for the women's restroom. I ran into a stall, and as soon as the door locked, I sagged against it, refusing to think about all the germs in this gross public restroom stall. I don't know how long I stood there, leaning against the door, trying to focus on not falling apart, when a deep voice called out to me.

"Oakley? You in here?"

"Westerman?" I answered in confusion, turning towards the door. He was definitely in the restroom—the *women's* restroom. "You realize this is the ladies room?"

"I'd hope so, since you're hiding in here, OT," he shot back, a grin in his voice that came from right outside my tiny stall. "You claim to be this 'true Southern lady', but I would assume a true Southern lady doesn't hide from her feelings."

"I'm *not* hiding," I scoffed, still not opening the door—I was, in fact, hiding. "Ladies use the restroom too, you know."

"Oakley." His voice got serious. "Jack thinks something's wrong, and I agree. The only reason he's not in here is because, apparently, Southern gentlemen don't enter the ladies room, even in emergencies. I'm not a Southern gentleman, as you've pointed out many times, so—"

"This isn't an emergency, Westerman." I crossed my arms and turned towards the door. "Can I not have a few minutes of privacy?"

"Oakley, the game's over, and you've been 'not hiding' for a half hour." His voice dropped low. "What's wrong, Oaks? Talk to me."

My arms fell to my sides, and though I couldn't see him, all the other noises faded away as I focused on him.

"It's Jack." The words barely escaped. "I can't pick it all up again. I can't."

Shuffling my feet, I waited for a witty remark to take my mind off it or a lecture on how that wasn't important. Instead, a familiar hand holding a phone came into view above the door, and *'Fishin' In the Dark'* overtook the stall.

Neither of us spoke, but I felt what he was trying to say. He didn't have words, but he knew what I needed. Slowly, I opened the door and faced him.

He stood there, arm still extended above us, a hesitant smile on his face.

"Thought you hated country music?" I said over the music with a strained smile.

"I like country music just fine. I just like to annoy you more." I shoved his shoulder, and he used the forward momentum to wrap his arms around me. I struggled for a minute, trying to push against his broad chest, but he tightened his hold. "Let it happen, OT."

"I'm not a hugger, Westerman," I grumbled but stopped fighting all the same.

"You're not a giggler either, but you giggle for me all the time."

"Shut up."

We stood like that until the song ended, his arms around me and my arms by my side as I let it happen. I let myself feel it all for a moment, even with the weird glances we were getting from women coming and going around us.

When the song faded and the noises of rowdy fans and the same chorus of a popular pop song we'd heard for hours came rushing back, we both pulled away.

"You can't control it, Oaks." His hands still held my arms, like he couldn't let me go all the way. "I'm worried about him too, but trying to control this will drive us both crazy. It'll be different this time, okay?"

I nodded. In my head, I knew it could be, but my heart wanted to run, to disappear before my family could expect me to pick up the pieces. I couldn't do it without him. I couldn't do it *alone*. When I glanced up, Jason looked at me with so much understanding.

"Jason, I—"

"Oh my hell, is that Jason Westerman?" a high pitched voice broke through the bubble, and Jason sighed as I jumped away from him, taking in the three giggling girls at the restroom's entrance. I didn't know how no one else had recognized the huge hockey player standing in the women's restroom, but these three girls in concerningly small tops, considering the cold air, were eyeing him like they knew *exactly* who he was. Instead of answering, he turned to me.

"You ready to go? Hunter should be with your family

down at the tunnel by now." He reached for my hand, but I stepped around him.

"Give me a second." I walked up to the sinks, and caught his eye in the mirror. He nodded once before readjusting his hat and making his way to the door with defeat in his steps.

"Ladies," he said softly as he made his way out, and I had a few seconds before I was surrounded.

"That was totally Jason Westerman!"

"We should get a picture—"

"Are y'all dating?"

"How did you snag him? Or is he still single?"

Wiping my hands with the paper towels and tossing them in the trash before adjusting the sleeves of my UT sweatshirt, I turned, and all three dyed blondes watched me expectantly.

"He's a person, not something you can 'snag' or fight over. Let him be," I said sternly. Two of the girls looked chastised, but the ringleader blinked at me.

"Oh, hun, that's what someone who got rejected by a hockey star would say." Her accent got snide and my jaw clenched. Then, I really looked at this girl, so desperate for someone to see her, to choose her. I felt sorry for her.

But she also pissed me off.

"No ma'am," I chuckled. "A piece of advice? Men like him can only pretend they're interested for so long, so I might focus less on others and work on what you have to offer. From your soul, not your body. No one wants to meet an amazing man and only have sparkly smiles and subpar insults to offer. It's embarrassing, *hun.*"

With that, I turned and left those girls to talk shit about

me for the rest of the day. The stupid grinning faces of Jason and Jackson met me outside the restroom.

"Not everyone can have insults that cut to the core, Oakley," Jack smiled, and the panic in my chest settled a bit more.

"Honestly, do you expect the average person to be on your level?" Jason chimed in, pushing off the wall and sharing a look with Jack. "And I am pretty amazing, eh?"

"Both of you shut it," I said, pointing a finger at my brother then at Jason. "You stood out here and listened, and *you* left me with those girls!"

I shoved Jason's shoulder for emphasis as they both chuckled at me. Looping an arm around my brother, Jason nodded towards where I assumed my family was waiting.

"Come on, Miss Feisty. Let's get you out of here before you pick fights with any more of my fans." Jason laughed before moving forward. Jack was not a physical touch guy, neither of us were, but when I saw the way he leaned against his friend, I knew.

Jason was holding him up, and Jack was letting him.

As the guys joked with each other, laughing about some movie quote I didn't get, I realized this was what Jason did.

When we met up with my family and he distracted them from my disappearance by exaggerating the story of my standoff with his fangirls, when he chatted with Hunter and laughed with him and Jack as if they were long lost brothers, when he pulled me aside and told me my car was unsalvageable, that he'd already taken care of getting the most money I could for it, when he looked at me with that freaking stunning smile, I realized it then.

Jason was the friend my family needed. He was what was different this time.

I couldn't do anything to take that away from them.

So, when he tried to sit next to me on the drive home crammed into my parents' car, I asked Mal to switch spots with me. When he asked if we could talk, I ignored it. When he offered to go car shopping with me, I said I didn't need him hovering. When we got back from Knoxville, I tried to pretend like the weekend never happened.

17

"There's no way in hell I'm wearing that," I told Ash as she held up the smallest silver dress I'd ever seen. She gave me a real good pout, but I was grumpy.

I was at one full week of avoiding Jason Westerman.

Jason Westerman was at one full week of trying to get me to stop avoiding him.

Momma had done the chemo runs this week, and that was what I'd felt most guilty about until the food delivery from Tucker's arrived on my door. My favorite brisket. I ignored the flirty text from Jason asking to join me for dinner. Even then, I didn't feel as guilty as I should have.

But when Jason sent me a link to a new song 'for my research', a car listing, and another dinner to my doorstep when he was out of town at an away game, I felt it.

I felt guilty for avoiding him.

But I wasn't going to stop. I'd been grumpier than usual, and all my roommates were concerned.

I was still searching for a car in my price range, hitching rides off Ash or using her car when I needed. I hated relying on her like that, but she was so ecstatic about it. The research position I'd accepted was a dream come true, and my roommates couldn't understand why I was so grumpy.

They didn't know that the creepy messages had kept coming to my social media account.

And coming and coming.

They were only making me angrier.

So, Ash was calling for an emergency mandatory Friday girls' night.

"Come on, Oaksy. You need a hot outfit and good live music," Ash argued, bringing the dress closer to me. "It'll snap you right out of this funk—unless you want to stop avoiding a certain hockey player..."

"I'm not avoiding him," I snapped. "Avoiding makes it sound like I usually spend time with him."

"You *do* normally spend time with him. That's the point, Oakley." Ash tossed the dress on the bed next to where I sat. "You two have been getting close, and it's scaring you. What happened in Knoxville that turned you into this angsty, hot-man-ignoring, scaredy pants gal?"

Everything.

"Nothing," I answered. "Why are we going out tonight? It really couldn't wait one more day, Ash?"

"No, it couldn't. Considering you've been grumpier than usual and Donovan is on another betting bender," she said, not even pausing when I huffed, "live music, bar fries, and distracting, hot men is exactly what you need. What *we* all need, *cara*."

No matter how much I rolled my eyes, protested, and just about begged, I found myself at a tall table in a crowded bar in the sparkly silver dress a few hours later. We'd come to our usual spot, the tables surrounding the dance floor and the ambience almost enough to make me want to stay.

Almost.

Annoyed and angry, I pulled my oversized denim jacket closer around me and crossed my legs, my white cowgirl boots kicking out as I took a long sip of water.

Because I was being obstinate.

And I was alone.

My friends were chatting around me, but I was alone.

Loud music blared, chatter battered incessantly against my head, and the general feeling of life around me settled in the air like a suffocating haze. People moved in slow motion. Fog filled my brain, and I couldn't stop looking at the door.

Like I was waiting for him.

I hated myself for it.

A hand landed on my shoulder, and I turned.

"Oakley, baby!"

The smell hit my nose with annoying familiarity, but I couldn't place the guy. I just wanted his hands off me.

"David!" Tess exclaimed, glancing at me with genuine apology in her eyes. "I didn't know y'all would be here tonight. Don't you normally hit Broadway?"

"Yeah, but I heard you talking about this place in the office and figured we'd try it out," he answered.

I internally groaned. David, the bar top, cologne cloud, handsy-drop-off forced date I'd dropped, blocked, and never thought about again. I watched him with disinterest when I felt the pull.

The hair on the back of my neck stood up.

Goosebumps snaked across my skin, and I fought a shiver.

I turned back towards the door.

The crowd parted, the haze in my mind lifted, and everything became clear as my eyes focused on him.

Jason.

In a dark blue button down and jeans that showed those hard-earned muscles, he stood with my brother and a few other smiling men I recognized from Jack's college days, scanning the bar like he was looking for something. For some*one*.

His eyes caught on mine, and he stopped looking. He focused on me.

Then, he smiled, like he'd finally found what he'd been looking for.

We stayed like that for a moment, the world moving around us, only focused on each other.

Then, that damn meaty hand clamped on my shoulder again. My gaze jolted to where David was looking at me expectantly. Tess blinked at me too.

"Hm?" I asked, unsure of what I'd missed.

"I said let's dance, babe." He bent down so his mouth touched my ear in a move I'm sure would be sexy if it were absolutely anyone else doing it. I shifted away, ready to give him a piece of my mind, when a very different hand landed gently on my other shoulder.

Jason was no longer smiling. I hadn't seen his 'genuinely

upset' glare in a while, and I'd rarely seen it used on someone other than me. And cyclists who hit me.

No, this glare was directed squarely at the man with his hand still sweating through the denim onto my shoulder.

"Babe, you know this guy?" Dave whined. When no one answered, he took a split second to grow impatient. "It doesn't matter, let's go."

He went to grab my hand, but I wasn't looking at him. I was hypnotized by the intimidating man towering over me. Slowly, he reached up and cradled my face, holding his thumbs on my temples. Those rough hands scraped softly against my skin, and I couldn't help the small gasp that escaped me. We were electrified, the only two people in the room, if only for a second.

"Dance with me, OT," he commanded.

"No," I answered sternly, doing nothing to move my face from his grasp.

"We need to talk, Oakley."

"We have nothing to talk about," I practically whispered, my resolve already wavering. "Go away."

But we stayed there, staring, until Dave jumped in again. He snagged my hand and pulled me so hard, I nearly fell off my chair.

"What the hell—"

"I would take your hands off her if I were you." Jason's voice was full of barely contained rage as he shoved himself between me and Dave. In his whole professional hockey career, he'd only gotten into two real 'drop the gloves' fist fights. Both times, he'd come out the unequivocal winner. I had no doubt he'd be fine.

Tess met my eye, and the fear there was the only thing that had me grabbing the brute behind me and dragging him to the dance floor and past the flock of overaged frat boys without throwing a single physical or verbal assault. I wasn't sure how I was going to get Jason to calm down, but he wasn't fighting to turn back around, and I called that a win.

We passed Jack, who was talking with Ash and Tae. He gave me a look with raised eyebrows, and I waved him off.

As soon as we made it to the hardwood, couples dancing around to some old school country band, Jason settled his hands on my waist, tugging me towards him.

I had no choice but to loop my arms around his neck.

Glaring at him, I waited, but he just glared back before huffing. "So, this is what the great Oakley Tennen does when she doesn't want to deal with something, huh?" he said gruffly, leaning forward so I could hear him over the noise. "Head in the sand?"

"I don't know what you're talking about."

"You know exactly what I'm talking about," he shot back. His hands tightened on my waist as we swayed in a small circle.

"Please elaborate, hotshot," I gritted out, involuntarily pulling myself closer as my jaw tightened. "You're the one demanding we talk."

"Because that's what normal people do, Oakley! They talk about things, about what they feel."

"Feel?" I scoffed, turning my head to look at anything but him, but he wasn't having it. Grabbing my chin, he turned me so I was forced to face him.

"Yes, Oakley, *feel.* Look at me and tell me you feel nothing when we're like this."

"Like what?"

"*Us.* When we're *us*, OT. Because I can't go on pretending I don't feel on fire when I look at those beautiful brown eyes. When you're glaring, or lost in thought, or listening to your music, or singing, or talking medical, or enjoying food you didn't make, it *doesn't matter*. I take one look at you, and I feel *alive*." He spoke forcefully, pulling me closer with every word until I had to tilt my head up to see everything I felt reflected in his eyes. "You can't control this, Oaks. Stop trying. Tell me you feel this too."

Yes.

My heart screamed, and I took in the space between our mouths. If I pushed up on my toes, I could show him how I felt.

No.

My head argued, showing me how it would feel when he left me behind for something better than the broken girl who couldn't even talk about feelings without arguing.

Because he was right. I couldn't control this.

When I pushed against his chest, surprise flashed across his face as I walked away. The doors to exit the bar were heavy, but I was determined as I raced out into the cold night air towards the parking lot. I didn't know where I was going, only that I needed to get away, away from Jason Westerman and all the feelings he brought out in me.

"Oakley! Oakley, what are you—"

I whirled on him before he could get too close and found his long strides had already eaten up all my distance.

"Leave me alone, Westerman!" I hollered before whirling back around and continuing towards the darkness. I had no idea where Tae had parked, or even how I would get into her car. I'd left all my stuff at the table inside, even my phone.

"I can't! Don't you get it? I can't leave you alone, OT." My steps faltered, but I kept going and heard a grunt of exasperation as a hand wrapped around my arm. "Would you hold on for a second and talk to me?"

Finally stopping my frantic steps, I turned and faced him. His eyes were blazing, and he didn't let go of my arm until I jerked it away from his grasp.

"What do you want?" I asked, crossing my arms in front of my body, willing the chills and anxious excitement at his closeness to *go away*.

"I think that's pretty obvious." His tone was pissed off. "You've been avoiding me ever since Knoxville, and that's not gonna fly. Why are you choosing to be blind to this? Unless you actually don't feel anything for me."

"Westerman—" I started, but the hurt in his eyes cut me off as his words did.

"Can you honestly tell me you feel nothing?"

"Jason—"

"No, you don't get to walk away like this, Oakley. You don't get to control the situation by avoiding it. You don't get to avoid feeling because it's hard. Maybe I should have let this go when it started, when you said you hated me."

"Jase—"

"But I kept going, and I fell for you." My heart stopped. He was frustrated, angry, and passionate all at once. "Do you even realize how beautiful you are? How insanely smart and quick witted and frustrating? How I couldn't stop thinking about you even if I tried? And you don't—"

"Shut up, Jason! Of course I feel something for you!" I practically screamed at him. "Of course I feel *everything* for you! You make me giggle and make me feel smart and pretty and calm and angry and scared all at once. I like when we're us, when I look at you and feel like I need to capture the feeling and hold onto it forever because it's the only time I don't feel exhausted by my life because *you* make me feel *alive!* Can't you see how terrified it makes me that I have no control—"

My yelling rant was cut short when Jason surged forward, which felt completely unfair, since he got to finish most of his. Trapping my head in his hands, he only spared one second.

One second to look in my eyes and see the emotion I couldn't hide anymore.

Then, his lips were on mine, and they were unforgiving. Like he always did, his hands cradled my face, his long fingers now threading through my hair as his thumbs rested on my temples. Every time he did that, I questioned if this tension between us was somehow, impossibly, *more.*

But feeling those hands hold my head in place as he smashed his lips against mine then feeling them turn my head so he could deepen our kiss, I knew it was more. It had always been more, and I'd chosen to not see it.

I couldn't be blind anymore.

When he pulled back, looking for a response to his brutal kiss, I answered.

Slap me sideways and call it Sunday, there was nothing

more I wanted in that moment than to give in to the tension thrumming between us. These feelings electrified me. They made me want *more*.

Of him. Of this feeling. Of *life*.

I grabbed fistfuls of his button down and yanked his lips to mine. I kissed him back with everything I had, and when he returned the favor, it felt a bit like our banter. We were fighting for advantage, still arguing even in our kiss. He would take control, turning my head this way and that as my knees weakened and his strength held me up. He guided me until my back hit a car then kept kissing and kissing as desire burned through my soul and let itself be devoured by his lips.

When I raked my nails lightly across his jaw, feeling the rough stubble under my hands, and he made a noise in the back of his throat as he kissed me harder, I thought I'd bested Jason Westerman.

But he wouldn't let me have the win. As he always seemed to do, Jason showed me it wasn't about winning or who had control. We had no control here, neither of us. He pushed a hand deeper into my hair, holding the back of my head firmly as he slowed us down. The kiss went from full passion, frustration, and anger to a whole lot of tender feelings. Like Jason had told me he would, he showed me he cared. That he cared about me. That he cared *for* me. When the kiss was too sweet, he pulled away.

Our chests heaved as we both struggled for air. My hands dropped to Jason's chest, and his came back to cradle my face. When I looked into his eyes, the soft sweetness mixed with determination jarred me.

"Oakley Mae Tennen, I don't care how scared you are or

your reasons for pushing this away. I'm done asking. I'm going to take you to dinner, and we are going to do *that* again, in a lot of different places, at all times of the day," he said in that beautiful gruff voice. His hands tightened around my face slightly, and I reached up to grab his wrists, steadying myself, anchoring myself to him.

For a moment, all my fears quieted, because I knew he had me.

"Okay," I whispered back, and he smiled. Oh gosh, did he smile.

"Okay?"

"Yep." I turned and kissed his palm before giving him a sassy look. "But I get to pick the playlists."

"Whatever music you want, as long as I get to bring the snacks," His eyes dropped to my lips, and he started moving in again when a slow clap started behind him. Jason whipped around to face Jack and Ash, who both grinned like fools, which meant I didn't even need to ask who'd coordinated this. My bubbly friend and my grumpy brother were in cahoots. Who would've thought?

"How long have you two been standing there?" I asked, my cheeks heating. Suddenly remembering I was leaned up against some random person's car, I jolted upright. Jason slung an arm over my shoulders and pulled me to him. I didn't miss that, while Ash hung back and stayed silent, she was bouncing on her toes and quickly tapping her fingers together, as if she wanted to clap but didn't want to make any noise. Her beaming smile said enough.

"Too long." Jack grimaced, dropping the hands that had disrupted our moment to his hips before he looked over to

Jason with the most serious look. "If you hurt my sister, you die. You hear me, Westerman?"

I opened my mouth to defend Jason when he just squeezed me close and looked down, holding my gaze as he spoke.

"You have nothing to worry about, Jack. I know this is a once in a lifetime opportunity, so I'm not gonna waste it. If I ever hurt Oakley, I'd deserve nothing less."

This was really happening.

Jason and me.

My heart started to soar.

Then, my brother grumbled at us.

"So, are you two gonna come dance, or do y'all need to go find a place to keep making out?"

18

"Hey, Ash, have you seen my white t-shirt—" I rounded the corner from the stairs to the dining area, where Ash sat, scrolling on her phone in said white t-shirt. "Never mind, found it."

She didn't even look up as she answered. "If you were planning on wearing this to your date tonight, then I have absolutely no remorse for stealing it." Finally putting her phone down, she glanced over at me. Then, she did a double take, letting out a whistle I hoped was a good sign. "Oakley, you trying to get that man to leave the house with you? He's gonna want to stay in and kiss on you for sure."

I blushed. Tonight, I decided to wear something that made me feel hot.

My favorite leather skirt that hit mid-thigh with a small slit on the side was paired with a light brown sweater with sleeves that puffed out before cinching at my wrists. Cropped at the waist, it did wonders for my figure while still keeping me warm up top. I'd added Momma's pearl earrings and the

209

white cowgirl booties I'd worn last night when we'd kissed in the bar parking lot.

They were now my good luck boots, and no one could convince me otherwise.

"You think he'll like it?" I asked hesitantly.

"Girl, he likes anything you do. Or wear. I'll accept your thanks for the silver dress that made this whole relationship happen later." She beamed at me, and I rolled my eyes.

"Thank you, Ashley. For the dress and the meddling," I grumbled. "Why do I feel so nervous?"

"Because this is a big deal. But don't worry, I saw him last night, completely entranced by everything you did. For some odd reason I can't even begin to comprehend, I think he even likes it when you sass him in that brutal, no filter way." Ash came over to me, grabbing my hands that had somehow started rubbing my temples. "Stop stressing, Oakley. This may be your first official date, but that man likes you. Genuinely likes you. Have you *seen* how he looks at you?"

"I'm working on actually accepting it." Tugging at the hem of my skirt, I blew out a big breath. "I've never felt this, but my momma was right. I'm not annoyed with Jason. I'm bothered. In a good way."

"Oakley, as your best friend and the certified household romantic," she was all seriousness, placing her hands on my shoulders and looking into my eyes, "I need you to let yourself feel all the feelings right now. You care so deeply for everyone around you, even if you try to pretend you don't. But as soon as they start to care back, you shut off. Becoming friends with you was..."

"What?"

"You chose to let me in, and I felt the moment you made the choice. It wasn't natural for you. You have a few people in your life you trust enough to let in. Everyone else is distinctly held at arm's length. Don't do that with Jason. Let him be there for you, especially..." She hesitated, and I decided to save her the trouble by pulling her into a tight hug. Her arms took a second to come up around me. "Oakley, we don't get many chances in this life to give ourselves fully to someone, let alone someone who deserves it. So please, don't let yourself get caught up in what stops you from being with him. Focus on the things that pull you towards him, what keeps you there. I've seen the way you are with him, and it's rare. So if you don't do it for yourself, do it for me, for all of us still searching for that."

Her words struck straight to my soul, and I felt a million different emotions. Pain for my best friend, who couldn't seem to let go of a guy who even *she* knew didn't deserve her. Fear at even the idea of giving myself to Jason, of letting him see every part of me and risking getting left behind. But the strongest emotion was the one I was learning it was possible to cling to.

Hope.

A knock on the door had Ash pulling away from me, shooting me a sly smile as she pushed me towards the door.

"Now, go enjoy the dinner that poor, sexy man has been begging you to get with him for a month." Her smile was a little watery. Grabbing her hands with both of mine, I squeezed tight, ignoring her surprised expression.

"Ash, if I deserve it, then so do you. Let's do it together. Let's go for the love we deserve," I said boldly. I saw her gearing up to defend Donovan, but another loud knock made her jolt a bit.

Groaning, I turned to shout at the door, "Hold your horses, Westerman!"

"Not a chance, OT!" a muffled shout came through the door. "It's finally date night. Let a man be stoked. I've made it, baby!"

I couldn't hold back the stupid grin that crept across my face as he let out an obnoxious holler. I turned back to my dear friend and watched as she took in the giddy smile on my face. She gave me a soft smile back and a nod.

"Okay, Oakley. I'll stop putting it off. I'll figure it out. I promise." She spoke with a gentle confidence, and any response I had was interrupted by another impatient knock. "Now go, before we have a giant hockey player breaking through our door to get to you."

She gave my hands a final squeeze before letting go and shoving me towards the entryway.

I didn't have time to say anything back to her before the nerves hit. Jason and I kissed last night and texted all day. My head had been filled with him more than usual since we'd said goodbye at Tae's car in the bar parking lot. Now, we were going on a date.

An actual date.

Despite everything swirling in me, I opened the door with a small smile on my face. There Jason stood, fist poised to knock again, a bouquet of daisies in his hand.

"Hey, Oakley Tennen," he said gruffly, moving his hand and rubbing the back of his neck before dropping it to his side. His eyes took me in, a small smirk lifting the side of his mouth when he noticed my boots.

"Hey, Jason Westerman," I replied. I allowed my eyes to do the same, taking in his dark brown button up, the color matching his mischievous eyes, his light wash jeans that fit too well. "How are you?"

"Right as rain." He chuckled.

"Hey, that's my line!" I laughed too, grateful he had broken the tension. Jason stepped forward so he stood just inside the doorway. Reaching his free hand around my waist and pulling my body to his, he did that infuriatingly endearing thing where he would truly look at me, as if taking inventory of every feeling I was trying to keep trapped in my mind, before he placed a gentle kiss on my lips.

Closing my eyes, I let go of the door and wrapped my arms around his neck, kissing him back before he pulled away slowly.

"I've been waiting all day to do that." He smiled. "Can I have my own line if I'm not allowed to steal yours?"

"I guess it's only fair." I giggled, eliciting a full smile from Jason. Before he answered, he pulled me impossibly closer, moving his mouth to my ear.

"You take my breath away, Oaks. Every. Single. Time," he whispered, and a shiver coursed through me at the brush of air against my ear and the words it carried. As soon as he pulled back, I moved my hands to cup his face, letting my fingers feel the stubble slowly growing into a beard.

"That's quite the line, Westerman," I said breathlessly.

"It's the truth. Now, we gotta run if we're gonna get a

table." He pulled back, filling the space instead with the flowers in his grasp. "These are for you."

"How did you know I love daisies?"

"I might've asked Jack," he admitted sheepishly. "I might've asked Jack a lot of things."

The thought that he made enough effort to go to my brother and ask him questions, ones I'm sure Jack gave him a hard time about, made my heart flutter.

Taking the flowers from him, I turned to put them in the kitchen, but Ash was there, grabbing them from my hands. "I'll put these in a vase for you! Now go. You're not officially on a date until you leave the house!" She smirked mischievously, shooing us.

I barely had time to turn back to Jason before he grabbed my hand and tugged me through the door. In a matter of seconds, we were on the porch, the door closed behind us. A huge, dorky smile was on his face as he dropped my hand, offering me his elbow.

"Now that we are officially on a date, may I escort you to the car, Miss Tennen?" he asked, bending a bit at the waist. I rolled my eyes at his ridiculousness, but my beaming smile must have given away how much I was loving every second.

"I guess so, Westerman. Do I get a hint?"

"Oh, bless your heart. Of course not."

I didn't have many expectations for my first date with Jason Westerman.

That was a lie. In my head, I might have thought he

would flash his money a bit, take me to a restaurant so nice, it would make me wildly uncomfortable to be there, we would have a really boring conversation until we argued, and that would break the ice. Then, the rest of the date would be fine until he dropped me at my door with a chaste kiss on my lips because he would be trying to prove himself a gentleman.

When we ended up going to my favorite fried chicken restaurant in downtown Nashville, talking about everything and nothing as if we had never heard of an awkward pause in our life, my expectations weren't met.

They were exceeded.

"You're lying!" Jason exclaimed as I grinned at him from across the booth, taking a sip of my root beer. It's a known fact that fried chicken goes best with root beer, and who am I to argue with tradition? "There's no way."

My soft chuckle barely carried over the old school country music filling the restaurant. This place was always packed, all ages filling the old worn booths with Johnny Cash and Tim McGraw to keep them company. The lighting was dim, and the décor was ancient and very southern, but the food and classic country atmosphere was more than worth it.

"It's true, Westerman. Why is it so hard to believe?"

"Maybe because you, Miss Always-In-Control, snuck into a concert?" He shook his head before taking a quick sip of his own root beer. "I mean, you're already the coolest chick I know, with the sass, the fishing, the nursing, the playlists. With how freaking smart you are, how funny, caring, absolutely beautiful inside and out..."

"Do you really see all those things in me?" I whispered

before I could think better of it, dipping my eyes to avoid him.

Hearing Jason describe the woman he saw healed a part of my soul I didn't even know was broken, a piece of myself that had felt too feisty, unseen and overlooked.

I was pulled from my thoughts when Jason reached across the booth, his warm hand covering where both of mine were clasped together on the table.

"And more. There's so much you don't let people see." He smiled nervously. "I want to be one of those people you let in, Oaks, because I think one of the greatest experiences of my life would be to truly know Oakley Mae Tennen."

Tears pricked my eyes, and I blinked rapidly, trying to force them back. I wasn't a crier. I didn't know what to do. I hardly heard the waitress come over with the bill as I tried to keep the damn tears from flowing over. By the time I had successfully subdued the impending waterfall, Jason had already paid for our meal and stood next to the table, hand extended to me.

"Can I show you something?"

The way he looked at me, I would've said yes to anything. Those contradicting, complicated eyes were filled with both nervous energy and boyish excitement. Slipping my hand into his, I laced our fingers together as he pulled me to his side. A sigh escaped me at the simple feeling of a man squeezing my hand tight before leading me out of my favorite restaurant and into the chilly night. This felt different. This feeling of lightness filled my chest, keeping me floating. It felt like sunshine.

That sunshine feeling stayed with me as we pulled up to

an ice rink. Jason got us both a pair of skates and took my hand again after we'd laced up. It was impressive how he only made three jokes about me not being dressed to ice skate. He then claimed it was the cold that made his cheeks red when I responded he would have to be in charge of keeping me warm, since he didn't give the right dress code.

I was still grinning from the knowledge I could make him blush when we reached the edge of the ice.

"How did you swing this?" I asked, looking around the empty ice rink. This wasn't the arena where the Rebels played, so I had to guess it was one of the practice facilities. Glancing over at Jason, keeping my hand firmly in his, he just gave me a smile and a half-shrug.

"I think you'll find a hockey player always has a way to get on the ice." Stepping forward, he tugged my hand as his blades shifted into the ice, barely even gliding as he waited for me.

Taking in a deep breath of icy air, I took a step into Jason's world. As soon as my skates hit the ice, he pulled me forward even further. The fluid motion of pushing the blade into the ice, pushing off, and repeating the movement came back to me. After a lap, I couldn't contain my smile. This right here, the feel of the frozen water beneath my feet and the cold air rushing past my face as we kept a leisurely pace, was all the best parts of my childhood. When I saw Jason's smile, I could see the best parts of the future too.

"Catch me if you can, Westerman!" I taunted, yanking my hand from his and racing away. I heard his deep laugh of surprise as I dug in, pushing my skates into the ice. My legs strained against my skirt, and my skating skills were nothing impressive, but a grin still spread across my face as crisp air flew across my skin. I felt the moment Jason decided to chase after me. It didn't take him long to catch up, but he didn't grab me right away. Instead, he circled me, fluidly crossing one skate over another, moving so fast there was no chance we would collide at my current pace. Then, when I inevitably lost steam and slowed down, he skated away. I turned to him in confusion, only to brace myself when I saw the mischievous grin seconds before he turned and skated right at me. He stopped a few inches from me, digging both skates in and hitting my bare legs with a spray of ice.

"Jason!" I yelled, giving him a playful glare.

"What? You're too hot, Oaks. Thought I'd help with a little cooldown." He winked then skated backwards so he was still facing me. Digging my skates in, I followed, and we chased each other around the rink, laughing our heads off like a pair of idiots. Finally, Jason snuck up behind me, looping those strong arms around my waist and picking me up as I screamed and laughed. He spun us in a few circles before setting me to my feet, but his big hands lingered on my waist. I felt so out of sorts, breathing heavy as I leaned back into him, but I'd also never felt so comfortable.

So safe.

With a deep breath, he released my waist and grabbed my hand, pulling me along as we began skating laps again. We kept quiet for a while, enjoying skating, when I felt his eyes on me.

"What?" I asked. He hadn't pulled his gaze from mine. His smile grew softer as he finally glanced away. Now, I was staring, taking in the way his cheeks were tinted red from the cold and admiring how at home he seemed here.

"And she skates," he muttered. "I figured you could, since your dad is such a hockey fan, but watching you skate is probably the hottest thing I've ever seen."

I laughed, letting my head tip back as I took in the absolute awe in his voice.

"Oh, shut up, Westerman."

"I'm serious."

"I'm sure my subpar skating is way hotter than the beautiful women you've gone out with before," I muttered before I could think better of it, and even I couldn't deny the bitterness lacing my voice.

"Oakley," Jason said sternly, pulling us to a stop. In a ridiculously smooth move, he pivoted in front of me, bits of ice flying from where his blades dug into the ice again. Using both hands to cup my face, he tilted my head up until my eyes had no choice but to meet his. "We went over this. I want to be with you."

"But why *me?*" The words rushed out. If we were going to do this, I needed to know. "I'm not an easy person."

"First of all, that has a lot of complexities to it, so hold that ridiculous thought. Second, I feel pulled to you, Oakley. It's like you're the sun, and I can't help but want to stay in your orbit, get as close as I can, even if it burns me." He sighed. "I want to be around you all the time. I want to know you, OT. I want to be the type of man you want to know."

My hands reached up to grasp his wrists as I let his words sink in. I pushed up and pressed my lips lightly to his. When

I pulled away, Jason kept his eyes closed, leaning forward until his forehead rested against mine.

"Why me, Oaks?" he whispered. "Why did you decide to stop hating me and give me a shot?"

"Because I feel just as pulled to you," I whispered back. "I tried to stay away, Jason. I tried to push you away. Tried to convince myself you only felt anything because you loved my family. Tried to see only the worst. But I couldn't, because you forced me to see the real you. You make me feel things I've only ever heard people feel, but it's more than that. It's how you care for your people, how you make sure I feel seen, how you give me butterflies with one look. I feel like I can be myself, like I can trust you with my fears and everything with Jack and my family. Even when we fight, it's the most at home I've ever felt. I want to stop pushing away how I feel every time I'm near you."

"How do you feel?" he asked, breathless.

"Safe. Fulfilled. Like the missing pieces of my soul finally found their way to me." I chucked hesitantly. "That was really cliché."

"Is it cliché if I feel the same way?" he asked, pulling back to look me in the eye. "Oakley, I've lived in a world where women only want me if they get everything *except* for me. With you, I've never worried you want to be around me for fame or money."

"Jason, I seriously don't—"

"I know you don't care. That's one of the reasons I was so drawn to you. You didn't fall at my feet because I can shoot a puck at a net."

"To be fair, you are one of the best in the nation at shooting a puck at a net."

"I am pretty amazing, eh?" He smirked, some of that cockiness I'd come to adore coming back. "Oakley, I don't know where this will go, but I know where I want it to go, and not because I'm close with your brother or because I care about your family. It's because of how strongly I feel about *you*. I want to be the person you come to first with your worries and your joys and when you start talking medical. I want you at my hockey games, wearing my jersey. I want to bring you daisies and go fishing together. I want to hold your hand during family dinner and get teased for how whipped I am and let you pick the music. I want you to meet my Grams and be in my world as much as I'm in yours until it becomes one world we're living in together. Officially. As a couple. And I don't want to scare you, but—"

"Okay," I interrupted him, my heart close to bursting with every word.

"Okay?" he asked, his eyes searching mine.

"Yep." I leaned closer, my lips barely hovering over his. "You have no idea how much I want all of that and more, Westerman. But right now, I need you to kiss me."

Grinning, he looked into my eyes one more time before moving even closer. "As you wish."

"'Princess Bride'," I barely had time to whisper before his lips were on mine, taking and giving and filling my soul. There was no pressure in my chest, no overthinking, no compartmentalizing how I was going to add caring for Jason Westerman into my life. There was just warmth.

He kissed me, and I was soaring.
He grounded me yet he helped me to fly.
My man, the contradiction.

19

"Alright, Miss Tennen, here is your lab space." A lab assistant, Joy, pointed to the small table towards the back of the lab where I would be working.

In the two weeks since our first date, Jason and I had spent every available moment we could together, which wasn't as much as I found myself wanting. Sometimes, he would come over after practice, or I would stop by his place after I woke up if I was working the night before. We'd planned to go out with Ivy and Colin for Halloween but ended up inviting them over to watch 'Hocus Pocus' at Jason's apartment instead. He insisted it was 'an absolute classic' and was horrified I'd never seen it, and yet he didn't complain when I fell asleep cuddled against his chest within the first fifteen minutes.

Now, at the beginning of November, we were only getting busier. When he was out of town, we FaceTimed every night we could. Our schedules were getting harder to coordinate. When he was home, we talked, watched shows, went to the ice rink, made food—well, Jason made food while I sat on the counter—and couldn't seem to keep our hands off each other. Jason was keeping his word on getting to know me and kissing me in multiple places multiple times a day.

I wasn't complaining.

It was Jason who encouraged me to start working at the research facility sooner rather than later. This time, he'd asked what I wanted before giving his unsolicited advice. Since I was assisting the project, I would work Thursday and Friday days, while still working two night shifts a week at the hospital. Now that Jack's cancer colony count had gone down significantly, his inpatient chemo was only one day a week, and the surgery was still scheduled for December if every-thing kept going well. Jason and I went with him when we could, but Jack insisted he didn't need us to go as much. He was letting Momma go with him, which freed up more time for us to hang out as siblings rather than the sibling/nurse dynamic we'd been trying to navigate.

It was busy, but it still left me with the weekends and some nights open to be with Jason when he was in town. When he wasn't, you know, being a professional athlete and playing hockey games across the country.

I went from pushing him away to wanting to spend every spare second with him faster than I thought possible. He kept joking it was all part of the irresistible charm. I would never let him know I agreed. Reluctantly, of course.

The only downside was, the disturbing fan messages were getting worse. I got at least ten a day for a while, each varying in their threats, and I'd thought about deleting my social media entirely. But then Jason would ask why, and he'd feel responsible. It was all empty words anyway. People could be brave behind a screen, but real life carried on.

Now, I was looking at my new desk, where I would be able to change a small part of the world. I gave the lab assistant a small smile. She didn't return it.

"I'll let you get started, Miss Tennen. Hopefully, this won't be too difficult for you." The odd tone of her voice startled me. Turning to take her in, her dark brown hair in waves similar to mine and her petite stature, something set me on edge. When I looked into her eyes, there was an iciness that worried me. I wouldn't think the research area of medicine would be competitive.

"I should be fine. Thanks."

She paused, looking me up and down as she adjusted her lab coat. "Just because you're pretty doesn't mean you're worthy. Don't try to reach above what you deserve, and you won't get hurt."

With that, she spun around and left me speechless. I'd always heard of coworkers who immediately hated their peers, but I'd never had it happen to me in the workplace. There was a feeling in my chest I didn't like—not pressure, but an ickiness that seeped through me with her hurtful words.

Trying to push it down, I sat at my desk. There was a note from Dr. Grouse welcoming me to the facility, thanking me for taking on this opportunity, as well as my login instructions. Well, at least somebody wanted me there.

As soon as I had successfully logged on to my computer,

my phone buzzed. I grabbed it, looking for any sense of comfort. Steeling myself for another hostile message but hoping for anything else.

Thankfully, my man was a mind reader.

Westerman: Hey, OT. Ivy has been blowing up my phone asking for your number to plan a girls' night. Looks like she wants to do it tonight, but I told her you were booked.

Trying to fight a smile, I typed out a response. I'd hung out with Ivy a few times other than Halloween, gotten lunch or dropped the guys off at the arena for an away game, but it was always with Jason and Colin there. Her infectious energy balanced my quieter demeanor perfectly.

OT: What do I have tonight, Westerman? Since you apparently know my schedule better than me.

Westerman: I'm wounded. How could you forget our important plans tonight?

OT: You cooking and then watch one of your movies?

. . .

Westerman: Yes. Dinner and movie night. Set in stone. A national holiday. So I'll tell her no for you?

OT: Send her my number, Westerman. Plus, I'm spending the majority of what is normally girls' night at your hockey game tomorrow. Ring any bells?

Westerman: I have a vague memory of this.

Westerman: Doesn't mean we have to abandon our plans tonight, tho.

OT: Jason.

My phone buzzed again as another text popped up. I switched over to the new thread.

UNKNOWN: HEY GIRL

UNKNOWN: Okay, so I'm thinking we get a bunch of cute fall treats and maybe some apple cider or even hot cocoa, because let's be real, it's getting CHILLY, and we could do my place, but it's kind of in the middle of being babyproofed so if it's not too much to ask, maybe we could possibly do it at your place? I can bring everything, I'm just so excited to finally meet your cute roommates!!!!!

I had to laugh at the way Ivy couldn't contain her excitement—ever, it seemed.

Oakley: Hey, Ivy. Let me add the other girls to this chat, and we can coordinate the details.

I knew Ash would take over, so I added her, Tae, and Tess to the chat. They were immediately off and running when I explained the idea. Putting their chat on silent for my own sanity, I switched back over to my text thread with Jason.

OT: Thank you.

Westerman: So I'll see you tomorrow? Ivy texted, and apparently I'm now going to a chill, team bonding, "this is our season" boys' night with some of the guys.

OT: She's even bossier than I am ;)

Westerman: Maybe you shouldn't be friends.

OT: You're the one who said you wanted me in your world.

Westerman: I said that so you would kiss me, and it worked so...

OT: You're annoying.

Westerman: I'm kidding. I've decided I don't want you in my world, I just want you with me always, bc, turns out, I'm clingy.

OT: Okay, Westerman, calm yourself.

OT: What if I come over tomorrow and we can spend the whole day together before your game?

Westerman: I guess I can wait that long.

OT: Big baby, I can feel you pouting from here.

Westerman: Can't blame a man for wanting his woman.

Westerman: I'll let you get to work. You've got this, Oaks. You

*were meant to change the world. I'm always rooting for you.
*salutes**

Feeling too giddy to do more than heart the message, I put my phone down and focused on my task board. I had so much to get done, but excitement at the prospect of building this program from the ground up instead of dread filled me.

Eight hours, three impromptu meetings, one quick working lunch with a very bubbly Sierra, and five different potential program structures later, I headed to my car, feeling exhausted but more fulfilled than I had in a while.

My phone buzzed with an incoming call, and I smiled when I saw the name on the screen.

"Westerman, you seriously can't go a single day without me?"

"Oakley," he choked out.

"Jason? What's wrong?"

"Are you off work? Sorry if I called when you were in the middle of something. I just needed to talk to you, so if it's a bad time-"

"Jason, what's going on? I'm almost to my car." Clicking the key fob, I opened the driver's side door and slipped inside, worry building rapidly in my chest. "You're scaring me."

"I'm sorry, Oaks. It's Grams." His voice shook a bit, and he swallowed before continuing. "She had a fall. She's in the hospital and says she's fine, but the doctor I spoke with said a nursing home is the next step. She forgot that Gramps died, that I moved out. She tried to leave the hospital, said she had to get me to practice."

"Oh my. Oh no, Jase."

"I know. When she came back around, she agreed the nursing home was probably for the best, but, I-I just—"

"Wish you were there?" I asked. Grams was so important to Jason, and that made her important to me.

"She's all I have, Oaks. She's all I've got left."

"You're wrong, Westerman. Let me show you I care too." My mind raced through how I could help him. "Do you want me to fly out there? I can check on her. I know your schedule is crazy the next few days, and I could get someone to cover—"

"As much as I appreciate you offering, we've got a lot going on this weekend. I called the nursing home, and they won't have a spot for her until next weekend, so..." He paused, and I let him think. "Okay, you don't have to say yes, especially because you're so slammed, but I don't have any games next weekend. I could ask Coach if I could take Saturday and Sunday to go see her. Maybe, if you'd want to, you could come with me? If it's too much, you don't have to—"

"I'll make sure I'm all set at the lab and we'd have to be back by Monday, but I'm coming."

"Okay. Okay. Let me talk to Coach, but are you good if I book flights?" he asked, that bit of nervousness in his voice making every other doubt in my head fade away.

"Of course, Jason. Do you want me to cancel girls' night tonight? I can come over and—"

"We both already have way too much going on to bring the wrath of pregnant Ivy onto our heads." I heard him sigh before his voice shifted. I could practically feel him decide to try to not worry about it anymore. "Anyway, tell me about your day, Miss World Changing Researcher."

A smile crept onto my face in spite of myself. This man couldn't help but be obnoxious. It made me happy.

The whole ride home, we chatted about my day, his day at practice. I told him how Mal had officially dumped the Letcher boy because he refused to go fishing with her. He told me how he was excited for me to finally see him play, how every home game reminded him of his Gramps, how they had a tradition of waking up early on gameday and watching the sunrise. He explained his Gramps was an avid hockey fan and measured his life in games and regular seasons through playoffs. I told him how proud Gramps must be of him. He told me he knew, and he tried every game to play in a way that would make Gramps proud. I even told him about the strange interaction I had with Joy, and he agreed it was uncalled for, but then that turned into him talking about how beautiful I was and how charmed he was by me.

When I pulled up to my house, we were laughing about the time I tried to give a fish I'd caught to my childhood crush, who had promptly run away like his feet were catching fire. It was then I realized not all boys were going to be the one for me.

"OT, you do know about the playoff tradition, right?"

"Westerman. You're asking a girl born and bred in Nashville if she knows about the throwing of catfish onto the ice?" I turned off my car, grabbing my bag and phone. "You're the transplant here, Mr. Canadian."

"That was a pretty dumb question, eh?" He chuckled. "I love your strange obsession with fishing. It's nice and quirky."

"Like how you're obsessed with quoting random romance movies for every situation. Nice and quirky." I giggled at his outraged noise and stepped into the driveway, closing my door behind me. "Don't forget about the muffins."

"Now, Oakley, if you make fun of my muffins one more time—"

"Oakley!"

I looked up to see Tess bounding towards me, her hair looking more red than blonde in the fading light. Dodging the phone at my ear and the bag looped over my shoulder, she wrapped her arms around my neck in a big hug. When she pulled back, the joy in her eyes was threatening to burst.

"I haven't seen you all week! You've been spendin' all your time at the hockey boyfriend's apartment—we have a lot to catch up on." She grinned from ear to ear, and it honestly felt good to hear her happy chatter. "Your cute friend Ivy just got here, and *girl*. Our livin' room looks like a fall Pinterest board."

"Do you ladies refer to me as 'the hockey boyfriend' behind my back?" Jason's voice came through the speaker.

"It was hockey prick before you won me over, Westerman," I giggled. "And I refer to you as the hockey boyfriend to your face, so calm down."

Tess' eyes widened, and a smirk took over her normally innocent face. "Was that a giggle?"

"Tell her I'm the master of Oakley giggles."

I rolled my eyes. "Westerman—" Out of nowhere, my phone was snatched out of my hand. Tae had apparently parked behind me, and she was grinning as she brought the phone to her ear.

"Hey, hockey boyfriend. It's Tae. We actually had a roomie meetin' and have some rules we need to discuss with you." She gave me a wink before she started towards the house, a giddy Tess trailing after her.

I stood in the driveway, stunned as a chilly wind whipped across my face. I wrapped my arms around myself, pulling my gray overcoat tighter around my body. The shock of the moment began to fade away, and a warm feeling spread through my chest.

Jason called me when he found out about his Grams. He asked me to go with him. Not his teammates, who I knew he loved and trusted, not his agent or any of his other million friends.

He called me.

I was able to care about him and not have a complete breakdown.

And he bothered me endlessly. In all the right ways.

"Should we snap her out of it?" Ash's attempt at a hushed voice made it through my hurricane of thoughts.

"This man of hers really wants to say goodbye. I even tried hangin' up, and he just called back, so I don't think we have a choice." Tae's southern twang rang loudly through the windy night.

My eyes popped open. I had been so deep in thought, I hadn't even realized I'd closed them. Readjusting my bag strap on my shoulder, I made my way to the porch, shoes crunching on leaves that had fallen from our oak tree in the process.

Making it up the porch steps in record time, I snatched the phone from Tae's hand. Her eyes widened slightly in shock before her whole face lit up in a knowing smile.

"Oh yeah, she's got it just as bad." Then, she threw me a wink before an equally excited Ash grabbed her arm and dragged her in. "Hurry up your goodbyes with your man, sugar! We're ready to get this girls' night started!"

When I gave them a stern look, they both just laughed before entering the house and leaving the door wide open, no doubt so they could eavesdrop.

Shaking my head at their antics, I raised the phone to my ear.

"Westerman?" I asked hesitantly.

"I'm here, Oaks." His voice instantly made my smile grow wider. "Those roommates of yours are a tough crowd. I thought playing professional hockey was the hardest trial of my life, but turns out, my harshest critics are four southern women?"

"Okay, first of all, Ash grew up in the north. So she's adopted into the south, and I'm not your harshest critic." I paused then amended my statement. "Anymore."

"Whatever you say, OT." He laughed, but something in me wanted him to know I was serious.

"Really, Jason. I don't want you to think me judging you is always how it's going to be. That's not—it's something I'm working on. I know I can be cold, but I don't want to be your harshest critic."

"Oakley." Now, he sounded sad. "One of the things I love about you is your brutal honesty. You won't say something if you don't mean it. You won't do something unless you believe in it. I never realized how much I needed that until I met you, how much it makes me a better man to know just existing isn't enough to deserve you. Now, don't get me wrong, 'You aren't a prize to be won.'"

He paused, waiting, but I couldn't place it.

"Dammit, I know this one!"

His small chuckle broke up the tension a little bit.

"'Aladdin'. I'll add it to our movie list. Anyway, you aren't someone I can be surface level with. That doesn't work with you. Dammit Oakley, you make me want to be the best man to ever exist just so you'll look my way."

"We're supposed to be saying goodbye." I struggled to keep my emotions at bay, embarrassingly vulnerable.

"I never like saying goodbye, not to you." He paused. "My grumpy little love hater."

"They didn't." I felt a keen sense of betrayal.

"Oh, they did. I have a feeling your roommates are going to bring me tons of good teasing material." Another deep voice called out to him. "Yeah, coming. Sorry Oaks, guys' night is starting. But I'll check with Coach and let you know about the tickets. I'll see you tomorrow, yeah?"

"I should probably get to girls' night. I'm here for whatever you and Grams need." I gave a sad smile he couldn't see. "And Jason?"

"Yeah?"

"I want to do more than just look your way."

"Well, that's a good sign, because I've been looking your way since we met, and I don't think I can go back from *more* now." He sighed like the world still weighed on him. I wanted to do nothing more than take all the hurt away. "Bye, OT."

"Bye, Westerman."

I hung up, trying to tamper down my emotions as I joined the girls in the house. When I shut the door and stepped into the living room, I jolted to a stop.

Our living area was simple. We had an L-shaped couch that backed against the walls closest to the entryway, creating a perfect viewing space, since the couch faced the TV mounted on the remaining wall next to the stairs.

We had a coffee table in the center of the room, and Tess had hung twinkle lights when we first moved in.

But now? The room was almost unrecognizable. Strings of fake fall leaves hung across the ceiling, intertwined with the twinkle lights. Neutral-colored pillows and blankets spread across the floor, and the coffee table had been pushed against the wall with the TV, a beige tablecloth spread across the top. The Martinelli's bottle should have seemed out of place, but it fit in with the charcuterie board, brownie tower, and hot cocoa bar. How she had made all that fit on the coffee table caught my attention.

The measurements just were not adding up.

My mental calculations were interrupted by a pregnant torpedo who wrapped me in the tightest hug her belly would allow. When she pulled back, Ivy's face was as animated as ever.

"Oakley! It's so good to see you. Now that we get some girl time, I want to hear the *whole* story of you and Jason from your side. You know how detail-less those guys can be. Jason shares more than Colin ever has, but I feel like he left so much out! I didn't want to ask in front of the guys, but now, you can tell me everything!"

Ash let out a little snort. "I can guarantee you, Jason gave you a more detailed account than Oakley will." She came to my side with a brownie in hand, giving me the sweet treat. "But that's one of the reasons we love her so much. What's our Oakley without a little mystery?"

I rolled my eyes playfully at her, taking a bite of the brownie.

"In other news, I broke up with Donovan."

20

fter I finished choking on my brownie long enough for Ash to tell her story, I was stunned. And proud.

I found myself bundled up with the other girls, sipping hot cocoa from my fall mug, wrapped in a cozy brown blanket as we took in her every word.

"He actually cried?" Ivy asked, appalled.

"Oh, hun, he normally cries. This was a manipulative sob," Tae interjected. "But Ash stood her ground."

Ash smiled shyly at the floor. She didn't seem embarrassed, just unsure. So, I tried to give her something I hated but I was realizing everyone needs: an opportunity to feel.

"Ash, how do you feel about this?"

"Oakley, are you asking about *feelings*?" Ash and the girls each gave me a matching look of shock, except Ivy, who glanced around, confused.

"I'm guessing she doesn't normally ask about feelings?"

Ivy leaned over to Tess and asked in a loud whisper. Tess giggled before glancing over at me.

"Our sweet friend Oakley? She normally doesn't acknowledge that feelings exist."

"Calm down, y'all. Can we focus on Ash?"

I was completely ignored as Tae chimed in.

"It's like pullin' teeth to get her to share her emotions." Tae giggled, flipping her golden blonde hair behind her shoulder. "But ever since a certain hockey player has been around..."

Rolling my eyes, I turned back to Ash. Though she was smiling at the interaction, her hands were clasped tightly in her lap, and she looked about five seconds from tears. I may not have fully understood why she felt so deeply about love and romance, but I understood that she did. And I was learning that understanding was everything.

Shuffling over, I wrapped an arm around her. The whole room stilled at the action, and I could feel Tess and Tae realize something was wrong.

"Ash?" I asked, and she wiped her tears before taking a deep breath.

"All I want is to be in love, to be more to someone than I've ever been to anyone." She sniffled, pulling away from me and wrapping her arms around herself.

"Ash, you're more to us." Tess rested a soothing hand on Ash's arm. "You know we all love you so much."

"But I've never had a *man* love me for me. I see these couples at work, building their families, or how Jason looks at Oakley, and I can't help but want that, you know?" she said with a watery sigh, trying to hold the tears in.

"Ash—"

"I'm not jealous. Okay, maybe a little. I'm genuinely happy for you, Oakley. I promise. I've never seen you so, so—"

"Light?" Tess suggested softly, giving me a smile.

"Exactly. I know I seem all bubbly and happy all the time, but I'm lonely. I just... I want more."

"Is it weird if I cut in here and add my two cents?" Ivy asked hesitantly. I didn't know she knew how to be hesitant. We all looked at her, an off-white blanket wrapped around her round belly and petite frame, the blanket bunched around her neck pushing her short blonde hair up around her ears.

"Go ahead, girl. We're a house of open opinions." Tae lightened the mood a bit, and Ivy smiled a bit more confidently.

"As you've all learned in our short acquaintance, I'm happily married and expecting this little squirt any day now." She rested a hand on her belly, smiling contently before zeroing in on Ash. "But it was a hard road to get here. The guys I dated before Colin were absolute asses. There were eight months between my last relationship and when I met Colin, and those eight months of being single were what made me ready for him. I learned that even though I wanted to meet the love of my life so badly, wanted my own little family more than anything, I wasn't ready. For context, my parents are pretty checked out, always have been, and I found myself trying to fill that void with any slightly willing guy. But those eight months, I *chose* to be single, and I realized that void couldn't be filled with any type of man or idealistic love. It could only be filled by me, by learning to love myself and become a woman who would be able to properly take care of the love I deserved when it came my way, if that makes any sense."

"How?" I'd never heard Ash sound so small. "How do you do that?"

"I have a feeling you and I are pretty similar, Ash." Ivy smiled. "Self-reflection. Acknowledging what the problem actually is. Making goals. Doing things for you, not because you think it will make someone else happy. Putting effort into your other relationships to prove to yourself you can."

We all sat in silence, trying and failing to not stare at Ash.

"It's not just about the love you let yourself receive. It's the love you tell yourself you can take. If you can only give yourself a tiny bit of love, what makes you believe you have the capacity to receive more from someone else?"

A quiet understanding filled the room. I looked at each of my roommates and saw the same epiphany happening in each of our eyes. Ash, the hopeless romantic who wanted a love she feared she would never find. Tess, our sunshine girl whose only focus was a job she didn't love and her friends, searching for something more. Tae, the southern princess who, while fun and free, kept herself from going deeper.

And me, the grumpy love hater, who'd decided to give a man who turned my world upside down a try.

We were all different, and yet, we were all the same. We were all human, all craving to feel like we belonged.

"I think we need a group hug," Tae exclaimed, throwing

her arms out. Laughter broke through the group, and we leaned forward, wrapping our arms around each other.

A warmth spread throughout my chest. This was happening more often now. Instead of the pressure and the panic that seemed to always be teetering on the edge before, ever since a certain hockey player started knocking down every wall I had put up, I felt all the good in my life. I felt the light.

"I'm sorry," I muttered. Each girl pulled back and looked at me with confusion. It was Ash who spoke up.

"What are you sorry about?"

"I just... I'm always negative about your feelings. I think it's because I've avoided mine for so long? I don't know. Trying to force you to think logically when that's the way I cope with emotions isn't fair." I grimaced, trying to convey how I felt. "I'm not good at saying how I feel. But Jason—"

"I was wonderin' how long she'd go without bringin' him up," Tae whispered to a giggling Ivy, and I shot her a look.

"Shut up. Jason forces me to let him take care of me. It used to piss me off when he would tell me how I felt, but he showed me he could change and be what I needed while still being his obnoxious self. He made me see I hold everyone at a distance, and it's not fair to you, Ash. It's not fair that I push you away yet expect you to solve your problems in a way that isn't you. You're magic and romance movies and bubbly happiness, and you deserve to keep seeing the world that way." I gave her a small smile, and the light started to come back into her eyes a bit. "But I still agree, this breakup was long overdue."

"Cheers to that!" Tess raised her hot cocoa mug high.

"Oakley, you're my best friend. We may rumble about our stances on love, but you're one of the best people I know. I'm so happy you're falling for a guy who deserves you while also being so jealous a hot man is obsessed while also getting why he would be obsessed—you're amazing." Ash wiped her remaining tears as she smiled at me. "Now that we've had the emotional heart to heart part of this evening, we should turn on a cozy romantic movie. My go-to is definitely the 2005 'Pride and Prejudice', but it's spooky season, and Ivy, you are the master planner... Ivy?"

We all glanced at Ivy, who had been uncharacteristically quiet for the past several minutes. Her hands rested on her stomach, her face scrunched as she exhaled slowly. After a few seconds, she looked up.

"So, um, okay. This was not part of the girls' night agenda, but I think my motivational speaking skills might have put me into labor."

We all jumped up to help Ivy stand, but as soon as she did, a gush of fluid hit the blankets. Of all the things from girls' night, Ivy's water breaking was actually the thing most in my comfort zone. Feelings were hard. Fluids and contractions, on the other hand, I could do.

21

"Ivy!" The burly defenseman rushed through the doorway, panic written all over his face. When his eyes fell to his wife, already hooked up to the monitors as the anesthesiologist prepped the epidural, his face turned even more panicked.

Ivy was sitting up in the bed, one hand keeping her balanced and the other holding her stomach. She was breathing through a contraction and didn't even notice her huge husband hesitantly moving towards her. I gave him a quick smile from where I stood, supporting Ivy's shoulders while the nurse finished messing with her IV fluids. Of all the nurses Ivy could have, I was glad it was Anita. She was like the unit mother. She and Ash were pretty close, and she had helped me through many hard shifts with her bright smiles. She was perfect for Ivy and Colin.

"Hey, Colin. Glad you could make it," I joked as I watched him try to wrap his head around everything. "She's already dilated to a five, which is great. It means she's halfway there. She decided to go ahead and get the epidural. She'll be way more talkative in a few minutes."

"Colin?" Ivy sounded so small. I shifted to the side and motioned for Colin to come closer, allowing him to bend down and meet his wife's gaze. The instant shift from sheer panic to caring was amazing to watch.

"I'm here, baby. I'm here. What can I do?"

"Hold my hand."

He laced their fingers together as she struggled through another contraction. The anesthesiologist glanced over at Anita and me.

"Oakley, Anita, how're we looking with those fluids?" he asked.

"Just finished up, John. All good on our end," Anita answered before glancing over at me. I gave her a look that said, *Do you want to take over now?* She gave me a shrug that said, *No ma'am, you've got this.*

Then, she gave me actual words.

"If you want to talk them through this part, I'll prep the peanut ball so we can get this sweet baby here." She put a hand on my shoulder, giving me a squeeze before going to the other side of the room, letting me know I wasn't overstepping, even though I wasn't currently on the clock.

"Okay, Ivy. John here is going to place your epidural. There will be a pinch when he inserts that needle, but it'll be over in a second. That's the main numbing medication. Then, he'll tape down a very thin tube that connects to the epidural pump. That pump pushes the medication through to get you nice and numb for your whole labor. Does all that sound okay?" I asked, glancing at both Colin and Ivy. Colin gave me a nod, and all Ivy could give was a thumbs up while she stared at the floor, squeezing Colin's hand hard.

Making sure Colin was good, I stood and moved over to Anita in the corner of the room while John walked them through the epidural.

"I'll step out, give them some time to themselves," I whispered, glancing at the couple as they pressed their foreheads together and muttered to each other. Anita gave me a bright smile, but the hint of mischievousness in her eyes set me on edge. "What?"

"Oh, nothin'. I've just never seen you connect with a patient like that. You finally let yourself feel it," Anita drawled with a wink when I couldn't find the words to respond. "And there's a ridiculously good lookin' man on the other side of the curtain. Don't think I didn't recognize him as that boy Ash teases ya about—especially since every time he's peeked around that curtain, his eyes've been fixed on you like he couldn't look away."

"Now Anita, I thought we were friends." That deep voice reached from behind the curtain, and it took me two seconds to hop around and find my Jason, a gray henley stretched across his chest, dark jeans molded to his thighs. It took another two seconds before he wrapped me up in a tight hug.

"Get outta here, you cute kids. Take care of our Oakley, boy, or bless your heart, because you'll have to go into hidin'." Anita shooed us out the door. We made it to the hallway, and I gave a small wave to my slack jawed co-workers. Ash had always openly teased me about dating and how much I hated it. Now, here I was, trying hard to look like I didn't have damn stars in my eyes in front of everyone I worked with.

From the way Ash was giggling with one of the other nurses, I wasn't doing a good job.

"Thanks for helping her, Oaks." Jason scratched the back of his head nervously. "You have no idea how stressed Colin was. We had to talk him down from calling 911."

"I don't know what more 911 could've done than two labor and delivery nurses," I chuckled with a shrug.

"Well, I knew you were amazing, but watching you in action was a whole other level." He stepped closer, lacing his fingers with mine. I had to tilt my head back to look at him. "You know I love it when you talk medical."

"Oh yeah?" I teased, moving my head a bit closer to his. "All this talk of epidurals and dilation does it for you?"

"I don't know if you've noticed, OT, but pretty much everything about you does it for me." His smile reached his eyes, and my chest got that warm feeling again. "I'm glad I got to see you tonight."

"Don't get all sentimental on me now, Westerman. People 'round these parts don't know the hockey player is actually pretty clingy."

"I can be tough and an absolute simp for my girl. I'm complex like that." He smirked. Our faces shifted even closer, his hand tethering me to the moment until our bubble was properly burst.

"Oakley, you gonna introduce us, or are you just gonna keep makin' eyes at each other?" one of the nurses called from where she was charting.

"Oh, hush, Julie. I'm enjoyin' the show just fine from here." Aspen, a nurse chatting with Ash, laughed.

"We're gonna go chat in the waiting room—without an

audience." I rolled my eyes, pulling Jason along with me. "Bye, y'all!"

"Bye, Oakley!" they chorused gleefully. Meddlers, each and every one of them, but I let myself smile at the way they joked with me, like I wasn't just the "unfeeling" nurse on the unit.

When we finally made it out the double doors to the waiting room, I was shocked to see we were definitely still going to have an audience.

The waiting room was full of men.

"Uh, Jason—"

"Yeah, so, when you called and said Ivy was in labor, pretty much the entire team was with us." He shrugged, scratching the back of his neck like he always did when he was nervous. "Not exactly how I imagined introducing you to the team, but here we are. Guys?"

All eyes were already on us, multiple sets zeroed in on Jason's hand gripping mine.

"This is Oakley."

I didn't get starstruck. I never felt that way with Jason. He was always just Jason. Extremely annoying and arrogant at first, but just Jason. But when the entire professional hockey team of your home town approaches you, you get a little overwhelmed. They were a group of men with missing teeth, thick thighs, and a wide range of facial hair, and they were *intimidating*.

The team captain, legendary forward and all-star player Peter Olsson, shook my hand and said in his thick Swedish accent, "Ah, so this is your little spitfire."

Once I understood this wasn't a fever dream, I picked my jaw up off the floor.

"Spitfire?" I turned to Jason and raised my eyebrows. He grinned.

"Oh, I didn't give you that nickname, OT, but it fits."

"Jason has never talked about the same woman twice. He was, how do you say it in English—not settling down? But he talked about you a lot after he met you, mostly how you frustrated him. Then, he was determined to be near you. Though you didn't make it easy, sounds like." Peter chuckled as Jason turned uncharacteristically red.

"Thanks for that, man."

"Oh no, there's more. The week when you, what do the kids call it, "ghosted" him, he was miserable. Missing shots, falling like he was learning how to skate. Embarrassing. And grumpy. Never seen Westerman grumpy. The week he finally got you, he scored a hat trick *and* he was more obnoxious than usual."

"Is that even possible?" I asked, and Peter and I chuckled like old friends.

"Hey!"

"Aw, calm down, Westerman. Your obnoxiousness is growing on me." I gave his firm chest a little pat. Peter grinned and stepped to the side to let the other guys meet me. Over the handshakes and joking, I heard Peter speak to Jason.

"Should we get used to having her around?"

"If I can convince her I'm worth it, she's not going anywhere."

22

"Oaks..." a soft whisper danced across my skin. Lips pressed gently against my neck, and a smile crept across my face as the world came to life around me.

I leaned back, arching my neck to give him more skin to kiss.

"Westerman?" I asked, even though from the way his stubble lightly scratched at my skin and the way my body sought to get closer, I knew it was him.

My eyes fluttered open, and when those soft kisses lifted from my skin, I turned my head so I could see him. A corner of his gray comforter was tucked up to my neck, and when he propped himself up on his elbow to look down at me, more than half the blanket fell to his waist.

What a blanket hog.

After getting back from the hospital last night, we'd sat on the couch and held each other, too many emotions running through us to stay awake. We got a text from Colin saying Ivy was still only dilated to a seven around midnight, and he promised to update us in the morning. Soon after, I drifted into a semi sleep, cuddled in Jason's lap and content to never move.

Then, I woke up in his arms, in his bed. Even though I couldn't remember it, I smiled at the thought of him carrying me. Jason kissed my smile before giving me a lazy one of his own.

His eyes were puffy with sleep, and the way his hair was messy and sticking up all over his head made him look more rugged, but the sparkle in his eyes made him seem more like a boy.

My man, the walking contradiction.

"Good morning." He smiled, pressing another soft kiss to my lips. I leaned into it then shifted so my body fully faced him. "You ready for the sunrise, Oaks?"

"I'm ready for this day with you." I grinned.

The more time I spent with Jason, the more I could read his looks. The way his eyes lit up when he thought of a good movie quote was different from the way his eyes lit up when he talked about Grams. His eyes crinkled when his smile was genuine, and his laugh was short when he didn't actually think it was funny. Right now, when his eyes twinkled, he was up to no good. "Westerman, whatever you're thinking—"

His hands were at my sides, tickling me as I squealed.

"Jason!" I couldn't stop myself from laughing loudly. "My brother is across the hall."

That thought sobered me instantly, and I pushed his hands away as horror washed over me.

"Oh no. Oh *no*," I groaned, sitting up and turning away

from Jason. With my feet hanging off the edge of his giant, Jason-sized bed, I let my head drop dramatically into my hands.

"Don't be stressed, OT. This isn't the first time we shared a bed, and nothing inappropriate happened." I felt the mattress shift as he clambered to the floor, kneeling in front of me. "Now, move your hands so I can see your gorgeous face."

I dropped my hands and rolled my eyes. Jason's face was all tease, his eyes sincere. He was like a puppy.

"Jason. I feel like a mess, and I bet I look even worse."

He cocked his head to the side, like he was considering my words. Then, his hands were on my hips, pulling me to the very edge of the bed, searing through my skin and stealing my breath. The heat of his hands seeped through my shirt, branding me as his mouth moved to my ear, and my heart legitimately skipped a beat.

That could not be healthy. As a medical professional, I should be concerned.

"You take my breath away, Oaks." I could feel the smile in his words as he whispered to me. "Every. Single. Time."

"Every time?" I whispered back. He pulled back to face me before answering.

"Every single time. Even when your mascara isn't on your eyelashes anymore."

"Jason!" I exclaimed, my hands going to my eyes, which were probably smeared with black. I didn't get to do much damage control when suddenly I was being lifted.

I thought maybe we would have a romantic moment. He would lift me and set me softly on my feet before kissing me.

I forgot I was dating Jason.

Not only was I airborne, but I was being tossed. Once he'd settled me on his extremely muscular and extremely uncomfortable shoulder, I completely dissolved into giggles.

"It's gameday, baby!" He laughed with me, and I tried to keep the noise down as we passed Jack's door. It was kind of impossible when a 6'4" hockey player was tickling your side any chance he got.

When we got to his giant window, he finally hoisted me back over the great wall of Westerman and set me on my feet, his hands still resting firmly on my waist. I reached up, looping my arms around his neck and pulling myself even closer.

Glancing at the window, something changed. His infectious happiness left, and he wore my least favorite Jason look.

When his brow furrowed and his eyes dropped, Jason was sad.

I put a hand to his cheek, forcing his gaze back to me.

"What just happened in your head?" I asked softly. He shook his head, like he was shaking away the feeling.

"I'm happy you're here." He kissed my forehead, and I gave him a look he just chuckled at. "Fine, Oaks. I was thinking about what my life would be like without you. I just...I don't have a good track record of people choosing me because they actually want *me*."

"That's not true," I argued, indignant for him. "Jack—"

"Has become like a brother, but even he left for a bit because I was an asshole."

"Your grandparents—"

"Were forced to take me in. I know they loved me, but it wasn't easy. Even the people I love the most, they've all left me at some point. I have this idea stuck in my head that if I keep most of my relationships surface level..."

"It doesn't hurt when you get left behind," I finished for him, and we looked at each other with new understanding.

My heart ached for the little boy who felt like no one wanted him and the man who felt like people used him for the things they could gain, not the things he had to give. In his gaze, I saw his understanding of the girl who felt abandoned by her family when she needed them most and the woman who felt left behind as everyone else moved on.

"I was also thinking." He shifted on his feet, nervous. "Grams says I get defensive and push too hard when I'm cornered. I don't want to push too hard with you, especially when you need answers or we have a misunderstanding at the end of a long ass day, because we will. I want to be the one you turn to when you don't know how to handle it, not the one you don't know how to handle."

"Jason," I whispered as I pushed forward, barely touching our lips together in a soft kiss before looking into his eyes. "Despite everything, you are becoming that person for me. The one I turn to. You have a gift for pulling emotions out of me no one else can."

I trembled with all the feelings coursing through me when he leaned forward and placed another soft kiss on my lips in place of words.

"Do you remember the first conversation we had when we didn't yell at each other?" Jason finally asked, and my head cocked to the side in confusion. "On your parent's porch?"

"You didn't understand any Southern sayings."

"That would be because Southerners don't know how to say what they mean." He rolled his eyes, and I gave him a small smile before he turned serious. "Kind of like you, OT."

"Hey! That's—"

"True?" Jason interrupted, and I gave him a glare he quickly kissed away before resuming his speech. "What if we had a phrase to let the other person know we aren't okay? We're not attacking, there's no need to get defensive, but we're not okay. That way, I'll know you're processing instead of steamrolling you. You'll know I'm not angry at you and it's not an attack."

My heart tumbled at the thoughtfulness. It was genius, for both of us.

"Since you already say 'right as rain' all the time, that's out—"

"Actually, that's what I say when I'm not okay," I explained.

"Wait, but you said that when I picked you up for our first date." He scrunched his face in an exaggerated pout. I couldn't help myself. I leaned forward and kissed him again.

"I believe *you* said it on our first date. You know, when you tried to steal my line?" I grinned. "But I still would've said it, because I was excited and nervous and damn near breathless. I'm not quite sure when your presence started doing that to me."

"Probably when I called you a puck bunny, eh?" He grinned as I groaned, seizing the opportunity to nuzzle into my neck, causing me to giggle and squirm. When I finally got him to keep his lips to himself, I couldn't keep my smile in anymore.

"Westerman. That was the moment I decided we were enemies." I shrugged as my voice got serious. "It was probably when you made me smile. That first dinner at my parents' house."

His hand stroked my face, pushing my hair behind my ear before threading his hand back into my hair, letting his thumb rest on my temple.

"I told you I was right as rain, but I was losing it." I smiled softly again then let myself really look at him. "We *should* use it as our phrase. Despite being a major pain in my ass, with you, everything is right as rain. On our first date, you told me I'm the sun, but that's not true."

"Oakley, how many times do I have to tell you? I get to decide how I feel about you—"

"Hear me out. Because you love a good analogy, it's rubbing off on me, and I don't know how I feel about that, but here we go." I took a deep breath, suddenly nervous. "You're the sun, and I'm the moon. Your light is so bright, I have to embrace it, even when I want to hide in the darkness. Even when I turn away from you, I know your light will always find me, because we're connected. The sun and the moon, pulled together by an invisible force. You'd think they'd hate each other because they're opposites, but when you think about it, they're similar."

I gave him a sly smile before I added, "We're so similar. We're both so stubborn."

His expression ranged from touched to confused to giddy. That was my man. Always a swirl of different emotions, a walking contradiction with his manly yet boyish personality. He was like the leaves on the trees. Sometimes, he was green, sometimes red, but most of the time, he was somewhere in between. He changed and moved between two feelings at the same time, and he was teaching me it was okay to feel more, to let go of that control and just *feel*.

With a stupid smile, he leaned close, and before his lips touched mine, he whispered, "Pride and Prejudice, 2005."

Then, his lips were on mine, and everything felt right.

When he pulled away too soon, he sobered again with a sigh.

"I know we both have a lot going on right now. You're starting this new job, dealing with everything with Jack and your family, and a million other things. Everything going on with Grams has me on edge, the season is starting, and we have a real shot at the cup this year." Jason reached up, assuming his usual position cradling my face. I leaned into his palm, the peace of our morning surrounding us. "But I have to tell you, I'm so damn excited for you to come to my game. Being with you is something I never knew I needed, Oaks."

"Being with you is something I never thought I'd want, Jase." I smiled when he stole my move and rolled his eyes. "But now? You really are my sunshine, Westerman. You pushed your way right into my life. As much as I hate to say it, I'm so glad you did."

"Can I get that in writing?" he responded with a smug grin. I barely had time to throw him a sassy look before his lips were on mine.

This was us. This push and pull was *us*, and it made me feel so damn alive.

When we finally pulled apart, we settled onto the couch that, at some point, Jason must have turned to face the window. When I snuggled into his side, he reached his hand to the side table, and it came back with one of Gram's muffins. My eyebrows raised when he offered it to me.

"What? I can wake up early to do something sweet for my woman." He shrugged as he handed me his phone, already open to his music app. "Plus, I get too excited to really sleep the night before home games. I didn't want to wake you up."

As we watched the sunrise, my favorite calm morning songs playing, eating one of the best muffins I'd ever had, I could finally name the strange feeling that had surrounded our blissful morning. As rays of golden light coasted over us, coating the fall trees with fire in reds and oranges before reaching me and Jason with its warmth, for one of the first times in my life, I felt it.

I was truly, one hundred percent, without a doubt *content*.

Not looking for something to go wrong, not waiting for the inevitable storm, not terrified.

Content.

And I prayed it would last.

23

I should have seen it coming.

But I was too caught up in Jason to let anything burst my bubble.

Another message from a fan account. They were getting more aggressive, stalking us more; this one included a picture of Jason kissing me before I got in my car that morning.

YOU ARE PLAYING A PART NOT MEANT FOR YOU. LEAVE HIM ALONE.

Everything went on high alert. I glanced around, as if the culprit would show themselves simply because I was scared, but there was no one, nothing except a crisp fall breeze and the rustle of dead leaves blowing across the pavement, feeding my paranoia.

"All good, Oaks—Oakley?" Jack called from where he

was waiting by the door. No matter how many times I told him to walk in, he refused, said it wasn't polite to my roommates for a man to go barging in. He was a gentleman like that—grumpy but a gentleman.

"All good," I called back, hoping my voice sounded steadier than I felt.

This was some crazy fan who wanted Jason. They just wanted to scare me.

A small voice in the back of my head whispered this was more, that I should tell someone. They were obviously following us, or at least following Jason. This could be dangerous...or it could be a sick joke. As I started walking towards the house, I took in my brother—how he leaned against the pillar on the front porch, the way he still favored his leg that hadn't fully healed. It was his eyes that made me block the account and lock my phone screen.

Again.

When he glanced up at me, I didn't see the brother I'd grown up with. The light in his eyes had dimmed, like everything happening muted his shine.

It terrified me—if we didn't lose his body to the cancer, we would lose his spirit to the fight. I knew my brother, and I knew he would never want to live a shell of a life simply for the sake of being alive. He would want to live.

"Oakley?" His concerned voice reached me again, pulling me out of my thoughts. "Are you sure you're okay?"

"Sure, Jack. How are you feeling?" I deflected, unlocking the front door and pushing inside.

"I'm alive. That's all I can ask for right now." He

shrugged, limping his way to the couch before collapsing in a heap from the effort.

"Jack, using crutches or a wheelchair again doesn't mean you're weak. It's—"

"To conserve my energy, I know. I just...I can't control much. I'm sure we'll get to a point where I can't control whether I have the strength to walk." He ran a tired hand through his hair. "I don't feel like myself at all, and that's killing me more than the cancer."

"Jack," I whispered, sitting down next to him. "You are still the obnoxiously stubborn first-born child who forced all his siblings to join his army and launch an attack on the neighbors because the Fulton boy pulled my ponytail at school."

"We won."

"Only because it was an ambush."

"Sure, Oakley." His small grin faded quickly. "I wish I felt motivated enough to take on a neighbor kid, but it's like all my energy is draining-"

He was cut off by the sound of pop music, getting louder by the minute as footsteps and off-key singing came down the stairs. With a jump and a spin, Ash treated us to our own private concert for a few seconds before noticing us on the couch and stopping abruptly.

"Sorry, Oakley! I thought I was the only one home!" She turned down the pop song blaring from her phone before coming over and taking a seat on the other side of Jack. "*Oddio,* Jackson! Have you been sleeping?"

"Good to see you too, Ash," he grumbled, shooting me an exasperated look, but a small twinkle was back in his eye.

Interesting. "Glad to see you haven't stopped starting conversations with compliments."

"Oh hush, you grouch. You have bags under your eyes so dark, they might as well be drawn on. Don't give me that attitude. I'm just concerned." Her words were annoyed, but she grinned at him like she couldn't help it. I wasn't sure when in the times they'd interacted they'd developed this unlikely friendship, but the way they dove into a comfortable conversation, I was happy it happened. I didn't care how. I'd been so worried about them both, but they didn't have only me to lean on.

Deciding to leave them to their conversation, I stood and made my way into the kitchen. As soon as I walked around the counter, my phone buzzed in my hoodie pocket.

I opened my phone to a picture of a sweaty, smiling Ivy and a tired, grinning Colin. Ivy had her arms wrapped lovingly around a little bundle.

Ivy: Our sweet girl was born at 6:30 this morning! Anita was AMAZING!! Sorry it took a while to text, we wanted to enjoy the moment! HOLY SMOKES, WE'RE PARENTS! Anyhow, I'm so sorry I won't be there, but enjoy your first official NHL game as a girlfriend of a player! I'm sure we'll be able to cheer together real soon :)

I couldn't help the rush of happiness I felt, knowing everything worked out. One more weight off my shoulders. Typing out a quick response, congratulating her and asking if she'd like a visit from the girls, I put my phone back in my pocket and opened the fridge, imagining Jason holding a baby. My cheeks warmed at the thought, and I tried to shake away the feeling as I heated up some squash soup. When I brought three bowls out to the living room, balancing them on a cookie tray, Jack stopped mid-sentence to look at me.

"Oakley, did you cook?"

I didn't appreciate the shock in his tone.

"Nope, the hockey boyfriend's been sending leftovers home with her pretty much every night since they started dating," Ash jumped in. "It's like he knows you hate cooking or something."

"Well, enjoy the fact that I didn't make this, because Jason is a surprisingly good cook." I handed bowls and spoons to two of the most important people in my world.

"That's actually not surprising," Jack said as he started slurping soup. "You know his grandparents owned that bakery for years, right? He grew up helping in the kitchen."

"Yeah, he loves to make things from memory and be a showoff about it." I grinned as I slurped my own spoonful. "Did he tell you about Grams?"

"Her fall? He texted me yesterday after he got off the phone with you. He was nervous you were going with him to be nice." He shrugged. "Don't worry. I let him know I've never expected to see you so in love with someone, so it was probably because of that."

I dropped my spoon into my bowl before shoving his shoulder, probably harder than someone with cancer should get shoved.

"Hey," he grunted before focusing back on his soup.

"You can't get mad at him for speaking the truth, Oakley," Ash chimed in. "You are twitterpated, infatuated, totally in love."

"That was a lot of romance book talk."

"You can't deny it. You've got the eye sparkle thing whenever he gets brought up."

"The eye sparkle thing?"

"You used to just blush, back when you were 'enemies'," she said with some exaggerated quotation marks while trying to balance her soup on her lap. Jack calmly reached out and steadied her bowl, and I reached for my spoon again as she kept talking. "But now you're together, you've got this magic sparkle. It's a whole other side to you, Oakley."

I thought about that for a second. It was true. Jason hadn't changed me or made me a whole new person. He'd helped open a side of myself I had a hard time letting out. It was a side that embraced emotions.

He had his faults. He was cocky. He pushed and got defensive. He bothered me to no end.

I think I loved him for it.

My spoon clunked back into my bowl as the realization settled over me. I was falling in love with him. I'd never felt this way before, so I didn't recognize it until Ash and Jack so blatantly pointed it out. This was all happening so fast. All this felt beyond my control. I barely knew him.

As soon as that thought entered my mind, my heart thrust it back out. It was a lie. I did know him. He did things with purpose, a man who felt things and protected and gave his loyalty to his people. A man who wanted to be seen for who he was. And I did. I saw him.

I was in so deep.

The pressure in my chest started to grow a little bit. Okay, a lot. My phone buzzed, and I quickly reached for the distraction.

Westerman: Hey, beautiful lady. My place or yours?

Smiling, I started to type out a response before he texted again.

Westerman: Okay, I couldn't wait. I'm headed to your place and I'm picking up food to carb load before the game. Can I use your bed and your snuggles to take a pre-game nap?

OT: Okay, superstar. Go ahead and steamroll.

OT: Also, Jack and Ash are here and we just ate, so don't worry about grabbing extra.

Westerman: Sorry about the steamroll, not sorry about the food. I know you probably reheated the soup I made you.

Westerman: Bed and snuggles?

OT: *I'm rolling my eyes at you.*

Westerman: *I can feel the sass from here, just the way I like it.*

Westerman: *See you in 30.*

"And that, ladies and gents, is the twitterpated, infatuated look Oakley Mae Tennen never dreamed she would wear." Ash sighed while Jack stared at me with an indiscernible look on his face. "It looks good on you."

"What?" I asked, focusing on Jack's face.

"This is real for you, isn't it?" Jack's look was the one he'd get when we were kids, when he was serious.

"Jack..." I was unsure what he meant.

He shrugged then looked to Ash.

"Talk to her, Jack." Ash nodded at him. What in the world was going on between them?

"I'm sorry," he started, his voice thick with emotion. "I left when you needed me most. I knew that hurt you, but I couldn't..."

"It's alright—" I tried to find the words, tried to stop him before he could bring up that pain again.

"It's not. I didn't realize how much it left on your shoulders, or maybe I didn't care until I was the reason it fell on you again." He glanced at Ash before looking at me again. "When I saw how they all looked to you, how you were keeping it all together, how you pushed Jason away even though you felt something for him...when you asked me not to call you Oaksy?"

His words caught on my old nickname, the tension and unspoken scars between us stretching so tight, we were on the urge of exploding.

My first instinct was to wrap my arms around my waist, to turn away from him, to turn off the hurt and go cold. I wanted to tell him what he'd done was unforgivable.

But I didn't want to live that way anymore.

I reached out, my hand landing softly on his arm, and his eyes shot to mine, filled with hope.

"When I asked you to come to Boston, I thought I could face everything I'd left behind," he whispered. "I thought I could finally be a part of that world again."

"That world?" I asked, confused.

"The one where I was responsible for more than myself. Every day, I risked my heart breaking by losing someone I loved, and I couldn't face it."

"So you broke our hearts instead by leaving us behind?" I said softly, trying not to snap at him. Hurt overshadowed the hope in his gaze.

"I wanted to fix it. I wanted you to come to Boston, to meet my friends, to see what life could be outside the pressure to hold it together for everyone else," he explained, each word costing him. "I wanted you to meet Jason. I knew you would be good for him, that he would be good for you. He's as loyal as they come, funny, carefree. You've always needed that. But he showed up at the bar a complete mess. I didn't want him anywhere near you, and I hated that I felt that way.

Then, I saw how much you wanted me back home, how much it had hurt you when I left, and I knew I couldn't do it. So, I took you far from Jason, cut you out of my life again, and left for base. It was easier—"

"To feel nothing than to feel the pain," I finished for him. "That's bullshit, Jack, and you know it."

"I know," he sighed, running a hand through his short hair. "I know. But Mal actually tells me about her life now. Hunter texts me back when I ask about football practice. I want my sister back too. It feels like I stole something from you by accident by keeping you away from Jason all those years ago. I—" He grimaced. "I've had a lot of time to think lately. I think... I just..."

"Spent that time trying to fix the past to avoid the future?" Ash added quietly. Jack looked at her, his gaze filled with sadness, then back at me.

"I don't even know what a future would look like, Oakley," he whispered. "I want to make sure my actions don't ruin *your* future. Ash says I'm making amends—"

"Which is ridiculous, because you're not going to die, Jack," Ash interrupted, and this time, there was nothing quiet about it. "So figure out how to be alive."

"You don't know that," Jack retorted, his anger growing. "Not even the doctors can promise that. So yes, I want to make sure my little sister and my closest friend are taken care of in case I'm not here to do it. I'm fixing things with Hunter and Mal. It was wrong of me to leave, especially after everything with Momma. Now, I need y'all to be okay if my body gives up."

Tears welled in my eyes, and I wrapped my arms around

my brother. Neither of us were huggers. He was the stoic soldier; I was the grumpy love hater. And yet, I'd been giving out hugs more and more to the people I loved.

His body relaxed into mine as I whispered, "I forgive you. You don't have to worry about me, Jack. You're not alone, even when you don't want to remember. I'm here. I promise."

My words, reminiscent of the ones Jack would tell me when we were kids, echoed between us. Ash stood, placing a hand on Jack's shoulder then mine before giving me a small smile and leaving the room, leaving us to this moment.

Once Jack composed himself, he sat back and stared at the blank TV for a moment. Then, he spoke, filling in the years we'd missed, asking me about my life. Just the two of us.

And I listened. For the first time, as the weight lifted from my brother, it didn't settle on me. As he talked, my name wasn't the only one he mentioned. He explained how he was worried about Momma and Pa, how Jason had always seen him at his weakest, how Ash had become an unexpected confidant, how he was scared Hunter wouldn't fully forgive him until it was too late.

But this wasn't my burden. This was my opportunity. After a while, Jack's eyes started to droop closed. I waited for his breaths to deepen before shifting his long, thin body to lay on the couch, grabbing one of Tess' decorative fall pillows to put beneath his head. Just as I pulled a blanket over his body, a loud knock sounded at the door. Panicked, I shot a look at Jack's sleeping form, but he didn't move.

With anticipation moving my feet forward, I opened the

door, quickly treated to strong arms wrapping around me, my feet leaving the floor as Jason kissed me like he hadn't seen me for days. His arms held me up, and his hand shifted my shirt so his rough palm slid along my bare skin, sending shivers across my body as I kissed him back. When he pulled away, he dazzled me with a full smile.

"How's my girl?"

"Right as rain."

He drew his eyebrows together, and I could tell he wanted to ask a million questions. Instead, he lowered me back to the floor, rubbing circles on my back.

"Food and talk?" he asked.

"Then nap and snuggles, I guess."

His smile was infectious. Grabbing his hand, I pulled him past a sleeping Jack, who he eyed with sadness, up the stairs to my room, where we sat on my floor, ate pasta and chicken, and talked about everything.

It felt so *easy*.

After a nap wrapped up in him, I kissed my handsome hockey man, pushing him by the lapels of his gameday suit against his car as I did, before sending him to work. I took a seat on my couch on the porch and watched the leaves fall from our tree. I touched my fingers to my tingling lips and thought about how fast things could change. Then, Ash asked me if she could borrow my cowgirl boots, and I smiled at how some things stayed the same.

24

"How you feelin', Oaksy?" Tess asked over the noise of the crowd. The hockey arena was right in downtown Nashville, full of live music and life. The energy from the bar crowds merging with the excitement of hockey fans was contagious and made me even more nervous as we trailed Ash and Tae to get in line.

"Tess, this is a lot," I choked out. Tess looked a bit stunned but quickly recovered.

"Which part is a lot, hun?"

"This is a big season for Jason. I want to be a good hockey girlfriend and I don't know how to do that, and he's just... He's—"

"Everything?" She gripped my hand harder. "Oakley, carin' is the hard part, and you two have already come so far. Now, it's time to do life together. Not that I know much, but I'd imagine this is the fun part. Still hard, but fun. Plus, he's really hot, and you're about to see him in his element. I can't imagine anythin' sexier than that."

Tess had a way of saying such non-innocent things in an innocent Southern drawl that had me throwing my head back laughing.

"He is pretty damn sexy. This is goin' to be so different from watching him on TV."

The time we'd been together, I hadn't gone to a game in person. There was always a scheduling conflict or it was out of state, and I think we both wanted this night to be special. He hadn't even played yet, and I was so proud of him.

"How's he feelin' about the season so far?"

"Like a kid at Christmas every time he gets to play. We got up real early to watch the sunrise like he used to do with his Gramps." I smiled as I thought about all our little moments throughout the day. *Normal* moments.

"Oh, we definitely noticed you never came home last night." She gave me a sly smile.

"Nothing like that happened. He's sticking to being a gentleman for now. I'm not ready for that, and he hasn't pushed." I rolled my eyes at her. "But waking up with him and having a quiet morning together, it was..."

"He must be a real good kisser if he's left you speechless," Tess teased.

"It's more than that. He made muffins and threw me over his shoulder and—" I smiled as I reminisced. "He let me pick the music."

We'd reached the entrance, and our conversation melded into the excited chatter of our friends and the crowd as we squeezed to present our tickets and find our way inside. Ash insisted we get there to watch the guys warm up, and I couldn't say no to additional time watching Jason in a hockey uniform.

As Tae roped us into a discussion about cowboys versus hockey players, which was a dangerous conversation to have so loudly, given the venue, Ash dragged us to our section and marched us right past our seats to the plexiglass. The players were already warming up, and it took me only a few seconds to spot the one who belonged to me.

Jason, on one knee as he stretched next to Colin, was laughing at something the stoic defenseman had said. In the next second, he easily got to his feet and started skating towards the shooting line.

Frozen next to two young boys with signs and a little girl clutching a puck to her chest, I let myself take him in.

A bit of brownish blond hair poking out the back of his helmet, his jersey caught in his hockey pants, his broad shoulders even more massive in his shoulder and chest pads—I was gone.

Dressed down Jason was good looking.

Chef Jason was cute.

Date night Jason was handsome.

But hockey Jason?

It was more than how hot he looked in a jersey. It was the way he glided across the ice like he was born for this, the way he smiled at his teammates, how he focused on the goalie and analyzed everything with joy. My heart pounded as he got to the front of the line, grabbing a puck and picking up speed down the ice like he owned it. He went top shelf, over the goalie's right shoulder, so fast, the goalie couldn't respond fast enough. He grinned at the goal then let his eyes travel across the stands, much like the day I watched his practice. But this time, I wouldn't wait for him to come all the way to me.

I stepped up to the glass and pounded on it with my fists.

"Westerman!" I hollered, though there was only a small chance he'd hear me over all the noise. Somehow, like he could sense me, his eyes latched onto mine, and I let my fists flatten onto the plexiglass as a ridiculously wide smile took over my face. He returned my grin and skated over, raising a gloved hand to match mine as his eyes raked over me.

"Hi," I mouthed.

"Hi," he mouthed back. Nodding towards my jersey, he grinned proudly. I rolled my eyes before giving him a shrug.

"Hey, Tae," I called, not taking my eyes off my hockey player. "Can you take a picture of us?"

I barely heard her enthusiastic reply as nerves flooded me. I turned around, pushing my wavy hair over my shoulder, letting him see the WESTERMAN displayed proudly across my back.

This was something told me he wanted.

Being a part of his world.

Cheering him on in his jersey.

He wanted me. And oh my stars, I wanted him just as much.

When I faced my friends, their grinning faces told me all I needed to know about Jason's reaction to my choice of jersey. I smiled as Tae took a billion pictures on my phone, Ash and Tess wearing matching giddy expressions.

When I turned back around, the girls still snapping pictures behind me, Jason was shaking his head. I gave him a shrug and mouthed, "What?"

Before he could answer, another player called to him from where the team exited the ice. Jason turned those sparkling eyes back to me, giving me a wink before skating backwards.

Right before he got to the other edge of the ice, still skating backwards, he raised two fingers to his helmet and gave me a mini salute. I gave him one back.

Only once I returned it did Jason turn around and follow his team.

The noise of the arena came back to me, piercing my bubble but not my sunshine.

The game was fast and physical. Jason told me the team was looking good this year, and he wasn't wrong. The Rebels cut through the opposing defense, fast passes and consistent plays keeping me on the edge of my seat, hands clasped under my chin. Tae laughed at my intense stance as she sang along to the songs and forced Tess to share popcorn with her. Tess ate a few small handfuls of the popcorn but was more than happy to cheer and boo anytime the crowd did. Ash kept making connections to some hockey romance book she'd been reading. Everything was romantic through that girl's eyes.

I'd texted my family group chat the picture of me and Jason and checked back after the first period. Jason had been playing well, but the scoreboard still showed 0-0.

Momma: The way he looks at you, my girl.

Pa: Happy for you kiddo.

Jack: Do you have to send that in here?

Jack: I support you two, but I have to listen to your giggling and making out way too often. Keep your love off my phone.

Momma: Wait, have y'all said you love each other???

Mal: Momma's shrieking again.

Mal: Please put the woman outta her misery and tell her you did.

Mal: Also, tell Jason he should've taken a slapshot off that pass from Olsson.

Pa: Your boy looks good, Oaksy. Could get a few more shots on net, but their goalie is having a night

Hunter: Oakley has been in love with him from day one. We all know this.

Hunter: Go rebels.

I rolled my eyes affectionately at each of their texts. These were my people. As I glanced at the ice, I felt a pang in my chest when my eyes settled on number 26.

He was one of my people too.

The second period started quickly, and Jason flew across the ice. On an intercepted pass in the neutral zone, he took the puck and the other forward in an odd man rush to the opposite side of the ice, and I knew he saw the play before it happened. With one defenseman to try and handle them both, Jason slapped a quick pass across the front of the defenseman, who lunged to try to intercept—but Jason was counting on that.

He passed it far enough in front that the opposing defenseman lunged too far, allowing for the other forward to slap the puck back to Jason who shot it right above the goalie's shoulder. I jumped to my feet, cheering at the top of my lungs, my girls screaming with me. I watched Jason pump his arms in the air as he shouted in victory. His teammates crowded him, a collision of jerseys and sticks and helmets banging together as the team celebrated. Once the players started to skate away, Jason let his eyes drift to the stands, catching on me for a moment. He nodded, smiling bigger than I'd ever seen before he turned to return to the bench.

I stayed standing, energy buzzing through me as I watched the man I loved accomplish something so difficult, something he'd worked at even when the world told him he wasn't wanted.

But he *was* wanted, and he was mine.

<h1 style="text-align:center">25</h1>

After an intense third period, with plenty of dirty plays from a desperate opposing team, my voice was hoarse as we exited the stadium. Arm-in-arm, us girls laughed and chatted our way back to the parking garage down the road.

"When Jason had to go sit in that timeout box, I thought you were going to fight the referee yourself, Oaksy," Ash giggled.

"That was a stupid call," I groaned. "My Pa says Geleski is known for flopping like he's trying out for the swim team, and of course, he's starting the season strong. Jason barely tapped him, but 'oh no, Geleski's down, it must have been slashing'. Such a weak call."

"Don't worry. The whole arena could hear you screaming *Justice for Jason*," Tess added.

Even though I scoffed and returned with a joke, I couldn't help but grin. Being there to support Jason added a whole new level to the hockey game. Pa's dad had been stationed in Minnesota for a while when he was little, and he'd quickly fallen in love with the game. So, when I wanted to learn more about the sport Jason played, Pa pulled me into watching highlights with an almost religious fervor.

But watching my man show off his hard-earned skills and finish with a 3-1 win while I wore his jersey, knowing there is so much more to him than those sixty minutes, was something else.

The girls dutifully dropped me off at Jason's apartment with a range of jokes about having fun but not too much fun. We'd agreed meeting up at his place after Jason's game made the most sense, since it would give me time with the girls and Jason could handle the media without having to worry about finding me in the crowd.

Only when I got into his apartment did I remember Jack was staying with our parents for the weekend, since he had chemo on Monday and Momma wanted to baby him for a bit.

It was just me and Jason.

The thought filled me with something new, something that threatened to grow too big to control.

Looking out at the city lights, I tugged on the sleeves of my jersey and instinctively reached for my phone. Choosing my *When Life Feels Like A Sunrise* playlist, I set my phone on the counter.

The sweet strains of Ingrid Andress' '*More Hearts Than Mine*' filled the air, and I heard the keypad beep as Jason opened the door, clad in his suit he'd worn to the game. Inhaling a sharp breath, I kept my eyes focused on his reflection in the window wall, not turning around yet. I watched as he took in the jersey, his name splayed across my back, shaking his head like he was trying to clear it. Then, his eyes darted to my phone playing music on the counter, and he smiled. I waited for him to come to me, to say something to get me to move. Instead, he walked to the counter and turned off my music.

Whirling around, I shot him a dirty look. I didn't say a word, terrified to break the tension between us. Instead, I said a lot with my glare.

As if he also felt the need to keep the tense silence going, he raised a hand to placate me as he grabbed his phone from his suit jacket, and a song I didn't recognize started. I tilted my head in question before curiosity won and I stepped toward him, closing the gap until we were chest to chest. I reached for his phone, the sappy song one I didn't recognize, but my eyes snagged on the playlist title.

Music for my OT.

It was simple. It was everything. Glancing up at him, the vulnerability I saw there made everything spin.

"You made me a playlist?" I whispered. Jason and his suit and after-game glow were overwhelming.

"I want to be a part of your music," he whispered back, his head leaning in until we were a breath apart. "If you'll have me?"

"I think you're becoming my music," I whispered, closing my eyes as I pushed up on my toes, pushing my lips softly to his. His hands landed lightly on my hips, and there was something about having only those two points of contact that made the kiss sweeter.

After a moment, I pulled back, looking into his eyes

before speaking. "That penalty in the second period was bullshit."

He laughed, throwing his head back, eyes crinkling around the corners as he shook his head at me.

"I know, rough call. What about that goal in the third?"

"That top shelf shot would be predictable to anyone who's ever watched you play," I teased back, giving him an eye roll for good measure. "Or if the goalie hadn't checked out after an okay first period. So, as usual, a mildly impressive performance from 26."

"Does this mean I'll see you at more games, OT?" He tugged at the edge of my jersey. "You look pretty damn beautiful wearing my number."

"I don't know if your fans can handle my screaming." I smirked, leaning into him a bit more. But then, I let my smile fall, running my fingers down his chest. "Are your ribs still bothering you?"

"I'm good, Oaks," he said, but I pinned him with a look. "My right side is a little sore from that hit in the first, but it's nothing an ice bath can't solve. It's a part of the job, OT. And I'm okay."

"I know, I know. Makes me want to get out there and throw some fists is all."

"Now that, I'd pay to see. My money, as usual, is on my feisty girl."

We both chuckled, but I sobered as I thought about this part of his life.

"I just hate seeing you get hurt," I admitted, puffing out a breath. His hands crept up to my hair, his thumbs rubbing those little circles on my temples.

"Is it too much?" he asked softly. When I looked up at him, taking in the way his head tilted towards mine, eyes seeking to understand, I felt myself breathe.

"It scares me, but you love it. And anyone who watches you play can see you were meant to do this." I grabbed the lapels of his jacket again. "I hate that you get hurt, but it won't stop me from being with you, not anymore. Now, hotshot, what do you want—"

I didn't even get to finish my sentence before he pulled my head forward, fusing our lips together. We kissed for a moment, heads tilting further as we both sought to deepen the kiss. Then, his hands moved into my hair, taking control and pushing harder against my lips. I reached my hands up around his neck, pushing up on my toes and gasping while he sighed. In the background, I faintly heard the song change. I pulled back, my nose scrunched in confusion.

"Is this—"

He surged forward, cutting me off with the strong press of his lips on mine as *'That's Why We Fight'* by Ella Langley played in the background. The song from his Canadian Thanksgiving. The song that played when he told me he dreamed about taking me out. That it was a good dream. The song that played when I realized I didn't hate him anymore.

I pulled back again, needing to acknowledge everything. "Jason."

He looked down at me, a smirk on his lips. "What?"

"You're still infuriating," I started, and he rolled his eyes. "But I really like you, sunshine boy."

"You're still annoyingly bossy," he responded, dragging

his intense gaze across my face. "But I more than like you, OT."

My eyes widened as I registered his words, and before I could panic, his lips were back on mine, his kiss willing me to just feel. I pulled back for a second, but Jason knew me too well. Before I could get a word out, he gave me a stern look.

"Oaks, I'm trying to help you not freak out right now, so whatever you're about to say, is it about something *other* than that?" When I shook my head, still awestruck, he grinned. "That's what I thought. Can you shut up and let me kiss you now?"

I nodded quickly, and he chuckled before pushing into me, more passion and heat behind it than before. Our bodies flush, we turned so when we tumbled backwards, my back hit the counter between the bar stools. In a second, Jason's hands moved from my hair to my waist, hoisting me up onto the counter so my head dangled above his. I smiled down, moving my hands from his neck to his jaw as I pulled his face towards mine, one of his hands firmly on my waist and the other one traveling back up my body to cup my cheek and push my hair out of the way, leaving goosebumps in his wake. He chuckled when I nipped at his lower lip, and his smile pressed into mine as he wrapped his arms around my waist and pulled me even closer.

Jason surrounded me—his masculine smell, his strong arms caging me in, his "more than like" making my heart pound faster and faster. Everything was changing, but maybe it would turn into something beautiful. Something breathtaking, in all the best ways.

26

"Did y'all land okay? Is Jason bein' a gentleman? Are you nervous? I think I'm nervous for you. This is a big deal." Momma's southern drawl deepened with her rapid fire questions. I blinked, taking in the big sign that said, 'Welcome to Calgary', shifting the sleeves of my hoodie with the hand that wasn't holding my phone to my ear. "Are you panickin'? Pa says I'm scarin' you, but you're not sayin' so—"

"Momma," I interrupted her. "You're not scaring me, but you're not helping."

There was a moment of silence on her end, easily filled with the noise of the airport around us—travelers pulling luggage, kids chattering loudly to parents, couples pointing out their bags on the carousel. I turned away from the sign, fiddling with the handle of my carry-on and scanning the crowd for him.

"What can I say that will help?" she asked hesitantly, and

I knew she'd used the mute function Mal taught her last week to converse with Pa before speaking to me. "This is the first time you've ever done anythin' like this, sweetheart."

"I know, Momma, but it feels…" I trailed off, looking for the right word as my eyes finally snagged on Jason. He was standing with his hands on his hips at the luggage carousel, waiting for his checked bag filled with souvenirs from Nashville for his Grams that were too clunky to fit in his carry-on. He turned, meeting my gaze with his. A soft smile lit his face, and I returned it with one of my own. "It feels right when I'm with him."

There was a pause, and Jason turned around to grab his luggage as it came around the bend.

"I can't tell you how happy it makes us to see ya like this, Oaksy." Momma sniffled, trying to hold back the waterworks. "We love you a whole lot, and all we ever wanted was for you to let someone love you the way we know you can be loved."

As she spoke, Jason made his way over, backpack slung over his shoulder and luggage in his hand. Using his free hand, he tugged me closer before letting his hand rest on the small of my back. I smiled up at him like the lovestruck fool I was.

"I know, Momma. We gotta go, but I'll talk to you when we get back." I was already moving the phone away from my ear as she hurried her goodbyes.

After hanging up, I looked back up at Jason as I slid my phone into my back pocket. He grinned, pressing a quick kiss to my forehead and laying that charming smile on me.

"You ready to see Lethbridge, Alberta, Miss Tennen?" he asked, wrapping his arm around my shoulders.

"Okay, Westerman, let's see your roots."

He gave me a laugh before guiding us towards the automatic sliding doors. After we got the rental car and headed onto the highway, I took in the land Jason Westerman called home. Once we exited the city, listening to my *Out In The Country* playlist, I took in the wide open skies as Jason told me stories of his childhood. We laughed as we compared his Canadian country upbringing to my American Southern one. He unfortunately didn't have the fishing passion I did as a kid; he was more into chasing sheep and riding horses.

As the country tunes accompanied our soft conversation, a nervous energy started to take over my easygoing man. When we pulled into the outskirts of Lethbridge, I reached over and laced my fingers with his.

"Jase, you okay?" I asked softly, noticing the clench of his jaw.

"I'm worried about her, you know?" he replied, squeezing my hand.

"Now we'll be able to figure out the next steps." I squeezed his hand back. "First, we'll go in there, and y'all will have some quality time together. Then, we can assess her mental state and what you want to do about it. Do you have legal capabilities to move forward with that?"

He gave me a nod, taking a deep breath. "Gramps made sure everything was in order as soon as he got diagnosed. Before his mind slipped, he wanted to make sure we were taken care of." As he choked out the last bit of that sentence, we turned onto a long dirt road, grassy fields on either side, with a small white house at the end of the lot. "For a long time, I was ashamed of how we lived, poor and rough and off the land. Only once I left did I realize how much I loved coming back here. But it feels different this time, having you here."

He looked over at me and smiled, fighting back the tears threatening to make an appearance. I'd never seen Jason cry. For all the times he'd seen me fall apart and picked me back up again, I hadn't had the opportunity to do the same. So, when he pulled the car to a stop next to an old pickup truck, I let my free hand rest against his cheek, my thumb swiping away the tear that escaped before it reached his stubble. I tried to convey how much I understood. How uncomfortable I'd been when he'd first come to my parents' humble home. How I wanted to be there for him too.

"Is it okay I'm here?" I whispered, realizing how precious and rare this moment was. Jason was the sunshine, but that didn't mean he didn't feel the rain too. He laid his big hand, rough from hockey and life, over mine and pressed it against his cheek.

"Oakley, I don't think I'd be able to do it without you." He took another deep breath. "The thought of losing Grams, of being where she and Gramps raised me, taking care of her without him? It wasn't supposed to be like this. But knowing you're with me, that the two most important women in my life get to meet each other? That's everything, Oaks. That's everything right now."

Now, tears pricked my eyes, and I leaned forward, letting my forehead rest against his as I closed my eyes and felt the peace of being wanted. Not just needed, but wanted. We sat like that, just breathing, just being there. When we pulled away, I untangled my fingers from his and fully cradled his face. His scruff was rough under my skin, but his eyes were soft as he took me in. Tentatively, I leaned forward and pressed my lips to his in a gentle kiss, letting it say more than I could.

I think I love you, Jason Westerman.

I let the way he smiled against my lips and kissed me back say what my heart couldn't help but pray to hear one day.

I think I love you too, Oakley Tennen.

When we pulled away, I let my thumbs rub over his cheeks again, completely in what Ash called my twitterpated love mood.

Movement caught my vision, and I barely had time to say his name before an elderly woman wearing a Rebels sweatshirt and dark sweatpants came hobbling down the porch steps as quickly as her uneven footing would take her. He turned, catching sight of the woman, and flashed me a grin before he flung his door open. His boyish wonder and the sight of him lifting her off the ground as she laughed made me giggle. They had the same laugh—strong, like it was overflowing with joy.

Stepping onto the dirt road and closing the car door behind me, I tucked my hands into the back pockets of my jeans as I rounded the hood. As soon as Jason set her down, the petite woman patted his cheeks like he wasn't a huge, hulking hockey player.

"Oh, Jay, my handsome boy. You sure you aren't missing practice to come see your Grams?" Her voice was gruff, like it had seen a tough life and fought through it. The lines on her face said the same.

"No, ma'am. I got it all arranged." He smiled endearingly down at her. "Grams, there's someone special I want you to meet."

When he turned, reaching a hand out towards me, I took it, putting my best smile on. Grams' eyes narrowed.

"Ah, this must be Oakley." She nodded curtly, and the sweet Grams who'd greeted her grandson was gone, a fierce protector in her place. "We'll see how special you are. Just because he says you're special doesn't mean you deserve him. Any girl can see his money and fame and want some of that glory without the man behind it. He's more than that, and I doubt that's fully understood by any woman he dates."

"Grams..." Jason said cautiously, but I tugged his hand to stop him.

"Mrs. Westerman, I care about your grandson. Despite him enjoying pushing my buttons, you have raised an extraordinary man. He sees my flaws—and I assure you, I have many— and he shows me they can be more than a weakness. He tries to understand, even when all he wants to do is push. Ma'am, you don't know me, but Jason does. I think that opinion should count, since he'd never put up with someone who was here for his salary or fame again. I should know—it was our first argument, and I held it against him for a long time." I paused, and Grams took the opportunity to place a hand on my arm.

"Save your breath, girl. I know my boy loves you, which means I'll have to. I have to do the job of protecting our boy for myself and Bob now that he's gone." She gave Jason a sly smile he simply huffed at. "But I appreciate your gumption. Jase said you were a fiery one. I like that. Better than the ditzes he dated in high school and college."

"Grams, really?" The tension dissipated as Jason scoffed and offered Grams an arm, keeping my hand tight in his grasp. "On that pleasant note, let's get you inside. The wind is starting to chill. You might be getting snow soon."

She swatted at him but ended up taking his arm. As we made our way slowly up the porch steps, Grams started mumbling.

"What was that, Grams?"

"Oh, nothing, dear. I gotta get the muffins in before Bob gets home. You know he gets that big smile when he smells us baking, even though he spends all day at the bakery. Make sure you get that algebra done first, you hear?"

My heart broke when Jason turned to me, devastation and questions in his eyes.

"Sure, Mrs. Westerman. Let's get those muffins going," I said, hoping to pull her back to reality without breaking hers. Her eyes met mine, and the tenacious woman who'd attacked my intentions seconds ago was gone. Confusion in her gaze, her eyes drifted to my hand clasped in Jason's, and then the clarity came back. In all my training, I'd never seen a case early enough to watch the switch happen so clearly.

"Oh, good idea, Oakley! Jase, I'll start the muffins. You get your girl settled. I want separate rooms, you hear?" She released Jason's arm and hobbled into the house, the battered screen door slamming shut behind her. Jason turned to me, and the pain he felt slammed into my soul.

"Can I access Nurse Oakley for a second?" he asked, barely getting the words out.

"Of course," I said, giving him a nod.

"What's your diagnosis?"

"I'll have to spend some more time with her to say for sure, and I think we should schedule an appointment with her primary care doctor, who can give an official diagnosis," I started then took a breath. Jason's hands shifted to his hips as he nodded along. "But from that interaction, and the way she bounced between being here and somewhere else, *sometime else*, I'd say at least dementia. She's confusing realities, seeing us as we are but fitting us into a past memory. It's going to feel like her memories are deleting backwards."

As I spoke, he ran his hands over his face and turned to look out over their property.

"I've been trying to get her to move for years, or at least get some renovations." He shook his head in frustration. "She refuses, says it's the only home she knows. Doesn't want anyone coming in and messing with her space. We got lucky she was hosting her knitting group the day she fell, but she's so isolated out here, Oaks, and I'm all the way in Nashville. I can't help her if...if she were to—"

Surging forward, I wrapped him in my arms. How do you decide how someone is going to live the years they've got left? When do those decisions get taken away from them?

"Do you still like it when I talk medical, Westerman?" I asked softly, trying to make him laugh but only getting a weak chuckle.

"I should say no, but it's actually easier to accept coming from someone I trust," he said softly, and I held him tighter.

After a few minutes, he turned back towards the house, his hand rubbing my back like giving me comfort was somehow comforting him. He gave me a strained smile, so different from the one he'd given only moments before, when his world hadn't been irrevocably altered.

27

After an early supper of Grams' famous muffins, a warm, creamy noodle soup, and mashed potatoes, courtesy of Jason, we moved to the living room, where Grams pulled out old photo albums. Apparently, she'd been waiting for years for Jason to bring home a girl so she could embarrass him properly. Throughout the evening, she faded into a past reality every couple minutes. At first, Jason would shoot me a panicked look, and we would try and bring her back without correcting her.

It was a tricky balance, but I didn't see the need in making her relive the death of her husband or the estrangement and probable death of her only daughter. The talk of Jason's mom was especially difficult on him, and he winced every time Grams brought her up. Things got better when we moved to the photo album, since she had tangible proof those memories were behind her.

"And this is when my husband bought Jason his first hockey stick. He was such an angry boy back then, if you can believe it! My happy boy, all angry at the world." She clucked disapprovingly. "But hockey pulled him out of that dreadful darkness. It was one of the first times I was happy my Bob was hockey obsessed."

Jason's eyes met mine over her head, and he winked.

"Oakley's happy Gramps trained me to be hockey obsessed, eh, Oaks? She loves it," he teased, his accent growing stronger the longer we were here.

"Keep telling yourself that, Westerman." I rolled my eyes. "My Pa taught me about the game, thank you very much. Bobby Orr is more my guy than these flashy new hotshots."

They didn't need to know how recently I'd discovered Bobby Orr.

"Oh, old school. My Bob would've liked you," Grams declared, wagging her finger. "Now, Jason, dear, could you fetch your Grams some more tea please? My creaky bones don't love getting up and down once they're settled."

"Of course, Grams," he replied, pressing a kiss to her temple before standing and giving my shoulder a quick squeeze as he left.

As soon as he was out of earshot, Grams' sharp eyes caught mine, and she shifted her body to face me head-on.

"Now that he's not mother-henning me, we can have a blunt discussion, woman to woman." Her gravelly words instilled the fear of God in me like nothing else. "We better do it before my mind goes again."

I stared at her, shocked.

"You think this old lady didn't realize she was losing it, eh? You kids don't give me enough credit. My health is failing, and I know it's only a matter of time before my mind goes too," she stated, like she had come to terms with it—unlike her grandson. "My sweet Jason loves with his whole heart. When he wants something, he isn't afraid to fight for it, to give his all to get it. That's what makes him so successful in life but also so unsuccessful in love. When he commits, he commits. He's told me you're a loyal person. I can see glimmers of that, but I also see a caveat. You have assessing eyes, my dear. You care for my grandson, that's for sure, but you haven't let your heart fully commit. I reckon you're on the lookout for a reason to leave before you can get left. To not be hurt at any cost, even the cost of my grandson's heart. As the woman who raised him, the need to protect him is all I can act on. Does that make sense?"

"Mrs. Westerman—"

"I don't want an excuse, Oakley." She huffed then looked down at the picture of Jason in her lap. His young grin beamed up at us. "My boy is light, but he's had darkness. When he started high school, he fell behind. Comprehension didn't come easy to him, and even though he was good at hockey, he wasn't great yet. So, the kids picked on him, told him he was stupid, that his brain must be too small to function. It hurt him."

A memory flitted in my mind—Jason, hands covered with flour and my hands in onion juice in Momma's kitchen.

"That's the best insult you could come up with? Did you get hit in the head at practice?"

"You keep saying stuff like that, like you think I'm stupid."

No wonder every time I'd said something like that, he bristled. He fought back. He'd never said why.

"For a while, he was lost, didn't know how to deal with the hurt. Then, he decided he was going to work harder. He might not have God-given book smarts, but he can read a room, a person, understand what someone needs and try to be that for them. He works harder than anyone else. After everything with his mother. After we lost Bob. After that mess when he first got into the league. He's worked so hard, and he loves playing, but his life isn't always stable. It's full of change. He can be traded, he can get injured, he'll be gone a lot, and you will have to constantly adjust to new schedules, new teammates, new routines."

I gulped. This wasn't a new concept to me. I knew about his professional life, but hearing it spelled out so clearly, all at once, all that change frightened me. Grams paused, watching my mind move through a million thoughts. Then, her eyes got impossibly sharp, and she delivered her final warning.

"I won't always be around to protect him, so I'll leave you with this. If you continue to drag this on and never fully commit to him the way I know he's committed to you, it will send him somewhere too dark for my darling light to go. If you love him, love him fully. Build a life with him. Defend him from it all, the way you defended yourself to me. He sees it all with you, but can you see it with him? If you can't—" She grasped my hand, hard. "Please let my boy go in peace before you break him."

My world blurred around me as her words hit me.

I was in love with Jason.

I loved our life now.

But it wouldn't always be this way.

Could I survive if everything changed?

Jason gave me space to think, and it made me fall even more in love with him.

I knew he wanted to ask about it, to talk through all my thoughts. His eyes bored into my head as we said goodbye to Grams in her new room at the assisted living facility when she hugged me tight and asked me to come visit again soon. Jason had been unsuccessful in convincing her to come to Nashville; she'd put her foot down on staying in Alberta. She said it was her home, and she was too old to move countries. Jason kept trying, even up until we had her fully moved into her new room. I let them have their argument, their hugs and laughs. I smiled and laughed with them, but my mind wasn't fully present.

"Oakley, are you okay?" he finally asked when we loaded our luggage into his car in the Nashville airport parking garage. I'd faked sleeping on the way to the airport. When the plane touched down in Nashville after I spent the travel time working on my presentation for work and we grabbed our luggage, making small talk about the most surface level things, I saw the determination in his eyes, the frown that marred his handsome face.

It hurt my heart, but Gram's words stuck with me. I loved him, but was I committed to him? Could I handle all the changes? It was only fair to him that I figured it out.

"Fine," I answered, mindlessly rearranging our luggage to avoid eye contact.

"That's not your line, OT," he joked, trying to break the

tension. I met his eyes and crossed my arms, closing myself off.

"There's a lot going on in my head, Jason." I scuffed my foot against the floor as my hands went to my temples. Like always, Jason was there, pulling my hands away and doing it for me. It took everything in me not to lean into him as his strong thumbs softly circled my skin.

"What happened, Oakley?" He peered into my eyes. I took a deep breath and closed my eyes, willing the tears to not fall. Why was I getting so emotional?

"Can you open your eyes, Oakley?" I shook my head quickly, and he rubbed his thumbs over my cheeks before placing a quick kiss to my forehead. "Please, baby?"

I looked into those dark eyes, and a sense of safety came over me, a sense of peace. Suddenly, looking into Jason's eyes felt the same as looking at the trees, and it struck me: like the falling of the leaves, things with Jason would inevitably change. They would never stay the way they were right now. Would I even get to see him throughout the season? What would we do if he got traded? What if he wanted to party hard after his team won the Stanley Cup and be free of me? What if they didn't win; how could I even help him get through that kind of loss?

"I'm overwhelmed," I finally admitted.

Jason sat with that for a moment, swiping away the few tears that had escaped down my cheeks.

"Is every change this hard? Even the good change?" he asked gently, and even though I knew he was trying to understand, those words cut. I took a step back, fast enough that his hand fell from my face. "Oakley, I meant—"

"I don't know. Jason. I'm trying," I insisted, my arms spreading out to my sides. "I want to let myself care for you, to roll with the change because we're together, and being together is enough. I want to embrace a life together, but I don't know if I can give you that. I don't want to hurt you, to send you somewhere your light can't shine."

At that, he stood straighter. "Grams said something to you, didn't she?"

"Uh—"

"She would always say that. Her biggest fear is me falling into darkness again, one where my light can't shine," he muttered, almost to himself. "Oakley, I love my Grams. I've put her through some rough times, and she's overprotective now, but do you know what she told me before I left? When she was clear and in this reality? She said, 'that pretty American girl from the South matches your worth.'"

Sniffling, I held myself together as his words hit me.

You will find someone who matches your worth, and that's when you'll be grateful you put in the hard work to be worth something.

How did I reconcile those encouraging words with all the fears Grams had brought to light?

"I'm scared, Jason. It's all going to change, and we can't stop it," I tried to explain, and then frustration took over. "How can you be so calm about this? What if we never see each other most of the year? What if we become strangers because we're both so busy living our own lives? Doesn't that scare you *at all*?"

Jason shook his head, hands on his hips, waiting for my

outburst to finish before he started his own, matching my exasperation.

"Of course it scares me, Oakley! But you're too wrapped up in your own head to see I'm working every day to not let my past and my scars affect us, to stop us from being all we can be. You won't even let me help you buy a car, dammit! You're so closed off, how can I even find a place in your life?"

Now, it was my turn to explode, my turn to give back all the feelings welling up inside me, and there was nothing I could do to stop the words that flew from my mouth.

"I know. I *know*. You don't think I get that, Jason? I hate that I'm so terrified of losing us, I can't live in the moment. I hate that I *love you* and I can't even express it. I hate that my momma was sick and I felt abandoned, and it's all happening again. I hate that I'm so scared of hurting you, I can't think straight. I can't help it because this is bigger than anything I've ever felt, and I don't know how to deal with it. So yeah, I'm sorry I'm a mess, but I want this more than anything, and—"

Reminiscent of our first kiss, he shut me up by pressing his lips to mine. It was quick and hard, and when he pulled back, I didn't know what to expect.

"We have a thing about arguing and screaming big feelings at each other in parking lots, OT."

I took a deep breath and thought back over my words.

I hate that I love you and I can't express it.

"Shit. That's not how I wanted to say that," I huffed, annoyed at myself.

"It was very '10 Things I Hate About You'," he smiled. "We're gonna work through this, Oaks. You and me? We're in this together. No matter what changes come our way, we'll face them. We'll figure it out, because I want this more than anything too."

"You're not gonna break up with me because I hate change?"

He chuckled, shaking his head. "As long as you're not gonna break up with me because my life involves a lot of change," he answered confidently, but there was still a touch of concern in his gaze.

"Well, I guess the free hockey tickets and home-cooked meals will have to make up for it."

He grinned. "I want to make this work, Oakley, to spite you."

I rolled my eyes, but a small giggle escaped my lips, and that was all the encouragement he needed.

"Thank you," he started, and he pressed a short kiss to my lips.

"For getting stuck in my own head again?" I asked, annoyed at myself for even starting this whole conversation.

"Thank you for opening up, for sharing what's going on in that beautiful, stubborn, over-thinking head of yours," he answered with a smile. "And Oaks?"

"Yeah?"

"I love you too."

28

When Jason left for his away games the next day, I kissed him goodbye and told him I loved him. He said it back, promising he'd try to talk as much as he could.

But the away series was against New York, and Jason needed to dial in. This team was their biggest competition, the other favorite for the Cup final this season. He knew this three-game series would set the tone for the rest of the year.

"I'll miss you so much," he'd said between kisses. After a moment, he'd pulled away, cupping my cheeks to try and keep the chill air away. It didn't do much; we were both flushed from the cold air and from each other. November was in full force, and Ash was already playing Christmas music daily. "I don't know how much I'll be able to call, but I could—"

"Jason," I'd reprimanded, giving him the glare he loved so much. "Focus on the game. I'll be okay."

He'd looked so sad, and even though he'd gone away for

games before, even though I knew he was in love with me the same way I was in love with him, it broke my heart. We'd grown closer. Jason knew how to read me like no one else.

He knew to give me space if I was listening to my *If Screaming Was A Song* playlist, and he knew he was welcome to show me all sorts of affection if I was listening to my *For Spite* playlist (previously named *Ash's Sappy Love Music*), which had quickly become a favorite.

Sharing my thoughts with him was like listening to my playlists: a safe place. But right now, I needed to let him focus on the game and hold myself together so he could be all he was meant to be.

I missed him from the moment he gave me that final kiss goodbye.

Despite both of our promises, the next week was harder than I could have ever expected.

I threw myself into work the next day. I gave a compelling presentation on my Music Tones Psychotherapy program, won over multiple stakeholders, and ensured the start of the program for the research team. Once again, that lab assistant sneered in my direction. Somehow, the fax I needed to get sent ASAP mysteriously got lost. The meeting location changed on my calendar, but thankfully, Sierra had wanted to walk to the meeting together, and I made it to the right place on time. I'd never had a coworker sabotage me before. When I tried to call Jason that night, he was at practice. When he tried to call me back, I was asleep. I texted him and he texted me, but the responses were so spaced out, it wasn't even a coherent conversation, just an occasional "I love you" and "that goal was shit" text to let him know I was thinking about him.

The cheap car I'd bought for myself was already making a weird rattling noise. Jason had threatened to just buy me a car if I chose a shit one, and I had chosen a shit one. But it was an affordable shit one, and being wrong combined with the looming pressure of Jason doing something so big for me added stress every time I turned the car on.

We lost a baby the next night. I sat in my rattling car for an hour before I felt like I could drive home. It was my patient, and everyone was aware this baby had some serious complications, including a heart defect and possible lung issues, but that didn't make it any easier. My heart wrenched for the mother. It tore apart. It was too much.

When I woke up that afternoon, I slid on Jason's Rebels sweatshirt and made a cup of tea. Jason's game started soon, and I wanted nothing more than to hear his voice and wish him luck. But he wouldn't be able to talk for a few hours, so I sent a quick text, feeling like the clingy girlfriend I'd always made fun of.

Taking my tea to my spot on the front porch, I settled in and watched the leaves. They had all died at this point in the season. It seemed like yesterday, they were green and full of life. Now, they are dead and gone.

The bench shifted as Ash settled herself beside me, criss-crossing her legs and leaning her head against my shoulder.

"You wanna talk about it?" she almost whispered, her curls tickling my neck. "I watched two whole Christmas movies, and you didn't even complain I didn't wait until after Thanksgiving."

I shrugged, half to convey my thoughts and half to move her head off me. Unphased, she readjusted and snuggled closer.

"I miss him so much, Ash," I whispered. The wind whipped across my face, stinging my eyes and making me shiver. "I'm trying to figure out how to love and support him while chasing my own dreams. I want to be as good for him as he is for me."

"That's a lot to figure out, but if anyone can do it, it's you," she declared with a smile, sitting up again to face me. "I wouldn't worry too much about Jason. That boy is head over heels for you, and you're just as bad. You glow when you're with him, Oakley. Our grumpy love-hater *glows*. And that sunshine hockey player? He glows right back. You bring out the best in each other."

A tear or two may have escaped as I hugged my best friend tight, showing her how much those words meant to me.

"Thank you," I said, though words couldn't express all I felt. "Thank you for sticking by me."

Ash just chuckled, running a soothing hand over my hair, and I let her. It felt kind of nice.

"You're my best friend, Oakley. I want to see you happy, and watching you discover this piece of yourself that not only feels but feels with passion? It's been beautiful." Now, Ash was sniffling too. "Thank you for letting me be a part of your life."

We sat there for a moment until Ash's phone rang loudly in her lap. After wiping away her tears, a frown instantly marred her pretty face. Glancing down at her phone as I wiped at my own eyes, I also found myself frowning at Donovan's name flashing across the screen.

"What's going on there?" I asked cautiously. Ash declined the call and blew out a breath, tucking her hands into the sleeves of her sweatshirt.

"He's upset he didn't think to dump me first." She shook her head. "I feel so much peace about this, Oaksy. I was forcing that relationship so hard because it felt like the only way."

"The only way to what?" I asked.

"The only way to feel loved." She stated, and there was still longing there but something else too. "I know that wasn't love. That was laziness because I didn't want to be alone. I've felt more love from you and Tae and Tess and—uh, other people, than I ever felt from Donovan. I'm finally ready to figure out what I want. So thank you, Oakley, for always being a true friend and showing me I can be myself. Maybe also for being brutally honest, even when I wasn't ready to listen. Now, I feel like I'm ready to be myself and be proud of it. So thank *you*."

She took a deep breath, and when she exhaled, a big smile graced her face. In that moment, as I watched her take control of her life, I was so grateful I'd chosen to be myself with Ash, to be honest and somber and sassy, because it was genuinely *me*, even though I tried to tuck those parts away. Without that authenticity, I didn't think Ash and I would be the people we were growing into or the close friends we'd become. I reached over, grabbing her hand and giving her a smile.

"That's amazing, Ash. You're so much stronger than you

know." I gave her hand a squeeze then raised my eyebrows. "Who are these mysterious 'other people', huh? You said it like you talk about your romcom boys."

Her cheeks went pink as she stammered. "Uh, nobody, really—"

"Have y'all been crying out here?" Our heads jerked towards Jack's voice. We were so wrapped up in our conversation, we didn't even see him make it up the drive and lean against one of the pillars framing our porch. Looking past him, I could see Tae and Tess chatting with Ivy, helping her get her sweet baby out of the car. "It's getting too cold for that. Why don't you cry inside like normal people?"

The pink on Ash's cheeks darkened.

"Is that where you like to have your cry time, soldier?" Ash joked. I smiled, especially when Jack's cheeks pinked right up too.

"Who even says *cry time*?" Jack muttered.

"Oakley!" Ivy shouted from behind Jack. "Sorry, I have to keep moving. These baby carriers are no joke. Could you scooch over there, Jack? The game starts in five minutes, and my husband slash baby daddy has already texted me twice to make sure I made it here safely. I lied saying I already had instead of worrying him with the great diaper explosion. My arm is about to fall off, and I don't need any of you to carry it, but I need all you to get a move on so you can ooh and ahh at my cute baby and let this momma prop her feet up and watch her hot husband at work. Oakley, I think you need some hot Jason Westerman ice action. It's so hard having them away!"

With that, Jack shifted to the side and let the Ivy Whirlwind rush through. Tae and Tess smiled at us, stopping to exchange a few words about the drive over and some analogy Tae had thought of for her freelance piece on the scam of dating apps. It was still in the beginning stages, so it made no sense, but she shrugged happily and hopped inside. Tess, sweet as ever, gave me a quick hug as I stood and silently wiped away an errant tear from my cheek. Ash followed her inside, and I wandered over to Jack.

"How are you really doing, Oakley?" he asked, all that big brother concern in his eyes. "Jason treating you right?"

"He's amazing, Jack," I replied with a sad smile, and the pang of missing him struck me. "Having him gone is hard."

"You miss him?"

I nodded.

"You told him how you feel?"

"Yes, Jack, he knows. He says he loves me too."

"Of course he loves you. You're Oakley," He stated it with such definitiveness, like there was no other option, and hugged me to his side. I grasped his hand that landed on my shoulder, taking on most of his weight as we shuffled inside.

"How are you really doing, Jack?" I asked as we passed through the front door. He sighed.

"We can talk after the game. For now, let's focus on the good." He sounded so tired, and I knew whatever was going on in his head couldn't be covered in the few seconds we had before entering the living room. Jack was more private than I was, so I'd make sure we could have some time alone to talk. We both needed it.

Once I got Jack settled on the couch furthest from where Ivy had settled in with her baby, warning them both it would not be good for a cancer patient and a newborn to be close enough to swap germs, I distributed hand sanitizer and a glare that had everyone nodding at my instructions.

Then, the game started. Settled between Ash and Tess, Ivy and Tae playing with baby Olive on the floor and Jack scooted as far as he could without being excluded from the circle, I took a breath.

My mind went from one worry to another as I took in Jason. Biting my lip, it hit me how inherently beautiful he was, and my heart beat faster.

The game started, and Jason had a few sloppy passes and off-net shots. The girls all commented on it, save for Ash, who squeezed my hand in support. Jack grimaced at his best friend's performance. He was having an off game.

Sensing my stress, Ivy placed a squirming Olive into my arms. I peered down at those sweet eyes and let those little hands grab my fingers—it did the trick. Finally calmer, I thought about what it would be like to hold my own baby someday, Jason standing beside me. The thought startled me, but then, it settled. I didn't know what the future would hold, but I knew who Jason was. I wanted a life with him. That was all that mattered.

A life with him.

It was there, with thoughts of a future with Jason in my head, that he finally got the puck, racing down the ice with momentum.

The next second, the opposing defenseman rushed him. Before Jason could even turn his head, he was slammed into the boards. The hit was high, dirty.

The whistle blew, guys from both teams yelling and throwing fists. Ash's hands covered her mouth in shock. Tess put a comforting hand on my knee, the girls on the floor cussing out the other player.

I waited, holding my breath as they cut the camera back to Jason. "He's not getting up," I whispered.

He was too still, arms splayed to his side, and when they showed his face, the world in chaos around him, my hockey player just laid there, eyes closed, blood dripping down his cheek.

"Get up, baby," I pleaded, a little louder. "Jason, get up."

Jack came over slowly, as if he was in shock himself. Ivy carefully took Olive from my arms, and the girls made space for Jack to squeeze in next to me.

I barely noticed any of it. My eyes were locked on the screen as two medical personnel raced onto the ice, checking his neck and covering my view of him.

"Jack, he's not getting up," I repeated, shock overcoming me. The screen cut to a replay of the hit, and I took that moment to glance at my brother. "He's not getting up."

"I know, Oakley. I know," he said, sitting stoically beside me.

No one spoke. I clasped my hands together, praying he would be okay, that they'd give us some sign.

Finally, the camera cut back to him being helped to his feet. He glanced at the crowd, who cheered loudly, and gave a small wave. The medical team started assisting him, but he waved them off and skated back to the tunnel. Before he exited the ice, he gave a little two finger salute with a sloppy smile.

A breath escaped, and then the tears came. He was okay. A little dazed and maybe concussed, but he was alright, okay enough to let *me* know he was okay. I wanted to call him, needed to contact him in some way.

As I opened my phone, multiple messages buzzed through my social media, each from a different username.

YOU HAVEN'T LISTENED.

IT WILL BE OVER SOON.

THIS IS YOUR FINAL WARNING.

I didn't have to go through the accounts to know that they were all the same. But it was the next message that sent a real chill through me. Because this one came to my phone number, through my texts.

UNKNOWN: END THINGS WITH JASON WESTERMAN, OR WE COME FOR HIM.

UNKNOWN: YOUR FAMILY AND FRIENDS ARE NEXT.

"Oakley? What the hell—" Jack's stunned voice pulled me away from my phone. When I glanced up, his eyes were wide, his face pale. I shook my head quickly. Hopping off the couch and walking to the kitchen, I ignored the messages and dialed Jason's number.

I knew it would go to voicemail. He was still in the middle of a game, even though he was off the ice.

When his voicemail beeped through, I had to say something.

"Hey, Westerman, I-I'm praying you're okay. Please call me when you can. I need to hear your voice right now. I need-I need to see you. I'm sorry we haven't been able to talk; it's been so hard, but I believe in us. I need you to know that. I love you, Jason. That's what matters. Please, call me when you can, and we can talk about everything and nothing. I want to make sure you're okay. I love you, sunshine boy."

I hung up, knowing I wouldn't hear from him for a while. The thought killed me. Jack limped into the kitchen, leaned against the countertop, and folded his arms, ready for a facedown.

"How long?"

"The first time was after your first chemo."

"Does he know?"

"No."

"Does anyone?" he demanded.

"You." I crossed my arms.

"Oakley, why—"

"I knew what I was doing when I started dating Jason, okay? Crazy fans are a part of the package."

"No, they're part of the problem." He rubbed a hand over his head. "Jason knows how to handle this stuff. He's had crazy fans before. He deserves to know."

"I just..." I sighed. "I didn't want him to have one more thing to worry about."

Jack didn't answer.

"I know it's stupid. I—"

"Oak..." His words came out gasping. "Some-something's wrong—"

I took a step closer as he put a hand to his chest, heaving like he couldn't catch his breath. Panic shot through me. I put my hands on his shoulders, trying to steady him. "Jack!"

His eyes rolled to the back of his head as he collapsed into me. I grunted as we both fell to the floor, and I tried my best to keep his head from slamming into the hardwood. Time slowed as my brother's body started convulsing as I sat there, stunned. It was that movement that shocked me into action, my training taking over as I grabbed his head to try to prevent a concussion.

"Ash!" I screamed. "Call 911!"

I didn't hear a response; I just tried to focus on my brother and keeping him from hurting himself.

Ash hit the floor next to me, laying the phone on the wood as she tried to assess the situation. She helped me turn him on his side as I kept my hands tight his head.

"Ma'am, can you explain what's happenin'? We have an ambulance en route to your location." The dispatcher's voice barely reached me over the panic. I blinked hard, forcing myself to go clinical. This wasn't Jack. This was a patient.

"I have a 27 year old male seizing. Spontaneous, n-no previous signs or symptoms I'm aware of except for shortness of breath immediately b-before he lost consciousness," I stammered then turned my attention to Jack. He'd paused seizing for a second, only to start again, this time making noises. "Jack, Jack!"

I tried to wake him, interrupt the seizing, something. But nothing helped him.

"Ma'am, are you a trained medical personnel?"

"Yes, ma'am. I'm a registered nurse with BLS training. I'm holding his head to prevent a concussion and we have him on his side in case of vomiting," I stated quickly, fighting to keep my grip on his head as his body fought against mine. I barely registered the crowd of friends behind me, Olive's soft cries mixing with Jack's grunts. "He-he's my brother. He's been doing chemo treatments for osteosarcoma. Bone cancer. I don't...I don't know... What do I do— I don't know what to do—"

"Keep on with what you're doin', ma'am. The team was nearby and is at your location. They should be enterin' any moment now." As she spoke, I heard knocks and then the unlocked door slammed open.

"Paramedics entering!"

"In here!" Ash yelled.

As soon as I'd given a frazzled report to the paramedics and they took over, I scooted back, my knees still on the floor and my breath coming out in pants. Ash wrapped her arms around me as Jack's seizing finally stopped. His eyes didn't open.

"Get up," I whispered. "You can call me Oaksy again. Just please, get up."

He didn't get up.

One man I loved had gotten up from a hit tonight, but I wasn't sure the brother I loved would ever get up again.

<h1 style="text-align:center">29</h1>

firm hand landed on my shoulder, shaking me awake. I had fallen asleep sitting up in a chair. Glancing around, it all came rushing back to me. The game. Jason. The messages.

Jack.

Jolting upright, I took in Jack's unconscious form and did a quick scan of the vitals monitor. His heart was still beating. He was alive.

"Oakley," Pa said, his hand still on my shoulder. They'd come to the hospital as soon as I'd called. Poor Mal had been at a friend's house, forced to sleep over there until things calmed down and one of us could get her. Momma was asleep on the couch behind me. I'd never forget the way she fell apart when she saw the tubes and wires attached to her son.

The sound of her sobs would stay with me forever.

"Oakley," Pa tried again. "Why don't you get out of here for a little bit? He's stable for now."

I looked at Jack again then back at Pa, at the tiredness in his eyes. I nodded numbly.

"I..." I took a deep breath. "I could go grab Mal? Would that be helpful?"

Pa nodded slowly, as if he was chewing on a thought he needed to spit out soon.

"What?" I snapped.

"I want you to do what you need to do to deal with this, Oaksy. We appreciate how much you handle all this stuff, but it's been brought to our attention that you take it all upon yourself."

"Who—"

"Obviously that hockey player you're in love with." Hunter took up the whole door frame with his hulking figure, a backpack on his shoulder; he must've driven all night. "I thought Oakley was supposed to be the smart one."

"She's givin' a whole new meanin' to the sayin' 'stupid in love'," Momma groaned as she rose from the couch, darting past us to hug her son.

"I didn't realize all y'all had an opinion to share," I grumbled as I gave him a tight hug. "I'm glad you're here, Hunter. I don't... He almost..."

"You saved him, Oakley," he said softly, putting a hand on my shoulder and looking into my eyes. "How are you feelin'?"

"Right as rain," I whispered, and my heart ached for Jason. I wanted him here more than anything. I had a vague memory of my phone ringing, of getting texts, but I hadn't had time to check who'd called. I was praying it was Jason, that someone told him what was happening when I'd been too shocked to do anything other than hold my family together.

Ignoring the piercing gaze of my younger brother, I turned to my parents and gave them a small smile.

"I'm gonna go get Mal. I'm sure she's been going crazy." I grabbed my bag Ash had shoved into my hands when she'd loaded me up to follow the ambulance. Tess and Tae had followed in another car with Ivy and baby Olive in tow, and though they didn't stay long, their support meant everything.

"Drive safe, Oakley Mae," Momma said with a sad smile, and Pa wrapped an arm around her as they updated Hunter. I left the room quickly, not needing to relive it all again.

Digging through my purse, I found my keys and phone. As I waved to the nurse at the ICU desk and walked out to the parking lot, I finally checked my phone. The messages were overwhelming, but I took a deep breath and started at the most important.

Westerman: Hey, OT, I got your voicemail and tried to call you back. Give me a call when you can.

Westerman: I love you too.

Those texts must have come through right after the game ended. A few more came in around midnight.

Westerman: Hey, what's up with all the Tennens ignoring me? I really want to talk to you, Oakley. I know you might be asleep, I'm done with all this phone tag. I need to talk to my girl.

Westerman: I even tried calling Jack to get to you, but His Grumpiness didn't pick up the phone either. Please call me.

I hadn't checked my missed calls yet, but I imagined there were many from him.

Westerman: Ash called me. My flight gets in tomorrow morning. I'm on the earliest one, and then I'm headed straight to the hospital. I'm so sorry, Oakley. I'm coming as soon as I can, baby. I love you so much, and we'll figure this out together. See you soon, praying for Jack.

Taking in a deep breath, I typed out a quick response. It didn't deliver, so I assumed he was still in the air.

OT: I love you too. I need you. See you soon, sunshine boy.

There were a few messages from the unknown number I promptly ignored. Of course, now they were asking for money like the scammers I knew they were. Next, I skimmed the texts from the girls and Ivy checking in, asking to know how they could help. Ash texted to say she'd be back soon with food for my family and to let me know she'd called Jason. A wave of gratitude for my best friend washed over me. Then, I called my sister.

"Oakley?" Mal's tearful voice came through the phone as I reached my car, unlocking it and quickly getting in.

"Oh, Mal. I'm on my way to pick you up. Can you send me your location?" I asked, trying to stay strong. She sniffled a yes. "I love you, kiddo. I'll see you soon, okay?"

"Okay. Just..." She choked back more tears. "Can you please hurry? I don't want—I don't want to get left behind again."

The tears I'd been holding back started to flow over, and everything was too much.

"You won't get left behind."

"Promise?"

"Promise. And guess what?"

"What?"

"I'd go fishing with you over anyone in the universe, Mallory Louise Tennen." I could hear her smile as she chuckled. "Even if you are a brat."

"Shut up and come pick me up, please."

***

We were almost back to the hospital when my phone rang, interrupting our duet to 'Tennessee Whiskey', a picture of Jason smiling and hugging me so tight, I was basically in a headlock, flashing on the screen. He'd taken the picture and set it as his contact photo after one of his hockey games before we went to see Grams. Before I could even speak, Mal grabbed my phone and unhooked it from the music.

"Jason!" she answered excitedly, the volume on my phone turned up loud enough that I could hear a surprised, "Hey, little Tennen."

My heart couldn't help but melt.

"Are you comin' to see Jack?" Mal asked expectantly, her voice getting watery with emotions again. "Yes, sir, I'm okay."

His response was muffled, and we were about to turn into the parking lot when she glanced over at me, took a minute to consider, then turned back to her conversation with my boyfriend.

"She's Oakley. She's tryin' to be strong for everyone, but she's feelin' too many emotions right now," she reported solemnly, as if I wasn't in the car. "You don't even want to know how many sad songs we've listened to on this car ride. Can you hurry and get here? You're the only one who can make her smile without havin' to play '*Fishin' in the Dark*' for the freakin' millionth time."

There was a nice little eye roll in that speech, and I gave her one right back. Sometimes, I forgot my sweet little sister was also a sassy teenager.

When I parked, I gave her a look.

"Ugh, Jason, she's givin' me the look." She snickered at whatever he'd said. "Yeah, that one. I'll give her the phone, but you're comin', right? Okay, see you soon!"

She handed the phone over and opened the door, hopping out and slamming it shut behind her. I put the phone to my ear, opening my door and following her lead.

"Hey, Jason," I said softly. I didn't realize I was holding

my breath until I heard his gruff voice come through the speaker, full of emotion. My chest finally loosened at the sound.

"Hey, baby." He blew out a breath of his own. "I'm at the airport, heading for my car. I'll be there in twenty minutes max, probably closer to fifteen, depending on traffic. How's Jack?"

"He's okay. Stable right now, but they're waiting for him to wake up, and then they're gonna run even more tests." I grimaced, turning to walk after Mal as she did a weird skip walk towards the sliding glass doors. Shaking my head and smiling softly at her antics, I turned my attention back to Jason. "How are you feelin' after that hit?"

"I'm fine, Oaks. Just worried. We haven't talked all week, and then I couldn't answer until after the game, and when I couldn't get a hold of you or Jack, I didn't want you to be worried about me. Then Ash called, and I... Dammit, I'm so sorry, Oakley."

I looked up at the sky, looking for answers. "I don't know what to do. The whole family is here, and hopefully, we can pull through—"

"Oakley?" Mal's voice snapped my attention forward, the fear laced in that one word chilling me to my core.

A woman in a ratty sweatshirt held my sister against her body, her arm wrapped tight around Mal's shoulders.

A gun to her head.

I watched Mal try not to cry as she bit her lip, looking at me like I was her only hope. I froze, the phone still to my ear.

"You've not been good at listening, Oakley Tennen." She used a lilting voice, sing-songy, as she pressed the gun a little harder against my sister's temple. The movement wore my shock off, and recognition flowed over me. Frizzy dark hair hit her shoulders, blonde roots peeking out the top. Her nose was turned up, like she couldn't have thought less of me if she tried. She'd given me that exact look so many times before.

"Joy?" I asked, not understanding why my lab assistant had a crazed look and a gun pointed at my little sister.

"That stupid cover didn't get us far anyway. You never left anything useful at work, Oakley. You were useless. You've always been useless."

"Oakley? What's going on?" Jason's confused voice filtered through my phone. Joy must have seen my reaction to his voice, because she grinned.

"Oh, you won't need that phone where we're going. Hang up. Now. Or your sister learns what real pain feels like."

My mind went a million miles a minute. I glanced around, taking in the way her arm was tucked, her body turned. She knew where the security cameras were and how to hide from them. I opened my mouth, but something hard pressed into the small of my back. A rough voice whispered near my ear.

"Unless it's the hockey player." I turned my head slightly, not taking my eyes off Mal but catching the man in my periphery—tall, gangly, in the same uniform of ratty clothes, but I couldn't catch his face. He pressed harder, and the object jabbing into my back became identifiable as another gun.

"Oakley? Oakley? Are you okay?" Jason's worried voice struck me again.

"It doesn't matter if it's him. He'll pay more if he's a little scared first," Joy declared, baring her teeth menacingly at me. "Hang. Up."

The way her voice warbled, eyes laced with an unhinged edge, I knew she would hurt Mal.

"Right as rain," I said quickly before holding the phone where they could see it, my hands going up in surrender. I hoped the cameras would pick up my movements, especially when the man yanked the phone out of my hand, cursing when he realized I hadn't hung up. He pressed closer to me, shielding the gun at my back with his body.

"Put your arms down," he grumbled at me, and I slowly lowered my arms. "That idiot was never smart. He'll never understand what's happening fast enough to stop it. Let's go."

With that, he tugged on my arm and tried to turn me, but I held a hand out towards Mal.

"I'm not going anywhere without my sister. You let me hold her hand, and we'll follow you," I demanded.

"You think you have any power here? I told you she was a stuck up princess." Joy waved her gun slightly, pushing forward with Mal, whose tears flowed down her face. My heart broke, and I didn't even know why this was happening.

What did these people want?

"Let's go," the man ordered again, pulling me towards him. Mal cried out, reaching for me as the determination to not let her out of my sight fought with my fear that listening would keep us the safest.

I reached for my sister one more time, and in that moment, a security guard burst through the doors. He looked at us, and the confusion on his face told me he couldn't see the guns.

"Guns! They have guns!" I screamed. "Mal get down!"

The security guard reached for his holster, but he was too slow. When the man behind me raised his weapon, I wrenched away from him.

He pulled the trigger, and I pulled Mal from Joy's manic grip. Panic gripped me tight as I tugged her to me, wrapping my arms around her body and dragging her to the pavement. We hit the ground hard as the security guard shot back. Maneuvering my body to shield hers, I cried out when I saw the guard hold his chest, crying out as the bullets hit him.

When the guard stopped shooting back, Joy's gun was in our face.

"Get up! You ruined everything! You ruined everything!" she screamed as she pulled me to my feet. I kept Mal in my arms, holding her as she sobbed, her gaze locked on the body lying too still in front of the hospital doors. "Shit, Rob, we gotta go! Go, you idiot!"

The man, Rob, stood transfixed on the security guard he had shot. Joy screeched at him again, and his glazed eyes slowly turned to us. When I finally saw his face, the signs that this man was out of his mind wasted on some kind of drugs were glaringly obvious, his fingers fidgeting by his side and around the gun. I knew his face. It clicked all at once: this man in his threadbare t-shirt on a cold October morning, herbal tea spilled at his feet, standing next to the bike he had used to run me over.

Jason was right. He had been aiming for me.

My mind raced, and I had no idea how we were going to get out of this.

Rob snapped back to whatever reality he had been operating under before, a shaky hand running through his stringy blond hair as he took off running.

"Follow him, or I'll shoot!" Joy yelled, a manic spark in her eye, so we listened.

I grabbed Mal's hand and squeezed it, trying to give her the hope I didn't feel. We stumbled to our feet, a rough shove from Joy sending us staggering after her partner.

"No matter what happens, don't let them separate us," I told Mal as calmly as I could, our breaths uneven as we followed a sprinting Rob. Whatever their plan had been, it was falling apart. They didn't attempt to hide their guns, running down the main sidewalk by the hospital in a mad sprint. The hospital edged a strip of wooded area, and as sirens sounded behind us, Rob glanced back with fear in his eyes and made a run for the trees.

"No! The car is the other way!" Joy screeched, turning us with another shove, leaving Rob to follow. Whether he did or not, I didn't know, because a police cruiser came speeding around the corner, sirens wailing, heading for the front of the hospital.

They didn't know where we were.

Time stood still as I tried to process that this was happening. This was real.

And I had no idea what to do.

Joy turned the gun on us, scrambling for a plan.

"Here's what's gonna happen. You are going to walk calmly to that black car, the one parked by the street lamp. You are not going to run, or scream, or do anything unless I tell you to. Do you understand?"

Pulling Mal behind me, I simply nodded, trying not to

show how fast my breaths were coming. Joy nodded towards the car, and I shifted so I was between the gun and Mal as we started slowly walking, praying someone would see us.

"Faster," she hissed.

"If we go too fast, they'll notice us," I hissed right back. "Then you'll never get whatever you want."

"I would've had everything if you'd stayed away."

"You wanted the research position?" I asked, appalled. All this over an entry-level job? There was no way she was that desperate.

"No, you stupid bitch. You took Jason. He's *mine*," she practically growled, turning when she heard Rob protest loudly, hissing for him to be quiet. "He gave me everything. When I left and he found out, I didn't care. He never even tried to get it back. But Rob lost all our money, and they came calling. I knew I could do it. All I needed to do was make him believe I loved him again, and all my nice things would be back. I'm meant to have nice things."

I tried to make sense of it all. She was obviously broken, maybe high, but something stuck out to me.

He never even tried to get it back.

"Rachel?" I asked hesitantly as we made it to the black car.

Her silence was my response.

How in the world did we end up here?

"When do we get our money?" Rob groaned, unlocking the car. He turned to face us, his expression darkening into anger. "You said this would be fast. We take them, we call the hockey player, and he pays. You messed up. Again."

"Shut up, shut up, shut up!" Joy/Rachel yelled. "You

messed up! You messed up when you couldn't take her out with that stupid bike! I got us here! Shut up, shut up, shut up!"

The shock that *this* was Jason's ex-girlfriend rolled through me as I took in these two. The edges were fraying between them, whatever drugs they were on making them unpredictable.

But it also made them malleable.

My heart was beating too fast, the fear causing my hands to shake.

I whispered to Mal, "When I squeeze your hand, you run to the cops."

She turned to me, her scared brown eyes wide. They were exact reflections of mine.

"But you said—"

"Do it."

My tone left no room for argument. Our situation gave no room for mistakes.

She gave me a small nod, and I turned to the psychotic pair, keeping Mal behind me.

"Did you send the messages?" I asked, keeping my voice strong. "Why didn't you say you wanted money from the beginning?"

"I didn't need you to give me money. I needed you out of the way," she snapped, huffing a breath. Rob held his gun loosely, twitching at every mention of Jason.

A thought came into my head as I watched him. "So you could be with Jason again?" I prodded, testing how much I could get her to say.

Frustration instantly turned to rage, fists clenched at her

sides. Rob watched the interaction with weary eyes, but he wasn't reacting big enough. Just a small twitch. I hadn't factored in the slower processing time. Who knew how much it would take to get him to fully distract her?

"You were never good enough for him," she hissed, taking a step closer, so close, we were chest to chest. I took another step back, creating some distance. "A little poor girl from a sad family with a sick brother? He only ever paid you attention because he pitied you. Because he felt forced to. One of his stupid charities."

Tightening my grip on Mal instinctively, I pushed her farther behind me. Glancing over at Rob, I took a sharp breath when I saw the focus in his gaze, how his eyes were bouncing between me and Joy. Or, I guessed, Rachel. I wasn't sure if either of those were her real name.

But if I kept pushing, that confusing gaze of Rob's would turn angry.

And that anger would allow Mal to escape.

Just maybe.

"Oh really? Then why didn't he come back to you?" I tried again to get an outburst out of her while slowly inching me and Mal closer to the front of the car. At the movement, Joy's eyes narrowed. She stepped closer, the gun in her hand raising slightly. I felt Mal tremble behind me, a small sob escaping her lips. Desperate, I shouted at the madwoman, "He doesn't love you like he loves me! He's mine now!"

Those narrowed eyes widened with a wild, raw kind of insanity. She became completely unhinged, her body trembling as she stepped so close, we were breathing the same air.

The cold wind whipped between us, sending our hair flying as she exploded.

"You're lying! If he knew it was me, he'd come crawling back, you bitch," she screeched, flailing her hands, the gun carelessly flying around us. "Jason thought I was a fan instead of the woman he used to love. I couldn't reach him. He didn't understand he's mine! He's mine, mine, mine!"

If I hadn't been so terrified, I might have felt proud as I watched the pieces fall into place. Joy lost her mind, shoving her finger in my face, screaming and hollering all her delusions.

Rob finally stepped forward, protesting loudly.

"Baby girl, but *we're* together! I told you to stop saying that," he raged. The anger in his voice reminded me that while these two were almost comically stupid, they were also insanely dangerous. "You're so obsessed with him. So obsessed, but you're *mine*. I thought you just wanted the money. For us. This is bullshit—"

She turned to him slowly, pure hatred in her gaze.

I pushed Mal and myself further to the front of the car as they started arguing, trying to give her a straight shot to the cop cars. Glancing slightly over my shoulder, I caught a glimpse of people running and shouting near the entrance to the hospital. Rob's rage-filled holler pulled my gaze back to the danger in front of us. I shuffled another step into the open, hoping to give them a direct line of sight to us.

A short pause in their screaming, and I heard cops calling our names. I heard a gruff voice I knew too well, and for the first time since I saw that gun against Mal's head, my heart soared with hope.

Westerman.

Waiting until Rob turned away from Joy in frustration, until they were so lost in their anger, they weren't paying us any attention, I squeezed Mal's hand hard before letting go of her completely. Pride and relief flooded me when she took off, sprinting as fast as her legs could take her.

Horror replaced it when Joy quickly turned and raised her gun.

Then, confusion when footsteps came back towards me, and horror again when Joy grinned.

"Ah, Jason. Perfect," she seethed, and I could see the exact moment her sanity snapped completely. "If you don't want me anymore, you can't have anyone. Goodbye."

I didn't even think when I jumped towards her, shoving at her shoulders as she fired.

"Oakley, no!"

"Put your hands up!"

"Drop the gun!"

We hit the ground hard, rolling to a stop as the gun was knocked loose. I gasped, ready to feel the pain.

But when I scrambled to my knees on the rough pavement, loose rocks stabbing into my skin and the strong wind blowing cold around us, I didn't feel anything.

She'd missed me.

But had she missed Jason?

Frantically, I searched for him as several officers came swarmed us. The police got to work holding down a stunned Joy and hauling away a screaming, thrashing Rob.

Then, my eyes landed on him.

And I could breathe. I raked my gaze over his body as he

pushed past the police swarming us to get to me, but he didn't look hurt.

Jason crouched before me, nodding for the officer on his heels to speak as he held my gaze.

"Ma'am, did you get hit anywhere?" he asked quickly, keeping an eye on his companions as they cuffed the two screaming attempted-kidnappers. "Do you require medical attention?"

"No, sir. I'm-I'm okay," I answered, but I couldn't pull my eyes from Jason's. "Mal? My sister? Where is she?"

"She's okay, Oaks." He reached for where I still sat on my knees. "They have her. She's safe."

I nodded slowly, and all at once, it hit me.

We could have died.

We almost did.

Shivers raced over my skin as I imagined how differently this could have gone, how my life could have changed if things had shifted even a millimeter.

How so many things had already shifted inside me.

Words flew at me, people trying to get my attention. To ask me questions. To try to understand.

But my head was underwater. The words muffled and indecipherable, it felt easier to not try to understand any of it.

To let the shock take over.

So, I let the world fade away around me, trying to forget the gravel digging into my palms, the chill of the air against my skin, the crunch of the dead leaves under shoes, the sound of the sirens signaling to all that something here was *wrong*.

It was easier to let it all go and forget to feel.

Strong arms wrapped around me. They lifted me, holding me close and bringing me behind a line of police officers. Those arms held me as we walked far from the people who almost took everything I'd ever loved.

I couldn't do it.

I felt the moment the numbness took over, the moment my heart decided *enough*.

I didn't hear when Jason asked me again and again if I was okay.

I didn't respond when Mal wrapped her arms around me and cried.

I didn't react when my parents sobbed as they heard our story.

I didn't cry when the police took my statement.

I didn't feel anything, because it was easier than feeling everything.

I tried to look to the trees for comfort, the nature that had always brought me peace.

But the leaves were all dead.

They were *dead*.

30

The numbness didn't go away, not even when some clarity came the day after we'd been held at gunpoint.

Rachel Robins, alias Joy, and Robert Marshel, wanted con artists and drug dealers, were arrested and awaiting trial. Living in a drug-induced haze, being chased by gangs and collectors for Rob's gambling debts, Rachel had decided to solve their problems by regaining her prior 'relationship' with Jason Westerman, the one in which she had access to his connections and money. I guess she knew something I didn't, because from the beginning, she'd targeted me as an obstacle. She even sent Rob to run me over with that bike, a half-assed attempt to take me out. When that failed, they got more invested. We learned she'd dyed her hair and gotten a job at the research facility in a dual effort to get rid of me and became more attractive to Jason—to try to *become* me.

But when I didn't listen to her anonymous threats, she

snapped and decided to kidnap me for ransom. She even admitted she'd hoped Jason would simply choose her instead.

The security guard was dead, shot and left to die because of greed. He had a name— Jonathan Winter—and a family. His wife was hysterical, his daughter inconsolable, all the lives involved irrevocably changed forever.

My head hurt from it all. I couldn't sit still. I couldn't think. I'd hardly spoken to anyone. Mal was holding up well, despite everything. She cried every few hours or so, but she seemed calmer after giving her statement to the police.

I wished I could say the same.

Now, I was pacing in Jack's room as he watched me from his hospital bed. While we'd been held at gunpoint, he'd woken up.

Ash had brought me new clothes and food for everyone. She sat next to Jack, somehow the one helping him eat. They exchanged a soft smile as she spoon-fed him chicken noodle soup.

"You gonna talk to him?" Jack rasped, still weak as he nodded towards the doors. "He thinks it's his fault."

"It's not," I snapped, huffing out a quick breath. "But I can't do it right now, Jack."

"Can't do what, Oaks?" Jason's voice struck me, so small and sad compared to his usual strength and sunshine.

Turning, I barely glanced at him before heading out to the hallway for this conversation. We were not having it in front of my family, who'd spread out around the room in various stages of sleep and hushed conversation.

"Thank you for calling the hospital and the police when that call cut off. But you don't have to be here anymore. In fact, you should go. You need rest, and I need space to process—"

"No," he said, shaking his head and putting his hands on his hips, glaring at me with those eyes I could lose myself in.

"No isn't an option. I'm not asking you." I crossed my arms, trying to block him out.

"I'm not asking you either. I'm staying with you. You can't push me away, especially not right now—"

"Yes, I can!" My voice trembled as it rose. He reached his hands towards me.

If he held me, I would give in.

His eyes pleaded with me, those damn beautiful eyes. "Please—"

I held out a hand, stopping him, putting space between us. "No. I can't let myself care about you."

The ringing in my ears kept getting louder as I kept talking. I couldn't meet his eyes, swirling with every emotion I couldn't face.

"I can't. He's sick and I can't save him. She almost hurt the people I care about most. I couldn't stop her. I-I couldn't —" A deep breath.

Refortify. Reground.

Breathe. Continue.

"She almost took you too, and that would kill me more than anything." My mind flashed to those moments when I heard his voice, when she raised that gun, when panic and heartbreak and devastation I'd never felt rushed through me like wind through the leaves, rustling every one of my deepest fears.

A hand tilted my chin. I let it. I was weak.

And I was breaking.

Shattering into a million pieces.

"But I *love* you." Now, his voice trembled as his hands cradled my face. "I'm not leaving you. Don't push me away. Please. Don't break what we have."

A loud alarm sounded, followed by a shout and footsteps running towards us, but I was numb.

What we had was already broken. I couldn't be there for him when I couldn't even be there for myself. I was dead inside, and nothing could grow there anymore. The cold was here, and all that was alive and growing was gone.

Pushing his hands away, I felt nothing.

When I turned away from him, I felt nothing.

When he yelled after me, I felt nothing.

When he went silent and didn't chase after me, I felt nothing.

Because I had broken it.

And I knew living without us would break me.

Everyone leaves eventually.

31

Jackson Oliver Tennen's heart stopped beating seconds after I walked back into his hospital room.

My older brother, who held me when I cried, who told me we could take on the world as two kids who had to grow up too fast. Jack took me fishing when I was fourteen when the boy I liked made fun of how I talked. Jack took me to work when I didn't have a license. Jack took me to Riverfront Park when I was sixteen and terrified because Pa had changed jobs and Momma was going through chemo. Again. He was at every sports game, every school event, silent and stoic as ever. But still, he was there.

Jack had fought so hard to find his place in life. And then, in a single moment, it was over.

I watched, completely helpless, arms wrapped around my own waist, as his heart fully stopped, as a stranger's voice declared they couldn't find a pulse.

The ringing in my ears got louder, and I barely noticed Momma sobbing and clinging to Pa, as close as they could get with the nurses and respiratory therapists and doctors surrounding my big brother, who'd never looked so small. I barely noticed Hunter standing behind them, his hands on his head and shock on his face, Ash at his side, hands over her mouth and tears streaming down her cheeks. There was something in her eyes, a feeling I knew all too well. I couldn't look too long at Mal by the door, sobbing in the arms of a stunned Jason, who'd followed me right into heartbreak.

This was real. He was leaving us again.

For two minutes and fifty seven seconds, my brother, soldier in the United States Army, skilled engineer, grumpy soul, giver of all he had, the strong Jackson Tennen, was gone.

Then, a nurse who barely reached my shoulder wearing a camo scrub cap, took two AED pads, slapped them on his chest, yelled "clear", and waited for the others to stop giving CPR. Then, she shocked him. Nothing.

Again. Nothing.

She did it again. Then, his heart started.

His eyes didn't open, but he had a heartbeat.

Sound came rushing back to me. Momma's shocked sobs, Pa's tearful whispers of gratitude, and the steady sound of the monitor picking up Jackson Tennen's beating heart came through loud and clear.

I'd never heard more beautiful music than the beating heart of someone I thought I'd lost.

Of what was once gone getting a second chance.

32

"When will he get to go home?" Tae asked from across the kitchen, stirring her pre-work pasta as I finished up my reheated soup.

"Next week," I replied with a soft smile. "Momma isn't letting him out of her sight. They said the seizures and the cardiac arrest were a result of the chemo and the stress on his body. His body was trying to do too much, so now he gets to be coddled. His surgery is pushed back until they can reassess."

I thought about the two weeks since my brother's heart had stopped. So much had happened. Mal had asked to get help, and I was so proud of her. Hunter had found me a therapist too before he went back to school, but I hadn't called the lady yet.

It felt too big right now. It all felt too overwhelming.

Tae and Ash had burned sage in our townhouse in an effort to "ward off medical emergencies from occurring on the premises". Even though we'd all laughed, it actually did make me feel a bit better.

I'd taken time off work and just started going back to meetings at the research lab, doing everything remotely until further notice. Dr. Grouse apologized thoroughly for letting Joy into the facility, instituting a new mandatory background check policy for all positions. The poor man had been just as conned as the rest of us, and since she was a lab assistant, she'd been able to fake her résumé and credentials easier than should've been possible. Still, he was excited for the breakthrough I'd had about the connection between heartbeats and music.

Jason had tried to call the first day after everything. When I didn't answer, he left me a voicemail I listened to when I needed to hear his voice.

"Hey, OT. I know you asked for space. I'm going to do my best to respect that. I'm so sorry about Rachel and everything that's happened with Jack. Everything about the last few weeks has been hard for you and for us. I understand that. But I want to make something clear, Oakley Mae Tennen. Even if you choose to leave me, it should be your choice and not influenced by others. I need you to know I love everything you are with everything I am. You give me everything I never knew I could have. I wouldn't be the man my grandparents raised me to be if I didn't tell you that you are, without a doubt, the most beautiful, stubborn, giving, loyal woman I have ever known. I love you. I miss you, baby. Please come back to me. It's been too long since we've argued. I miss my moon girl."

It was the sappiest voicemail I'd ever heard, and I missed him more than anything, but he was right. I needed this time to figure out where to go from here.

"You still going fishin' today?" Tae asked softly, pulling me back from my zone out.

"Yeah, Mal was real excited about it. Pa is coming too, so it'll be a fun time. Get us all out of the house and doing something normal, I guess." I shrugged, downplaying how much we all needed this. "Have you seen Ash today?"

Tae grimaced, which told me enough.

"She picked up another shift last night. I don't know why she refuses to see Jack, but she's watched Pride and Prejudice more times than I can count, and she won't talk to any of us..." Tae shook her head. I couldn't explain it either. It was like Ash's sweet heart couldn't handle it all, but instead of running to her friends, she escaped into work and movies. She was like a ghost of herself, barely smiling and avoiding all mention of my brother.

But with every text I avoided from Jason, I felt less and less able to comment.

"I actually have to go if I'm gonna meet them on time. Have a good shift tonight, Tae."

She smiled gently as I grabbed my bag and walked out the door.

As I got into the car, I finally opened the text Jason had sent that morning. Since that voicemail, he hadn't called or texted. But a few days after the voicemail, daisies had shown up on my front door. No note, just a vase of daisies.

A few days later, Tupperware holding a variety of meals

appeared in our fridge with my name on them. I knew any of my roommates would've let him in, and my heart beat faster as I thought of him here without me knowing, of his smile and his beautiful soul in the same kitchen I stood in, separated by time and my pain.

In a grand gesture meant to provoke a reaction, a car was delivered the next day. It was affordable, got good gas mileage, and wasn't too flashy or showy but with seat heaters and a working gear shift. It was perfect and completely ridiculous. I snapped at the delivery man, telling him it was a mistake, but then he handed me a printed email he was instructed to bring if I resisted.

It was simple, and it was everything.

"Oaks,

Take the damn car. Sell that piece of shit and donate the money to your momma's choir or to buy Mal a gift or put it towards Jack's recovery, whatever selfless thing will make you feel better. It's a nonrefundable purchase, baby, and I hope it makes you angry enough to talk to me again. I'm not going away. I'm not leaving you. Please don't leave me. Take the damn car.

Your Jase"

As soon as the paper was in my hand, the delivery man escaped. I had no choice but to take the car, and I was boiling. I typed out every style of message, from scathing to mildly angry to begging to see him and thanking him for taking care of me when I couldn't take care of myself. The urge to call him was so strong, I threw my phone across my room. I was fighting the feeling that I'd become like every other person in his life with the way he'd turned to material things to win me back, even though I knew this wasn't that.

Then, today, right when I needed him more than anything, he sent me the playlist, the one he'd made for me.

Westerman: Playlist: Music for my OT

Westerman: I love you. This is our overtime, and I'm willing to fight for it. I can't wait until you're ready to fight with me again.

It put away any doubt that Jason knew me, because it meant more than the car ever would.

I didn't even attempt to stop the tears streaming down my cheeks. Steadying my breaths to keep back the sobs, I hit shuffle. He knew my heart. This was everything. The tears increased when 'Fishing in the Dark' started playing through the new car's speakers. But after a moment, I smiled.

Pulling into the parking spot, I checked to make sure it didn't look like I'd been crying to 'Fishing in the Dark', 'That's Why We Fight', and 'What Hurts the Most' on repeat.

When Mal hugged me tightly and whispered, "It's okay to cry with us", I fought back new tears and knew there was no hiding from my family.

Pa silently gave me a tight hug then handed me a new hook to start attaching to the end of my pole. I'd kept the pole Pa gave me after I graduated high school. It was simple and black, and I'd always loved having it in my hands. An immediate sense of peace flooded through me as I strung my hook and attached my lure.

On the edge of the river, Pa and Mal set up three foldable camping chairs and a cooler. We quickly cast our lines into the water and settled in. Soft music played from a speaker, but I couldn't focus on anything but the water. It was still, not a ripple across our part of the glassy lake. This was one of the last days we could go fishing before it got too cold, and even then, the cold air nipped at my nose as I pulled my jacket tighter around my body.

After a few moments of chatter between Mal and Pa, they turned their attention to me.

"How you doing, Oaksy? Really?" Pa asked, and Mal gave me wide eyes, failing to hide her concern.

"I'm—" I took a breath. "It will be fine" or "I've got it handled" were on the tip of my tongue. That was what I always told them, but it wasn't true. "Honestly? I'm pulling myself back together. I'm terrified because I feel so numb. It's like my heart couldn't take it anymore. It turned off. It hurts, but it's a dull pain, like someone is trying to talk to me but my head's under the water. I know it's there, I don't want to hold it in anymore, but I don't know how."

"Wow," Pa whispered after a moment, something like awe in his eyes. "I know you're hurting, but I don't think you've ever been so open with us before. I...I never want to see my little girl broken, but I think all this opened the part of you that hides your feelings, the part of you that has always been so closed off. Your momma and I know we had a hand in that."

"Pa—" I started to argue, shaking my head.

"No, Oakley. We didn't realize how much landed on your shoulders, how much responsibility you felt until you closed yourself off completely and we didn't know how to fix it. You wanted some sort of control, and no one can blame you for that." He sniffled, wiping his eyes with the back of his hand. In that moment, I saw my parents in a different light. Part of me resented them for how they'd failed us all, how they'd failed me. But now, looking at Pa as he struggled to find his next words, it hit me.

He was human too, and he didn't know how to deal with this wild life any more than I did. His voice cracked as he continued.

"I wish we could go back and take that load off you, but we can't. We tried to make this time different, to be there for you all with Jack's chemo, the way we weren't before. We were so worried you'd stay closed off, but then you met Jason. The way you gravitated towards him, the way he lit you up, even when you claimed you hated him? That—*that* was magic, Oakley."

The mention of Jason made my heart ache.

"Pa, I don't know how to fix it with him. I closed off, I shut him out. When things were crashing down and I couldn't stop it, I pushed him away. How do I fix that? He doesn't deserve someone who lashes out when things get hard." I'd cried all my tears away. Keeping my eyes on the water, I couldn't stop the words that tumbled out. "I feel like things are changing too fast, and then they're gone forever. I can't get my peace back. Because no matter what, I can't go back to how my life was before Jason. I can't even go back to how things were with Jason two weeks ago. It's gone, and I feel abandoned by it all."

With that dramatic outburst, I leaned back in my chair and let out a long breath. It was only a moment before Mal spoke up, her voice holding more wisdom than any fifteen year old should possess.

"I don't understand all this relationship stuff, but honestly? You're bein' stupid, Oaksy." She met my surprised gaze with a nonchalant shrug. "Anyone with eyes can see you love Jason, and he loves you. It's actually kinda gross but also cute, I guess? The point is, after everything that happened, you made sure we were all okay and we let you. So why the double standard? Why can't Jason take care of you too? Why does things changin' mean you can't be happy anymore? Nobody left you behind this time. In fact, Jason's trying to stay, and you're the one leaving him. It makes no sense, and I think you'd be really sad if you didn't end up with Jason forever. He's your person."

Pa nodded at Mal, pride shining in his eyes before turning to me.

"I don't think any of us could say it better than that, Oakley Mae. But if I could add, sometimes, things have to change to make room for somethin' new. I know it hasn't been easy, but the changes and growing pains you've been facing have made room in your heart for a real relationship." He sniffled again, his voice breaking. "Almost losing Jack, right after having those—those...after what happened to my girls and feeling so helpless through all of it... I know it feels like a piece of you died when that gunshot went off and again when Jack's heart stopped. A piece of mine did too. We can't get that piece back, but we do get to choose what replaces it."

Their words hit me hard and fast. Could I really get to choose this? To control what filled the horrible hole in my soul that was left behind?

Closing my eyes, I tried. I focused. I let it go, and I replaced them.

Jack's heart stopping.

I replaced it with him fishing with us, completely healthy, a smile on his face and color in his cheeks, maybe a sweet girl with wild curls at his side.

The gun held to Mal's head.

I replaced it with her graduating high school, ignoring a boy staring moony-eyed at her, planning to change the world.

Walking away from Jason, the devastation on his face and in my heart, leaving him behind in the very way I was terrified he'd do to me.

I replaced it with coming home from work to music playing, rings on our left hands, my man cooking before we get ready for his game.

Yelling at Jason, pushing him away, telling him he's stupid and being rude and scared.

I replaced it with whispered I love yous, seeing all he can give, all I can give too, letting him hold me after a hard day and holding him right back.

A life. A life I couldn't have if I didn't accept that things were changing, that they had *changed*. That they will change. That I could choose to stay despite it all.

And finally, *finally*, I felt ready.

"Should we tell her that her line's pullin'?" Mal whispered. Pa chuckled.

"Let her have her moment. If she hooked 'im good enough, he'll be there when she's ready."

33

fter fishing until we lost daylight, which wasn't by any means the prime time for fishing but the time that worked and felt oddly symbolic, we had successfully caught and released five fish. For the weather and time, it was the best we could've hoped for.

The way Pa and Mal both hugged me tight before saying goodbye healed another small part of my soul. When I climbed into my car, I knew what I needed to do. Our whole relationship, Jason had been coming to me—breaking down my walls, trying to get through my issues and give me the love I needed.

It was my turn to go to him. Not meet him halfway, but go completely to him, and I couldn't go empty-handed.

But when I pulled up to his apartment complex a few hours later, the sweet old valet gave me a sad smile.

"I'm sorry, Miss Tennen, but he left about two hours ago. He had his old skates with him, and when I asked if he was headed to practice, he said no," Bill explained slowly. "He's done that for the last two weeks if he hasn't had a game at night or been away. He even goes after afternoon games."

My initial disappointment faded as I took in his words. I had a feeling where he could be.

"Thank you. I appreciate your help."

"Miss Tennen?" he said hesitantly, and I turned back to him. "I don't know all that's been going on between you two, but he hasn't been as happy since you stopped coming around. I hope to see you more often, along with Mr. Westerman's smile."

"Me too," I agreed with a small smile, jogging around the front of my car and heading towards the practice rink as the darkness of a fall night took over the city.

Needing some courage, I turned on Jason's playlist and tried to go over what I could say. But when I entered the empty practice facility using the code he used our first date and saw the low set of his shoulders, the solemn expression on his face, the defeat in his eyes as he pushed lazily around the rink, all the words left me.

But I couldn't be scared of whatever this conversation would bring. I couldn't be scared of change. I couldn't try to control this. Not anymore.

I stepped onto the ice as he rounded the bend across the arena. His eyes snapped up and met mine. His face was guarded, and it hurt that I couldn't read his expressions.

When he made it to me, stopping nearly five feet away, we were both breathing heavily, anticipating this conversation.

"Hi," I breathed slowly, unsure where to begin. "How are you?"

"That's what we're starting with, eh?" Jason muttered, crossing his arms defensively, but his words were soft, full of hurt. "How do you think I am, Oakley?"

"Jason, I don't even know where to start." I held the Tupperware closer to my body, trying to hold myself together. "There aren't words to say how sorry I am, how selfish it was that I cut you off like that. I didn't want to hurt you—"

"But that's what happened, Oakley. You hurt me. I know not all of that was in your control, and I can't even tell you how much it's been eating me alive that it was my past that put you in danger." He shook his head, as if holding back the anger. "When that phone call cut off, it felt like I'd *stopped breathing*. Another person I loved was leaving me, taken from me. And when finally I got you back, when you were safe, you shut me out. I'd watched you get held at gunpoint, dammit. You literally jumped in front of a bullet for me; then, you wouldn't even look me in the eye? You told me to leave? Do you...I mean, do you blame me? I would."

The sorrow in his eyes overtook the anger in his voice, and my heart broke as I realized how much this weighed him down.

His eyes glanced down at the Tupperware in my hands, finally noticing what I was holding.

"Are those—"

"You know I'm not a good cook or baker or anything," I interrupted, trying to stop my voice from shaking. "I know you'll let me pay you back for the car."

"It was a gift," he started, gearing up for a fight. He wasn't going to get one.

"I know. So is this." I reached across the space between us, and as soon as they were in his hands, I wrapped my arms around my waist, unsure of how he would take it.

"Grams' muffins?" he whispered, almost reverently. "Did you make these?"

I nodded slowly, and his eyes widened in shock.

"I don't blame you for any of it, but I couldn't do it, Jason. It was too much to almost lose you; I'd never felt fear like that in my life." Jason watched me, jaw clenched, and I knew everything in him wanted to steamroll, to comfort or argue, but he was holding back. I loved him for it. "A piece of me died that day. When Rachel shot that gun. When Jack's heart stopped. When I shut you out. But I realized a piece of me was dying long before everything that day. It started dying when I met you."

He blinked, hurt slashing violently across his face. I hurried to explain what I meant.

"That was a good thing, Jase. I was holding onto this idea that it was all on my shoulders, that if I cared *about* anyone instead of *taking care* of them, they would leave and I would get hurt." I swallowed, looking at the space between us, knowing I needed to say this before either of us could come any closer. "You started breaking down that wall the first time you looked at me with those damn eyes, because you *saw* me. I shut down because I didn't know I could choose what filled the piece of me that was gone, the piece that didn't want anyone to care. But you've been showing me this whole time. I didn't realize it was you,

Jason. You'll always be what fills my heart, and I *choose you*."

"Oakley..." Jason whispered my name like a prayer, but I kept going. He needed to hear this. I was offering him my heart and soul, giving him every piece.

All I felt was hope. No fear. No all-consuming thoughts I was going to get left behind.

Hope.

"I don't want to be so scared of change that I'm scared to live. You taught me that change can be beautiful, that it's okay to feel more than one thing at a time. You taught me to look past the flaws and feel connected to someone who makes me feel. You taught me to find someone who matches my worth. So, even if you decide this is too much, and you...you don't want to do this anymore, I can respect that. But I'll always love you because you taught me how to truly live."

I looked into those eyes swirling with so many emotions. When he slowly put my muffins on the ice, my heart dropped.

It was over. He'd rejected this. Us.

Then, he smiled.

With one push of his skates, he closed the distance between us, holding my face in his hands.

"Oaks, we taught each other." Tears formed in his eyes as he peered down at me. "Before you, my only purpose was to be good at hockey and be there for Grams. But something was missing. When Jack called me, I felt like maybe this was the 'more' I'd been looking for, to be more than a man who lived for himself."

His voice shook, and I reached up, gripping his wrists,

anchoring myself to this man, to this moment. I clung to every word. With a small grin, he took a deep breath before continuing.

"Then, I ran into a true southern woman in a parking garage who wasn't scared to call me on my shit and make me work for it. My world started to shift. What I felt in that moment? It didn't end. For once, I wanted to be near someone who didn't *need* anything from me. It made me want to be someone you *wanted* in your life. More than anything, I want *every part* of me to belong to you. But I can't do that without you. As terrified as I am to lose you, I'm more terrified I'll never get to really have you, not the way I need to." He paused, giving us both a second to steal a breath. "There is so much between us already and yet not enough. Because we haven't completely figured out how to do the hard stuff yet. I—Oakley, I didn't know how to handle the past few weeks."

"I didn't either. I still don't," I whispered. "I should've talked to you. I wish I would've been brave enough to handle it with you. I want a life with you. I want to fight with you, roll my eyes at you, choose you when things are changing all around me."

I took a deep breath, stepping away from Jason and letting his hands drop from my face. His eyes were confused when I pulled out my phone, but then I handed it over.

Hesitantly, he took the phone from me, and I nodded encouragingly. He looked at the screen, and then I was in his arms, my feet lifting off the ice as he crushed his body to mine.

We spun for a moment, his skates moving with our

motion, until he gently lowered me to my feet, resting his forehead against mine.

"You made me a playlist?" he asked in a whisper, his voice straining with emotion.

"No, I took the playlist you created and made it ours," I answered, smiling through the few happy tears that escaped. "'*Our OT Is Worth It*' is a working title, but I need you to know. You're worth it, worth facing the change. You're worth changing my life for. And I love you more than I ever thought was possible."

"Things are always going to change, and we can't stop it," he said, tugging me closer. "But you'll never get left behind, Oakley. I'll be right there with you, showing you how beautiful the change can be."

A tear escaped as Jason smiled, and I wiped it away before pulling back to really look at him.

"I know. You're my music, Jason. You're my music and my trees and my safe place." I smiled. "We're so sappy right now."

"Hell yeah, we are," Jason laughed then kissed my forehead before looking at me intently. "I love you. Even when everything's changing around us, remember that. We'll do life together, Oaks. We won't get left behind ever again. It's better than any dream I've ever had, because this is real."

Moving his head slowly, he gently touched his lips to mine. It felt different, like change and arguments and emotional rollercoasters and sunrises before hockey games and fresh baked muffins and late night talks wrapped up in each other with music in the background after a long day.

When I pushed back and kissed him hard, loving him as fiercely as he deserved, we let ourselves be both lost and found in each other. My chest tightened in anticipation.

Everything was shifting.

And I was ready.

EPILOGUE
1 Month Later

The air was brisk as it wrapped around me, fall gone and winter fully taking its place. I settled into my couch on the front porch, watching my weathered oak tree standing strong amidst the weather. Warmth seeped into my hands as I gripped my mug, taking sips of tea.

"Oakley, what do you think?" Dr. Grouse's voice came through the phone, tension filling the silence.

I heard a huff from one of the interns. He didn't agree with anything I said and had a habit of thinking more about logistics than others' feelings. Despite how he treated me, I understood him on a level he'd never understand.

"I think we should push towards the connection aspect of the research. There's a right way to do this, like Henry stated, that we can do as we consider the feelings of the participants and make sure they're comfortable as well."

Another small pause but no more huffing.

"Thank you for that insight, Oakley. I appreciate that you're able to see the humanity in our work as well as the efficiency piece. I'll let you get back to your holidays, but thank you for taking the time to work out this issue."

"No problem. Have a great holiday break, Dr. Grouse." I took a sip of my tea. "You too, Henry."

This time, I had both men happily saying goodbye before I hung up the call and settled back into my cozy space.

I couldn't fathom working in a hospital after all that had happened. I couldn't ever go back to being the cold, unfeeling nurse who'd treated her patients like a controlled formula. So, I quit labor and delivery and went full-time with the research position. Anita and Ash tried to convince me otherwise, but in the end, they understood. Direct patient care nursing was never where I was supposed to be. It had started as my way to take care of everyone how I thought they needed it, but strangely, research allowed me to connect and take care of them better than ever before.

It helped me push past my fear of emotion in a way I'd never been able to.

Successfully interrupting my peace, my phone buzzed from its spot on the couch next to me.

Hunter: How was it today?

I smiled at my younger brother's thoughtfulness as I typed out a response. After everything that had happened with me and Mal and Jack, he was trying to be as involved as he could be. Momma and Pops hovered, and I'd had to tell them to back off a few times. I was getting better at accepting being cared for, but I still had my limits.

Oaksy: It was good. Mostly discussed coping with panic. She shared some interesting research I can send your way.

I'd only been to counseling a few times, but so far, the sweet lady was helping me see things from another point of view and understand how to process my emotions. Even things I'd witnessed at work, like the traumatic births and deaths, weighed on me. I didn't even realize how much I hadn't processed. It had built and built and built until it was too much. Now, I was finally brave enough to face it.

And she gave me research articles, which was my favorite part.

Hunter: That's more your thing than mine, I'll have to hear the Oakley recap in normal people terms tonight.

Oaksy: How's the drive? Got an ETA?

Hunter: About an hour out; just stopped for some gas. What time are y'all getting there?

Oaksy: We're heading out soon. Will probably get there around the same time. Excited to see you.

Hunter: Same. See you soon, Oaksy

Locking the phone screen and setting it down beside me, I took a deep breath. So much had changed. Things were getting back to normal with the girls. Ash still refused to come with me to visit Jack, but otherwise, she was dedicated to working on herself. She was trying new things and learning to be comfortable without a relationship. I knew there was more to her strained relationship with Jack, more I wasn't seeing between them.

We had our first girls night a few weeks after everything, and it felt different, other than the fact that I came voluntarily. We were closer. I appreciated Ash's off-key singing as she ate her cheesy fries. When Tae forced us to pose for a picture, I found myself smiling and laughing. Tess found little moments to make sure I was doing okay and avoided the guys constantly trying to get her attention.

I let myself love those little moments. Embrace them. Find the beauty as life went on, moving and changing around me.

Jack was calling me Oaksy again. He was struggling to find where he fit in his new reality, but I had faith he'd find it. He wasn't running from us, and that was all I could ask for.

My thoughts were interrupted again when the bench

groaned under the weight of a hockey player. Smiling as I took in Jason, his hair wet from a shower and a Rebels pullover tight across his chest, I sighed. He wrapped an arm around me, pulling me close and placing a kiss on my forehead.

"Hey, Oaks."

"Hey, Westerman." I tilted my head up and gave him a quick kiss. "How's Grams?"

"Good. She says hi and expects you to talk longer than five minutes next time she calls."

"It was your Christmas call with her, and I stole her grandson for the holidays." I gave him a stern look, which he smiled at. "I know we'll see her for New Years, but this felt big."

"It is big, Oakley." He pulled me even closer, and I laid my head on his shoulder as his soft words reached me. "One of our firsts, but not one of our lasts. You know what they say. 'When you realize you want to spend the rest of your life with somebody, you want the rest of your life to start as soon as possible'."

"Jason." My tone was the equivalent of an eye roll.

"When Harry Met Sally."

I nuzzled in closer and watched my tree. The branches were completely barren, nothing even hinting at growing. We didn't often get snow before January, so they were empty.

That used to make me sad. The leaves would seem beautiful and colorful during the fall, but really, all that change was killing them. They died, and they were gone.

But now, with Jason's arms around me and the future in front of us, I saw them differently.

Because the leaves don't just change. They fall. They leave and make room for new life, for new growth, for time to take its sweet ideas and whimsical fantasies and help the Earth keep moving forward. Realizing change was only a step in the process was just the beginning. Learning to *accept* the change helped me to embrace the fact that better things would come to fill the empty spaces. I let my passion change from working full time as a nurse to completely changing my career and making room for a research job I loved. I let my inability to show emotion change, realizing that life is short, and made room for making sure the people I loved knew what they meant to me. I let my fear of being left behind fade away and made room for finding something to stay for. I let my hate for a certain hockey player with a strange mix of defensive arrogance and sunshine joy change into respect and admiration, making room to fall helplessly and fiercely in love with him.

After the leaves fell, that was when I could finally breathe again. Because what had been holding me back was dead and gone, and all that was left was room to grow.

"Oakley?" Jason gently stroked my hair, pulling me out of my thoughts.

"Hm?" I snuggled in closer. He laughed, pulling me tighter against him.

"Can we make a quick stop before we head to your parents?"

I gave him a questioning look, but all he did was give me a smile.

After a small debate and a really unfair tickle war, I

found myself at the practice rink again, a cocky hockey player lacing up my skates.

Once we were on the ice, the two of us skating in a contented silence, I knew life wouldn't always be as simple as holding Jason's hand and gliding through the challenges. It would be hard, and it would break me and build me back up.

But it was possible, because I had people who were with me, even when I couldn't see them. I was never alone.

That was what family was.

With that thought, I turned to the man I loved.

"Hey, sunshine?"

He turned to me with a smile. "Yeah?"

"Thanks for being my music."

"Thanks for being my everything."

Now I really did roll my eyes.

"Always have to one up me, huh?" I teased.

"Nope. Just happy with you."

I leaned forward, kissing him deeper this time. He returned it even stronger, showing me everything I never thought I could have. His hands went into my hair, and when we finally parted, gasping for breath, I smiled.

I was happy everything shifted, happy everything had changed. Because without it, I wouldn't have him.

I didn't know everything that was coming, but with him by my side, I wasn't scared anymore.

Because life *was* oh, so beautiful after the leaves fell.

The End

OUR OT IS WORTH IT PLAYLIST
(formerly Music for my OT)

That's Why We Fight (feat. Koe Wetzel) by Ella Langley

Fishin' in the Dark by Nitty Gritty Dirt Band

What Hurts The Most by Rascal Flatts

Easy by Camila Cabello

Feels Like by Gracie Abrams

God, Your Mama, And Me by Florida Georgia Line and the
Backstreet Boys

All To Myself by Dan + Shay

I Could Use a Love Song by Maren Morris

Lady Like by Ingrid Andress

Me and You by Mike G and Leyla Blue

Honey, I'm Home by Shania Twain

You Proof by Morgan Wallen

I'm A Survivor by Reba McEntire

Chemical by Post Malone

Keeping Score by Dan + Shay and Kelly Clarkson

True Love (feat. Lily Allen) by P!nk

I Feel It All by Feist

Exhale by Sabrina Carpenter

Risk by Gracie Abrams

The View Between Villages by Noah Kahan

.

Acknowledgments

I think I'll say this every time, but I can't believe I'm writing the acknowledgements at the end of a book I dreamed, wrote, revised, and poured my heart and soul into. Jason and Oakley have lived rent-free in my head for the better part of two years, and now they get to live in yours for as long as you'll have them. This book is full of the things I love most about a Nashville fall. Changing leaves on the trees, hockey games, nights out downtown with the girls, cozy nights in wrapped in blankets, and twinkle lights. All the magical twinkle lights.

But amidst the fall and the angst and heartfelt moments, I hope this book made you feel seen. Writing this book was a cathartic experience, as I found myself trying to figure out my life the same way Oakley was. There are so many amazing people that contributed to this book, and I'd like to take a moment to thank as many of them as I can.

First, to my publisher, Azala Press. A huge thank you to MK and her team for taking a chance on my little fall hockey romance and not only seeing my vision but believing in it. The cover? Are we kidding? Thank you for turning my very descriptive "whimsical, fall, but like moody and there needs to be a tree" into a masterpiece. The love you have for these characters and the care you took with them made all the difference. Thank you from the very bottom of my heart.

To my editor, Alexa. Bless you for adding all the necessary commas and taking out all my unnecessary ones. It was tedious and I can't express how much I needed your keen eye to bring this manuscript to the next level. You are amazing!

To my alpha and beta readers, how can I express my appreciation adequately? Truth is, I can't. You took the time to read a very, very, very rough version of this manuscript. You pushed through the plot holes and inspired new scenes (the hallway moment was all you), keeping me on track and pushing this story to the best it could be. Jason and Oakley quickly became yours, and the way you continued to champion them even though you had to wait a full calendar year before even knowing when you'd have them again (I am SO sorry). Finally I can give them to you, and I've never been happier.

To my fellow Creatives That Cry, we started our little writer's group when I had just finished the early version of this manuscript. You encouraged me when I felt hopeless, you laughed with me when I made a querying mistake, and you always believed that I could publish another book. Each of you bring something unique and special to my life, and I appreciate it more than I can express.

To my family. My siblings, who market my books to all their friends, get angry when I don't talk about getting a book deal enough, and who ultimately inspired the close relationships of the Tennen siblings, I love you all. Thank you for being my biggest fans, even though I write romance books you're scared to read.

My parents, thank you for more than I have space to list in a whole book, let alone the back of this one. To my mom, my number one alpha reader/cheerleader/best friend. Thank you for listening to every new idea and plot twist and always pointing out the pieces of me I wove into my characters. For believing I could do this even when I didn't. To my dad, for telling everyone he works with to buy my book and introducing me to hockey at a young age. I don't think this book would have been possible if you didn't teach me to love the sport – sorry I wrote a kissing book about it, love you!

To Tessa, the Ash to my Oakley. The amount of random "what if I did this" and "what do you think about" texts you suffered through deserve an award of their own. You inspire me, and I appreciate you more than you know.

To Lexy and the other amazing girls I've met when I moved back to Tennessee as an adult, your support has been insane and invaluable. More than I can express. Thank you.

Finally, to the reader picking up this book. You took a chance, and I am so very thankful. You're the reason I get to keep doing this crazy thing I love to do. I hope you felt all the emotions as you read this book and wish you very happy reading.

About the Author

Ella Justice is a Tennessee girl with a passion for emotional rollercoaster love stories. She loves hanging out with family and friends, listening to music, being in nature and cozying up with a good book during a rain storm - and Tennessee has plenty of those. When she's not working in the nursing field or reading and writing, Ella can be found watching anything and everything hockey. She is grateful for the chance to share the stories always bouncing around in her head with the world. Happy reading!

Check out Ella's social media for updates on book releases and new info!

@ellajustice.author